BLUE HURRIC

John Dyson

Blue Hurricane

Futura
Macdonald & Co
London & Sydney

A Futura Book

First published in Great Britain in 1983
by Futura Publications, a Division of
Macdonald & Co (Publishers) Ltd
London & Sydney

Copyright © John Dyson 1983

ISBN 0 7088 1894 3

Typeset by Elanders Computer Assisted Typesetting
Systems, Inverness
Printed and bound in Great Britain by
Hazell Watson & Viney Ltd, Aylesbury, Bucks

Futura Publications
A Division of
Macdonald & Co (Publishers) Ltd
Maxwell House
74 Worship Street
London EC2A 2EN

For Lucy and Kenneth

L.J.

CONTENTS

1 : DEAR MOTHER

The Solent bristled with whitecaps and my old lady rolled like a demon. Legs braced at the wheel, I steered one-handed and clutched the deck-head with the other. Short, steep waves stormed through the Needles Channel, heaving against the spring tide. The odd one broke over the gunwale, sluiced along the deck, spilled over the cabin top on the roll. The water would find the leak over my bunk and soak my sleeping-bag, but in this kind of sea I could not leave the wheel to do anything about it. Yarmouth lay on the bow, the tide sweeping me over towards the Isle of Wight shore: it would be a short run in.

Weekend yachtsmen out in force were getting their money's worth. Away down towards Cowes, yachts in a club race for Solent Point were hard on the wind, shouldering through fisty waves like riot police marching through a crowd. Smaller boats barely made headway, stopped by every wave and left wallowing because they did not have the momentum. It took more than a Solent lop to worry my old girl, a retired Scottish fishing-boat, but that didn't stop her protesting as she corkscrewed rheumatically across the shipping channel where the ebb ran strongest and the waves were highest. The steadying-sail would have helped, but it hardly seemed worthwhile for a four-mile dash and from the moment I had left the shelter of Lymington River I had been regretting it. But it was great to be at sea again, feeling the gallant diesel throbbing under my feet and hearing the rattle of the ensign in the wind.

Out of nowhere a wave peaked alongside. *Windycap* scooped up half a ton of green water on the up-roll. It swept the deck, jetted upwards under the wheelhouse door, cascaded into the sea as the other gunwale dipped. This was getting a bit too punishing. I altered course three spokes to starboard to bring the nose up a bit, aiming to get into smoother water as quickly as possible; then I would turn up the coast to make the harbour entrance.

The change of course brought an Enterprise-class sailing dinghy into view. Half a mile away, it was having a wild roller-coaster ride as it ran up from the Needles with the wind dead aft. Another sail on the Solent is unremarkable and I did not pay it much attention, but something triggered my subconscious when it planed off the top of a curling wave, and I looked round just as it fell into the succeeding trough and disappeared.

Peering out of the spray-flecked side windows, I saw the pale blue diamond of Terylene sail lurch back to the vertical, rattling in the wind and shedding clouds of spray as the water was shaken off. Then it fell over again.

Righting a capsized dinghy in this ugly sea would be difficult. So early in the season, the water would still have a wintry chill. Concerned, I swung the bows round to starboard again and headed for the spot. With the waves now hitting her on the bow, the old girl reared like a wild horse. Spray rained on the wheelhouse window and I started the revolving Kent screen to get a clear view. Through the spinning Perspex disc I saw the blue triangle flutter upright again, then flop over at once. There were no other boats nearby. Only the parade of racers beating down the channel with the tide under them, and a Thoresen ferry turning through the Needles entrance on its way in from Normandy.

Righting a sailing dinghy is hard work at the best of times. In cold water you get numbed and tired quickly and after two or three attempts you feel knackered. A cable away, I saw the sail heave into the air once more only to be knocked flat as a wave rolled over the semi-submerged hull. Two figures, bright yellow in

10

sou'westers and buoyancy-aids, struggled in the water. One of them lifted an arm and waved it slowly in the recognized signal for help wanted.

I cut the revs and weighed up what was a tricky situation. With the tide on the stern and the wind on the nose, rescue would be difficult. Doubly so with the boat rolling her guts out. Getting men single-handedly up her high sides would be a hellish job. And all the time the capsized dinghy was drifting down the middle of the shipping lane, heading for the open sea on the strong ebb.

Keeping just enough way on for steerage, I worked to within twenty feet of the dinghy, then slid the door open and stuck my head out. Both men lifted their arms wearily.

'Can you get us out?' one of them called.

No chance. But I made encouraging signals, switched on the VHF radio, pressed the tit on the mike.

'Coastguard, coastguard, this is motor vessel *Windycap*, do you read please?'

They came back at once, the voice getting clearer as I adjusted the squelch.

'*Windycap, Windycap*, this is coastguard. What's up, John?'

The big wheelhouse, sticking up on the deck like a telephone kiosk, was acting like a sail and we were rapidly going past the stricken dinghy.

'Coastguard, this is *Windycap*. I am standing by a capsized dinghy in rough seas off Shingles Bank but getting survivors aboard will be tricky. Is the Yarmouth I.R.B. operational, over?'

It was Ted Allan's voice on the radio. He was a drinking chum from way back and knew I wouldn't call out the inshore rescue boat unless it was essential.

'Negative on that, John. The I.R.B. is busy on a rescue, over.'

'Roger, Ted, I'll have a shot at it myself, over.'

'Is it a helicopter job, John?'

'Stand by, Ted, I'll let you know. Over.'

'Roj, coastguard standing by.'

I clipped the mike on its hook and left the set running. *Windycap* had jilled fifty yards beyond the dinghy. Unworried by the Solent's temper, the car ferry was now flying up the channel towards us. Shoving the throttle forward, I spun the wheel and lurched the heavy old boat into a rock-and-rolling turn to bring her downwind of the casualty, then nosed gently alongside. I flung the door open and clambered out on deck, the wind tearing at my hair. The inflatable dinghy was lashed to the deck. I cut the ropes and knee'd it over the rail, keeping hold of the painter. Mercifully, it landed upright. I shouted to the dinghy-sailors to swim for it and as they struck out to cover the few yards to the inflatable's low, torpedo-like sides I reached into the wheelhouse to adjust the helm. The ferry was altering course, leaving us plenty of room. No worries.

The bow had fallen off the wind so I gave the engine a spurt to bring her up again. One dinghy sailor had rolled himself into the inflatable and reached out to take the rope which the other was passing him. They wanted to save their boat: who could blame them? Then the second man crawled, exhausted, into the inflatable and I hauled it alongside.

Pale and shivering, they were both in their early twenties, probably students. One had a beard that dripped with water as he crouched to throw up the coiled end of their tow-rope.

'Where is it fast?' I asked.

'Round the mast.'

'Okay, lie flat and keep your weight down!'

Hitching the thin Terylene line to the stern bollard, I scrambled into the wheelhouse and, with a backward glance to check that the inflatable was falling astern with its rope clear of the prop, I edged the throttle forward and got the procession under way.

The sailing dinghy was now bottom up, its mast

pointing straight down. Its bailer, floorboards, rudder, paddle and other loose gear had been threaded together on the mainsheet and floated behind. Gently the tow ropes tautened and we began to move.

To head directly for the shore would bring the seas on my stern. There was a good risk my boat would be pooped by a breaking wave, or that the inflatable and the sailing dinghy would surf on to the stern deck. But to keep heading out to sea would be disastrous in another way, for the two men lying prone in the inflatable desperately needed some warmth inside them. The only safe course was to take the waves on the port bow and edge slowly into the sheltered water behind the long shingle spit on which Hurst Castle stood, jutting like a breakwater into the Solent.

The old girl had hardly settled down to the task, and I had just reported to the coastguard that I had the incident under control, when a more worrying problem arose.

The fleet of racers that had been tacking down the Solent with the tide threw about on the mainland shore and in close formation knifed towards us on the star-board tack. Each yacht was hard pressed under a mass of sail – big low-cut genoas that hid from the helmsmen's view everything lying to leeward – and every man in every crew was sitting to windward.

Smoking along at a good nine or ten knots, sails as taut and sharp as Concorde wings, the leaders were in a tight bunch racing neck and neck. Straight for us.

Swearing under my breath while watching the tall, leaning sails loom nearer, my mind raced but came up with no answers. A round of grape-shot through their sails would have done the job, but I had no cannon.

The seas were nasty, peaking sharply with angry ridges that were torn off by the wind. Foam streaked the troughs and hollows. I was unable to increase speed because of the two small vessels I was towing, but if I turned towards the oncoming yachts to present a smaller target there was every chance the inflatable would either flip over as it breasted a crest and the wind got under it, or founder beneath a breaking wave.

The nearest yacht was half a cable ahead of the others and it surged past my bow in a blaze of rainbow spray. As the sturdy old fishing-boat was revealed behind the leech of the genoa, the helmsman's jaw dropped like a brick. I saw him mouth a four-letter word, then one of his crew jumped to leeward to see what other boats might lie ahead. A supertanker perhaps.

But the next three yachts were in a tight bunch and bearing down fast. Steam gives way to sail, true. But what could I do? Every captain is obliged to keep a proper look-out. What if I had been legitimately at anchor with the proper signals hoisted? Or in distress? This was one of those crazy combinations of circumstances I had observed a hundred times on this crowded and dangerous stretch of water.

All the crew except the helmsman of the yacht leading the trio would be looking aft, at the second yacht which was trying to eat through to leeward. In the heat of the contest, any thought of keeping a proper look-out would have gone overboard with the water creaming along the lee deck. The third yacht had no way of seeing through the two in front.

Legally, I should have hoisted the proper signals. Two black balls on the fore-stay, for example, to show that my ship was not under control. Balls to that. A forty-five-foot boat was plain enough.

Leaving the wheel for an instant, I fumbled beneath the wheelhouse seat for the big brass foghorn and belted out five short blasts: maritime language for 'Watch yourself, mate!' The lads in the inflatable stuck their heads up in surprise and I pointed to the phalanx of what looked like speeding icebergs cutting down on us.

I jerked the throttle back and dragged the gear lever into neutral, then shouted to the lads astern to paddle up, and turned sharply to starboard. They were sailors enough to recognize danger when they saw it, and leaned out, one each side, paddling with their hands, to tuck the inflatable closely under my stern. Like massive darts, yards away now, all three yachts hurtled for the bull's-eye.

Then a horrified face appeared round the luff of the second sail in the line. There was an urgent shout. The yacht's helmsman pushed his helm hard down. The yacht rounded up but there was another yacht to windward of it. They collided with a loud crack and a thunder of flapping sails. Crewmen cursed and waved their fists, dodging sheets whipping frenziedly in the wind, and clinging on for dear life as the yachts dipped their long tapered snouts head-first into the waves.

I recognized *Blue Chip*, a former Admiral's Cup contender, and an Australian yacht called *Didgeridoo*. The third yacht, black with a gold stripe and a red flash on its sail, was a little further back. When its helmsman saw the chaos and glimpsed the stocky MFV rolling heavily dead ahead, he altered course to leeward, just sufficiently to miss by inches a collision that would have sunk him.

But the overturned Enterprise sailing dinghy still floated low in the water on the end of its tow-line, forty feet off my starboard quarter.

Frantically I tried yelling a warning to the helmsman but he was standing up behind his large chromium steering-wheel hurling abuse and not looking ahead: a tall, ginger-headed fellow with a face as red as his foul-weather suit. I heard him shout, 'Can't you see we're bloody racing ...!'

His complaint was broken short by a loud bang. The whole yacht twisted beneath him as its keel struck the line between the swamped dinghy and *Windycap's* stern. Momentarily the racing yacht seemed to stop dead in the water, throwing its crew on their beam ends. The helmsman all but measured his length in the cockpit. Caught by the rope, the bow of the yacht rounded up and crashed

15

with a splintering crack into my sturdy bulwark. There was another loud cracking noise, like a green branch breaking, as the sailing dinghy was dragged into the black yacht's hull and slammed against it. Then the tow-line snapped with a twang and the yacht surged on, laying off on a starboard reach to bring the hole in her bow clear of the water.

As the wreckage of the sailing dinghy bobbed into view, I read the name written in gold on the big yacht's black transom: *Go-Faster*.

Go to hell, I thought.

Twenty minutes later, in smoother water, I cut the throttle and turned into the wind and pulled the inflatable alongside. Exhausted, shuddering with cold, the dinghy sailors would never have made it to the rail without the help of a boarding ladder. When one of them started to haul in the new tow-rope we had fixed to the dinghy I shoved him roughly below.

'Get your wet things off and use my sleeping-bags, or you will be dead of hyperthermia.'

'But I need to ....'

'Do as I say: move it!'

They looked like a pair of corpses found face down in a river, their hair plastered down over their skulls, eyes bright and sunken, skin the blue tint of an all-over bruise. Amazing what cold water can do in a short time.

When I hauled the sailing dinghy alongside I saw it was a mess, one side stove in and only the buoyancy compartments keeping it afloat. The mainsail was ripped from tack to clew, probably due to being towed through the water.

In the cabin I found the survivors still shivering and too embarrassed to climb into the bunks, so I bullied them. I gave their limbs a brisk drubbing with a towel then pushed then into the bunks; my sleeping-bag was dark with wet stains from the leak in the deck but it would do the job. Then I picked my way through the chaos in the galley and warmed some milk while keeping

16

a weather-eye outside in case we drifted on to a mud-bank.

'Do you want some cocoa in your milk, to give it some body?'

'Mmmm, please!'

'Where did you sail from, Lymington?'

They nodded. I showed them the locker where they would find dry jeans and pullovers.

'But don't get dressed until you're properly warm: stay wrapped up for at least an hour, right?'

'How is our boat?' the bearded one asked.

'In bad shape, I'm afraid. I'll get you back to Lymington, then you can haul her out and take a look.'

Leaving them sipping cocoa and looking perkier, I ran *Windycap* the short distance up the coast to Lymington. In calm water just inside the river I stripped off to my shorts, scrambled down into the inflatable and managed to get the sailing dinghy on its feet and empty of water: it would sail again, but the repairs would make it too heavy to race.

I cruised slowly into the town quay, careful because the tide was now nearly dead low. The two lads had stopped shivering and dressed in my clothes. They came up and shook my hand, Mark and Jon from Oxford. They thanked me profusely but I was brisk: I had spent three hours at sea and now I was back where I started. My Rolex said eleven-thirty. With luck I would still make the Post Office in Yarmouth before it closed at one for the weekend.

They wanted to know how to get my clothes back to me and I gave them my Post Office address.

'Or you can bring them back yourselves when the wind drops,' I said. 'I live on board this bag of nails. Look for her against the harbour wall, I'm never far away. Come and have a drink and I'll tell you a thing or two about carrying too much sail.'

They looked suitably chastened. 'What's your name?'

17

'John Montgomery. I'm the lifeboat mechanic at Yarmouth. Or was, until yesterday.'

They shook hands again, stepped on to the quay, and hauled their boat clear. Then the bearded one gave my bow a push out and for the second time that morning I motored down Lymington River and set a course for Yarmouth.

The moorings at the piles in the harbour were already filling up, although it had only just gone noon, as yachts turned in to shelter from the Solent's angry mood and their crews settled down for an afternoon in the pub. As I nosed between the piers, engine in gear but only just ticking over because you never know what sailing dinghies you might find upside down just inside, the British Rail car ferry was preparing to leave and the queue of cars was already growing long on the quayside. The fairway was clear so I increased revs a little to make ground against the last of the ebb gushing out of the Yar, and turned the bows towards my mooring buoy. Picking it up single-handed was tricky but I did it all slowly, walking forward with the boat-hook and scooping up the buoy rope just as *Windycap* lost way. I looped the rope over the kingpost, walked aft, put the helm hard over, gave her a burst to kick the stern into the harbour wall, then went astern to stop her and chucked a warp up to Dick Johnstone who had seen me come in and had strolled along the quay to lend a hand. A slouching figure in a faded blue anorak, a battered white cap that looked as if it had been bombed many times by seagulls, and short seaboots, Dick was the assistant harbourmaster; we called him the Yarmouth hobbit.

'Morning, John! Bit fresh out there today, by the looks.'

'Thanks, Dick.'

I killed the engine and heaved in on the warp which Dick had dropped over a bollard. In a few moments *Windycap* lay snugly at home and I scrambled up the vertical steel ladder to where he was waiting, a loud hailer in his hand for giving berthing instructions to incoming boats.

'What a bloody morning,' I complained, dusting the ladder's slime off my hands. I described my brush with the racing fleet and Dick shrugged philosophically. A twinkle-eyed ex-mariner, he had seen it all before.

'Well, there's seamanship and there's winning races,' he said, 'and they don't go together any more. Every one of that fleet out there today is carrying too much sail, and when the mast goes over the side they expect the lifeboat to come out and get 'em.

As he spoke he waved his loud hailer towards the harbour entrance and I saw the familiar orange and blue lifeboat coming in with a yacht under tow, its mainsail in tatters and a broken cross-tree dangling halfway up its dangerously wobbling mast. Then, as Dick began to walk off, he remembered something and put his hand in his pocket.

'Almost forgot, telegram came for you.'

'Really?' I said, surprised. 'See you in the pub for a noggin later?'

'Not me,' he said, as I ripped the envelope open. 'This place is going to be like Piccadilly Circus all afternoon.' But Dick was an incurable old gossip and the telegram had been burning a hole in his pocket all morning. He was already fumbling in his pocket for the horn-rimmed specs that were repaired in two different places with insulation tape, and when he had put them on I handed the telegram over. It said:

JOHN MONTGOMERY CARE HARBOUR-MASTER YARMOUTH + MEET ME ABOARD DEAR MOTHER COWES MARINA 17:30 SATURDAY + JAMES BLOM

'God himself, eh!' Dick muttered.

'That depends.'

'On what?'

'How religious you are.'

'Well,' Dick said, pausing as he folded his specs and

slid them into his top pocket, 'if I was you I would say a little prayer in any case. You can call it insurance.'

The old green double-decker bus lurched round the leafy back lanes like a car ferry in a sea-way. Lush new grass rippled in the fields like acres of parachute silk. Glossy new leaves on the trees twinkled as they twisted in the wind and caught the sunlight. Now and then I caught glimpses of the distant Solent, its blue-green water corrugated by the wind but with fewer whitecaps now that the tide had changed. The leaning white diamonds of sail were getting an easier time of it.

The bus made frequent stops and seldom topped twenty miles an hour. It was hard to control my patience. For the hundredth time I regretted not bringing my car to the island instead of garaging it on the mainland to save ferry bills; whatever happened, the damn thing always seemed to be on the wrong side of the water.

The summons to a rendezvous aboard the motor cruiser *Dear Mother* was mysterious but I did know a little of what it foretold. The meeting, I suspected, would be the hinge on which my new career would open. Or close. For Major James Blom was chairman of the local County Planning Committee and in his hands he held the future I had been working and building towards during the three years since I had bought myself out of the Army.

My ten years in the service had given me a lot besides a trade and a practical experience in the art of staying alive and making out. I had gone in as a boy entrant and completed my course in motor engineering, then stepped sideways into the Parachute Regiment and made it to Staff Sergeant. It had been a good life, because I had been smart enough to discover that, under the guise of adventure training, a young soldier willing to do dirty work for rich and/or successful officers – in my case, pulling on ropes and tuning engines – can make the Army work for him any way he likes.

Sailing and engines had become my whole life. I had crewed in the Sydney-to-Rio lap of the round-the-world sailing race, in the Army's boat; I had led the engineering team supporting a long-distance powerboat race from England to Monte Carlo; on the strength of my handiness with a tool-box I had driven in a Land Rover through the Amazon jungle. It had been a great life, with the odd nightmarish parachute jump thrown in, but when I reached the ripe old age of twenty-eight I began to chafe. The Irish problem was becoming too ridiculously tragic and interfering with my sailing. Life as an NCO was too limiting; it was time to be my own boss.

Saving my pennies and throwing in all the capital I could lay my hands on, I bought myself out of the Army and invested in the hulk of a Scottish fishing boat which some mates had helped me to sail down from Peterhead to Yarmouth.

There, with a permanent mooring on the harbour wall, I had landed a job as full-time mechanic to the lifeboat. Every spare moment, day and night, I had devoted to fitting out my boat for business. There was always extra pocket money to be earned by ferrying boats for yachts-men who had become weatherbound and were unable to sail back to their marinas on the mainland. The owners left their boats in my charge and went home by ferry and train, and I would take their boats to their moorings on my days off in the middle of the week. Several times I had been requested to take the ferry across the Channel and bring boats home from France.

Now my own boat was pretty much as I wanted her. For a lone wolf like myself, she was a comfortable home, with a large saloon amidships, a well-equipped galley, and a chart room. But what made her different from any other boat was that I had converted her large foc'sle into a self-contained workshop. With South Coast marinas and boat harbours jammed full, and most boats left at their moorings all year round, my plan was to offer a boat-repair-and-maintenance service that would under-cut boatyard prices because my workshop was mobile and my overheads minimal.

But that was only half the project. Two or three hundred small boats nosed into Yarmouth harbour every summer weekend; a fair proportion of them would suffer mechanical problems of one kind or another, and because the shops were closed over the weekend, yachtsmen would have no opportunity to shop for spare parts and supplies. This week I had bought a barge, now lying in Southampton, which I would moor at the harbour wall and convert into a floating provision shop and chandlery, accessable by dinghy and open virtually round the clock all weekend. The range of stock would be small, prices high. I had been in Lymington overnight to talk with a naval architect who was designing the conversion. Now only the bureaucratic hurdles remained.

Three months ago I had written to the Isle of Wight council and formally applied for planning permission. Various officers had come down to talk about it, and my being a lifeboatman had made them sympathetic to the extent that when they built walls in my path they showed me how to get over or around them. Feeling confident, I had given notice to the lifeboat secretary and pushed on with my plans, the whole season in front of me. With an assistant working in the shop I could build up the yacht delivery side, spend the off-season on engineering and maintenance jobs cruising *Windycap* to wherever there was a job. I would be my own man, accountable to nobody, and working with what I liked best in the world: boats and engines.

As the bus cut out of Newport and trundled past the prison, the ruffled silver expanse of the Medina estuary opening out to the right, I reviewed what I knew about Major James Blom, horticulturalist, business wizard, local politician. His nurseries over in Hampshire were known country-wide, the slogan 'Blom's Blooms' fam-

22

iliar on television adverts, and on the large boarding in his nurseries that caught the eye of every traveller on the A3 just outside Portsmouth.

A few years ago he had linked up with a shrewd City man and they had built up a chain of shops which, though small, stood in every High Street as neighbours of Mothercare, Marks & Sparks and Kentucky Fried. Their clever money-making idea had been to marry the selling of flowers with greeting cards, chocolates, and boutique knick-knacks. I had just about kept them in business myself, for three months straight, when my own mother had been desperately ill. The shops were called Dear Mother and there was even one in Cowes. As I walked down the street from the bus station I saw its window flagged with headscarves patterned with anchors, dish-cloths bearing the international code of flag signals, and bunches of roses, tulips and violets. From any Dear Mother shop you could telegraph flowers and so-called personalized gifts anywhere in the country. Chocolates, flowers, greeting card saying Dear Mum, Hugs and Kisses, Luv Son.

Yuk.

My deck-shoes were springy on the pavement and I pushed on through the weekend shoppers feeling like I did when hunched in the thunder-belly with my parachute in my lap waiting for the signal to jump.

The day's racing was over and the marina was packed but *Dear Mother* stood out like the big wheel at a fairground. She was a fast motor launch with a flying bridge and swept-back Cinemascope windows, like scores of others that littered the South Coast marinas. But once you clapped eyes on this model you never forgot her. From stem to tuck she was coloured a vivid mauve. Her name was painted in thick gold scrolls three feet high on either bow and across her broad stern. The curtains shading her big windows were also gold, as were the squabs set around the well-deck abaft her tall super-structure. I had timed it just right and as I got nearer I saw that the vessel carried a pink water-ski boat in chocks on her fore-deck. It was called *Get Well Soon*.

Feeling decidedly ill, not to say embarrassed, at being seen within a mile of such nautical vulgarity, I stepped aboard. The well deck in her stern had the air of a balcony of a high-rise luxury apartment. All it needed was a wrought-iron gate and a dovecote. A floor-to-ceiling panel of smoked glass revealed a cocktail party in full swing in the saloon but there seemed to be no way of getting in and I struggled for a few moments before somebody on the other side slipped the catch that allowed the door to roll sideways on well-greased bearings.

'Is Major Blom aboard?' I asked politely. Smoke and shrill chatter rolled over me like fumes from a diesel with dirty injectors.

'Jimmy!' somebody called, 'You're wanted!'

'Who wants me?' The fruity voice emanated from the forward end of the saloon.

'I do,' I answered, rather more crisply than I intended.

The conversation died to nothing like a wave running up a beach and the ten or twelve people pressed shoulder to shoulder in the saloon registered mild curiosity and astonishment. At the same time an avenue was cleared down the length of the dark purple carpet and a large figure standing at the far end of the room, between the steering console and a cocktail bar, turned and stared with ill-concealed impatience as if I were collecting for Christian Aid Week.

'And who the hell are you?'

'My name is Montgomery.'

'Ah. You'd better have a beer, I suppose.'

'Thanks.' There it was, the instant pigeon hole. Clearly Major Blom was not the man to waste gin or whisky on NCOs. The major opened a fridge door, shouted 'Heads!' and with a powerful, well-aimed throw hurled

24

a can of beer at me. I caught it neatly, one-handed. A girl in tight trousers and high-heeled sandals clapped, giggled, and gave me the eye.

'I'll be right out,' Blom called to me, then finished pouring his drink and pushed his way across the saloon.

The handshake was wet and cold because he had been handing out ice cubes with his fingers. His eyes, meeting mine for a milli-second before sliding sideways, were hard, bloodshot, and set in deeply wrinkled and bruised-looking pockets of flesh. Like kidney stones, I thought. He must have been good looking once, in an Army & Navy Stores sort of way. Now aged about sixty and reeking of after-shave, he looked like a government health warning against cholesterol. His rig was what you might call Cowes Executive: navy double breasted blazer buttoned across a double gut, its shoulders speckled with dandruff snowing from a thick head of grease-blacked grey hair, narrow club tie, white shirt, grey slacks, dark blue deck-shoes. Despite the slack and puffy features behind the grey military moustache, there was something formidable about the man. He reminded me of the headmaster at my old prep school, the type who demanded the highest of standards. In others.

Dipping my beer can in salute I wished him good luck and took a long swallow, NCO style. Standing like Lord Louis with one hand in his blazer pocket, the major searched the crowd of boats with his eyes.

'I'm waiting for my idiot son, did you see him?'

'I'm afraid I don't know him.'

'Bloody fool knocked his boat up in the race and got disqualified, so he's arguing with the race committee. Sit over there.'

I sat on a gold-flecked cushion while the major remained standing, moodily rat-tat-tatting a heavy gold signet ring against his tumbler of pink gin.

'So you got my signal?'

I felt like saying no, I just popped in for a quick one,

but I nodded dutifully and smiled again.

'Yes sir.'

The deference tickled him and now that he knew I knew my place he visibly relaxed.

'Look here, old fellow, I always like to help you lifeboat chappies along a bit. You do a splendid job. You know I'm on the National Committee of course? And when I saw your application came up in Planning Committee I took a personal interest, so to speak. Follow me so far?'

'I'm grateful for your interest,' I said carefully, wondering what was coming next.

'That's the ticket.' He gulped his gin and again glared searchingly along the floating gangway that stretched between the moored boats to the shore. 'Where is that boy, sod him? Always late! No, it's a creditable scheme you put up, with a lot to commend it.' The major sat down heavily beside me, turned sideways with one ankle thrown across his knee. 'The thing is,' he went on, 'I would like to sound you out on it, if you follow me. For example, the pontoon thing, how would you moor it to the wall and build a gangway that adjusted itself with the tide?'

These were questions I could answer easily, and for ten minutes I elaborated on the fine points of my proposal. Not just technical factors, like moorings and gangways, but commercial ones, too. Had I done market research into demand for the bread, petrol, shackles, torch batteries – and no doubt French letters, eh? Ha, ha! – which I would be selling? I made precise, soldierly answers and told him all I knew. It reminded me of the intelligence debriefings after border patrols in Northern Ireland when the first rule of survival was that you made any answer you could think of as long as it was an answer, otherwise they sent you out again to get one.

Though patronizing, the major's tone was encouraging. And if this was what was meant by going through the bureaucratic hoops then I was content to coo the right noises in my pigeon hole. But that feeling did not remain for long.

Having extracted all the information he wanted, the major changed his tone and spoke more earnestly.

'Look here, Montgomery. There's nothing much wrong with your scheme as far as I can see but it won't wash, I'm afraid. I had you along here to see if there was some way I could help you make it work, but I don't see any glimmerings of hope at all. You see, the planning committee met on Thursday and in fact your application was thrown out. I'm sorry, but there it is.'

Pole-axed, I could only open and shut my mouth like a stunned fish.

'It's simple enough to explain but very difficult to solve,' he went on, looking along the pontoon again with restless, indifferent eyes. 'I'm afraid you overlooked one essential requirement. In this country you can't open a shop without a water supply. It's the rule of the land. And as you probably know, there is no water main along the quay.'

'Jesus wept,' I muttered, appalled.

'Thing is,' he continued smoothly, 'I hear you've been working on this project for some time and this will be a setback. But if you come up with something else I might be able to help put you on the right road, eh?'

He stood up and smiled, wiping his moustache with a white handkerchief dragged from his sleeve.

'Though I must say, if I was in your shoes with my own boat I'd be off to the South Seas so damn quick .... Thank God, he's here at last!'

The major had spotted something over my shoulder. He opened the glass door to the saloon and called in, 'Charles, fire up the rockets, would you!' Then he added with a pleased smirk, 'Ladies and gents, my ah-sole-heir approaches!' But he slurred the words to make the meaning quite different and was rewarded by gin-sodden guffaws and Babycham giggles.

Turning, I saw a tall, ginger-headed fellow about my

own age standing on the gangway and chatting with a group of people clustered on the stern of a moored racing yacht. He wore a cream silk shirt with matching slacks, and blue deck-shoes. As I watched he tilted his head over a gold lighter which he had removed from a little velvet pouch, and lit a filter-tip cigarette that he cocked upwards in his mouth like a bowsprit as he drew heavily.

I recognized him at once. The last time I had seen that pale, narrow, hollow-cheeked face was only that morning, when he had bawled 'Don't you know we're racing!' from the cockpit of his yacht *Go-Faster* as it smashed into the capsized sailing dinghy.

The major had flared with contemptuous peevishness at sight of his son. Now he put his hands round his mouth and shouted hoarsely, 'Come along, you little beast! You're keeping us waiting!'

The son jerked as if he had been shot, said about two more hasty words, then walked briskly along to the berth. His father shouted to him as he approached, 'Get rid of that bloody weed and take our bow lines, for God's sake.'

'Sorry father. Christ, we're pushed for time.'

'I know that, you fool.'

The deck underfoot trembled as first one then the other powerful diesel thundered into life, jetting a cloud of blue smoke into the air. It was only as the son stepped aboard, and I looked for an opening to make a courteous and heartfelt goodbye, that our eyes met. I read astonishment in small, pale eyes framed by ginger eyelashes so short and bristly that I wondered if he had had an accident with the flame of his gas lighter. He aimed his cigarette at me between thumb and forefinger, as if he planned to throw it into my face like a dart.

'You! You're the vandal who nearly wrecked us in Hurst Narrows. God, what are you doing here?'

Major Blom put it all together in his mind and boggled.

'Is that right, Montgomery?'

'In a manner of speaking.'

'I've got a hole in my hull you could put your head through,' the son said hotly, his face flushing the colour of new anti-fouling paint. 'You caused a collision of three yachts: don't you know that steam gives way to sail, you arsehole?'

The major rounded on me as well.

'You are a disgrace! I will be in touch with the inspector....'

Facing him squarely and speaking in measured tones, I said, 'At 10:42 hours today I was rescuing two lads from a capsized dinghy. They were near to unconsciousness due to exhaustion. There was no time to hoist proper signals to indicate that I was not in control. Three racing yachts bore down on me without any sign of a look-out being kept. I had to sound my foghorn to get their attention but I was still hit. When the collision occurred my vessel was stationary. This hot-shot nincompoop bowled clean over the top of the dinghy which was upside down in the water. If I had not got the men out in time they would be dead.'

'Balls!' the son snorted.

'Is this true?' the major demanded angrily.

'Ask him!' I retorted. 'You seem to be God Almighty around here.'

'You can't talk to me like that!'

'Is that the unanimous decision of your bloody committee?'

'Remember your position, Montgomery.'

'Ha!' I scoffed. 'And what is that supposed to mean?'

'I can terminate your employment any time I choose simply by picking up the telephone,' he growled. Then he turned to his son.

'Do the racing committee have these facts?'

'Of course not, father, it's a pack of lies.' The younger man's expression had suddenly become stiff, almost frozen, as if he were steeling himself. I realised that he was afraid of his father. Then a sneaky look come into his narrowed eyes and he added with a barefaced sneer, 'In my crew there is a Q.C.'s son, a journalist, two stockbrokers, a merchant banker and a sailing-school instructor. They were all witnesses.'

I pushed between the two men and stepped on to the narrow floating pontoon which bobbed under my weight.

'As far as I'm concerned,' I said with all the outrage I could muster, 'you can stuff your witnesses, your job and your boat up your spinnaker chute!'

As a lifeboatman I had free entrance into any club-house on the island, with the notable exception of the Royal Yacht Squadron. I made straight for the bar of the Island Sailing Club where I bought a pint and took it out on the balcony. With rattled nerves, I fumbled for my pipe and tobacco. I had just got it going nicely when Robert Cochrane, the racing secretary, came out to join me.

'And who has ruffled your fine feathers today, young man?' he asked, with a knowing look and a sympathetic smile.

I said nothing but pointed my pipe at the violet monstrosity now beginning to move from her berth. Rob chuckled.

'Yes, Ronny has been regaling us for the past couple of hours about some collision in the Hurst Narrows but nobody saw the name of the launch he says virtually cut him in half.'

Setting down my beer, I said tightly, 'I can tell you that, Rob. It was me.'

'Good heavens, what were you up to?' Rob was genuinely shocked, until I told him the whole story.

'It figures. These racing people need to be taught a lesson from time to time. Too many of them think they own the Solent. Ronny is such a prick.'

30

'Is that his name, the son?'

Rob nodded. 'I was at school with him years ago. We used to call him Floribunda. Good God, look at that!'

Dear Mother had got herself wedged across the narrow channel between the rows of moored yachts. People on the bows of their boats were desperately trying to fend the high-sided motor cruiser off. Steering from the flying bridge, Major Blom shoved the red-knobbed throttle levers all the way forward, trying to dig his way out of trouble with brute power. As the engines tore the boat free it wrenched a pulpit off a small cruising yawl and bent its stanchions. The transom of a pretty wooden folkboat splintered and the ensign on its varnished jack fell into the water. Still accelerating, the big motor cruiser sped too fast into the fairway, where a Mirror dinghy crewed by two youngsters threw about just in time to avoid being cut in half, and scraped all the way down the larger boat's hull. Major Blom and his son shouted and waved their fists at the children, who were white-faced, confused, and utterly in the right. Beside me, Rob breathed out with a long, shuddering sigh and held his face in his hands.

'There goes our Vice Commodore,' he said.

'Can't you read the riot act to a pig like that?'

'No chance. It was his money that bought the new dinghy sheds. So now he is Vice Commodore.'

'The air gets fouler every day around here. Maybe I will do what he suggested and push off to Tahiti.'

'Well, give it a few weeks,' Rob said seriously. 'Didn't you see the *Telegraph* this week? The Dear Mother shops are in hellish trouble. Ronny has lost a packet on that up-market magazine he has been running. They're desperately trying to salvage themselves. Both their boats are on the market, and that is significant.'

Rob was one of the back-room boys who knew yacht-racing politics inside out and had no illusions about sacred Cowes. Retired early from the Navy with a back injury, he lived in Yarmouth and had been one of the first to get me known by the inner circle, so the lifeboat job and a number of delivery assignments had followed naturally upon one another. Now I told him my troubles, and how my pet project which he had blessed had been scuppered by an idiot local authority law.

'Will you fight it?' he asked thoughtfully.

'It bears thinking about. Meanwhile, I'm unemployed. And broke.'

'Footloose and fancy free, eh, you lucky blighter.'

'Depends on how you look at it,' I replied, feeling brighter for having shared my troubles.

'Something will turn up: I'll keep my ear to the ground, don't worry.'

Gripping the Sunday morning paper in my teeth I went down the ladder backwards, stood one foot on *Windycap's* stern warp to draw her closer in, then stepped aboard. As the boat fell back on her mooring I slipped out of my seaboots and went below in my socks. The coffee was percolating on the gas stove. I slapped half a dozen rashers in the frying pan, broke in a couple of eggs, then took the coffee off the other flame and set up the pyramid toaster.

A few minutes later I was sitting on deck in the calm morning sunshine, my back against the wheelhouse, with all the ingredients of my Sunday morning treat around me. I started with the coffee, to relieve the murky pounding in my head, for I had followed up my two beers in Cowes with half a dozen pints in The George during the evening. Seagulls flew shrieking to perch on the rail and eye me hopefully as I drew the plate of bacon and eggs towards me and spread out the front page of the newspaper with the plate of toast holding down the corner that fluttered in the rising breeze. Ah, luxury!

The harbour had the air of a busy camping-ground. Boats packed the mooring-trots and lay six abreast along the harbour wall. The slick-smooth grey water pouring out of the Yar was alive with tenders and inflatables as weekend yachtsmen rowed to and from the shore, fighting the tide. Crews were out on deck, industriously sluicing muddy water over everything, though quite why they did it in harbour was something I never properly understood, especially on a Sunday morning when bubbles rising around every hull signified busy use of hand-pumped flushing apparatus. Some boats were already hauling in mooring warps and pottering out to sea. A French cutter was motoring in through the entrance, its crew tousled after an all-night crossing. There was a mighty splash and a dismayed shout as a black Labrador leapt out of the cockpit of a Westerly and with difficulty was hauled aboard, dripping muddy water and slime. The first ferry of the day was just coming into view as it headed in from Lymington.

Finishing my bacon and eggs, I sat back with a sigh, the paper unread on my knees. I would miss all this. A small cloud, promising winds to come, passed over the sun, dimming the brightness of the scene, and my spirits darkened with the sudden recollection of the previous day's events.

What puzzled me most was why Major Blom had summoned me all the way to Cowes just to tell me that my planning application had been thrown out. His 'call me father' attitude to lifeboatmen rang about as true as a teredo-infested rudder post. Did he want to crow over me, or did it give him a sense of raw power over individuals that somehow satisfied his ego?

The seagulls wheeled around, jabbering, as I tossed my coffee dregs into the sea, scooped up my plates, and went below.

To a foreign eye I suppose the cabin looked chaotic but to me this was home, my nest. I had everything the way I liked it. The wide and extra-long bunk was on a shelf behind sliding panelled doors, Dogger Bank style, above and behind a dinette upholstered in dark-blue leather cloth; its far corner was where I tossed my dirty clothes.

When the pile could be seen above the level of the table I knew it was time to make a trip to the coin-op laundry. Opposite, was the full-size chart table and a big galley. The dark mahogany glowed in the soft light coming down through the skylight, and the old brass ship's lanterns hanging from the deckhead gleamed like solid gold.

Beside the companionway leading down from the wheelhouse a low door led aft into the engine room. Forward, there was a small coal stove which kept me warm in winter, a door leading to the heads, another small cabin with two bunks, and the large for'ard workshop with its work benches, racks of chocked tools, storage bins for timber and sail cloth, and the steps leading up through the wide hatchway.

For a moment I stared around despondently. Would I have to sell her? She was my dream ship, the love of my life. Only my car, garaged on the mainland, had an equal place in my affections. With the kind of blank future I faced, it seemed doubtful that I could afford to keep both my love and my mistress.

Feeling sorry for myself, I tipped the rest of the hot water out of the kettle into the washing-up bowl and was rinsing the dishes when the boat lurched and a voice asked if there was anybody aboard. It was one of the dinghy sailors I had rescued, standing shyly on the stern with the clothes they had borrowed rolled up under his arm.

'Hello, come on down,' I called. 'How do you like your coffee?'

'Milk and sugar, thanks. Great!'

I cleared a space for him to sit among the sailing and motor-racing magazines that littered the settee and spooned Nescafé and sugar into two tin mugs.

'Sorry, you'll have to tell me your name again.'

'Jon,' he said, running his fingers through his blonde beard. 'Jon Van Blommenstein.' Then, seeing the lift of my eyebrows, he added, 'My father was a South African.'

I filled the kettle from the pump, put it on the burner, then sat opposite the visitor and took a pipe from the rack on the bulk-head.

'You had bad luck yesterday. Was she your boat?'

He shook his head. 'Mark is pretty upset, but he knows he made a bad decision and is being philosophical about it. We were lucky you happened to be in the area.'

Jon Van Blommenstein was about twenty-three, as tall as me but slender, with delicate hands and bright blue eyes. He grinned engagingly as he caught my eye, saying, 'I was petrified, I can tell you.'

'So was I, when those bloody fool yachts came at us.'

The kettle changed its tune and I got up to bring the coffee.

'Actually,' he said, 'there is something I want to ask you. I believe you make a business of delivering yachts?'

'Now and then,' I answered. 'How did you find that out?'

'Rob Cochrane is a friend, and I asked him last night if he knew of a reliable and experienced skipper who wouldn't rip me off.'

Good for Rob, I thought, lighting up my pipe.

'What's the job?'

'It rather depends on whether you are free.'

'Whether I am free rather depends on what the job is.'

He bought time by sipping his coffee but I could see his mind ticking.

'It's my grandfather's boat, you see. He lives in Sardinia and needs to sell the yacht to raise cash so he wants it brought home as quickly as possible to get a good price for her early in the season.'

'Why not sell her down there?' I asked.

Jon looked a bit embarrassed.

'To tell you the truth he's in financial trouble and he

35

wants the money here in England.'

'Sounds like I ought to put in for danger money.'

'Oh no, there's no question of bailiffs or anything like that. Not yet, at any rate, I promise you.'

'Fair enough. Would he pay my fee and expenses?'

'Certainly. You can work out an arrangement, I'm sure. He's a decent old guy, very honourable. He wrote and asked me to find somebody but I've been tied up finishing my thesis at Oxford and I've left it all rather late.'

The boat, he said, was a thirty-foot motor sailer. Just right for the Med. It had a shallow draught, so we could bring it up through the French canals. It would be a lovely trip, especially at this time of year. There was only one snag. Jon himself would crew, though I had to get the boat as far as the French coast alone. It wouldn't be difficult. He would meet me in Toulon in a few days, when his work was finished. I gauged him afresh, for I didn't lightly commit myself to three or four weeks in a small boat with a stranger. But I liked the look of him: he seemed handy and shrewd, and obviously had a sense of humour. A beam of sunshine blazed down through the skylight. My spirits lifted. What a chance to get out of this place!

'From our point of view there's only one problem,' he said.

My heart all but stopped.

'What's that?'

'How soon could you start?'

I glanced at my watch, then at my half-finished coffee, and pulled a mock face.

'That leaves me a bit stuck,' I said. 'I can't commit myself to anything until I've finished this.'

His face fell.

'What do you have to finish?'

'Just my coffee.'

He laughed. 'Right,' he said, 'it's a deal.'

2 : FERRARI

Southbound on the autoroute, cruising at ninety. The hot, bright sun flaring through the windscreen grew hotter and brighter by the minute and was keeping just ahead of the black rainstorm that had chased me all the way down from Paris. Taking short-cuts over the hills, the torrential rain had occasionally come close enough to breathe damply on the back of my neck. Then the road would straighten and I could speed out into the sunlight. I was praying for a clear run with no roadworks.

In an early summer downpour an open-top Austin Healey is not the most comfortable car in the world. My windscreen-wiper was out of commission, so I would have to slow right down. Worse, the car had no roof at all, so I would have to stop and dress in the yellow sailing suit that had been designed for protection against gales in the Channel. In hot weather, close against a hot engine, I would melt like chocolate in a Cellophane wrapper once I got into those heavy waterproof leggings and the jacket with wave-proof collar and cuffs. If the rain was really as bad as it looked I would have to get rid of the woolly tea-cosy hat that kept my hair from blowing in the slipstream and exchange it for a lifeboatman's sou'wester with ear-flaps.

The countryside looked green and fresh enough to eat. I could almost taste the sweetness of the Côte d'Or air being sucked with a hawking growl into the trumpets of the four carburettors. Fields of sunlit yellow mustard glowed to the left of the unwinding ribbon of white concrete as if thinly spread with dairy butter. Opposite, tailor-made fields pin-striped by vineyards were getting hot sunshine and heavy rain simultaneously, creating the taste you pay for in a bottle of Burgundy.

Every forty-five seconds at this speed put dreary England another satisfying mile further behind: small-minded England and its petty bureaucracy that had brought all my dreams crashing about my ears. It was my home but I couldn't get away from the place quickly enough now – though ninety would have to do, for I had no desire to begin my new life with a speeding ticket.

Although I had told Jon Van Blommenstein that I would be ready to move as soon as I had finished my coffee, it had not been quite as easy as that. My boat had to be laid up at cheaper moorings on the trots in the middle of the harbour. The naval architect drawing plans for the barge had to be bought off and the barge itself sold back to its previous owners, leaving a hefty hole in my pocket. Then there had been trouble with the French dockside and railway workers going on strike and the cross-Channel ferry sailings had been erratic, but I had finally caught the Tuesday night boat from Southampton to Cherbourg, kipping on deck in my sleeping-bag, and now I was feeling the cobwebs being ripped away by this exhilarating buzz down the empty motorways of France where the long-striding engine was in its element.

The fat racing-tyres sizzled on the concrete. The low-slung exhausts bellowed a happy, burbling sound. And six thousand moving parts in the engine, assembled lovingly with my own hands, made the most beautiful music of all. The familiar alarm-clock dials on the metal facia confirmed what I was hearing. Tach steady on four and a half thousand revs, oil pressure looking good, temp normal, charge-rate okay, no warning lights showing. All well in the engine room.

A small Renault hugged the fast lane ahead. I floored the accelerator and even from that speed the car cata-pulted satisfyingly.

Astonishment registered briefly on the other driver's face as I split through on the inside at about one hundred and twelve. His car floundered in the slipstream like a cardboard box and he caught a brief glimpse of a dusty, mud-streaked, saucepan-coloured bullet. When it was designed in the early fifties the Austin Healey was the epitome of a handsome and functional sports car; now, in an age of boxy little beasts that ran on a mere sniff of petrol, it still turned heads on the road.

Not that my Healey any longer bore more than a token resemblance to the car Donald Healey had drawn on his dining-room table. Its lightweight 100-S body had been going cheap after being wrapped around a tree at Brands Hatch. Since then the front end had been patched as many times as a pair of gardening trousers. The neat little oval grille that distinguished the racing 100-S from other Healeys had long ago disappeared and now there was just an open mouth with a radiator behind it.

The bare alloy bonnet was domed on the passenger side to accomodate the turbo-charger and was held down with straps of frayed army webbing. Like silver tulips, eight carburettor intakes jutted through the bonnet in two rows of four. The car's wings were flared over wide mag-alloy wheels and Dunlop intermediate racing-tyres. For lightness when racing the car had never in its life been fitted with bumpers.

At first, being a bit of a romantic and believing that boats and cars have personalities, I had given the car a name: *Ma Biche*, my darling. Then I discovered she had a personality right enough, and when I got to know its true nature I pronounced the name in the English way. The car was a bitch.

Below the belt she made you writhe because her exhausts ran just beneath the floor and at full chat they glowed red-hot. Above the belt you were exposed to wind and rain that flicked your ears like wet towel-ends. If I loathed this car it was with a loving passion; if I loved her it was with burning hatred. I had built her, nursed her, kicked her, even slept with her – on a freezing Yorkshire moor when the fuel-pump packed in at 2am. I had raced her, wrecked her, and started all over again with a five-litre Chevy engine salvaged from a class one offshore powerboat that had gone the wrong side of a buoy in the Cowes – Torquay Race two summers ago and driven up a sandbank. The engine happened to have a turbo-charger but the tremendous power it would provide was too frightening and I had adjusted the waste-gate to by-pass it.

The car was a sod to drive. She was bad-tempered, treacherous, difficult. But she had a heart of gold, and as I bowled down the autoroute with the sun in my eyes – typically, no visor – I was sufficiently drenched in self-pity after my bad news weekend to imagine she was my only real friend in the world.

The Renault was a tiny speck in the cracked rear-view mirror when I stopped pedalling and slowed to ninety. The tyres synch'd over the concrete slabs like fast-ticking wristwatches and gentle vibrations came up through the small steering-wheel of laminated elm and bored-out alloy. A lumbering lorry in the slow lane seemed station-ary in the landscape. Then a low-flying magpie came at the windscreen like a bomb, turning away at the last split second, and I thought of the old rhyme, 'One for sorrow, two for joy ....' The road became straight and level, the roofs of a large town over to the left, fields and the usual shelter belts of poplar trees to the right.

Suddenly, like a firework going off, the mirror seemed to explode with brilliant light.

Twisting my head round, I looked up the barrel of a dark blue Jaguar XJ-S that was so close a brave man could have jumped from the Healey's tucked-in tail on to the Jaguar's long snout. On full beam, the double headlights began to flash imperiously, but I would not be spoken to like that and I hesitated, tingling as my blood quickly came on the boil.

It was just as well, for a streamlined shape howled through on the near side, then another – a green Porsche sniffing the trail of a red Ferrari Dino.

Startled, I glanced in the mirror again and jumped as

a third car, its horn blaring, overtook on the near side. A polar-white Corvette Stingray doing at least a hundred and twenty.

Then the Jag vanished from the mirror and hammered after the 'Vette, its only noise the steam-jet whistle of rubber on concrete and an exhaust murmuring like conversation in a library.

The four super-cars formed up in line abreast across three lanes, slowing sharply though not braking. Like my battered Healey, they all had GB plates and all but the Corvette were right-hand drive. I flashed my headlights and waved my fist over the windscreen. They blared their horns derisorily; one had an air-horn that loosed a few bars of Colonel Bogey into its slipstream.

I was aware of oncoming cars in the other carriageway being braked hard as their drivers saw what must have looked like the starting-grid at Le Mans bearing down on them.

Then, at about 35mph, the Ferrari Dino sounded a triple blast and all four cars took off, leaving a cloud of blue smoke in the air and eight parallel lines of black rubber on the road.

There was traffic ahead, so the formation changed as neatly as the Red Arrows, the red Ferrari and green Porsche leading the white Corvette and blue Jaguar in a tight four-square group. My dusty Healey might be a bitch, but nobody had the right to treat her that way.

I tucked the Healey's stratocruiser nose six inches from the Jaguar's rubber bumper and got my first thrill of revenge. From the jerk of the driver's head as he looked in his mirror it was obvious he hadn't expected to see me there. The formation changed again to line ahead, passing a pair of cars running abreast. The Jag moved right to get a look ahead but when it tried to get back in the line I was already there, pressing hard on the American Corvette.

A small saloon tooling along at seventy hogged the middle lane. I pulled out of the line, accelerated, and overtook it on the inside. For a split second the brown Citreon GS became the jam in a 110mph sandwich.

Now I was in front of the Corvette, abreast of the Porsche but inside of it. Ahead, a yellow flashing light showed a lorry pulling out of the slow lane to overtake another. The fast lane was the only clear road. I gritted my teeth and held the power on. The Ferrari Dino accelerated but the Porsche left a gap, hardly longer than the Healey but just long enough. With a twitch of the wheel I nipped into it with about one second to spare. Alarmed, the tear-drop shape of the Porsche fell back, out of the running.

At this speed on such a first-class road the driver of the Ferrari Dino 308 would be relaxed, possibly even steering with one hand while he beat time to the stereo with the other. Six feet behind I cursed and sweated, struggling to concentrate every ounce of muscle and will-power on keeping the Healey going in a straight line. The whole car was alive. Every rivet danced in its hole. The thunder of four hundred and fifty brake horse-power trailed behind like a vapour stream. The Healey had been built to take a souped-up A90 taxi engine; now it bulged with power and it took a strong man, and a brave one, to keep his foot down.

Touching a hundred and twenty, with a clear road ahead, the Ferrari began to slow. Through the strange kind of telepathy that passes between drivers having a dice on the road, I was persuaded not to overtake. Then the Ferrari took a slip road, braking hard. At the toll booth there was a delay because I did not have the right money, but the other car was clearly waiting for me as I accelerated along some dual carriageway to catch up.

Ahead lay the town of Mâcon. Overhead-banners in the streets proclaimed an imminent wine fair.

Unnaturally loud in the dim and shuttered streets, our engines crackled and spat as the Ferrari led at a sedate and modest pace. The two cars attracted many glances, all curious, some envious: the Ferrari – dynamic, soph-isticated, the best modern motor-engineering can devise; the Healey – battered relic of a once-gracious era.

A white-helmeted gendarme on a motor-cycle peeled out of the traffic and followed at a distance, turning back as we crossed a bridge over a wide river on the far side of the town. On the far bank of the Sâone the Ferrari turned off right, taking a rural road southwards, parallel with the river. The road was empty, lined by poplars. The Ferrari snapped ahead with a busy howl as if fired from a rubber band. Under hard acceleration the Healey danced all over the road; the wheels would spin at sixty. The *chausée* was very *deformée*, and the judder as I hit sixty from a practically standing start in six seconds flat was like driving over a badly built level-crossing.

Flashing the lights I pulled out to pass. The Ferrari weaved across the road, blocking.

That was rude. And dangerous.

I feinted. The Ferrari weaved again. Slicing down a gear I turned the Healey's biscuit-tin nose the other way. From 85 mph the car leapt ahead swiftly enough for my backbone to feel the pattern of the seat-stitching.

A girl passenger in the Ferrari looked back worriedly as the Healey moved up. She turned and said something to the driver. Instantly the Ferrari weaved back across the road. The girl opened her mouth to cry out but I avoided collision only by savage braking and throwing the Healey into the gravel on the far side. Cursing, I weaved back through the Ferrari's slipstream as feathers of smoke drifted from the skid-marks my wheels had left on the tarmac.

The road led into a rural village. Farmhouses with large hen-cluttered yards and immense barns of mossy brick and tile lay on the outskirts. Poultry scattered as both cars whined down through the gears, and the road narrowed, and the tarmac became pot-holed *pavé*. The village centre was a market square, empty but for a handful of dung-spattered cars and a fountain that was not working. Waving restlessly in the sultry air as the thunderstorm advanced, plastic streamers hung in the open doorways of half a dozen shops and cafés facing a mediaeval church across the square. Beyond them was a Total service station. The Ferrari braked sharply and veered into it.

I stopped in the street outside and switched off. My blood was up. That kind of driving on a racing circuit would have meant instant disqualification. The other driver was a madman and I intended to tell him so. After five hours at the wheel I didn't allow myself even the luxury of a stretch, but strode across the forecourt and rapped on the Ferrari's curved tinted window. Its engine was still burbling.

More insistently I rapped again, determined to deliver a piece of choice Anglo-Saxon advice.

The electric window rolled down evenly and a man put his head out. I registered slicked-back gingery hair, pale eyes, and cream silk cuffs turned back from chamois leather driving-gloves. It was Ronald Blom.

'Boo!' he said loudly, and let out the clutch. The Ferrari sprang away. I was left stooping ridiculously over a car that was no longer there.

A man in a blue work-coat came out of the office wiping his hands on a rag as I stood stupefied in the smoke.

'Monsieur?'

I ran to the Healey, fired the engine before my feet hit the pedals, and was severely embarrassed as the spinning wheels danced on the cobbles, slewing the car broadside across the first of three sharp bends as the road twisted out of the village.

In the open country ahead there was no sign of what might have been a Red Arrow cleared for take-off. Then, too late, I realized that the farmyard wall on my right ended abruptly and the main road peeled off. As it came into view I glimpsed the red speck of the Ferrari, rapidly diminishing. I was in third gear, doing well over sixty, and the unexpected bend was as greasy as a skid pan because there had been cattle on the road. I yanked the wheel round and stood on the gas.

Then I felt the Bitch start to slide.

Beyond the turn-off was a patch of bumpy bare earth as large as a tennis court where half a dozen men in blue dungarees and flat hats were playing the French version of bowls. I was dimly aware of *boule*-players leaping for their lives as the massive trunk of a plane tree crossed and recrossed the end of the bonnet.

In a cloud of dust that spiralled upwards like a small tornado, the Bitch came to rest in the middle of the *boule* game.

The game would have ended prematurely anyway. As snatches of 'Colonel Bogey' trumpeted on a distant horn there was a loud swishing noise from behind. And with a barrage of raindrops as big as acorns the thunderstorm that had been trailing me finally caught up.

The sofa was an old friend. I woke to the sounds of busy traffic and the whirr of a highly-bred outboard-motor. Bright sunshine streamed through the dark green shutters leading to the balcony. The flat was on the fifth floor of a modern block right on the Quai Stalingrad in the old port of Toulon. Blinking in the brightness, I rolled out of my sleeping-bag and took in the view, a feast after winter on the Solent. Deceptive as always, the Mediterranean was calm and blue, tinselled with silver where its mirror-surface flashed in the clear light. Directly below me, a dozen yachts were moored to the quay, a couple of them flying red dusters. The wide mosaic-patterned pavement was thronged. Tall Africans stood among the crowds, like ebony lighthouses, selling leather hats and carvings. To the right was the great naval arsenal of Toulon, to the left the yacht harbour and moorings for tiny, brightly-coloured fishing-boats.

Wet and starving, I had thrashed the Bitch into Toulon

just before midnight to find Julian with company. He had come out of his bedroom to greet me with a towel round his middle, an evident anxiety to return to his pit with the least delay, and a self-satisfied grin that I knew of old.

'Beer and eggs in the fridge, plonk in the bottle, and bed where you find it,' he had said, 'and if you want a job tomorrow I can fix you up.'

Then his bedroom door had snicked behind him and after a glass of red wine I had stretched out on the sofa and drifted to sleep with visions of leaping *boule*-players before my eyes.

Now the flat was empty and I opened a can of cold beer and attacked Julian's eggs with butter and a saucepan. I broke the nose off the new *baguette* he had left for me and took it out on the balcony with the beer and scrambled eggs. Sitting in an alloy-frame deck-chair I ate off my knees and watched the yachts, fishing-boats and St Mandrier ferries moving in and out of the port past the warships, feeling a surge of contentment at the first touches of hot sun on my bare shoulders.

A couple of times a year I had done delivery trips to or from the Med for Julian Simpson-Potter, a young and well-connected ex-Para officer who, like myself, had made the army work for him. He had bought himself out of the regiment as a captain and then set up a yacht brokerage and charter business on the Riviera. And if the home comforts I was enjoying were anything to judge by, he was doing nicely, thank you. With luck, I thought, I could stick him for a few more jobs through the summer. Driving boats on the Med was a more attractive proposition than the dole queue in England; in any case, the dole would not go far with a mouth and a petrol tank to feed.

As I forked eggs into my mouth and chewed on the crusty bread and watched the contrast of the peaceful harbour and the crowded quayside, I wondered what Julian had lined up for me today. With luck I could fit it in before going to Nice and taking the ferry to Corsica; then I would connect by bus and ferry to the northern tip of Sardinia where I had to meet Jon Van Blommenstein's grandfather. It was a complicated way to go, but according to Jon it beat the long and tedious way through Italy, and as I was in this lark as much for the fun and interest as for the dough, I had decided to take his advice. Julian had gone out early with his girl, muttering about helping some English journalists to take pictures, but while I sat out on his balcony in my briefs and soaked up the sunshine I was in no particular hurry for him to come back.

Fetching Julian's binoculars, I swept them idly over the yacht club marina that lay on the far side of the town basin, protected from the bay by a high sea-wall. Leisurely I ran the glasses over a number of boats in turn, looking out for British flags and admiring a couple of ocean cruisers, their rigging sprouting growths of baggy-wrinkle to protect their sails from chafe on long ocean crossings. Then a flash of red caught my eye. Not ordinary red but *rosso chiaro*. Ferrari red. I focussed more sharply. At the top of one of the boat-launching ramps, surrounded by admirers, was a red Ferrari Dino 308 GT4 2 plus 2.

Then I glimpsed a speck of metallic green and the glasses located a Porsche 928 parked on the sea wall. On the road beyond was the streamlined iceberg-outline of a Corvette Stingray, and behind it the refined dark blue Jaguar XJ-S.

Well, well.

It was a ten-minute stroll around the harbour to the marina, the pavement burning beneath my thonged sandals, and I soon wished I had put on rather less than jeans and a t-shirt. The Dino had one door open, so it looked like a lame butterfly. Striking a tense pose against its door, jutting her chin as if determined to find a ship with which to go down, was the girl who had played the castanettes to Julian's organ all night, a model with brassy eyes and enamel lips who wore little besides a deep sun-tan and a look of satisfaction.

But the centre of attraction was neither the model nor the exotic car, which hardly rated a second look in this part of the world. Forty feet away a crowd of fishermen, yachtsmen and quayside loungers formed a guard of honour on either side of a tripod, set low to the ground, on which was mounted a Hasselblad camera with a lens as long as a machine-gun. Over its viewfinder stooped a lithe blonde with skin like soft suede. Her bottom wriggled with unconscious provocation as she focussed carefully. Then the shutter went off with a high-pedigree clonk and she stood erect, hands on hips, squinting at the car. The top of her bikini was no larger than a pair of black eyepatches, the bottom a tiny black triangle that dangled beneath her belly button like a storm-cone warning of gales to be expected from the south. It seemed to me that she was at the wrong end of the camera, and evidently most of the admirers around thought the same.

Julian came over, biting the ear-hooks of his sunglasses. I made to push past him but he held me back and we made a mock struggle of it.

'Leave her alone, you randy sod, she's a customer!' he hissed.

'After last night I doubt that you would have any services left to offer,' I challenged.

'You'd be surprised, you don't realise how we have diversified. But when I said I had a job for you, she was not what I had in mind.'

'If you think that would be work, old man, I'd be happy to relieve you of the strain.'

He shook his head admiringly as he ogled.

'I agree, but neither of us stand a chance, we're not rich enough by half. But she might speak to you if you say hello nicely and keep your hands in your pockets. Come on.'

As we approached, the girl flicked big tortoise-shell

sunglasses upwards so they rested on her hair, which was cut short in Peter Pan style. Her eyelids, weighted with false eyelashes, moved slowly up and down like bed covers being shaken out. Her eyes were pointed at the corners, almost Asian, and strikingly green. As Julian introduced me formally it was obvious from her amused expression that she knew something I did not.

'Fritz, this is a good friend of mine, John Montgomery.'

She did not shake hands because she was busy winding back a film.

'Hi! We met yesterday, I think.'

'We did?'

'Oh yes.' She waved a long, thin brown arm at the Ferrari. 'But it wasn't me who put you in the ditch, believe me.'

The sunglasses dropped down over her nose and she began to load a camera-back with film, turning sideways to shade it with her body. Julian drifted off.

'You looked as if you had wet your pants,' she said with a narrow look.

Discomfited, I shook my head and she stuck her tongue out with a little giggle as she saw that I had taken her seriously.

'If your boyfriend was trying to wipe me out he nearly succeeded,' I said stiffly, the thought only then occurring to me that perhaps Ronald Blom was trying to pay me off for spoiling his yacht race.

'Ronny can't bear to lose,' she said, 'and just for the record, he is not my boyfriend.'

'What is he, then, besides a maniac?'

'For the moment, he's my boss. I'm a freelance.'

'Is there a difference?'

The edge in my voice surprised her, but with both hands busy she could use only a slender elbow to indicate the tall figure whose back was turned to me as he talked with Julian.

'Better ask him,' she said pointedly.

Ronald Blom cut an elegant figure, if you admire the deb's delight style of being: dark blue Terry-cloth shirt, tailored cream slacks, blue canvas deck-shoes with white laces. An elaborately-battered panama titfer was pulled a shade low over his forehead. As I watched, he opened out a shooting-stick, set the point on the concrete, then sat on the seat and with arms folded rocked himself back and forth as if he were settling down to watch a gymkhana.

With a sideways kick I sent the shooting-stick flying out from under him. His pale arms shot into the air as he struggled to recover his balance and as he fell backwards heavily I grabbed him under the armpits to soften his landing, at the same time saying a loud 'Boo!'

'Christ almighty!' he shouted. He had not hurt himself but he had got one hell of a fright. His narrow face flushed and as he got to his feet the small brown eyes with the bristly orange eyelashes glinted with dangerous temper.

'Snap!' I said, grinning.

With an icy, four-letter glare he dusted the gravel off his hands and straightened his posh hat.

'You might have broken my spine!'

'I was driving the Healey you beat up yesterday – it was more than my spine you nearly broke.'

'I know very well what you are,' he muttered venomously. Then he became aware of the circle of curious onlookers, including Julian, who was gaping like a village idiot. He scooped up his shooting-stick and stalked away.

'Can't we find some place fresher?' I said to Julian.

He nodded, momentarily speechless, and led me to a quick-food shack with a number of tables set out under a dusty vine.

When he found his voice he said, 'What you need is something cold and wet. Preferably straight in the mush.' I waved him off as I would a blowfly and when he returned with two glasses of white wine I explained the events of the last few days, beginning with the collision in the Solent and the interview in Cowes, then telling the story of the dice on the road. The wine cooled my nerves and by the time I was through, Julian was no longer so up-tight. I refilled the glasses.

'Now, suppose you tell me what on earth is going on here. Looks like a curious set-up.'

Julian snorted through his nose.

'God, you can say that again. You know about *Go-Fast*, I suppose?'

'The magazine? Yes, of course.'

Half serious, half tit-and-bum, but mostly advertizing, it was a jet-set magazine in which the girl friends of Cowes yachtsmen I knew longed to see their names printed. It did for fast cars, boats and planes, not to say fast living, what *Vogue* did for fashion and *House and Garden* ... well, for houses and gardens. It was one of those heavy, glossy publications which were more important to be seen throwing out than actually reading. It was a magazine devoted only in name to the search for speed; its real meat lay in reporting the social whirl surrounding those who were champions of speed. And Ronald Blom, incredibly, was its publisher.

Julian told me how the magazine had been on the point of folding a few months ago when Ronald Blom bought himself in with seventy thousand pounds on condition that he could do things his way. He reckoned that he could use his City contacts and the old-school-tie brigade to boost advertizing. But his ship was sinking fast.

'The magazine is going down hill faster than ever and Ronny can't see the writing on the wall,' Julian added. 'The recent issues have been nothing but a Ronald Blom ego-trip – that's why he's down here, playing with the dolly birds and fast cars, instead of back in London selling advertizing. If you think Ronny is a prick you should hear what Phil has to say!'

'Phil?' I queried.

'The editor, Philip Fanselow. Over there.'

The Ferrari Dino, out of gear, was being manhandled along a jetty where Julian had arranged for a pair of swish vessels, a graceful schooner and a ritzy Italian power cruiser, to tie up as background for a group photograph of the cars. The other cars were still on the quayside, being dusted with soft cloths. Fritz was peering through her viewfinder as a small man dressed all in black, a large chunk of Mexican turquoise hanging from a silver chain round his neck, positioned the Dino to her directions. His face was deeply-lined and leathery, much of it concealed behind a steely grey beard and sunglasses. He had a nervous, tense look about him, as if at any moment he expected to stand on a land mine.

'Tell me what the hell they're doing. Do you know?'

Julian rocked his chair back and chewed on his sunglasses.

'It's a typical journo-type package. They borrow the cars from the importers in the U.K. on the strength of a car test and performance report that two motoring correspondents they have brought with them will write for the magazine. Then they photograph the cars in glorious Technicolour against a backdrop of Riviera scenery, to give the thing a five-star jet-set rating, and get even more mileage out of it by shooting a range of swimsuits with the cars, for the fashion pages. So the importers and manufacturers get a lot of publicity, the magazine fills a dozen colour pages, and the writers have a jolly time on expenses with the dolly birds. It's done all the time by the glossy magazines, and this would be routine except that now your friend Ronny has muscled in and is acting the *prima donna*. Phil has been in a rage ever since he got here.'

Two men came up to the little café and started pulling up chairs but Julian waved them over and as they sat at our table I was introduced to Alec Dempster and Graham Wilson. I recognized the names at once. Dempster, in his early thirties and developing a beer belly, insanely wearing a two-piece grey suit with a padded nylon rally jacket that had a yellow stripe down each side and Dunlop written across the back, was a top national newspaper motoring correspondent. Wilson, a tall and weedy younger man with long curly hair in need of a wash, a psychedelic t-shirt and owlish spectacles, was a specialist writer for one of the car magazines and I had often read his articles on engine tuning. They sat back and groaned about the heat. Julian brought them drinks.

'I reckon I've seen you before,' I said. 'It was my Healey you guys tried to burn up yesterday.'

They were both surprised and immediately interested.

'What happened to you?' Alec Dempster asked with concern. 'You just disappeared from view – I thought you must have had some trouble.'

'I did, in a way, a lot of trouble. I took a slip road and chased the Dino.'

'Did you catch him?'

'Yes, but the sod ran me off the road and nearly killed me.'

Dempster and Wilson exchanged looks.

'It figures,' Wilson said. 'He shouldn't be allowed out in a Mini, that man.'

The newspaper writer squirmed uncomfortably in his rally jacket and smacked his lips over the wine.

'Our Ron might be a fool but he's not stupid,' he said. 'Remember when the big Mercedes was so hard to get? I heard him ring up the sales manager. He said that if he was Princess Margaret ordering a silver Merc with black trim he would get one tomorrow, wouldn't he? Well, he said, this isn't Princess Margaret on the phone but I'll have hers.'

Julian laughed and even I had to smile.

'Did he get it?'

'Says he did,' Dempster shrugged, 'but I don't know.'

The four cars were now perfectly lined up on the jetty. Fritz was dusting her lens filters with an airbrush before shooting.

'I'd sooner get my hands on that Fritz than a silver Mercedes, any day,' I said.

The others nodded agreement.

'Elli Johansson, Swedish freelance photographer,' Wilson explained. 'She got the nickname in Washington and uses it as a by-line. She's bloody good.'

'And she can take good pictures,' Julian chipped in, mischievously.

We talked about the cars, and I told them all about my turbo-charged Healey. Graham Wilson had seen me racing a few times in club events at Silverstone. He was buying another round of drinks when Ronald Blom himself came over. Julian turned out a chair for him.

'You can't put this down as entertaining local detectives like you do on the paper,' Blom said meaningfully as Wilson came back with a tray of glasses and a fistful of small change.

I saw Alec Dempster's thick eyebrows arch in an Oh Jesus! expression as Wilson caught his eye. The young technical writer said nothing but handed the drinks around, leaving one on the tray which he held out to Ronald Blom, then drew back.

'What shall I put this one down as?' he asked.

'Anything you like as long as you quit waving it around in the sun!' Blom retorted.

'Roger,' Wilson said quietly and came back to his chair with a wink that only the rest of us could see.

As he drank thirstily, Ronald Blom studiously avoided my gaze. A pall fell on the conversation. In the shimmering heat rising from the stone quayside we could see the editor standing behind Fritz as she triggered shot after shot, pausing from time to time to make tiny adjustments or change camera-backs.

Shortly, Fritz started packing her gear while Philip Fanselow shaded his eyes as he searched around.

'Come on,' Alec Dempster said, draining his glass, 'we're needed back at the ranch.'

He and Wilson walked down to the jetty to help move the cars. Fritz came up lugging her heavy aluminium camera case and flopped down in a shaded chair next to Ronald Blom. Julian got her a drink.

'By the way,' I asked him, 'you said you had a job for me?'

'That power cruiser at the jetty has been chartered at Bonifacio. Do you want to take her over?'

What a peach of a job! It was an easy 12-hour run to the southern tip of Corsica, and from there I could get the ferry across the straits to Sardinia where my next job was waiting.

'When can I go?'

'Any time,' Julian said. 'There's just one thing ...'

Wait for it, I thought. This will be good. It was. Ronald Blom had pulled his hat low over his eyes and was dozing with his feet up on another chair. Julian leaned forward and tipped the hat into his lap.

'Wake up, old man! You want a ride to Bonifacio, that right?'

'Sure, as long as I don't have to do some stupid thing like scrubbing the decks.'

Julian looked at me, his expression divided between an apology and suppressed laughter.

'You've got a passenger,' he said.

As the blood left my face, Ronald Blom whipped round in his chair and stared at me, surprise turning to supercilious indifference.

'Don't worry about it, Julian,' he said, 'I'll keep an eye on what he does.'

Determined not to rise to him, I said we would push off in the middle of the afternoon.

'After dinner, wouldn't you say?' Blom looked not at me for confirmation but at Julian, who nodded.

'There's no hurry, John,' Julian said soothingly.

'Eight sharp, then,' I said, 'and remember you are the

passenger.'

'And you remember,' Blom said, getting up and patting his pockets, 'that I am passenger and not your bloody crew.'

Fritz had been listening with amusement to the needling.

'Why aren't you the one who wants to spend a night in a boat with me?' I asked her.

She raised one eyebrow as she got to her feet, saying out of the corner of her mouth, 'Keep your back to the wall and you'll be okay.'

Ronald Blom snapped his lighter and tilted the cigarette upwards in his mouth as he blew a stream of smoke into the air. Then he snatched the girl's arm and jerked her away, muttering archly, 'Poisonous little tart.'

Julian caught my eye and turned his palms outwards. I raised my fist to smash him down but he surrendered at once, uttering the one word in the world which, under the circumstances, was capable of saving his skin.

'Lunch?'

He had promised to be on board by eight o'clock but it was just touching midnight when I was woken by the hawking of the Ferrari's exhausts and Ronald Blom staggered along the marina gangway carrying an expensive leather grip in one hand and an open bottle of champagne in the other. After a long and boozy lunch with Julian, following hard on the heels of the long and boozy morning spent under the vine on the quayside, I had communed some more with his sofa, then run my usual precautionary checks on the vessel. I knew Julian ran only taut ships and everything would be as I wanted it, but I could not put to sea without making certain. Then, during the long wait until Blom turned up, I had listened to the stereo in the wheelhouse and finally fallen into a doze.

Ronald Blom had put away a few too many but there

56

was also a nervy look about him: the thin face was grey and tense, the eyes not sleepy but needle-bright and burning. He was not on drugs but the trip he had made had been to the Casino, and my guess was confirmed when I asked if he had lost a packet. He rounded on me, momentarily hysterical with panic.

'Not that much!' he snapped. Then he got a grip on himself and the old arrogance returned. 'Mind your own damn business – okay, what are you waiting for now?'

Having touched a nerve I backed down and invited him into the cabin. The power cruiser was not unlike his father's dreadful mauve thing, with a large deck saloon that had a steering position behind large, swept-back windows at its for'ard end. I started the engines, switched the navigation lights on and the saloon lights off, and Ronald Blom dumped his gear on the floor.

'I suppose you want me to take her while you cast off?'

'Please yourself,' I replied, 'but please put your clobber down below, out of the way.'

I threw off the stern-lines from the aft well-deck and coiled the ropes as the boat moved forward under the weight of her anchor chain. Then I went for'ard along the wide side-deck to the front of the flared bow where I put my toe on the electric windlass button and started getting the anchor in. It was a warm still night and the city lights wriggled across the water like long silver worms. The exhausts burbled happily. Ripples spread out from the hull where cooling water from the engines spurted into the sea, stirring up the reflections.

The anchor had barely bumped once against the bow rollers when I staggered backwards as the engine revs increased sharply and the cruiser began to surge down the dark lane between rows of moored boats. Blom chose not to hear as I shouted at the black windscreen and with memories of his father's boat crashing into the other vessels moored at Cowes still fresh in my mind I ran aft. The moored boats were rocking heavily in our high wake. I jerked the throttles upright in their gate so the way fell off immediately. The bottle of champagne had foamed where Blom had put it down on the navigation chart. The grip was still on the deck. I thrust it into Blom's lap.

'Put it below, will you,' I said tightly, 'and don't play the fool when there is a man working on the foredeck.'

'God, you're one of those Mountbatten types, I see. Just my luck!' He threw a sloppy salute and lurched past me. I put the champagne bottle in his hand as he passed and told him to fetch a cloth from the galley, then finished stowing the anchor while the boat lay quietly in the middle of the harbour.

Under way again, I aimed the bows for the gap in the breakwaters. The gaunt silhouettes of the warships slid by a couple of hundred yards to starboard. The sea was oily smooth, with only a slight swell outside in open water. I edged the throttles forward and soon the big boat was planing, leaving a broad flat wake that was swallowed up by the city lights astern. When clear of the land I set a compass course for the Straits of Bonifacio, reckoning that if we could maintain this twenty knots we would be in port by the middle of the morning.

Cruising so fast in such a big vessel gives a false sense of security, like tobogganing in an armchair. Spray flared from each bow in a high wall of diamonds that glittered in the star light. The diesels maintained an even, powerful roar that was muffled by the soundproofed engine room and the thick carpet underfoot. Compared with my old lady laid up on the Solent this was hardly like being at sea at all. Yet, for all the speed and elegance, I knew which boat I would prefer to be in should the sea turn really nasty.

Expecting my passenger to have crashed in a drunken stupor, I was surprised to see him return to the saloon. Not only had he exchanged blazer and tie for a blue pullover that said *Go-Faster* across the front, but he appeared reasonably chipper. I determined to be tolerant, at least until he forced me to be otherwise, and I offered him the wheel which he took with a downward twist of his mouth.

'Hasn't this thing got an auto-pilot?'

'Yes, but it doesn't help you stay awake.'

I made coffee, seeking frequent excuses to return for a quick look at the compass and a glance around the dark horizon. A small boat hanging a bright lantern to attract fish was a long way off to port, and the shore lights were still visible astern; otherwise the sea and sky were a bag of black velvet.

When I handed Blom his coffee he took it without a word and for the hundredth time I wondered how a man could get so far through his life without bearing the scars of being frequently punched in the mouth. I dipped my own mug and said Cheers, but all he did was grunt. Until, after a while, as if it was all a foregone conclusion, he said: 'You can run me over to Santa Teresa on the way in, it will save me taking the ferry.'

With an effort that required a very deep breath I managed to smooth down my hackles. No way would I go all the way to the northern tip of Sardinia when there was a ferry running from Bonifacio every couple of hours.

'No chance, I'm afraid,' I said. 'The wind tends to blow up nasty in the middle of the mornings through those straits and we would have it right on the nose. We're running late as it is.' Then, wanting to change the subject, I asked, 'What's the attraction over there, anyway?'

'Pal of mine has got a villa at Porto Cervo, so I'm going to give him a chance to throw a party. And do a bit of business.'

I was continuing to keep a wary eye on the compass but Blom steered a close course.

'That's the Aga Khan's place – have you met him?' I

asked.

'Oh sure, but he's got so much money he doesn't know what to do with it, poor chap.'

'Get him to invest some of it in your magazine.'

'God, that's just what I need, a miracle.' Blom ran his hand wearily through his ginger hair. 'I can't even sell my boat now because she's got a ruddy great hole in her bow....'

As he looked sideways at me I saw in the bluish glow from the compass light that he was actually smiling, though it was hardly the kind of smile I would stick on a poster.

'I'm going to sue you for repairs, you are aware of that, of course?'

I took a long, careful, unhurried sip of coffee. 'You see that dark wet stuff out there, with all the little waves on it? You know what you can do....'

'Prettily said, but you're a fool.'

A silence fell between us until, against my better judgement, I had to ask why.

'If you had any sense at all you would settle out of court and save the legal fees; they can set you back a bit, you know.'

'You assume I am the guilty one.'

'My dear chap, it's as clear as Big Ben on a sunny day. I'm going to screw you for all I can get.'

'It won't be much,' I said with a hollow laugh. 'Even if you catch me. I'm not rich.'

'Maybe not, but it's a very pretty old boat you have been working on for the past few years. Must be worth a lot to people who like that little ship stuff. There are a lot of them about.'

'Is that a threat?'

Blom licked his dry lips, checked the course with an abrupt movement of the chromium-plated wheel so the boat swayed heavily and I had to grab the console to keep my balance.

'You have to get your act together, Montgomery. You

are a born loser and not even smart enough to know it.'

'How come?'

He shook out a cigarette, lit it with the gold lighter, and made the gesture that was his trademark, tilting the cigarette upwards between his lips while dragging the first puff, and sliding the lighter back into its velvet pouch.

'I can tell you why, but you won't like it and you certainly couldn't ever prove it.'

'Go on,' I muttered tightly.

'Your planning application, for example. Don't you see how Father screwed you? As Chairman of the Water Board he has already got the engineers working on a new main along the quayside, ostensibly to service the boat moorings. And he's got the harbour board in the palm of his hand. It's all been cleared.'

There was a buzzing in my ears and I felt as if it had been me who had just drunk too much champagne and lost a lot of money at the casino.

'Tell me more,' I said thickly.

Blom checked the course again and chuckled, his eyes veiled by cigarette smoke as he turned to see what effect his words were having on me.

'I mean the mooring for the barge that he bought, of course. He has filed his own planning application already, though naturally, as a matter of form, he will step down from the committee while the matter is being considered by all his chums. We don't want anybody smelling a rat. There was only one thing he was not sure of, and that was the mooring-system the naval architect designed for you. That's why he had you spill the beans to him in Cowes on Saturday. And I bet you even paid your own bus fares, eh.? See what I mean, old son? You've been screwed. Comprehensively.'

Throwing his cigarette down on the carpet and grinding it in with his heel as he stepped down from the wheel, Blom pushed past me. I started to protest but he waved a hand cursorily, saying over his shoulder, 'You're the mariner, old boy, so you do the marinating, what? It's what you get paid for, I imagine, and you're going to need all the cash you can get, believe me.'

The wheel-spokes were warm and sticky from Ronald Blom's soggy palms.

Somehow, as I steered the big boat fast through the dark night, that was the most unspeakable insult of all.

3 : VILLA MADDALENA

The day began badly and got worse. All night I stood the long watch while Ronald Blom slept off the effects of the champagne. With the boat being steered by auto-pilot, I dodged below once to look at him and found him lying on a satin-covered double bed in the owner's cabin, curled up in a ball and twitching like a red setter dreaming about a rabbit hunt.

Around two in the morning the moon came up, washing the velvet sea with pale light and making the arrow-straight wake a track of tool-swirled silver. The red and green glow of the navigation lights faded as the moonlight strengthened, and from the wheelhouse the power cruiser's white bulwarks and cabin-top seemed almost luminous and milky-blue. Towards dawn the moonlight itself began to fade; the outlines of the boat around me became a hard grey, then a miraculous pink as the sky changed by the minute, throwing a magnificent peacock's tail of turquoise and gingery yellow high above the distant mountains of Corsica which blocked the eastern horizon. Raw-eyed but elated by the spectacle, I put on sunglasses as the sun flashed like a golden arc-welder over the water. The big cruiser thundered onwards over the faint billows of a silk-smooth sea.

My passenger shook himself out just before nine, when the sun was already a searing white orb in a hazy sky and the white cliffs of the southern tip of Corsica were growing larger and more distinct over the port bow. He came into the wheelhouse with a mug of hot coffee.

'That's welcome,' I thanked him. 'It's been a long night.'

'Oh, do you want some? There's plenty of hot water still in the kettle. Give me the wheel.'

Cursing myself for not knowing better than to expect a kind gesture from Ronald bloody Blom, I handed over sourly and made my own coffee.

The ancient fortress of Bonifacio and its remarkable harbour are among the wonders of the Mediterranean. From the sea you approach a wall of limestone as massive and as white as the cliffs of Dover but it has been so undermind by the sea for centuries that it leans outwards; perched on its brim, the walled town and castle dizzily overhang the sea lashing far below. Houses are so close to the brink that their drains are often as not merely holes in the floor – as many a tourist discovers to his cost, it is not always pleasant to put your head over the parapet at Bonifacio when there is a gale blowing.

When I returned to the wheelhouse, the cliffs formed an immense and seemingly unbroken wall across the bow and Ronny was peering through the salt-speckled windows with a puzzled expression. 'Where is the entrance?' he had to ask, peeved that he did not know the answer himself.

Saying nothing, I edged him off the wheel and drove the boat onwards towards the towering cliffs. At a distance of little more than a mile I could begin to see how the sea made a knife-thrust into the heart of the cliffs, then angled ninety degrees right to form a long, narrow fiord. The old town is on the splinter of land between sea and fiord. As the cliffs close around your boat you know how Ulysses must have felt when his fleet was bombarded with rocks thrown from these self-same cliff tops.

So early in the season there was no difficulty in finding a vacant visitor's berth at the marina. The port captain idly watched as I reversed the boat carefully into one of them and ran the anchor chain out neatly, struggling to hold the boat straight in the cross-winds eddying off the cliffs. When I had cleated down the last mooring-line and killed the engines he strolled along the floating pontoon to tell me to move to another berth.

Ronald Blom stepped ashore with his grip. There was hot water in the kettle but he was unshaven and unwashed. 'I'll go ashore and get some breakfast before the ferry comes,' he said. And walked away.

Acidly I thanked him for his help, then set about moving the boat by myself. It would take longer – but suddenly I realized that without Ronald Blom the sun was warm, the sea was blue, and it was going to be a lovely day. Feeling jaunty, I set about finding a fresh-water hose with which to wash down the deck and windows. When all was ship-shape, I cooked a double ration of bacon and eggs in the galley – the breakfast my passenger would have shared had he not been in such a hurry to push off. The ferry to Sardinia was not yet in its berth; with luck, I hoped, Ronald Blom was stamping along the dock-side starving to death.

For three hours I napped on a squab laid on the deck, then closed up the boat, left the key with the port captain as Julian had instructed, and took an early afternoon ferry the eight miles across the straits to the tiny port of Santa Teresa. I found a taxi and, with the map Jon Van Blommenstein had sketched on the back of an envelope for me, set out on the 90-minute ride to the place where his grandfather lived, confident that I would never see Ronald Blom again. But it was difficult to forget him: like something nasty on the bottom of your shoe, memories of a man like that tend to stick around.

Rattled like a dice in a cup, I sprawled in the back of the taxi, an old Fiat, and watched the countryside through half-closed eyes, trying not to dwell on how simply the collapse of all my hopes and dreams had been engineered. The driver steered with one hand, removing it from the wheel often in order to change gear because of the waywardness of the road; his other hand hung out of the window and drummed a ceaseless tattoo on the door panel. The simmering heat and the irritation of the staccato fingers kept my nerves a-jangle.

Whole areas of the tinder-dry country had been laid waste by fire. Where flames had jumped the road, the car raised dense clouds of ash and black dust. A grove of olive trees, gnarled and silvery, gave flickering shade for a few seconds, then the car was racing round the shoulder of a hill and in the far distance I saw the sea, studded with green islands and laced with dazzling beaches. The driver gestured with his steering hand at a far valley where clusters of buildings, some with curiously curved and slanting roof-lines, overlooked a smart little port crammed with expensive-looking yachts and power cruisers. He broke into a long explanation in which I caught only the words Costa Smeralda, Aga Khan, and Princesca Margarita. The centre of the village, contrived at fantastic expense to look like some sort of five-star *stazzi*, or Sardinian shepherd's croft, was Porto Cervo. Right now I could think of at least one good reason for not going near the place.

Cork oaks in various stages of undress crowded the dried-up streams in the valleys. Hedges of prickly pear made ragged lines up and across the stubbly slopes. The air roared through the open back windows, beating my face. It would have been a pleasant and attractive drive had I not been in the hands of a madman who squealed the balding tyres on every corner.

At last the car swung onto a tortuous side-road and after another few miles reached a pot-holed driveway that led through a gateway formed by tall white pillars overgrown by creepers. A small faded board announced my destination: Villa Maddalena.

An avenue of Australian eucalyptus trees shaded the drive and sprinkled it with brittle leaves that snapped beneath the tyres. The car stopped with an unnecessary skid, raising a cloud of dust that drifted against the two-storey, whitewashed villa. Its red tiled roof was mottled with moss. Green paint peeled from its dusty shutters. Flowering creepers spread up the wall to the eaves and hung outwards in bushy masses.

I paid the driver and got a receipt so I could claim the expenses, then the Fiat sped away with screaming engine and spinning wheels.

After the noisy and uncomfortable journey, the silence of the villa and its tall, cool trees came as a surprise. There was a wrought-iron handle near the weathered door leading into the house; when I tugged it, a bell tolled with a sharp, thunderous clang as if summoning monks to prayer.

I must have jumped visibly, for a quiet voice behind me said, 'I am afraid we do have a rather loud bell, so we can hear it in the garden. How do you do? I am Piers Van Blommenstein. You must be Montgomery.'

Like his handshake, his voice was firm, cultivated and friendly. He was erect, slim, elderly, wearing only khaki shorts and scuffed espadrilles; a trim Van Dyke beard, more white than grey, jutted from his chin. Though shaded by the wide brim of a battered bush hat, his sharp blue eyes could be seen weighing me up and I was suddenly on guard, as if in the presence of a major-general.

'How was the trip?' he asked.

'I think I'm lucky to get out of that taxi alive.'

Van Blommenstein smiled sympathetically and took my elbow, guiding me round the side of the villa. 'You must come and have a drink with us to recover from the experience.'

The view from the wide front terrace was breathtaking. A grove of olive trees fell away in a series of irregularly-shaped terraces to a cove of bone-white sand kissed by a blue sea. Out from the shore, a pair of low, hummocky islands joined by a sandy spit formed perfect shelter for the little bay; beyond them twinkled the eastern horizon of the open sea.

Van Blommenstein sensed my admiration. 'It's a beautiful place, we love it very much. Where will you sit – in the sun or the shade?'

Part of the terrace was shaded by a pergola of timber beams overgrown with vines to form a level roof. Beneath it, half a dozen folding-chairs were set around a table. The twin rows of shutters along the front of the villa were thrown back and white curtains in the open windows lifted lightly in the sea breeze. On every window-sill were red and pink geraniums in boxes; more grew in mossy ceramic pots standing on the low stone parapet around the terrace. The whole valley was a sun-trap. Feeling the heat settling heavily on my shoulders and rising from the flagstones underfoot, I elected the shade of the vine.

Van Blommenstein arranged three chairs nearer to the table. 'Yes, the sun is much too hot for comfort at this time of day. Please excuse me, I will fetch a bottle from the cellar.'

As the old man went inside, calling somebody's name, I sat back with a contented sigh. The air was twenty degrees cooler beneath the lush young leaves and the flagstones were comparatively chill and moist. The tensions of the past days began to evaporate like water spilt on hot stones. The gruelling drive south, the ridiculous driving-games, my unpleasant passenger on the boat: it all seemed a million miles away. I gazed at the magnificent view spread at my feet and let the silence be heard: the whisper of the breeze rustling the tall gum trees, the buzz of bees in the honeysuckle and bougain-villae, the delicate chime of a clock indoors announcing three o'clock, and a persistent little voice inside my head informing me that here was paradise. Then I heard the slap of leather sandals on the flagstones and I turned to see a girl walking over to join me. 'So you've come to take the boat away,' she said, ducking under the vine.

It was an odd choice of words, I thought, as I got to my feet and smiled a greeting.

'You could say that. How do you do.'

'Hi.' The accent was English, the manner faintly American. As she shook hands, Nepalese silver bracelets jingled on her wrist. 'How do you like our view?' she asked, flopping into a chair and propping her heels on the parapet.

'Sensational. I can hardly look away.'

Sweeping the horizon with a wave of her hand she said with real bitterness, 'Enjoy it while it lasts: soon it will be spoiled.'

The old man came under the pergola carrying a silver tray which he set down on the table. 'You met my grand-daughter I see. I'm afraid Kristy isn't very happy today. The boat you are taking away was our dream boat and we have had to sell her, you see.'

I muttered a defensive apology. The girl's resentment was understandable; I had been in the same frame of mind myself for long enough and was now trying to forestall a similar fate.

Van Blommenstein filled three tall glasses from a slender-necked green bottle speckled with dew. 'Well, it's not your problem, Mr Montgomery,' he said. In seconds the glasses, too, were filmed with moisture. He passed one to me and one to Kristy, then tossed his bush hat on a chair and lifted his own glass in a courtly salute. '*Prosit*, Mr Montgomery. Here's to a good voyage in our dream ship. And good luck to us, eh Kristy?'

Their eyes met over the rims of their glasses, sharers of some secret. 'We'll need it,' the girl murmured, tasting her wine. The old man shot her a keen look but made no comment.

'*Gesundheit!*' I said. The amber wine was light, fragrant, icy cold and completely delicious. As the cool, golden tang of it filtered through the dusty tissues at the back of my throat I gazed at the girl. She was as intriguingly perfect as the wine. Shoulder-length auburn hair, sun-bleached with blonde lights, framed clear hazel-coloured eyes, a freckled and attractively tilted nose, and a delicate though determined chin. It was a good-humoured and kind face, with the same zest and fresh intelligence as her brother's. When not actually smiling she seemed always about to, though her lips were sun-cracked and her expression had a certain wariness.

A few years younger than myself, she wore faded jeans and a man's patched work-shirt which hung out and was knotted in front, the sleeves rolled up high. Earth stained her fingers, a pair of sécateurs jutted from a hip-pocket. The pretty dusting of salt in her eyebrows, from a morning swim, was proof enough that this girl was no wallflower.

I was suddenly aware of Van Blommenstein's blue eyes fixed on mine. They twinkled good-humouredly as our glances met.

'Is the wine to your liking?'

'Simply marvellous,' I said.

Sensing a double meaning in my admiration, which I did not really intend to convey, Van Blommenstein followed my gaze and nodded, smiling in a pleased sort of way.

'Jon told us you were coming, but with the strikes in France we were not certain exactly when. I hear you saved his life: that was good work, he told us all about it.'

'Well, he was a fool to go out in that weather.' Embarrassed, I tried to shrug it off.

'Yes, he told us that, too.' As Van Blommenstein sipped his wine reflectively, perhaps pondering on what might have been, his grand-daughter set her glass down with an irritated jangle of bracelets and sat forward, her chin on her hands, staring gloomily at the beautiful view. When I asked about the boat I was to take to England, Kristy told me matter-of-factly that it was down at Golfo Aranci fuelled up and ready.

'I can run you to the port in the van when you want to go,' she said, with part of a smile, 'it's only half an hour away.'

Van Blommenstein refilled my glass. 'But you're not in a hurry. You will dine with us, of course, before you go.'

It was not a question but a statement and when I did not protest but made a conciliatory gesture, half gratefulness and half surrender, Kristy got up at once. 'Good, you can help me pick.'

The old man explained. 'We grow chrysanthemums here in greenhouses and air-freight cut flowers to all parts of Europe, mainly the top hotels. It's our business here, my life's work....'

There was a note of such wistfulness in the voice that I glanced round at him sharply and for the first time realized how hollow-eyed and shrunken with tension he was. As his voice faltered Kristy cut in bitterly, 'Not that it's going to continue much longer, at this rate.' Making a visible effort to be more cheerful, she drained her glass with gusto and stood up, pulling the knot in her shirt-front tighter and grinning. 'Do you mind helping out a bit? We would be awfully grateful.'

'Not a bit.'

Van Blommenstein stared after his grand-daughter as she carried the tray of bottle and glasses into the house. 'Kristy worries too much.... I die a little every time I see it.'

'What is she so worried about?' I asked curiously.

The old man tugged at his neat beard and said with both sadness and pride, 'Mainly about me, I'm afraid to say. If there were more girls like her in the world it would be a profoundly better place.'

I had come to the Mediterranean to begin a long voyage as a boat-delivery skipper and within twenty-four hours I was in Sardinia picking flowers....

Feeling cool in swimming-shorts and thonged sandals I walked with Kristy to a long, low-roofed, whitewashed building behind the villa. It was a big shed, dark and dusty. When Kristy snapped a switch, the bare electric bulbs illuminated cobwebs among the rafters, shelves of horticultural chemicals, three rotary diggers parked in line, piles of forks, sprinklers, hoses, back-pack sprayers and other gardening equipment. The earthen floor was carpeted with wilting leaves stripped from flower-stems. Down the centre of the building were long wooden tables. On one side of them were piled large cardboard boxes stamped 'Villa Maddalena' in red; on the other side were rows of tall green plastic buckets half-filled with water, a score of them holding armfuls of tall flowers of the kind I had seen on Julian's balcony.

'This lot I picked this morning,' Kristy said. 'Tomorrow, if we can get them packed, they will be sent by air to the big hotels and restaurants in Paris.'

The far end of the shed was partitioned up to the rafters. A large brass padlock on a heavy wooden door leading into the room beyond caught my eye.

'That's Opa's lab,' Kristy explained.

'Why the padlock?'

'It's like a plant hospital: tests have to be carried out in virus-free conditions, so it's only Opa who goes in there.'

The gravel drive continued fifty yards beyond the stone-and-tile shed to a shallow valley which was hidden from the villa by gum trees. In the valley were four greenhouses, not glazed in the conventional way with sheets of glass but covered by thick, semi-transparent polythene. Each one was about thirty yards square with a curious roof that looked like an enormous shimmering counterpane. As we walked nearer and I heard the dull clatter of large electric fans, I realized that the roofs comprised two layers of polythene with air pumped between them so that the top layers billowed upwards in long, rounded corrugations.

Kristy wrestled with the latch of the door leading into the first of the great polythene greenhouses; when she won the fight and opened up, I had to stop and stare in sheer amazement.

Now I knew how it would feel to be an ant on a Persian rug. Slabs of vivid colour were laid out in neat parallel rows, the brilliance distilled and given a striking purity by the filmy, almost opaque light that softened shadows so much they hardly existed. With the thin walls blurring the outside world while the translucent roof caught and diffused the harsh, hot light, I had an eerie sensation of suddenly finding myself underwater.

In ten-abreast rows with narrow walkways between, the flowers stood as tall as Kristy, their blooms brushing the bottom of my chin. With so many flowers massed just at eye-level it was like swimming in a heaving sea of colour. Thrusting out of the peaty soil on strong stems, they branched into half a dozen stalks, each one ending in a beautiful bloom. Some flowers were like big daisies, with double rows of neatly-formed petals around large yellowish centres. Others had so many rows of petals that their centres were obscured. There were flowers with feathery petals, flowers with petals like tentacles, flowers with shaggy heads that might have been hand-crafted from tissue paper.

But what hit me in the eye was the fantastic variety of colours. Every kind of yellow; at least ten shades of colour that I could only call white, yet each was different; masses of reds, pinks and mauves, as well as orange, gold, russet and even a pale apple-green.

'Every colour but one: can you guess which is missing?' Kristy asked, amused at my expression of wonder. Only when Kristy pointed it out to me did the gap become obvious.

'Blue. Nobody has ever grown a blue chrysanthemum,' she said.

'Why, isn't it marketable?'

'Oh yes, but it simply doesn't exist. It's one of the mysteries of horticulture, something to do with the arrangement of genes. A long time ago there might have been a blue chrysanthemum in existence because pictures of them figure on Chinese porcelain, but some

73

experts say this was because blue was the colour the ancient Chinese potters produced best, so they coloured most things blue. If it did exist at one time then it must have disappeared from the chrysanthemum colour-spectrum for a reason we can only guess at. When it turns up again whoever finds it will make a million....'

'Dollars or lire?' I asked disbelievingly.

'Pounds sterling.'

The heat wrapped around me like deep water as I followed Kristy between shoulder-high waves of rich purple and brilliant yellow.

'Be careful not to damage the heads as you brush past them,' she warned, moving with a careful grace and pausing every few seconds to inspect a flower for signs of wilt or some other disease.

In the space of a few minutes I learned from Kristy a great deal about what the Greeks had called the flower of gold.

The Chrysanthemum was the national flower of Japan, where it had been cultivated for three thousand years. It had become popular in England last century, so popular that now there were fifteen hundred chrysanthemum societies in the country. But that was amateur stuff compared with the big commercial operations. In England alone 150 million sprays were grown every year for sale in flower shops. One nursery in America cut a million flowers a week. Another sold to the flower shops every week four million cuttings in seven hundred different varieties.

When I looked incredulous, Kristy added that there were already thousands of different varieties, and three hundred new ones were discovered and registered every year.

'It's fantastic when you think that twenty-five years ago the spray chrysanthemum was practically unknown, but when the Americans discovered how to grow them all the year round they passed roses and carnations as the world's most popular flower.'

'It must be big biscuits.' I said.

'Yes, there are a lot of Jaguars and BMW's in the horticulture business. But if you can't pick and pack the flowers you might as well stop growing them.' She looked sadly at the blooms massed around her in silent ranks. 'They were ready for picking last week but we will get rid of less than five per cent. Only what Opa and myself can do ourselves.'

'Tell me about your grandfather.'

'Opa's been growing chrysanths all his life. At least, since he left South Africa to fight in the First World War and stayed to settle in Sussex. He was one of the first growers to make a success of growing the American spray varieties all year round.'

'But why Sardinia?'

'For the sunshine, of course. Twenty years ago, before the Aga Khan started the Costa Smeralda, you could buy land here cheaply because the Sards always considered coastal land to be valueless. It proved to be a wise move, when the oil crisis broke, because we don't need to heat our greenhouses here. And until the big resorts appeared there was no shortage of cheap labour. But now....'

For a few moments the girl's attention was arrested by a number of flowers, still in bud, from which she methodically nipped out the centre stalk with a thumbnail that I suspected was grown long specially for the purpose.

'But now?' I prompted.

'Now we're practically bankrupt, through Opa never tells me quite how bad things are. The business flourished for a few years, then turned sour, mainly because the locals can get easier work for better money on the Costa. There's been a lot of unrest. It's hard enough at the best of times finding Sard women who are thin enough for this job. These rows are six inches further apart than they would be in England, simply to allow local women to walk between them. But now we can't even get the fat women to work here.'

The petals of a white flower tickled my bare shoulder blades as I stood still, turning Kristy's guarded explanation over in my mind.

'Jon told me there was a bit of trouble – that was why you have to get your boat out of the country rather discreetly.'

'He shouldn't have said that!' Kristy protested hotly.

'But it's true; you would much prefer that I set sail after dark, right?'

Kristy acknowledged the accuracy of my guess with an indifferent shrug.

'I reckon there is more to it than labour problems,' I pressed. 'Who has got their hooks into you, the Mafia?'

Answering 'No!' with a curtness that dismissed the subject but did nothing to stop me wondering, Kristy stopped at a bed of whitish flowers that a painted stake in the ground named as Cream Bunting. 'This is what you can pick, if you don't mind,' she said.

Each stem poked up through a square of taut orange nylon netting that had been lifted upwards on iron supports as the plants grew taller. Above the level of the net, each of the stems branched out into up to a dozen different stalks, of which ended in a flower, to create what was called the American spray. To pick each one Kristy demonstrated how I had to reach beneath the net, snip the stem about five inches above the ground, then carefully withdraw it without damaging the stem on the net or bruising the flowers on the sprinklers, wires and rafters just overhead. Then the lower half of the stem was drawn through the hand to wipe off the leaves and it was placed carefully in one of the tall flower buckets half-filled with water.

Kristy worked nearby, picking a variety called Yellow Hurricane. With four buckets filled we took two armfuls each and carried the flowers into the dimly lit packing-

76

shed. It was tedious yet oddly satisfying work, bending and snipping and carrying, and talking with Kristy who had stripped to a bikini of faded yellow towelling and seemed happy to have some company.

Despite the fans drawing air out of the greenhouse it was stultifyingly hot and sweat rolled in gallons down my torso. Standing up and stretching to ease the ache in my back from the unaccustomed bending, I was suddenly enveloped in a cooling but suffocating mist that spurted from an overhead pipe.

Kristy laughed uproariously and through her giggles explained that I was standing so close to the temperature sensor that the heat of my body had set it off. Automatically it had reacted to the sudden heat by turning on the rain, and when I stepped away, dripping wet but feeling better for it, the spray abruptly stopped.

With thirty buckets filled and the sun beginning to dip towards the hills behind the villa, the light in the greenhouse was no longer sharp and pure but softened by the promise of a magnificent sunset. Van Blommenstein put his head through the door, his bare torso pink and glistening, his eyes deeply set from strain and fatigue.

'Well done – it must be gin time.'

'We'd better do the blackout, Opa.'

'It hardly seems worth....'

'Of course it is,' Kristy said brusquely. 'If you carry these flowers down, John and I will do it.'

The adjacent greenhouse was filled with half-grown plants just beginning to form their buds. At the end of each row was a large parcel of black polythene that had to be unwrapped and slid along wires to form a tunnel of darkness over every flowerbed. Kristy explained that in high summer when the days grew so long it duped the plants into thinking that winter was coming so they rushed into flower.

'I'm afraid it's a long job: normally we would have a couple of labourers to do it.'

It took an hour and left me feeling hot, sweaty and

dirty. Weariness had crept up on me like a drug and I couldn't help yawning.

'I'm sorry, I was on deck all night and the wine is sending me off.'

'What you need young man,' Van Blommenstein said in a fatherly tone as he met us on the terrace, 'is a well-earned swim.'

Minutes later white spray boiled from Kristy's feet as she struck out strongly for the island, some two hundred yards out from the shore. The warm water was flecked with gold and pink by the sunset as I splashed into it and crawled after her, swimming evenly and slowly because I was out of training for that sort of distance, most of my swimming in recent years having been limited to short dips in the Channel while wearing a life-jacket and helping survivors struggling for their lives. Kristy waited for me in the shallows, the last rays of the evening sun touching her slim and tanned body with a honeyed glow. As my reaching fingers grounded on the sand of the island's beach the hammering of my heart was not solely due to the unaccustomed exercise.

'Shall we stroll round the island?'

I nodded, too puffed to speak, and followed her up a short path to a pinnacle of rock. The seaward shore fell away steeply in a low rocky cliff. On the horizon a large and handsome schooner, its white sails catching the sun that had left us in the shade of the mainland hills, was making for the flesh-pots of Porto Cervo. The resort had been fitted so skilfully into the landscape a few miles along the coast that from here it could have been a city centuries old. I gestured towards it, asking, 'What are the neighbours like?'

'It's like having a holiday camp next door, only every guest is a millionaire,' Kristy said. 'The trouble is that it has attracted a lot of less exclusive developments along the coast so we get all kinds of strange people coming into our beach in their fizz-boats.' She giggled suddenly. 'One night my brother and I sent a parachute-flare up over the island: you have never seen anything like it, there were bare bodies leaping around in the bright light just like sand-hoppers.'

'Tell me about Jon. Why doesn't he help you to keep the show on the road?'

'He does try,' Kristy said with a trace of indignation that I should think otherwise. 'He is doing his finals in botany at Oxford and will take over here one day, if there is anything left. Opa is an old fashioned fellow in the sense that he believes education comes before anything else.'

'And when your brother does come back,' I said intuitively, 'your grandfather won't let him take a single decision because he will say all the books in the world don't mean a thing without experience.'

Kristy laughed and I knew I had guessed right. The old man was gallant and charming but in that old Boer way he looked as mulish as some of the Squadron yachtsmen with whom I had sailed as crew.

'Well,' I sighed, 'this place is really quite beautiful. I could live very happily on a small island like this.'

'There isn't much to live on,' Kristy said, stooping to collect a handful of dusty, stony soil. 'This stuff won't grow much, and you have to get fresh water.'

'Maybe, but it would be perfect for a marina,' I said, planning in my mind's eye the layout of a small and exclusive boat-mooring and repair yard, with a landscaped shoreline, white-painted pontoons resting on the green water, a gaily painted fishing-dory serving as a ferry to the mainland....

'But that would spoil the beauty of the place,' Kristy protested.

'Better to build in your own way something that suits it,' I reasoned, 'than let the property developers put up some monstrosity.'

Her tawny eyes suddenly bright and challenging, the girl stepped close and confronted me angrily. 'You know more than you let on, Mr Montgomery! Are you one of the sharks, too? Is that why you have come here?'

Flustered, I shook my head and must have looked confused, for she took my hand and smiled. 'I'm so sorry. You touched a nerve, I'm afraid. You see, that is just what is happening. A property company has been trying to get hold of this place for years and now it has won.'

'But isn't land here worth a bar of gold per square foot? If it were mine I'd be laughing all the way to the bank.'

'It's not that simple. When things started to go wrong three or four years ago Opa took out a mortgage. At that time he expected business to pick up again but it never did, even when he offered competitive wages. If Opa sells he must give the mortgage company first option, it's part of the agreement. Now the company is foreclosing on us because Opa cannot meet the payments. Why else would we be selling our yacht?'

'So it's got you over a barrel,' I observed. 'What sort of things went wrong?'

'Sabotage, for instance.'

'Really!'

'I'm not joking,' Kristy admonished crisply. 'Water is precious here and hard to get. It has to be brought down by pipeline from the mountains. Last year the pipeline was dynamited and we lost an entire crop. Opa has put himself body and soul into this place but already he's had two heart attacks....' For a second her eyes misted and she dropped her head, collecting herself. Then, aggressively, she changed her tone. 'Let's go, I'll race you to the beach!'

Kristy won handsomely and was waiting with a towel when I staggered out of the water. Grinning, she drubbed my back vigorously, then tossed the towel round my neck and without affectation spun on her heel so I could do the same for her. The girl's relaxed familiarity was infectious. In a fleeting moment of perception I saw myself standing on a deserted beach drying the back of a beautiful creature in a scanty bikini – it was hard to believe.

'It's obvious what you need to get yourself out of the hole,' I said.

'Tell me.'

'A blue chrysanthemum!'

Kristy laughed hollowly and said with a toss of her wet hair as I draped the towel over her shoulders, 'You might as well count on winning the football pools. Come on, let's get a drink. Cold gin and limes is just so good after the taste of sea water.'

Showered and feeling immeasurably brighter, I went to join the others in the drawing-room. I was crossing the stone-flagged hall when I heard the sound of voices raised in argument. Hesitating, wondering whether I should interrupt, I heard one man with a hectoring and heavily-accented voice which I did not recognize doing most of the shouting. But the words were indistinct behind the heavy door. Then it was snatched open and I was roughly shouldered aside by what at first glance seemed to be a kind of raspberry *gelati* in jeans. He was a big fellow, wearing a sweat-stained t-shirt of a shocking pink colour stretched tightly over hulking shoulders and a massive gut that gave the appearance of being supported from below by the cone-shape of his trousers. But he had not been as angry as he sounded. Encountering me unexpectedly in the doorway, he had not had time to wipe the smirk of triumph from a sallow, fat face that was beaded with oily sweat on the smooth forehead and cheeks, and grey with bristle-shadow around the puffy jaw and sneering lips. As his Roman sandals slip-slapped rapidly across the flagstones I went into the drawing-room. Lit only by the last lingering loom of twilight stealing off the sea, it was virtually in total darkness.

His expression set and pale, Van Blommenstein acknowledged my entrance absent-mindedly and then busied himself taking the large opaque glass shade off an elaborate brass oil lamp. Kristy, breathtakingly elegant in a dress of plain white, stood by the tall marble fireplace in an attitude of complete despair. She looked as if she had been back-handed across both cheeks.

'Oh that ... that fat pig!' she gasped.

'That will do my dear,' her grandfather said sternly. A match flared in his hands and with a deep breath and sheer will he stopped his hand from shaking as he transferred the flame to the wick. When it caught he turned the wick down low, shook out the match, and began replacing the glass funnel and shade, the soft light from between his hands emphasizing the deep ravines folded in the flesh of his face.

'Good evening Mr Montgomery, how was the swim? You know, I think we could all do with a drink.' He went stiffly to a trolley on the other side of the high-ceilinged room: a frail, neat, soldierly figure in a beige linen safari suit. As he stooped over the bottles his shoulders sagged momentarily, then squared again as, determinedly, he checked himself.

'Kristy, dear, we seem to have run out of limes. I wonder, would you....?'

Choking back a sob, Kristy stared speechlessly at her grandfather's cool demeanour, then ran past me to the door.

'You must excuse her.' Van Blommenstein regarded me gravely. I'm afraid we have both had something of a shock.'

'I'm sorry, but I understand it has come as no surprise.'

'That's true, the writing has been on the wall long enough. But you have just witnessed the death blow, Mr Montgomery. The final nail in our coffin. All our labour is now withdrawn. The flowers you picked today will not be packed, except those Kristy and I can do alone. And even if we work all night it would be impossible to meet a tenth part of our orders.'

'What is the trouble exactly,' I asked. 'Is it unions?'

'On the face of it, yes. The gentleman you bumped into in the doorway is Bruno Feraldi, our nursery foreman. A hard and cruel man, and a stupid one. I made a mistake when I employed him three and a half years ago. Nothing has gone right since. He has me completely at his mercy now.' Van Blommenstein stacked ice cubes in three tall, narrow glasses and splashed a good sock of gin over them. 'Now that he has got what he wants perhaps he will be a better man to know, who can tell?'

'Okay, two obvious questions....' The old man waved me down with impatience.

'Questions are easy to ask but hard to answer, Mr Montgomery. For example, why did I not fire the man? You must know that the union organiser, the shop steward, is the most difficult man of all to get rid of, especially when he has a private line to every petty official on the island and has backing from powerful financiers who want to get rid of me. Again, why does the man want the place closed, thus putting himself and his union members out of work? I will tell you, but it has nothing to do with trade union affairs. The man is being paid off by the merchant bank which holds my mortgage. In London.'

'London!' I exclaimed.

The old man nodded heavily, his blue eyes gleaming in the lamplight. 'Yes indeed, the City of London is far from being the example of probity it pretends to be, as you well know. My land is an attractive proposition for development of a big resort, and I happen to be something of an irritation, so....'

Red-eyed and pale, Kristy came in with half-a-dozen small limes which her grandfather halved with a serated knife, squeezed, and dropped into the glasses on top of the ice. Then he topped them with a squirt of soda, stirred, and handed one glass to me and one to Kristy. He lifted his own glass in a formal toast: '*Prosit*'.

'Cheers,' Kristy mumbled dispiritedly.

'Things aren't as bad as that, my girl?'

'Oh no....' Again that look passed between them, a signal on a secret waveband from which Kristy seemed to draw strength and encouragement.

Dinner might have been strained and tense but Van Blommenstein was relaxed and disposed to talk. On books, wild animals he had hunted as a boy, the Boer War, conservation. A lot of it would have gone over my head but he had a knack for getting you involved, making you think. Amazingly, he seemed genuinely interested in my limp opinions on such things as the world refugee problem, the oil crisis, whether it was fair to make Eskimos stop their traditional hunting of whales.

Then, over the simple but perfectly delicious meal of smoked ham, salad and fresh peaches, I found myself being gently quizzed about my own life. When I described my recent misadventures in Yarmouth, which I was now beginning to recognize as merely a temporary setback compared with the total collapse Van Blommenstein himself faced with such dignity, he leaned forward suddenly and pressed for details. Several times Kristy was on the point of saying something, but each time her grandfather moved in quickly with another question of his own. Kristy's attitude throughout dinner was strangely different: she seemed nervous, remote, worried.

As the delightful meal came to an end. the old man having eaten almost nothing, I sensed the couple drawing more into themselves, as if preparing to be alone once more when I had sailed away in their dream boat. I felt an aching kind of sympathy for them, but knew that pity was the last thing they needed.

Little did I know that Van Blommenstein was far from withdrawing. He was thinking swiftly and arriving at a decision that would affect all our lives profoundly.

It seemed to be only his old-world good manners that impelled him to offer brandy – or perhaps a glass of port?

I declined, sensing that I would be intruding.

'But I insist, young man,' Van Blommenstein said, bringing a crystal decanter to the table. 'This port is quite excellent and there will be few opportunities for Kristy and me to enjoy it in such pleasant company. Will you smoke a cigar?'

'May I smoke my pipe?' I asked, reaching for my pouch.

'Please, but why not try some of my special tobacco?' He drew a slender, silver-banded, small-bowled briar from the pocket of his tunic and filled it from a tobacco jar of fragrant inlaid wood which he pushed over to me. Kristy stood up to leave but he stayed her with a brisk movement of his hand.

'In that case,' Kristy said with a challenging look, 'I'll join you chaps in a glass of port.'

The old man's eyes twinkled as he poured her a glass.

'In fact,' he said, arresting my attention with a suddenly sharp glance, 'Kristy and I need your help.'

'Of course – tell me what I can do.'

With studied calm he struck a match and held it over the bowl of his pipe, sucking until the flame leapt four inches high. The blue eyes, narrowed against the smoke, were fixed on me like lasers. Waving out the match, he said, 'Let's top up your glass, then you can bring it along. There's something I want to show you.'

Walking slowly along the driveway towards the packing-shed, the night air soft and cool and the port lining my throat like liquid velvet, Van Blommenstein began his explanation.

'Do you know what a sport is, Mr Montgomery?'

'In horitcultural terms? No, I'm afraid not.'

'A sport is a genetic mutation which causes one particular flower among many to change its colour. Chrysanths are pollyploid, like carnations and orchids, which means they have more than one set of chromosomes, fifteen, in fact. This means that the potential for variation is immense. Among millions of white flowers of a certain variety something happens to the chromosomes of just one plant and for no apparent reason it turns out to be yellow. That's how the variety called Yellow Hurricane was discovered. One day it just appeared, as a sport.'

'But it could be any colour?' I asked.

'Oh yes, and the colour might appear on only part of a flower. You might find a red chrysanth with half its petals a different shade, pink perhaps. A clever grower can breed out the original red by grafting different plants and develop the pink until he gets a completely new flower, which is then propogated, tested, and grown commercially.'

Van Blommenstein stopped, breathing hard from the effort of the walk, and turned to face me. Even in the darkness I could sense the intensity of his expression.

'You see,' he continued, 'if the plant you have discovered proves to have stamina and all the qualities a commercial grower looks for, and if it also happens to be a rare or unique colour, the number sold every year can run into millions. If the grower registered the new flower with the international Breeder Growers' Association, which happens to be in Germany, he takes a royalty on every single cutting that is sold during the subsequent ten years.'

'As you said earlier, John,' Kristy interrupted, 'it's big biscuits!'

We entered the packing-shed. Van Blommenstein took a key from round his neck and snapped open the big padlock on the door to his laboratory.

'But you have to remember,' he said, one hand resting on the door before pushing it open, 'that it is only one in a hundred successful sports that makes any money worth mentioning, and only one in ten thousand that can make you rich. The whole thing is a complete gamble.' He pushed the door open and switched on the lights.

The room was large, whitewashed, with a glass roof.

Benches around the walls supported dozens of pots with flowers in various stages of growth, each marked with an orange tag on which was scrawled a number in black marking ink.

'This is the flower I would like you to take to France with you tonight,' Van Blommenstein went on, cupping his fingers around a bloom and inspecting it closely. 'It is six years now since I saw the first streak of colour in a flower I had been growing. I grafted scores of times but it was difficult to eliminate all the white. Can you guess what happened then? One of the grafted plants itself mutated and by pure chance I had the chrysanthemum of my dreams.'

His hand shook as he turned it palm outwards to reveal the flower cupped in his fingers.

'It's a perfect Blue Hurricane – a good strong colour, don't you think?'

4 : SMOKESCREEN

The yacht harbour at Golfo Aranci is a tiny haven enclosed by the crooked arms of two concrete break-waters that also serve as jetties. A dozen open-decked fishing-boats were pulled up on the untidy shingle beach. Yachts and cruisers moored stern-to in tight formation stirred in the night breeze. Kristy bumped the van over a ramp and drove along the western harbour wall.

'That's her,' she said, stopping with a jerk and point-ing to a pretty little thirty-foot sloop with a large dog-house.

The yacht I had to take to Toulon and then to England was a honey. I understood at once why Kristy and her grandfather loved her.

'Won't you show me the ropes?' I asked.

'It would be too sad. You'll find your own way around. The electrics are on the starboard bulkhead just inside the hatch.'

I opened the door and got out of the van. 'I'm sorry you can't sail with me. Won't you come?'

'Not possibly. I can't leave Opa.' Kristy looked tense and worried. Her hair, dry now after the swim, tumbled lightly down to her shoulders. I had a desire to run my fingers through it and hold her tightly.

I walked round to the driver's window and put my hand on her arm. 'I'll cable you tomorrow from Toulon. Don't worry about a thing.' Kristy's quick smile was part bravado, part wistfulness. I leaned forward and kissed her lightly on the lips.

Kristy's head jerked back as if her lips had been scorched, and she let out the clutch so quickly that the tyres squealed on the concrete. I heard her snort contemptuously, 'Be your age!' then the van hurtled backwards along the jetty. It weaved so erratically that my dismay became instant panic. But she made it safely to dry land, turned, and drove away with an encouraging toot-toot that went some of the way towards rallying my hurt feelings.

Standing alone on the dark pier, watching the van's tail light diminish, I thought about what Van Blommenstein had told me in the laboratory at the villa.

'It's only fair that you should be aware of the situation,' the old man had said, deftly cutting the stem of the blue hurricane four inches above the root, laying the flower on the bench, and turning the root out of its pot. 'The reason neither Kristy nor myself can take the plant out of Sardinia ourselves is that we are almost certainly being watched – by those who have driven us out of business.'

'Bruno Feraldi, you mean?'

'Perhaps, but there are almost certainly others. I'm pretty sure that Feraldi himself has got wind of what I have produced here in the lab and that's what worries me.' Van Blommenstein shook the loose earth from the roots of the plant and put it in a small polythene bag which he gathered at the neck and tied with a twist of garden wire.

'Just give it some air every day, to stop the condensation rotting the stem, and keep it in a cool place. Jon will know what to do when he meets up with you, and you can help him dream up a way of smuggling it into England.'

'Smuggle!' I said, astonished to hear the word in this context.

'Oh yes, that's the crux of the problem. You see, every plant imported commercially into any country must have a phyto-sanitary certificate issued by the agricultural authorities in its country of origin to show that it has been grown in clinical conditions and does not carry viruses or disease. To get such a certificate in a place like this is difficult, unless....'

'Unless your brother is secretary to the chief,' I broke in, meaning to be flippant.

'Exactly,' said Kristy. 'Bruno has an uncle in the local department and there is no way we could get it past him.'

Van Blommenstein had handed over the little plastic bag, saying, 'It will be safe enough in a good propogating house that Jon knows in England. Until then we trust to luck. And to you, Mr Montgomery.'

Kristy had picked one of the blooms from the discarded Blue Hurricane stem and threaded it into the buttonhole of my shirt.

'For luck,' she said with a smile.

After the insulated tensions and courtly hospitality of the villa, the outside world had seemed unreal. Only when the scattered lights of the port showed up, and Kristy drove past a big white ship loading cars and lorries for the overnight run to Civitavecchia, on the mainland, had she broken a long silence. 'We send a lot of flowers to Italy on that ferry.'

'Why not the blue chrysanthemum?' I had asked.

'We couldn't risk it. A new flower is like an invention. Until it has been registered, or patented, possession is ten-tenths of the law. Even then you can't be sure the cuttings won't be pirated and grown in places like Taiwan.' In the darkness of the small cab I had sensed the appraisal in Kristy's look as she weighed me up. 'Opa reckons you're trusty, strong-willed and ingenious. Is he right?'

'What do you think?' I fenced.

'All I want to see is Opa enjoying the success he deserves.'

'It seems a strange move, putting the flowers in the hands of a stranger: how do you know I won't grow it myself and make my own fortune, and to hell with you and your grandfather!'

'You could do that,' Kristy admitted, 'but you won't.

Opa's a good judge.'

Now, with the small plastic bag containing the plant wrapped in my wet bathing-trunks which were buried in a towel inside my small kitbag, the night suddenly had eyes. The yacht *Bonnie Jean* shifted under my weight as I stepped aboard. The main cabin, white with varnished deck-beams and fittings of oiled teak, had been fitted out with an old-fashioned craftsmanship that was rare in modern boat-building. Yellow squabs and brightly-coloured cushions covered the bunks. On the forward bulkhead, below a polished brass ship's clock and matching barometer, was a simple round frame with a water colour of the white, daisy-like chrysanthemum after which the boat had been named. I wondered whether *Bonnie Jean* had also once been a sport that had appeared by surprise in a grower's flowerbed.

The yacht had been cleared of personal possessions but there was nevertheless a great deal to be observed about her recent owners. In the fitted bookshelf there was a row of large, smooth holes in which Skipper Van Blommenstein had kept his pipes. The cushion covers were embroidered with patterns of different flowers and looked as if they might have been the handiwork of Kristy's mother who lived in Sussex. Empty screw-holes in the bulkheads showed that the cosy little cabin had once been adorned with mementoes and ornaments.

I made the usual pre-voyage checks – gas-leak sniffer, bilges, fuel and water tanks, sails, anchor chain with its inboard end shackled securely to the ringbolt. As Kristy had said, the yacht was in all respects ready for sea. This fact alone was a handsome comment on the capabilities and attitudes of the yacht's former skipper and crew.

The engine started easily and I let it run for five minutes while I familiarized myself with the charts of the area. Compared with an overnight trip in the English Channel this would be an easy voyage. There were no tides to worry about, no currents to speak of. I would not have to run the gauntlet of a score or more supertankers and other vast ships ploughing through the darkness like moving islands. There was no likelihood of sudden fog. No deathly shoals like the Goodwin Sands. No grey-bearded waves and driving spray to chill you to the marrow.

The coast of Corsica, which I would pass to the east, was clearly lit and in any case there were few offshore dangers. Even at night its high coastline would be clearly visible, more so once the moon rose soon after midnight. But I would have to keep a careful watch for fishing-boats – they had a reputation for steaming without lights and with nobody at the helm. It was also important to look out for signs of a *libeccio*, the wind which could howl out of the south-west with nearly hurricane force and churn the sea into a vicious trap of short, steep, seething waves. Unlike the powerful Italian power cruiser I had brought over, *Bonnie Jean* was a plodder: a slow, steady and sea-kindly little vessel that did not have the horsepower to run for shelter at first sign of a bit of wind. I estimated the voyage would take all of a whole day and a half, maybe two.

For the moment, the night air was balmy and the black sea barely ruffled. I steered for the dark gap between the pierhead lights. The bow lifted to small waves coming across the gulf on the land breeze. Then I was in open water, nudging the throttle forward until the boat reached a relaxed cruising-speed of about eight knots.

It was midnight. The large ferry had just left the quay and was moving across my bow, a pyramid of lights. I swung the wheel over to follow in its wake. Soon our courses would diverge, as the ferry headed east for Italy and I turned north for the Riviera.

Out here on the wide sea the fact that I had a horticultural miracle worth a potential million pounds sterling wrapped up in my bathing-trunks seemed unreal, but as usual the business of running and navigating a little ship of my own proved so absorbing that I soon gave the Blue Hurricane no more thought.

It was only a matter of minutes before I realised I had a problem.

It had been a long day with lots of wine, followed by a good dinner with more wine and two large glasses of port. There was no chance of being able to stay awake for the rest of the night and the next day would be a long one. After only a couple of miles my eyelids drooped and my head felt as if it was wearing a crown of lead. To continue in this state invited a night of torture, for there is no fiercer agony than trying to stay awake while having to remain at a steering-wheel gazing at the tiny figures of a hypnotically-swinging compass card.

The chart showed a small indentation in the coast of a high island over to port. There was a sandy bottom which would be a good holding ground for the anchor. Sheltered from the breeze, the bay would be as smooth as glass.

Fifteen minutes later, with the diesel at tick-over, *Bonnie Jean* nosed into the cliff-girt bay, its water so smooth that it reflected the stars. As the yacht lost momentum I went forward and dropped the pick.

It was one of those night anchorages cruising men dream about while they are stuck among the boats crowded into Yarmouth. Too sleepy to sit on deck and appreciate it, I waited long enough to see the yacht settle on her anchor chain. Then I scribbled down a compass course to steer if the weather blew up nastily in the middle of the night, forcing me to escape in a hurry, and stretched out on the starboard bunk with my head on an embroidered pink chrysanthemum.

For a few seconds my mind ticked off the familiar boat noises: the gulp of water kissing the hull, the faintest whisper of night air puffing through the taut shrouds, the squawk of a sea bird that ought to have been in bed with its head under its wing. In the far distance I thought I heard the murmur of an outboard engine: probably some fisherman heading out to sea for an early start.

I must have slept for barely half-an-hour. Something

triggered my reflexes. Before I was even half awake my feet hit the deck and I headed for the short ladder leading up the open hatchway.

From a distance of about three feet a bright, harsh light flared suddenly in my eyes. The beam seared my retinas like a blowtorch. I turned my head away, ducking behind my hands and seeing pink shadows. The beam followed, like a searchlight, and I realised it was directed by a man sitting in the hatchway, his feet on the top rung of the ladder just inside the cabin.

'Stand up, turn around!' the man said. There was a click, then a deafening explosion. The small cabin filled with smoke and the reek of cordite.

Blinded and now deafened, I shouted, 'For God's sake....!' The beam shifted from my face and centred on my chest. Looking past it I discerned the silhouette of the man's head and shoulders.

'Shut up and do as I say.'

The voice was English, high-spoken, decisive. The boat rocked as a second man walked heavily along the side deck. The forehatch opened and I was warned not to look behind me.

Recollecting the outboard engine I had heard as I fell asleep, I said, 'Okay, you followed me out here, I suppose. Just tell me what you want, then piss off.'

My skin crawled as the second man moved clumsily into the cabin. The voice from the hatchway was somehow familiar, but in my confused condition I couldn't place it.

'We want the plant you brought from the Villa Maddalena.'

'Talk sense,' I protested. 'What plant would....?'

A stunning blow from behind sent me crashing into the galley lockers. My arms were grabbed and twisted up my back. I was shoved forwards until my nose was squashed against the top step, a suede chukka boot with a hard leather sole positioned beside each ear.

'Now look, don't be a bloody fool....'

94

'I don't know what you want,' I grunted. A boot kicked me in the side of the face. First one side, then the other.

'Lift him up.'

The light drilled into my face again and I saw a pale hand reach out and point at the blue flower in the top buttonhole of my shirt where Kristy had put it. For luck. I summoned all my courage.

'You want it, you find it.'

The sharp edge of the torch slammed into my temple. I slumped groggily, all but knocked out. Through a haze of nausea and pain I saw the second man searching the cabin, the torch playing just ahead of him to provide illumination. Lolling against the galley lockers I watched the silhouette of his broad shoulders and large belly disappear into the fore-cabin and return a moment later with my sail-cloth kitbag. It was Bruno Feraldi.

He turned the bag out on the cabin table and his thick fingers went through my things. Sponge-bag, towel, clean shirt, passport, underwear, wet bathing-trunks ... Feraldi caught the polythene bag as it fell out and held it up in the light.

At the same moment I grabbed the leg of the man in the hatch and jerked him with all my strength into the cabin. He landed heavily with a gasp of surprise and pain. His gun clattered to the deck. The torch rolled away beneath the table. My hands scrabbled for the cabin light switch.

The light revealed Ronald Blom lying on the floor. He grabbed for the gun and directed it at my stomach.

Incredulous, I backed away as far as the bulkhead, straightening up and holding my hands out from my sides.

'Good God, it's Floribuna!' I said.

Blom flushed scarlet and for a terrible moment I thought he would shoot me. Then the anger faded and he grinned with some trace of humour.

'Snap again,' he said.

'What on earth are you doing here?'

'Having a party, as I told you.' Blom arched his back painfully as Bruno Feraldi helped him up. He rubbed his backside with his free hand and groaned.

'Hell, that hurt. Why do you have to be such a bloody hero?'

His tone became more conciliatory but the gun never wavered. I returned his baleful stare and remained silent. Then Blom twitched the gun at me and the big Italian approached, his black eyes contemptuous and cruel, the fingers of each hand rubbing ceaselessly against his thumbs.

'Next time you kiss my zulu cousin,' Blom went on, 'I should make a better job of it. She needs a man without his trousers on to bring her down a peg, though I'd be surprised if you had the balls....'

Bruno Feraldi was not all fat. His bunched fist slammed like a pile driver into my stomach. I fell down, retching and gasping. Blom's chukka boots hammered in my ribs, then smashed hard into my skull, and I blacked out.

Thump! Each step was as high as a cliff and as I went over the edge another limb cracked. Then my eyes blinked open in the darkness and I realized with relief that it was only a nightmare. But the terrible jarring did not stop. Sickening, agonizing – thump!

I thought I would faint. My body was in a strait-jacket of bruises but I knew now what was happening. In the trough of each wave the boat's keel was digging heavily into the sand. The weather had come up. A thin wind piped in the rigging. Big waves rolled into the bay.

Stumbling out into the darkness I saw angry waves peaking right alongside, breaking into smothers of foam only a few yards further in towards the beach. Each time the boat struck the bottom she heeled sharply. In a moment she would be swept by a wave and begin to break up. Sick at heart I punched the starter-button and was reassured by the vibration of the little diesel. With spinning head, stomach a ball of pain, I fought my way along the deck to the bows. The anchor chain stretched out at an angle into the oncoming waves.

I saw at once what was wrong. The chain ran out freely because the pawl that locked the windless ratchet had been lifted. My own mistake or deliberate sabotage? There was no time to think about it. The electric capstan was powerful and fast, one of Van Blommenstein's few concessions to old age, and I was thankful for it. Working it in bursts I managed to haul the bows round to face the waves, then I scurried painfully aft and kicked the boat ahead on the engine. Mercifully, the murderous jarring ceased and soon the boat was floating in deeper water.

In the lee of an island around the point I found sheltered water again and dropped anchor once more, this time making doubly certain that the pawl was securely locked in place. While the kettle boiled I dipped my head into a bucket of sea water then inspected myself in a mirror. It was the sort of face you see on Sunday mornings in a regimental guardhouse. Both eyebrows were split and bleeding, one eye looked like raw steak, my lips were split and the long cut where the edge of the torch had hit my temple had bled heavily into my hair. It made me ill just looking at myself.

I made the coffee black and strong but it would take more than caffein to remove the bitter taste from my mouth. How would I tell Kristy and Van Blommenstein that I had lost their precious blue chrysanthemum? I hardly dared face them.

What was it Ronald Blom had said, before the Italian laid into me? Something about a zulu cousin. It took more than just one cup of coffee to clear my head sufficiently to work it all out and be certain that the whole incredible link-up must be true. Blom could only have been referring to Kristy. Their surnames were similar, in the sense that Blom could well be an anglicisation of the unwieldy Boer family name, and Major Blom's business was also flower growing.

On the boat coming over from France, Ronald Blom had told me he had business to do in the area. His magazine was on the point of collapse and his father's business was also in trouble, so there were a million green-backed reasons for wanting to get hold of his grandfather's blue chrysanthemum.

If Bruno Feraldi had been Ronald Blom's man all along then perhaps it was Blom himself who had engineered the collapse of the nursery. He stood to get a handsome rake-off from the property company that wanted to develop Villa Maddalena's beautiful bay and its twin islands into a resort. Feraldi would have told him of my arrival, and of the fact that the boat was being taken away, so they had followed me out to sea in a high-speed Zodiac inflatable of the kind used in the gulf by local lobster divers, aiming to board me at sea; I had made things easy for them by dropping anchor and turning in. My suspicions as I boarded the yacht at Golfo Aranci had not been mere fancy: the night really did have eyes.

Dawn was casting a wan light over the sea when I took three Codeines, checked the anchor chain once more, and eased my throbbing head back on to the pink cushion.

When I awoke at nine the yacht rocked in a howling gale. The sea was calm because it was sheltered by the island, but the strength of the wind alone was sufficient to heel the yacht as she yawed back and forth on her chain. Out in open water the wind-driven waves were capped with white.

After a quick and stimulating ride into harbour, slamming into the head sea that diminished quickly as I got nearer the mainland, I found a café where I could sit under a wind-buffeted parasol on the pavement and have a succession of sweet, strong *espressos* with bread rolls and cheese. Food made me feel a little better and a lot braver but it was nevertheless with reluctance that I hunted for a taxi. It was the inevitable battered Fiat which took the hairpins like a motorcycle in a TT, the driver leaning into the corners with everything but a petrol tank between his knees.

On the outside of the corners the gusts whipped spirals of yellow dust into the air and threatened to blow the car over the edge. I closed my eyes and tried not to think of the steep precipices but opened them quickly when a lurch and a scream of tyres announced serious trouble.

There was a flash of sun on chrome, dead ahead. The wide front end of a Mercedes filled the windscreen. It was on our side of the road, on the outside of the bend, trailing a plume of dust as the offside wheels tore at loose stones.

Only the taxi driver's appalling driving saved a fatal head-on crash. For the taxi was also on the wrong side of the road, hugging the inside of the bend. The two cars shaved by, horns wailing. The Merc did not so much as brake. My driver hung his head out of his side window, looking back and waving his fist. The Fiat was all but off the road when I grabbed his shoulder and shook it furiously. He recovered, lurched the car into a straight line, and drove into the next bend at the same blind speed.

The back of my hand came away from my forehead running wet. I had been badly frightened. So had Ronald Blom, hunched over the Mercedes' big steering-wheel.

If I had been travelling in my own Healey I might have done a slick handbrake turn and given chase. But my courage failed at the idea of telling this madman at the wheel actually to drive fast. Now why was Blom in such a devilish hurry? Uneasily, I thought of Kristy and the old gent alone at the villa.

We smelled the smoke before we saw it. The driver

muttered worriedly to himself, wrinkling his nose, then the road breasted a rise and the villa's white gateposts stood ahead. Behind them rose an immense column of boiling smoke, its head dragged out by the wind into an anvil like that of a great thunder cloud.

The taxi stopped with a jerk that threw me forward. Fanned by the wind, the noble avenue of gum trees flanking the driveway became an inferno of hot flame. As I watched, a tongue of fire leapt high into the branches of a towering eucalyptus and its inflammable sap and tinder-dry leaves exploded in a fireball of crackling, snapping, white-hot fury.

I threw some notes at the driver and started to run, sore head pounding, pain stabbing.

The only way to reach the villa was by a round-about route through waist-high scrub. Too late I realised I was up-wind, and running a real risk of being overtaken by the fire. The noise was overwhelming: a crackling roar so violent it seemed that the world itself was splitting apart.

The villa was wreathed in thick smoke and flying embers. The polythene greenhouses were spotted with holes where sparks had landed and burned through. An acre of scrub below them was a blackened waste. The olive trees were skeletons. The fire had leapt across the hillside and was devouring spiky brown stubble and green bushes, eating its way at a fast rate towards the villa. Half a dozen men beat at the flames. Another had a weak hosepipe. The fire was winning.

I found a sack and joined the line of defence. Dust rose in choking clouds as I flogged the sack up and down into the flames. Pale in the smoke-filtered sunshine, fiery tongues advanced in spurts like waves of a rapidly-rising tide running up a beach. The roar and crackle of whole trees being consumed filled the air. There was an eruption of sparks as a branch fell with a crash on the taut polythene roof of a greenhouse. It lay there for a second, smouldering, then the material melted and it fell through into the flowerbeds below.

In the uproar I heard a firm, English voice. A girl. I peered into the stinging smoke and we saw each other at the same moment.

'John! Thank God you're here,' Kristy exclaimed. Blotched with soot and sweating like a stoker, she was pale and frightened yet cool and in control. 'Our water is drying up. There isn't enough pressure to supply the sprinklers and the hoses.'

'Turn off the sprinklers to keep the hoses going,' I advised. 'The flowers will look after themselves. It's more important to protect the villa and kill the sparks as they land on the roof.'

A burning ember landed under the arch of Kristy's foot and she flicked it away with a cry of pain. It left a black scorch-mark on her thonged sandal.

'We just don't have enough people,' she said desperately.

'Where are Bruno and his mob?'

'Need you ask!' Kristy turned away from me, cupped her hands round her mouth, and shouted orders in brisk Italian. The men flung their sacks over their shoulders and ran to the villa. By sign language I had the two garden-hoses played over the walls and roof. A maid in the kitchen filled pots and pans with water and passed them out to douse sparks that fell in dangerous places. I directed other men to protect the garage and the packing-shed in the same way. Soon the real danger was past as the trees became burned-out skeletons, their gaunt branches weeping wisps of bluish smoke. Although they continued to burn, tornadoes of sparks were no longer spiralling from them into the air. The fire raced on up the hill through the scrub. In the distance came the two-tone blare of a klaxon: the local firemen would be in time to stop the flames jumping over the road, but there was little they could do here.

'Signorina, Signorina!' The cry was high-pitched, hysterical.

A middle-aged Italian worker, wiping his eyes with one hand and holding up his trousers with the other, gabbled at Kristy. I saw her gasp then run off into the smoke. I followed as best I could, smoke tearing like acid at my lungs. Gagging, covering my face with my hands, I stumbled through the hot, stinging fog until it was cleared momentarily by a gust of wind and I saw a figure slumped in the doorway of the packing-shed.

Kristy was already there, cradling the old man's head in her arms, bending to listen to his heart. I ripped the lid off a cardboard box and used it as a fan to clear the air around him.

'We must get him out of the heat,' I said.

Kristy's breathing came in short, panicky gasps. 'It's another heart attack. Can you carry him?'

Van Blommenstein's face was ivory-white, his eyes screwed up, his breathing imperceptible. I eased him over my shoulders in a fireman's lift and followed as Kristy led me into the villa. Its whitewashed cement walls and stone floor were cool, pleasant and quiet. The large bed in a room overlooking the bay and its islands had a colourful Mexican rug on which I gently tipped the old man by lowering my shoulder until he over-balanced and rolled off. Kristy caught his head and shoulders while I straightened his legs.

'Opa, Opa....' Kristy wiped Van Blommenstein's dry forehead and took one of his hands. 'Opa, you'll be all right now.'

Silently I watched as Kristy soft-talked her grandfather back to consciousness. After a few moments I asked softly, 'What about a doctor?'

As if woken by the sound of my voice the inert figure stirred. The hand which Kristy held so tightly and affectionately began to clench. Van Blommenstein opened his bright eyes, looking up at her with pupils eclipsed by enlarged irises of brilliant pale-blue.

'Kristy, my dear?'

'Yes, Opa, I'm here.'

'Kristy, listen....' The old man's free hand groped towards the top of his head. 'Kristy,' he said again, his voice a mere whisper. Then his eyes closed and he lapsed into unconsciousness again.

Kristy looked up, frightened and puzzled.

'Maria's in the kitchen. Get her to phone for a doctor, quickly!'

I found the maid collecting up her pots and pans. She spoke sufficient English to understand at once what I wanted and ran to the telephone.

In the bedroom Kristy was taking her grandfather's pulse.

'It's incredibly faint. Where's the doctor? Why hasn't he come?'

I told her the doctor was on his way but she did not appear to listen. She loosened the old man's faded shirt, turning back the collar. I heard her quick intake of breath as her hand found the end of the leather thong on which Van Blommenstein had worn the key to the laboratory padlock.

'It's gone,' I said, with a sudden premonition.

Kristy patted her grandfather's chest, feeling for the key. 'It definitely is not here.'

'That explains a lot,' I said.

'What do you mean?'

'You haven't asked me why I am standing here. Remember, I'm supposed to be halfway to Toulon. I came back because your blue chrysanthemum was hijacked last night, and I nearly lost your boat in the process....'

Kristy shrugged as if the blue chrysanthemum was the last thing she cared about. I went on, 'But I think I'm right in saying that one blue chrysanthemum would be no good to another grower unless he also had every other single one. And there was more than one growing in the lab, right?' Kristy seemed confused but she nodded agreement. 'Does a blue Mercedes mean anything to you?'

'Our car? No, why should it?'

'Is it possible the fire was started deliberately?'

Kristy turned away impatiently. 'Don't be absurd!' Then she thought about it for a moment and asked sharply, 'What are you driving at?'

'Where were you when the fire started?'

'I was picking flowers.'

'Obviously the fire was a diversion,' I said. 'While you were fighting the flames somebody took the key from your grandfather and went off with the rest of the blue chrysanthemums.

There seemed no point in complicating the story at this stage with the fact that the theft of the flowers had been carried out by her own cousin.

Bemused, Kristy shook her head as if she could not bring herself to believe it.

The blue chrysanthemum in my buttonhole was wilted and crushed. I tossed it on Van Blommenstein's imperceptibly-moving chest.

'You stay with him, I need to look around.'

It took only a few minutes to confirm what I suspected. The laboratory door was wide open. Five pots which had held blue chrysanthemums rolled empty on the earthen floor. The sprays of blue flowers which had been cut from their roots lay on the bench. On the beach I found footprints in the sand and skidmarks where a rubber inflatable boat had landed, undoubtedly the same Zodiac that had come alongside the yacht during the night. On my way up the path again it was no surprise to find an empty tin can with a strong smell of petrol.

Ronald Blom had surreptitiously landed on the beach, started the fire on the down-wind side of the property, and raided the laboratory while everybody was busy fighting the flames. There, he had been surprised and confronted by his grandfather, for whom the shock had been too much. As the old man collapsed, Blom had raced away in the Mercedes which he had taken from the garage.

Twirling one of the stems of pretty blue flowers between my fingers, I returned to Van Blommenstein's bedroom and said to Kristy, 'I was right, I'm afraid.'

But Kristy was not listening. Her grandfather's fingers had caught her wrist in a strong grip and she leaned forward to hear his words.

'Kristy, my dear....'

'Yes Opa, I'm here. Just rest.'

'Kiss Jon for me ... God bless you.' The brilliant blue eyes were suddenly no longer lit from within. They became hard and glassy, reflecting the dim and cool light in the room dully, like pieces of china in a cabinet.

It was some moments before Kristy realized that her grandfather was dead.

5 : BLUE RINSE

The sound of revving engines drew me to the rear of the villa. Cars and motor-scooters milled round the open door of the packing-shed. As I watched, a man staggered from the shed bearing an armful of tools which he dropped in the tray of a three-wheel motorcycle truck. The nursery workers recognized a lost cause when they saw one. Having been told by their foreman that the business was folding and they were all out of a job, they were making off with a few last-minute perks.

The smoke had gone but the air still had a sharply-unpleasant tang of burning. The fire truck crew out on the road were stowing their hoses. Specks of black and grey ash on the driveway stirred like fluff as I strode briskly towards the shed. A young man on a Vespa, a power-drill on the platform between his feet and a garden fork over his shoulder, came slowly towards me. As he passed I wrenched the fork out of his grip. He wobbled and fell off with a shout that caught the attention of the others. I collected the power-drill and put it in the shed then turned to face them, leaning on the fork in the doorway with a nonchalance that I was far from feeling.

'Buzz off, chaps,' I said genially. 'Flake off home and mind your own business.'

Red in the face and shouting like a Facist, the Vespa rider made to reach for the power-drill but I blocked him with my body and presented arms in parade-ground style as if the garden fork was a rifle. Some of the older men sniggered and it was this that stopped the youth from taking a swing at me.

The ten or twelve men who faced me in a semi-circle

were peasant types, some bowed and shrunken with faces like old prunes, others clean-limbed and fresh-faced with that slicked-back Italian flashiness that makes a man astride a 50cc moped feel king of the road. Some were not nursery workers but locals who had seen the smoke and, with the kind of camaraderie that exists everywhere, had rushed to help fight the fire. Most were clearly uncertain about how far they could go in walking off with nursery property and regarded me with uneasy, defensive expressions. Even so, I didn't care for the proposition that I should hold the lot of them at bay with a garden fork.

Then the door of one of the cars opened and Bruno Feraldi got out. Like an NCO whose men had just won a skirmish, he had been giving them a bit of rope to enjoy themselves. If he was surprised to see me it did not register in his expression, which was warily confident. He said a sharp word and the boy who had been confronting me moved away, glowering. I swung the fork round and jabbed it into the hard-baked earth, then propped myself casually against its handle with my arms folded.

'Van Blommenstein has just died,' I told the foreman as he approached, adding for the possible benefit of the others and drawing a finger across my throat, '*Morto.*'

Feraldi looked unsuprised, as if he had been expecting the news, then instantly readjusted his features and looked perplexed.

'Kaput.... *Finito*?'

'Finito,' I said quietly.

Feraldi returned my steady gaze thoughtfully and nodded, then chewed his fat lower lip as if suddenly biting off a smirk.

'Is bad for the signorina, eh?'

'Yes, very bad.'

He gazed around at the melted polythene flapping in tatters from some of the greenhouse frames, at the

107

fire-blackened under-growth surrounding the villa, at the silent faces of the men watching him curiously.

'All is *finito*, I think.'

'Perhaps.'

Then his eyes focussed on the bloody scab on my forehead and he leered, touching his own temple with the tip of one finger.

'Very pretty you look.'

'Piss off!'

'The signorina: you take her England?'

'Perhaps.'

Apparently concluding that there would be plenty of opportunity to finish his business in his own time, the foreman barked a few harsh words at the men around him and they began drifting away to their vehicles. Bruno Feraldi could afford to call off his troops; for the moment his job was done. The horticulture business was in ruins so the finance company in London would not be getting its payments and now it could foreclose, handing the property over to its sister company for development. The old man was now totally out of the way: no more trouble from him, and his grand-daughter was bound to return home to London.

No doubt Bruno Feraldi was already planning his own slice of the action from the big hotel that would rise on the site. And that was not all, for he had helped Ronald Blom to get the Blue Hurricane which would soon be on its way to a safe nursery in England and officially registered by Blom's Blooms. I wondered how large the Italian's slice of that action would be. And, for that matter, whether he would ever see it.

For the moment, he and Blom had scored the perfect double and he could celebrate. But he had no wish to face me alone, not after what he had done to me on the yacht in the middle of the night, and as the men filtered away Bruno Feraldi suddenly realized his support had dwindled and he walked quickly to his car, fired up, and drove away in a cloud of black dust and ashes.

When the last two-stroke moped had buzzed after him down the driveway and its noise faded into the distance, the villa was suddenly quiet and desolate. The grounds an ugly black scar, every ledge thick with black dust, the whole place seemed to be grieving: paradise in widow's weeds.

Glumly I stowed the garden fork away in its rack and made my way back into the villa while turning over in my mind the best course of action.

With a head start of more than two hours, Ronald Blom was not worth the chase. The Mercedes could be anywhere in Sardinia by now, probably abandoned at an airport or ferry terminal. Blom himself, if he had made the right connections, could be halfway to London or meeting up again with his magazine team.

Meanwhile, I still had to get the yacht out of the country and I should move quickly in case the vessel was impounded as part of the old man's estate. But there was Kristy to consider. Her grief was discomfitting and I did not know how to handle it. In a single day she had lost her grandfather, the blue chrysanthemum, most of the greenhouses, and a whole crop of flowers. There could be no question of abandoning her to face it all alone, at least not before her brother arrived.

Indoors, I went into the drawing-room to get Kristy a drink which might help to steady her, and noticed a back number of *Go-Fast* mixed in with some *Country Life* issues in a heap on the sofa. On the cover was a picture of a Jet Ranger landing beside the swimming pool of a ritzy country house, a pair of silky Afghan hounds looking windswept in the rotor-wash. For the first time since arriving in Sardinia I suddenly recollected the delectable Fritz. Delectable but instantly forgettable, I thought, splashing brandy into a glass. A girl like Kristy would never go out of my mind, just like that.

But Kristy was not to get her drink, because the doctor arrived. The maid met him at the front door and escorted him into the bedroom. Soon afterwards I heard him make several telephone calls, including one to the Carabinieri. They came in half-an-hour, two inspectors in dark-blue uniforms and ghoulish sunglasses. They talked with Kristy, then sauntered round the greenhouses. From a distance I watched as one of them plucked a yellow chrysanthemum and installed it in his lapel.

An undertaker's hearse arrived, embellished with silver lamps, ornate fretwork and faded purple drapes which reminded me of the vulgar mauve power cruiser on board which all this, from my point of view, had started in Cowes. A simple coffin was unloaded and carried into the villa by an old man and a barefoot boy.

Wanting to spare her the sight of her grandfather being carried away in a box, I looked for Kristy and found her seated stiffly erect in the drawing-room, her face pale and drawn as she conversed in terse syllables with a local official who made notes in a large book.

'You're still here,' she said flatly. 'The police are taking statements and want to see you.'

'What did the doctor tell you?'

'Opa had a heart attack. The doctor is familiar with his medical history and says it could not have been anything else.'

'Were you expecting anything else?'

Kristy shrugged fractionally and turned away. When I asked what I could do to help she shook her head silently. I went in search of the police and found them conversing in low tones near their car.

One, coarsely shaven and wearing scuffed shoes, spoke a little fractured English. He was interested in how the fire might have started so I led them down to the footprints on the beach and produced the petrol can. No doubt they would find Bruno Feraldi's fingerprints on it, but as he was the foreman of the place it would amount to nothing as evidence. The second policeman studied the footprints on the beach and stirred them up with the toe of his shoe, successfully making them unrecognizable should any further investigations be required.

As we returned to the villa the coffin was being carried out. I watched it slid roughly into the rear of the meat wagon and the ornate doors slammed. The hearse drove away, followed by the police car, then the official and finally the doctor.

Kristy sat alone beneath the vine, staring out to sea. Large round sunglasses with tortoise-shell frames hid most of her face. I pulled up a chair and sat beside her, resting my feet on the parapet.

'They've all gone – the worst must be over now.'

'How can you say that? It's only just begun! I shall remember this day for the rest of my life.'

'Perhaps, but the pain won't be so hard to bear after a while.'

'Do me a favour and stop being wet,' she said tiredly. 'Patronising remarks like that don't help.'

'All right,' I said crisply, seeing an opening. 'If that's how you feel, tell me how your cousin Ronald came to be driving away from here not long after the fire started. In your car, the blue Merc.'

'That's ridiculous,' she said dismissively. 'In any case....' Kristy paused and turned to look at me, suddenly tense. 'What do you know about my cousin, how can you know his name?'

'I brought him over to Bonifaccio in the boat with me, the day I arrived – yesterday.'

Kristy's chair crashed backwards as she jumped to her feet.

'God, even you are in it! I might have guessed! You think you've found a friend, then everybody is an enemy. I trusted you. Thought you would help. But you're a shit like the rest....'

'Now hold on,' I protested.

'Don't touch me!' Kristy was near to screaming, her fists bunched tightly beneath her chin as she covered her body with her arms.

I had to shout to get through to her. 'Don't be a fool,

111

sit down!' She showed no signs of sitting down but she did stop the anxious sideways shuffle with which she had been retreating from beneath the vine. 'Shall I tell you what happened or are you going into hysterics? I am on your side....' I pointed to the scabs and bruises on my face. 'How do you think I got these? It was your bloody cousin who did it, last night on your boat. That's how I know his name, sod him!'

Kristy froze, a picture of confusion, guilt and grief. Taking her firmly by the arm I steered her back to her chair, set it back on its feet, and pushed her into it. She relaxed then, and had a little cry.

'I'm sorry,' she sniffed. 'I just didn't know what to think any more....'

I sat closer and put my arm around her shoulders.

'I can help you, if you let me. We'll sort this thing out together. But listen, neither of us can be strong-minded and intelligent on an empty stomach. Why don't you find something to eat and bring it out here while I fetch a bottle? Then you can tell me all about your abominable cousin and we'll decide what to do about him.'

Having something to do helped Kristy to pull herself together, as I had hoped. She went off with a wan smile and returned in a few minutes carrying a tray bearing a loaf of bread, butter, and an assortment of cheese and salami. In the middle of the tray was a narrow-necked vase holding a single Blue Hurricane on a long stem. I popped a bottle of champagne that I had found in a refrigerator and poured it into inelegant tumblers.

'We were saving the bottle for when there was something to celebrate,' Kristy said sorrowfully. 'It's been on ice for a very long time.'

'Your grandfather would want us to enjoy it,' I said, 'so let's drink to him, and to the damnation of Ronny.'

'No, not that,' Kristy replied with a shiver. She put the blue flower on the parapet so we could look at it. 'We'll drink to Opa, and to what might have been.'

I tilted my glass in a silent toast. Then I asked if she had reported the stolen car.

'Do you think I should?'

'It won't be too far away. You should make a routine report, otherwise you might never get it back. How much more you say depends on whether you want the police to get on your cousin's trail.'

'It wouldn't do any good.'

She was right on that point. Feraldi would have friends all over, and he obviously had money to keep them sweet.

'This island runs on back-handers,' she went on, 'it's one reason Opa was always struggling. He could never bring himself to do it. Bribes were against his principles.'

'Tell me about him,' I urged.

The wind had died and it would be another golden evening. A feather of ash drifted over the low table and Kristy waved it away, staring after it gloomily as it wafted over the parapet and was carried upwards on the calm air. Then, hesitantly at first, and in a low husky voice, Kristy began to tell me about her grandfather. How he had grown up on a country estate in the Cape Province, at an early age demonstrating an extraordinary rapport with Nature and remarkable green fingers. He had devoted his life to the study of botany and the development of horticulture.

'He never could remember the latin names,' Kristy explained, 'but there was nothing he couldn't grow. In the trenches in France he grew geraniums and pansies, using German helmets as flowerpots which he lugged around with him in a cart. Can you imagine it? And he was fantastically brave, too: he won the Military Cross and was mentioned in despatches at least a couple of times.'

'That doesn't surprise me,' I murmured, 'he looked the fearless sort.'

'Oh yes! He always claimed he was just collecting

113

some primroses but there happened to be a machine-gun post half-buried beneath a bank in the woods and he stormed it single-handed when his platoon was pinned down.'

One leave in England the young South African soldier had met Kristy's grandmother and after the war they settled in Sussex to grow flowers. The nursery had a lot of ups and downs but after the Depression it became successful.

'You see, Opa was much more than just a gardener,' Kristy said. 'Although he made a living on his hands and knees among the flowerbeds he had a very fine and brilliant mind. Some of his friends were men in very high places – politicians, generals, scientists, actors. He was a member of the Garrick Club in London, though he could not afford to go there often in recent years. He was always writing technical papers for the Royal Horticultural Society, and he used to judge at the Chelsea Flower Show.'

'Ronny hardly fits that superior kind of mould.'

'Well, Opa had two sons. There's Ronny's father, Jaap, who lives in Hampshire. And my own father, who was a bit younger. Daddy was brilliant and brave, everything his older brother should have been. In the Second World War he was twice wounded and came out with a DSO. His brother was a Mayfair soldier, a major in public relations or something safe like that, and didn't even go abroad until 1945. He married three times and even now he lives apart from his current wife. A dozen times the family has bailed him out of different scrapes but he has always managed to live like a lord. He has been in court for drunken driving, procuring an abortion, assaulting a traffic warden, and when Daddy was killed....'

'Killed! By his brother?'

'Oh no! He went to California in 1955 to study horticulture and was run down by a truck....' Kristy's voice faltered and I remained silent, sipping the cool wine a little at a time and reflecting on the bitterness and hostility she must feel towards her uncle. When she had got her breath back she continued: 'Mummy brought Jon and me back home to find that Uncle Jaap had somehow prevailed on Opa to make the nursery over to him to avoid death duties. The business was doing quite well then, and Opa had been very ill from the shock of Daddy's death, so it all made some kind of financial sense, though I was just a child and did not really understand what was happening.'

'What happened next?' I prompted.

'Within a couple of years Ronny's father sold the whole place to a property developer who covered it with neo-Georgian houses for stockbrokers. He made a packet out of the land sale, and used some of the money to buy a new place down in Hampshire. At the same time he changed his name to James Blom, mainly because he thought it would do him good commercially and because he had political aspirations, but Opa was broken-hearted because old-fashioned values like carrying on the family name really mattered to him.'

'What did your grandfather do?'

'He had enormous goodwill in the industry and it was not hard to get capital behind him to make a new start out here. Even after the dirty trick he had played, Ronny's father was always hammering on the door asking for more cash. In the end Opa disowned him and since then there has been nothing but trouble.'

'And Ronny?'

Kristy made a sour face. 'What do you make of him?'

Fingering the bruises and cuts on my face, I said, 'If I had got the gun before he did I would cheerfully have shot the bastard, believe me.'

Kristy's hand flew to her mouth. 'He had a gun! Good heavens, I had no idea he was that serious.'

'The man's a villain, and that is putting it mildly,' I said with feeling.

'He always was a bully,' Kristy admitted. 'When we were kids Jon and I hated his coming to our house: when I was about six, he tortured my pet hamster to death. Just broke its back across his knee then threw it into my hands. Ugh! Three years ago, when I was working in London, he borrowed the Mini I had bought with my own hard-earned cash. Without asking he just took it, and smashed it up. Then rang to tell me where I could collect it and when I tried to get him to pay for repairs he said that was what insurance was for, and if I didn't have insurance I was a bloody idiot. It was insured, of course, but I lost the no-claims bonus and the car was off the road for six weeks.' Kristy was silent for a time, dwelling on the memory. Some of the colour had returned to her cheeks. The indignation, and the unburdening of her troubles, was as good as a tonic.

I said I did not understand how Ronald Blom had got to know about the new flower.

'Weren't you keeping the whole thing under wraps?'

'Yes, but only up to a point. You can't keep much from your own foreman. The padlock on the door, alone, and the fact that Opa was always so careful about keeping it locked, must have been a signal that there was something interesting going on, something worth investigating, and I dare say he had his own ways of doing so. But you must know that when he first came we were not a bit worried. He was charm itself: efficient, knowledgeable, pleasant to work with. And he had a powerful influence on local labour. For the first couple of years Opa had full confidence in him and treated him terribly well.'

'So what went wrong, what changed him?'

'Who knows? Blackmail, perhaps. Or simple greed.'

'Or somebody made him an offer he couldn't refuse?'

'You mean the Mafia? I doubt it, though anything is possible on this weird island where everybody seems to

116

be in somebody else's pocket. In the end we were paying off Bruno to keep the labour sweet and he was undoubtedly taking a rake-off from the people we employed. It was mad, we couldn't win.'

'As a matter of fact,' I said, 'it was your cousin Ronald whom I had in mind.'

Kristy shifted in her chair as if the thought made her uncomfortable.

'You might be right. I know he was connected with the property company that wants this place; in fact, he probably took the idea to them, when he was working in the City. Once he had bought up Bruno, he would find out about the new flower quickly enough and he would want it, badly.'

'What about his father, smoothy-chops Major Blom?'

'That man is capable of anything. You see, the usual thing to do when you discover a sport is have it propagated by a nursery that specializes in selling cuttings to the flower growers, like us. As the finders of the flower we would get our thirteen per cent royalty on every cutting sold during a period of ten years, while the nursery gets the business. The finder of a really top-class successful flower could make a small fortune from royalties but the nurseries growing it would make much more from percentage on turnover.'

'What you are saying is that by growing it in their own greenhouses Blom's Blooms will get the best of both worlds, the big biscuits.'

'As far as Europe is concerned, yes. In America and Japan they would licence other nurseries and take a cut.'

After thinking for a few moments I said with deliberation, 'There is only one thing to do, you know.'

'I know what you're thinking,' Kristy said, 'but things are different in England and it is not so easy to take the law into your own hands. We could have laid poison for Uncle Jaap years ago. Few voters in Hampshire would know his real history because he has changed his name, and it would have been so easy to have tipped off an investigative journalist. But Opa would never stoop to it and I don't intend starting now. In any case, it's a bad principle to meet force with force.'

'Balls!' I snorted, but it was hardly the appropriate moment to argue the point so I said nothing and poured the last of the champagne. It had warmed in the low sunshine and now it frothed in Kristy's glass, spilling over the rim and flooding the table.

'Sorry about that,' I said, handing her the dripping tumbler. 'Tell me, who inherits this place?'

'Jon does, if there is anything left when the debts are paid. Ronny will dispute every penny but the will is quite clear and it is safely locked away in a bank in London.'

'You had better get in touch with him,' I advised. 'Jon can fly here direct instead of meeting me in Toulon and I will look after the boat for you. You should send a cable to your uncle, too.'

'Must I?'

'Well, you have to tell him sometime. And inform the Carabinieri you have discovered your car missing, too.'

'I suppose you're right,' Kristy agreed with a sigh. She went into the house and I heard her dictating a cable over the phone. With nothing to do but wait I took the Blue Hurricane out of its vase. The stem stood two feet high and had seven blooms. Their sky-blue petals were larger and softer at the outside, growing smaller and more numerous towards the centre where the daisy eye, a darker hue of almost midnight blue, was all but hidden by a thicket of tiny upright petals. It had no perfume, just a faint smell of paper money. In a few hours the flower I held in my hands would wilt and die, yet incredibly its lower half, now in Ronald Blom's hands, was capable of sprouting anew and growing a fortune.

'It looks a bit forlorn,' Kristy said as she returned.

I dropped the stem on the table and tried to think of something encouraging to say but was distracted by the sound of sandals slapping on the flagstones as Bruno Feraldi crossed the terrace towards us.

'Speak of the devil,' I muttered, wondering what mischief he was bent on now.

His mouth set in a grave line, the big Italian nodded a cursory acknowledgement and, ignoring me completely, addressed himself to Kristy who had flipped her sunglasses on top of her head and met his gaze icily.

'Scusi, Signorina, please. We are sorry for the dying of your grandfather.'

Kristy inclined her head a fraction of an inch.

'Thank you, Signor Feraldi.' Her voice was a husky breeze straight off the North Pole.

'And the fire,' he went on, waving his hands at the blackened landscape. 'Is unlucky thing, no? All is *finito*.'

'What do you want?' Kristy demanded.

The man's sallow, puffy flesh bulged out of his tight t-shirt like caramel custard with a thin skin on it. His bald head shone and from my seat below and in front of him I could see gold flashing in his teeth which I had a sudden urge to knock down the funnel of his throat. He bunched the fingertips of one hand in the palm of the other and said, 'The men, Signorina, they desire the monies....'

'Just a minute!' I interrupted sharply. Kristy frowned a warning which I ignored. With a kick I sent the empty petrol can scraping across the flagstones so it bumped Feraldi's shins. 'Yours, I think.'

The Italian's eyes bored into mine for a long moment then he kicked the can away. It bounced across the terrace and with a loud report hit a flowerpot containing a heat-seared geranium.

'Don't, John!' Kristy cried anxiously.

Feraldi shrugged his shoulders. 'We have many such petrol cans here.'

'But this one was used to start the fire, and you know

119

it,' I said, rising to my feet and stepping towards him, intent on settling a score of my own. I knew he could move quickly, and was waiting for it, but I thought I could handle him. Feraldi smiled thinly, glanced meaningfully over his shoulder, then stared back cockily, his head on one side and the tip of his tongue showing between his teeth. Following his look I saw three men lounging by the side of the villa. Alerted by the drumbeat of the empty can they faced us in a row, hands thrust deeply into the front pockets of their denims, shoulders flexed beneath tatty t-shirts.

'You had better sit down,' Kristy muttered in a tone that made only too clear the contempt she felt for my tactics.

'Now, Signor Feraldi,' she said, 'what is all this about money?'

'For the work, Signorina.'

'Your men, Signor, are not at work.'

Bruno Feraldi's elliptical head nodded. 'Si, Signorina. It is a question of....' He struggled for the right word in English then said it in Italian and looked surprised when Kristy understood.

'*Pagamiento licienziamenti*– he wants severance pay,' she told me.

'You can't pay that!'

'No, I can't and I won't,' she said, staring balefully at the Italian for a long moment. Then she drew a deep breath, pitched her voice high, and delivered a volley of rapid Italian.

'*Brutto schifoso ignorante questa non me la fai*– you ugly, repulsive, ignorant bum, don't try to put that one over me....'

It might have been a back-street whore in Naples screaming at a customer who had jibbed at paying his bill but it was Kristy, on her feet and red in the face as she advanced on Feraldi, her arms spelling it all out in wild semaphore. The foreman was shaken by the ferocity of her attack, all the worse for being in his own tongue.

120

When he tried to speak up Kristy shouted him down. When he waved his fist in her face Kristy slapped it aside. Her voice was a whip, her eyes threw knives that rooted the man, terrified and wide-eyed, to the spot. Sensationally she had become the Mother figure, the harridan in black who has every red-blooded Italian male gripped by the short hairs.

Listening with amazement to Kristy's performance I concealed my delight by drawing patterns with my finger-tip in the champagne that had run over the table. The blue petals of one of the flowers had turned a darker colour where it had been lying in the wet, and I moved the stem aside to make room for more doodles.

Suddenly I was aware of Kristy's tirade beginning to falter. I looked up to see Bruno Feraldi staring down at the table, eyes wide, mouth slack. Kristy also stared with an alarmed expression at the pattern of swirls I had drawn.

A blue pigment was leeching from the wet petals and staining the champagne a diluted pale-blue.

Kristy's colour turned ashen and she darted a frightened glance at the Italian who snatched the stem and rubbed the wet petals between his fingers. They came away stained with blue. He muttered a coarse oath, angrily flung the flowers at Kristy's feet, then spun on his heel and strode away.

Kristy was still staring intently at the flowers when, seconds later, there was the sound of a car racing away.

At a loss, I asked what was up.

'Isn't it obvious!' Kristy retorted waspishly. 'It's not really blue at all.'

'It looks blue enough to me,' I argued, wondering if shock had made her go loopy. 'In my opinion it is as blue as the deep blue sea.'

Kristy picked up the flower and rubbed the petals between her fingers as Feraldi had done, then held out her hand to show me the dark-blue stain. 'Look for

121

yourself – this flower has been dyed.'

6 : OLD TRAFFORD

Champagne always did have a crippling effect on the small intelligence I had been born with. Feeling fuddled and in need of a proper drink I paid another visit to the fridge in the kitchen and returned with a couple of cans of beer. Jerking the pull-rings I handed one can to Kristy who turned down her mouth, then I took a long swig on the other. The fresh cold taste, and the touch of sharp aluminium on my lips, did not really help.

'You had better explain in short words I can understand,' I told her. 'You can't dye a flower, of all things!'

Kristy snorted. 'Why ever not? Most of the carnations you buy in London are dyed. The nurseries grow whites and keep them in deep freezes until needed, then dip the blooms in alcohol-based dyes according to which colour the market demands. That way nobody is caught with a lot of pinks when there's a spate of funerals and everybody wants purple.'

'So the blue chrysanthemum could have been an ordinary white?'

'Yes, dyed with ink. Opa always wrote with an old fountain pen.'

'I find it had to believe it is as simple as that.'

'It's true,' Kristy said. Then, seeing the doubt on my face and making her mind up to make a clean breast of it, she added the clincher. 'I helped him do it.'

Stunned, I dropped into the chair and looked at her in blank astonishment. It couldn't be true, but judging by the scarlet flush burning her cheeks the truth was only too evident.

'I don't know what to say,' Kristy said, hanging her

head. 'It was Opa's plan. I helped him to make the decoy a few days ago.'

'Why, for God's sake?'

'We wanted Bruno Feraldi and whoever was in with him to show their hands. We wanted them to steal the decoy so we could get the real plants away from here the moment their guard was down. Up to yesterday there was no way of knowing just who were the trouble-makers and who were the real villains.

'When Jon telephoned and told us about you, Opa hit on the idea of having you take the decoy. He said it would seem more authentic if we were seen smuggling it out and that you looked the capable kind of chap who could handle it.'

Troubled, Kristy flashed an embarrassed look at me but her high flush was fading.

'Opa didn't even tell me about it until you and I came back from swimming last night. We had been arguing about it when Bruno Feraldi called with his bad news, but neither of us imagined they would go so far or that Ronny would have his own reasons for putting his boots in.'

Rubbing my bruised forehead I pondered Kristy's explanation and thought it rang true: it was just the kind of unholy deviousness the old Boer would contrive, though I would have preferred not to have been the pawn in his suicidal game. But there was no denying the plan had succeeded, and handsomely. Now Kristy knew exactly where she stood.

In trouble.

'Okay, just give it to me by numbers,' I said heavily. Counting on my fingers, I went on, 'One: you grow a valuable flower which has to be got back to England but Feraldi and his chums have not openly shown their hand so it is hard to know who or what to defend yourselves against, right?'

Kristy nodded and started to speak but I waved her to silence.

'Two: Van Blommenstein dyes a flower blue and Feraldi is allowed to see it. This is like lighting the touch-paper. You wait for the firework to go off.'

'Three: while waiting for the thing to go bang along comes John Montgomery, fresh as the last shower of rain. Oh, you think, he's made of stern stuff, this fellow. He can ride the rocket. We will ask him to smuggle the thing out so the enemy will spring their ambush on him.

'Wonderful,' I said scathingly. 'Thank you very much!'

'It wasn't my idea,' Kristy protested.

'Four: the rocket misfires. Blom wants all the blue flowers, not just the one he takes from me, so he comes back.'

'Opa knew he would.'

'What!' I paused, thinking on this new development and realizing that it, too, made some kind of sense. The whole strategy was in fact a deliberate trap. The old man waited in the shed to confront his enemy – and it turned out to be his own grandson. I shook my head in wonder. 'The stupid old bugger!' I said.

'Yes, he was always stubborn.' Kristy sighed. 'He liked to do things his own way.'

'And it killed him.'

'Yes. And it killed him.'

Tossing off the beer, I demonstrated my feelings by slamming the empty can on the table with a bang that echoed round the valley. Kristy brushed tears from her eyes and I apologized but she cried all the more, throwing herself into my arms and sobbing when I stood up and reached for her. My anger evaporated as I held her tightly, smoothing her glossy hair which gleamed prettily in the softening light. Until, after a while, she pulled away and noisily blew her nose. Then she smiled wanly and said how sorry she was, brushing my bruises with a tender touch of her fingers and asking if I would like a dressing for them but I told her not to fuss. She rested her forehead against my shoulder and closed her eyes.

'Oh John, the last few months have been so terrible, you wouldn't believe it. And now this....'

All the while, as we stood thus in the yellowing sun, a restless thought dodged in and out of the shadows of my brain. Something Kristy had said about dyeing flowers, something that did not add up. Then the thing flew out into the light. 'Did I hear you correctly,' I said casually, 'when you said you helped your grandfather make the decoy?'

'Yes.'

'Just one?'

'Yes....' Kristy's eyes snapped open and she looked up at me, suddenly tense. 'But that was the flower I put in your buttonhole. Where did this one come from, and the others which Ronald grabbed?'

'Exactly,' I observed drily. 'And why didn't your Opa let you in on his secret?'

Kristy faced me over the wine-stained table. 'Opa was busy in his lab until the early hours and I was up at five-thirty this morning packing the flowers we picked, for shipment. It was never our habit to see much of each other in the mornings, we were always so busy. But we stopped work around one and had a long lunch together while it was really hot. I expect he would have told me then, but....'

'But he didn't expect to die.'

'No, but he was always a bit psychic. When Daddy was killed in California Opa knew it long before our cable arrived. Often he would do things in the greenhouses on the spur of the moment and forestall some crisis such as an outbreak of wilt, or even a power cut.'

'What about you? Did he have a telepathic link with his grand-daughter?'

Kristy shook her head ruefully.

'That's a shame,' I went on, 'because if the Blue Hurricanes Ronny pinched were really fakes, we have to find out where your grandfather concealed the real ones. And we have to find out before Bruno Feraldi gets hold of your cousin Ronald and brings him down on our heads again.'

If the real blue chrysanthemum was still at the villa, I thought, finding it should not be difficult. If the flower was blue it could only be dyed a darker colour, and that should limit the field.

'Come on,' I said, taking Kristy by the hand, 'we had better look now, while the light lasts.'

The sun was dipping low over the hill behind the villa, the smouldering gum trees sending long, gaunt shadows over the ashes.

'It's not quite so easy,' Kristy said, 'The Italians prefer dark flowers, especially purplish ones. For us it was a lucrative market and we grew a lot of them.'

'Why purple?'

'For funerals, mostly.'

'But surely the earth will have been disturbed where the disguised flowers were transplanted,' I argued.

'Possibly, but you don't know how clever Opa was with his fingers.'

The telephone rang and Kristy hurried in to answer it. The maid had gone home. I gathered up the empty bottles and cans and followed. The two beer-can pull-rings reminded me of an old trick, and feeling the tremor of a little premonition that was all my own I tore the metal tags from each one, leaving a sharply-serated edge, then slipped the rings on the fingers of my right hand. It was as nasty a set of knuckledusters as you would ever find in a NAAFI tent.

I put the glasses in the kitchen sink and placed the empty champagne bottle in a bin near the scullery door. In an English country house I would have found gum-boots, riding-crops, hunting boots and old tweed sports coats with leather patches on their elbows hanging behind the scullery door. Here there were lifejackets, thonged sandals, tattered espadrilles, a walking stick with a silver ferrule, and the battered Great White Hunter's hat which Van Blommenstein had been wearing when he met me at the front door. Could it have been only a little over twenty-four hours ago?

The brim was floppy with age, the ribbon around the crown had faded in the sun. Idly I turned it upside down and with a sudden sense of excitement saw an oblong of folded paper tucked inside the sweat-stained band.

I unfolded it. Van Blommenstein had done his football pools, ready for posting.

As Kristy hung up I rejoined her and learned that the Carabinieri had found the Mercedes at Santa Teresa and she was to collect it tomorrow.

'So Ronny took the ferry to Corsica,' I said.

'The further away the better – I hope I never see him again.'

'Well, I wouldn't count on that,' I said. 'Especially when Bruno tells him he has got the wrong merchandise.'

The greenhouses were a forlorn sight. Sacks and tools used for fighting the fire littered the ground. In the gentle evening breeze the scorched and seared polythene fluttered uneasily. The silence was uncanny, as if the massed flowers knew they were doomed.

I had picked flowers in the first greenhouse, and helped to put up the blackout in the second, but I had not been into the other two. When Kristy stepped over the threshold of the third greenhouse I saw the reason for her doubts. There was row upon row of dark-coloured chrysanthemums ranging from vivid, funeral purples to shades of red so dark they were almost black.

The blooms of the nearest bed stood nearly as high as my shoulders and were overdue for cutting. I rubbed the petals of one between my fingers but it left only a faint yellowish stain. Dropping to my knees I parted the leaves, but the earth between each stem was beaten flat by constant watering from overhead sprays, and I realised that any ground disturbed with a trowel need only be heavily watered for all signs of the disturbance to be erased.

'This is only half of them,' Kristy said, 'there are just as many up the hill in Old Trafford.'

Momentarily my mind stuck like bad synchromesh. When I finally got it into gear I asked, 'What was that you said?'

'About what?'

'Old Trafford. What has Manchester United football ground got to do with it?'

'Nothing much. Opa always called his greenhouses after English football grounds. It was a sort of tradition because the first one he ever built was dubbed Crystal Palace. Soccer was one of his passions.'

'And what did he call the greenhouses here?'

'Old Trafford is the next one up the hill. This is Craven Cottage. The others are Turf Moor and Villa Park.'

Remembering how, just before he died, Van Blommenstein's hand had moved towards the top of his head, as if feeling for his hat, I took Kristy by the wrist. 'Come quickly, I might have the answer.'

We spread the football coupon flat on the kitchen table. 'Opa always did the pools,' Kristy said, mystifield. 'There is nothing unusual about it.'

'But never quite like this,' I said. Normally you would expect to find eight crosses in each vertical column printed on the coupon, representing the match draws selected by the punter. In the first column of this coupon there was only one cross, alongside the Manchester United v. Everton game. This meant that United was playing at home, at Old Trafford. The next ten columns had neat crosses in row one, while row twenty-four had five columns in rows three, four, five, six and seven.

'What does that prove?' Kristy asked numbly.

'The flowers are in rows ten abreast, right? Your grandfather has drawn a plan of one of the beds and these five crosses in the middle of row twenty-four are the disguised Blue Hurricanes.'

With shaking hands Kristy turned the coupon over. The name and address had not been filled in, but with a sense of humour Van Blommenstein had inked a large cross in the 'no publicity' box. In the space for writing the total amount of money being invested he had put 28p in large, underlined figures.

'Are the beds numbered?' I asked.

'Yes, the plan is in the study.'

The study, off Van Blommenstein's bedroom, was the den of a busy and efficient man with a wide range of interests. A large roll-top desk occupied the centre of a dark room lined from floor to ceiling with laden bookshelves. Under the window overlooking the bay was a long trestle table on which an Anglepoise lamp, microscope and brass telescope on a tripod stood amid a clutter of test tubes, horticulture magazines, and notepads. At one end of it was a three-tier wire basket filled with sales dockets and receipts. The books on the shelves ranged from the scientific to a complete collection of Laurens van der Post, South African yearbooks, back numbers of *Drum* and a large number of well-thumbed classics.

Kristy switched on the old brass desk lamp which had a shade of dark green glass. She looked around sadly for a few moments and then, from a filing cabinet behind the door, drew out a sketch plan of the greenhouses. In half a minute we had located bed number twenty-eight: third on the left as you entered the main door of Old Trafford. I returned the plan and rolled the drawer shut with a bang.

'Now we know,' I said quietly. 'Next question is what are we going to do about it?'

Looking sick and tired, Kristy avoided my eyes and stood at the window staring over the darkening sea.

'The funeral won't be for several days yet.'

'But your brother's exams finish when?'

'Tomorrow or the day after.'

There was a pleasantly-mellow aroma of pipe tobacco

in the room and I could visualize Van Blommenstein smoking as he worked at his big desk.

'The finest thing you can do in his memory,' I reasoned. 'is grow that flower. And that means getting it back to England and keeping it out of your cousin Ronald's thieving hands.'

'It's all very well to say that, but how can I leave....?'

'You can and you must!' I pressed. 'And start tonight while you've got the initiative. How long will it be before your cousin or that Eyetie meatball come back and start pushing you around? What will you do then, ring the Carabinieri who will hold you down while Ronny boots you in the face, like he did to me?'

As I put my hands on Kristy's shoulders two large tears rolled down her cheeks. My heart filled with affection and sympathy. The poor girl needed tenderness when all she was getting from me was harshness. But there was no other way.

'Kristy, you are on your own now,' I continued more moderately. 'Only you can get that plant back to England, and you will have to be devious about it because your cousin wants it more badly than you do.' A carriage-clock on the mantel put the time at six-thirty. It would be dark in half an hour. 'If you want me to help we can be away from here right now and in France tomorrow. But it is your decision.'

On the roll-top desk there was an assortment of photographs – Kristy's father in uniform receiving his medal from King George VI, a faded soccer team in striped jerseys and knee-length shorts grinning proudly beneath a hot South African sun, an elegant lady with Kristy's distinctively-pointed chin and high cheek bones. In the sepia-tinted picture she wore a gold brooch inlaid with rubies and beautifully crafted in the form of a springbok; the same brooch was pinned to the old leather picture-frame.

As I removed the brooch from the frame Kristy told

me in a small voice that it had been her grandfather's wedding present to her grandmother. I pinned it to the collar of Kristy's blouse.

'What you decide to do now,' I said theatrically, 'depends on whether you believe it is more important to bury your grandfather, or....'

Kristy's chin jerked upwards defiantly and she flushed, not embarrassed this time but angry, and tears again sprang into her eyes.

'That was a perfectly bloody thing to say.' She sniffed then went out. 'It's getting late, we'd better hurry or it will be dark.'

It was darkish on land but the sea was still bright: you would stop playing tennis and probably decide to go swimming. But there was to be neither tennis nor swimming for us. Kristy switched on the lights in the dusty packing-shed and took some plastic bags from a shelf. Nearby was a carton of small cardboard cannisters, each capped by a twist of blue paper. 'What are these?' I asked.

'Greenhouse smokes, for killing aphids. You light the touch-paper and retire gracefully, holding your breath and shutting the door behind you.'

'Poisonous?'

'Very, if you get enough of it.'

At the door of Old Trafford I let Kristy go ahead. 'Be quick, I'll keep guard from here.' She found her way rapidly to bed twenty-eight then counted down the ranks of plants. I saw some chianti-red flowers tremble as she pulled several plants up by their roots. She rubbed the petals of one bloom between finger and thumb and held up her hand to show me the dark red stain. Then she carried the five plants into the centre aisle, where there was room to work. Inspecting each by turn, she selected the best specimen, cut off the stem with sécateurs four inches above the root and dropped the root in a plastic

132

bag. From a nearby tap she let an eggcup of water dribble into the bag, squeezed most of the air out, then fastened its neck with a paper twist.

Standing by the greenhouse door I watched all this with one eye while keeping a careful look-out with the other. The sun was on the point of dropping fierily behind the hill and I kicked myself for looking at it as strange irridescent shapes danced in my eyes.

Kristy reached for the second-best plant to cut and bag when a movement caught my eye. This was no trick of the vision. Figures of men did not dance like spots before the eyes. He had stepped out from behind the neighbouring greenhouse and was partly silhouetted against the golden sky. The clink of a stone pointed to another man standing before the belt of low scrub, untouched by the fire, where he had been hiding. Then, striding out of the twilight shadows around the packing-shed, where he had apparently been concealing himself until Kristy made her move to collect the true blue chrysanthemum, was Bruno Feraldi.

With a sick feeling I realized the car must have been driven away by the fourth man, leaving the others to deploy themselves in positions where they could observe what we did. Now some signal had passed between them and they were advancing on us, converging like a sheriff and his posse who know they have got the outlaws cornered. In his right hand the big Italian carried a massive, rust-speckled revolver with a chined barrel – it must have seen service in the Abyssinian campaign, but there was no reason to doubt that it packed a wallop.

Seeing they had been spotted, the three men broke into a slow run. But a man with Feraldi's stomach was incapable of anything more rapid than a breathless jog, and this gave us valuable seconds. Thinking quickly, I told Kristy in a low, urgent tone what she had to do.

Coolly she scooped up the remaining plants, ran with them to a bench near the door of the greenhouse, and sprinkled them with the contents of a tin marked 2,4-D

– a hormone that in undiluted form would accelerate growth so drastically that the plants would die of exhaustion. The Blue Hurricane in the bag Kristy now picked up was the only one that could possibly survive.

In the corner of the greenhouse I noticed a rent in the polythene. I waited until the men had come past it then plucked a plant from the nearest bed of flowers – according to a labelled stake it was a variety called Flamenco – then plunged out through the hole in the wall and ran like a rabbit.

Feraldi cocked his gun but did not fire. The three men wheeled round and came down the hill after me. I dived among the pink, red and purple chrysanthemums of Craven Cottage, jigging along the walkways and trying to lose myself. It was like being a castle piece on a chess board. I could move up and down, and across, but not diagonally. I threw myself flat and tunnelled into a bed of tall flowers then froze, trying to regulate the panting that caused the blooms above me to tremble as if heavy traffic was shaking the ground.

There was a click and the entire greenhouse was flooded with light. Rows of 100-watt bulbs, backed by reflectors made of tin-foil pie dishes, were slung above each long row of flowers. I felt like an insect on a floodlight.

To let Kristy make an escape with the blue chrysanthemum I needed to delay the three men for only a short time, but I had already had a taste of Bruno Feraldi's viciousness once in twenty-four hours and it was an experience I had no desire to repeat in twenty-four years.

Breaking out of cover like a fox flushed by hounds I fought my way out of the flowers and crashed into the next bed, getting entangled in the orange net stretched tautly across the bed at knee height. Crimson petals rained like confetti as I struggled to get clear. Feraldi shouted. A man with shoulders like a lifeguard and a gold cross swinging from a thin chain round his neck pushed through the adjacent row to reach me. I managed to break clear, then he, too, was floundering like a fish in the net.

At the far end of the aisle the bulky figure of Bruno Feraldi was braced, aiming his gun with both hands. I was framed like a target in a tunnel. The gun went off with a bang as loud as a land mine as I leapt sideways, driving forward, jumping from row to row across the greenhouse. The other two were only yards behind. And gaining.

Over my head I saw one of the temperature sensors that controlled the misting-sprays. If the temperature rose they turned the water on to cool things down. A bit of cool was just what the occasion demanded. Praying that it would work, I put my lips round the sensor and exhaled with all the wind I could muster. It reacted after two or three seconds, squirting a needle-sharp spray in my face. Three parallel rows of flowers extending the entire length of the house were saturated in dense, stinging rain. I ran behind it, the water running down my face and wetting my clothes but providing necessary cover. When I reached the polythene wall the material was smooth and tough and there was nothing on which to get a grip. If you know what it is like trying to get into a bag of sweets, imagine what it is like fighting your way out.

Wildly I cast around for something with which to tear the material, but it was a tidy greenhouse. I fumbled in my wet pocket for my Zippo lighter. It had never let me down, not even in a Force 9 Channel gale with water flying like concrete through the air. When its high flame touched it the wall melted instantly. I dived through head first, hands and arms pointed like a diver's to widen the gap.

After the brilliance of the lights, the twilight outside seemed pitch black. Stumbling down the gentle slope through some bushes I came to the back of Turf Moor, the second greenhouse in the line of four, where I had helped Kristy put on the blackout. Again I burned my way through the wall, this time to get in. There was a shout as the flare of the flame was spotted.

Feraldi padded down the hill and switched lights on again. I hid in a long tunnel of thin black polythene, trampling some young plants barely a foot high and getting the mulchy smell of crushed vegetation up my nose. Until there was a flicker of light on the inside walls of the tunnel as the far end of it was lifted, and I had to roll out under the skirt.

The three Italians zeroed in.

Another blackout curtain was two rows away. I dived beneath it and sprinted its entire length. The temperature was in the high nineties, humidity about the same. Sweat rolled down my forehead and into my eyes. The weight of water in my clothes slowed me down. I had to think of something. Quickly.

Bursting out of the tunnel I ran ten yards left through a bank of young plants, then five yards right, and broke out through a wall of rust-coloured buds.

It was a lucky shot.

Bruno Feraldi was right in front of me, looking the other way. Long ago I had reversed the beer-can pull-rings on the first and second fingers of my right hand, so the sharp edges were uppermost. As Feraldi jerked round and lifted his gun arm my tin-knuckled fist raked his face. He reeled back with a shriek, clutching his torn cheek as blood poured down his jaw and stained his t-shirt. Feeling slightly sick and ashamed, I snatched the gun from his hand, let off a shot in the general direction of the two men running down separate aisles towards me, and made a clean exit through the main door, snapping off the lights as I went.

The van didn't have keys. For a panicky moment I thought I was sunk. Then I remembered how Kristy, before driving me down to the yacht, had found them in the glovebox. I went down the drive like a rocket, honking 'We won the cup' to tell Kristy I was on my way.

I prayed she could have the sense to stay put.

Hard driving helped me relax. I took the long way round in case I met Bruno's mates driving up to reinforce him at the villa but it meant an extra forty minutes at the wheel. I kept a close eye on the rear-view mirror but I seemed to be alone on the twisty road. All good Sards were in their pizza houses, cramped around tiny tables eating enormous pizzas washed down with rough wine. My mouth watered at the thought but I could not afford the time to stop.

The little van's headlights were weak and after the first ten minutes I slowed down, for there was no point in hitting one of the belled sheep grazing along the rocky verge and having to hitch-hike.

Turning back on the main road for the last six or to worry that I had made a mistake, for the detour might have given Bruno Feraldi time to arrange some sort of trap at the yacht harbour.

The road plunged down a short hill, wriggled across a narrow culvert in the dip, snaked up the other side in a double hairpin partly concealed by shrubbery. Glimpsing the whole picture in the watery headlights I dived the van like a Stuka.

It pulled out with engine screaming, bounced over the culvert and hit the first hairpin at sixty. I drifted round with squealing tyres, fighting the over-steer and letting the steepness of the incline act as a brake.

I had judged it nicely, but had made no allowance for the road-block around the bend.

A red and white pole of four-by-two was propped like a gymkhana jump across the road on a pair of crutches. Three feet in advance of it was a white metal disc with a red rim and the word ALT! in small black letters. There was no other warning, no light.

The van could not jump the pole so it had to go through it. My right hand snatched the hand-brake on hard, my

137

left hand whirled the steering-wheel to full lock. Then, as the van nosed sharply into the bank with both rear wheels locked solid, I slammed into reverse, released the handbrake, and stood on the gas.

Going backwards at thirty miles an hour, the van smashed into the barrier. With a thump that rang the bodywork like a drum the pole thudded against the rear doors, bounced upwards, slid along the roof, and dropped down in front of the windscreen.

At the same instant, a battery of arc lights came on. Through dazzled eyes and flying dust I saw a policeman with a sub-machinegun leap for his life as one of the crutches flew at him.

The sight of one machinegun was sufficient. I had no desire to get a burst of nickel-plated three-nought-threes through the windscreen. As the van jerked to a stop, my right foot pushing the brake pedal to the floor, I leapt out and threw both hands in the air, shouting, '*Inglesi, inglesi!*'

Surprise road-blocks on Sardinia are infamous. The island is still the haunt of bandits, mainly bank robbers, who elude capture easily. Not because they have the sympathy of local people who hide them, but because locals will never turn fellow Sards over to uniformed 'foreigners' from the mainland. The only hope of the Carabinieri is to spring ambushes at night on the off chance that a bandit will fall into their net.

Armed to the teeth, a dozen men in dark blue uniforms with silver badges and buttons stepped into the light. Would I be treated as an English tourist and told to push on? Or had the news of Bruno Feraldi's cut face got around? As a man himself operating outside the law, I doubted that he would call in the police officially. But there was an even chance the haughty-looking officer striding towards me, holstering a pistol big enough to melt down for pig-iron ballast, was the brother-in-law of whom Kristy had warned me. Feraldi would have had plenty of time to make telephone calls from the villa.

Whatever the reason for the road-block, I had no illusions of talking my way through. This was no genial bobby who had nabbed me for clocking eighty miles an hour on the Kingston by-pass. The officer had a thinly-chiselled face and eyebrows that arched under the sweat-band of his white cap. He took up a stance in front of me and with studied calm put on a pair of metal-rimmed sunglasses. Then he made a curt signal to his men to search the van.

With so many men the job did not take long. I could see the entire scene reflected in the officer's sunglasses. His face was an expressionless mask, like that of an astronaut on the moon.

After a few moments a constable spoke to him. The officer turned to me again.

'*Lei e Inglese*?'

I caught the last word and nodded vigorously. He held out his hand demandingly. I gave him my passport and driving licence. He buttoned them into the breast pocket of his tunic without looking at them, and my heart sank.

'*Nella sua macchina non ha il triangolo.*'

'What?'

'*Non triangolo.*' His fingers drew a three-sided shape in the air and I understood the van did not have the mandatory red warning triangle.

Well, they could hardly put me in jug for that.

I shrugged and said I was sorry.

Then a policeman searching the driving compartment shouted triumphantly and came over with Bruno Feraldi's gun. The officer squinted up the barrel then sniffed it, his nostrils puckering as they caught the sharp reek of fresh cordite.

'*E questo cos'e*?' The words were incomprehensible to me, but the question was clear enough – What's this then? The officer's cheeks drew back like curtains revealing the opening into which a coffin might slide for cremation. In the bright lights his nicotine-stained teeth gleamed like brass plaques. The lights glimmered away to nothing and he took off his sunglasses.

Escape was out of the question: I could see nothing until my night vision returned. There were armed men all around me. A car with a blue light on its roof reversed up and a sergeant pushed me into the rear seat, getting in alongside and offering a cigarette. It burned like a bush fire but I had to keep it going at least until the door was closed and the interior light went off.

At last, when I thought the roof of my mouth would peel off, the officer got in on the other side of me and told the driver to move. I drew strongly on the cigarette so the end glowed red then coughed hugely and, doubling up, managed to stub it against the touch paper of the fumigation bomb I had pocketed in the packing-shed at Villa Maddalena.

There was a faint splutter of salt-petre as it caught and I was sure it would be detected but the driver provided cover by crashing the gears and spinning the wheels on the gravel.

Cupping the smouldering cylinder in my hands, between my knees, I held my breath and waited for the thing to go off.

There was a sudden jet of thick, swirling smoke. As it spurted through my fingers I dropped the canister which rolled beneath the driver's seat. The car filled in an instant and jerked to a stop, nearly off the road. The sergeant beside me threw the door open and jumped out, retching. The officer tried to draw his pistol but my arms went round him in a half-nelson and I was able to rip open his pocket and snatch my papers.

Only when I had sprinted half-a-dozen paces towards the van did I dare to open my eyes fully and draw a deep, shuddering breath. Shots rang out as I flung the van in a wide, skidding turn. A couple of bullets hit the body-work and must have passed right through both sides. In the rear-view mirror I saw the floodlights go on again, effectively blinding everyone on the spot. As I took the first bend on squealing tyres I caught a last glimpse of the police car spouting a column of dense white smoke that billowed around it like steam from a burst boiler.

Kristy ran across the sand in bare feet, carrying her sandals and a kitbag of gear which she dumped on the bottom boards as the transom of the dinghy bumped her knees. I had rowed into the bay stern first to be ready for a quick getaway should I meet with a hostile reception.

'All set?' I asked in a hushed tone.

'Aye-aye, Captain,' she answered in a mocking whisper.

Phosphoresence danced like stardust off her toes as she shoved the dinghy out and clambered in over the stern. I put my back into the oars and skimmed the dinghy across the dark water to where *Bonnie Jean* lay on a short anchor chain. Secrecy was pointless now. It was more important to get away from shore and out to sea where we could lose ourselves.

'You've got the flower?'

'Of course,' Kristy smiled. 'You're not hurt are you? I was worried when I heard the shots.'

'Bruno couldn't hit a barn at five paces,' I said with a cockiness I was far from feeling. 'And you were right, he does have relations in the Carabinieri.' I told Kristy about the road-block, and how I had escaped. 'You'll be pleased to know that Bruno has got a sore face.'

'I saw it,' Kristy said with a shudder 'He's not very happy about it, either. But are you certain you're all right?'

'Perfectly, thanks.' It was nice to be worried about.

The stars were just bright enough to illuminate Kristy's face. The line of her mouth, which all day had been thin and straight, again curled upwards at the corners. Her eyes, previously sunken from shock and grief, shone now like wet pebbles.

141

'I was having fifty fits lying in the olive grove listening to it all,' she said. 'Thank God nothing happened to you.'

'Better get aboard,' I said, steadying the dinghy against the yacht's hull. 'We don't know how many brothers-in-law Bruno Feraldi has got. If there is a nautical tradition in his family, half the Italian Navy might be out hunting for us pretty soon.'

7 : FRITZ

There had not been the right opportunity to tell Kristy about the car, and when she came out of the *Bar Henri* where she waited while I collected it from the garage I introduced her with an elaborate formality.

'Meet *Ma Biche*,' I said, 'she and I have been the best of enemies for years.'

As pretty as the hitch-hiker princess of every lorry driver's dreams, Kristy laughed and pretended to shake hands with the door handle, saying '*Enchanté*'. When the door would not open she climbed in over the top.

'Will this old girl get us very far?'

'Careful what you say,' I warned. 'If this old girl hears you saying things like that she'll scratch your eyes out.'

'What do you mean?'

'She's got a mind of her own, this old bitch, as you'll find out. But I love her.'

I stowed Kristy's unremarkable kitbag, with its precious contents, in the narrow gap between the back of her seat and the large petrol tank that occupied all the boot space, then helped her to adjust the seat-belt. She sucked in her breath as my knuckles brushed her stomach. It was all I could do to restrain myself from giving her a kiss, but after the last brush-off I dare not risk it.

During the two-night voyage from Golfo Aranci Kristy had been relaxed, though drained to the point of exhaustion. Grief and anxiety had been pushed firmly to the back of her mind, and since leaving the villa with its desolate air and sad memories she had been more cheerful company.

The moment we were well clear of the Sardinia coast and certain of no pursuit from the fast inflatable, Kristy had made an acre of scrambled eggs and steered professionally while I demolished them with gusto. Unlike most of the girls with whom I had sailed, Kristy neither fussed when the wind blew her hair nor went into a faint when the heads needed pumping, and my heart warmed to her. Each of us slept while the other stood watch and steered, taking a circuitous route far out to the east of Corsica on the faint chance the the Carabinieri might have alerted a Naval mine-sweeper which would have been more likely to have searched for us in the direction of the Straits of Bonifaccio.

In the middle of the morning, the hills behind the Riviera coast a veiled smudge on the northern horizon, I had cut the engine and let the boat drift. We stripped off and dived over the side. Without affectation Kristy hauled her slim and golden body lithely up the rope ladder to regain the deck, then wrapped a towel around herself and found a far-away ketch to inspect through binoculars while I climbed aboard and dried off.

A breeze had sprung up and it was Kristy who suggested we hoist sail. Though slower, progress became infinitely more pleasurable. The hull cut slickly through the flat water and, with the breeze on the beam, the big genoa pulled strongly. Stretched out on the lee side of the cockpit in her yellow bikini, her face in the shadow cast by the fore-sail, Kristy dozed most of the afternoon and when the wind fell away in the early evening she helped me to stow the sails, looking fresher and brighter than I had ever seen her. The grub I had put aboard for my own voyage was scarcely sufficient for two, but Kristy made a fry-up of everything she could find, then took the helm as I navigated us into the *Rade de Toulon*. It had been getting on for midnight when we slipped by the gaunt warships and entered the harbour by moonlight, finding an empty berth at the yacht marina. Handling her neatly, Kristy turned the boat in the fairway, signalled me to drop the anchor, and ran her stern-first into the floating pontoon before killing the engine.

This morning, Julian Simpson-Potter had agreed to keep an eye on *Bonnie Jean* until I could return to collect her, and had eyed Kristy with open admiration and many questioning looks in my direction from behind her back.

'What about your friend Floribunda?' I had asked him. 'Has he been back lately?'

Julian shrugged with a look of pain, as if he did not want to be reminded.

'Haven't seen him since he went off with you. The *Go-Fast* people finished here yesterday and were planning to use the Paul Ricard racing circuit to do some speed testing. Good riddance, as far as I'm concerned, they were a pain in the neck.'

Now I thumbed the starter button and the five-litre Chevy roared like a Spitfire warming up for a dawn patrol. Shopkeepers rushed out of their doorways as if a liberation army had arrived. I turned the Healey's *art nouveau* front end into the traffic, taking the waterfront road, and in ten minutes we were on the outskirts of the city heading along the N8 coastal road to Marseille on the grounds that it was the route which lay furthest away from the Ricard circuit.

'Don't you think we should have the roof up?' Kristy suggested.

'Are you cold?'

'Not at all. Just feeling exposed.'

'There is no roof, I'm afraid. But even if your cousin does see you on the road he would have trouble catching up.'

'What, this old thing! You said Ronny was driving a Dino.'

'He will be in England now, planting what he thinks is the blue chrysanthemum.'

'Not if Bruno has been able to contact him.'

We were on a stretch of open road: telegraph poles and a railway line on the left, plane trees with white-painted trunks on the right. There were two lorries ahead, eight-tonners loaded with roof tiles. Coming towards us at a good lick was an articulated petrol tanker. I glanced in the mirror, then sideways at Kristy. The wind ruffled her hair forwards; one slender brown arm lay along the top of the door. 'All right then,' I warned her, as I snicked down a gear and floored the acclerator, 'hold tight!'

Instant lift-off! Pressed deeply into the upholstery by the g-force, it was like being squeezed out of a tube. I pulled out and flashed the headlights to let the driver of the oncoming tanker know that he was not seeing a mirage with an after-burner. Both tile lorries flicked past.

At eighty I changed to third with a quick thrust of the stubby lever and swung back to my own side of the road, twitching through the tanker's slipstream. We hit the far bend at a hundred and five, still accelerating. The Healey glued itself to the tarmac as if it had been poured out of a bucket. I sneaked a quick look at Kristy. Her knuckles were not clenched, always a good sign, but her eyes were like saucers.

Orange butterflies fluttering in the heat-waves over the road battered the windscreen like soft bullets as I lifted my foot off the gas, the engine note dying with a lingering whine like that of a Boeing taxiing into the apron. The drivers of a couple of little Renaults gave us the sort of brief, startled look reserved for low-flying jets as the Healey whistled past them and I tucked in behind a van as it ran up to a blind bend.

'Phew!' Kristy exclaimed. 'Do you always drive like that?'

'Only when I'm trying to impress, don't worry.'

'Where are we, Paris?'

'And that,' I boasted, 'was without the turbo-charger.'

Ahead was a country store, an *alimentation* which seemed to have everything from doormats to bottles of wine arranged on racks under a canvas awning out front. I drew up on the gravel. 'Are you hungry? I'll lay in a picnic.'

I went round the shop filling a wire basket: a loaf of sliced bread in Cellophane, margarine, jar of jam, two cans of Coke, cheese packaged in little parcels with pictures of Swiss mountains. Kristy met me at the cash desk and viewed my selection with horror.

'For heaven's sake put that rubbish back and let me do it.'

I carried the basket round behind her as she found a long loaf of crusty bread, portions of country cheese smeared on greaseproof paper, some meaty stuff out of an earthen jar, and a bottle of cheap red wine. It cost half what I would have paid for the stuff I had chosen myself.

We found a narrow side-turning that twisted up the hill between dark shrubs and skeletal outcrops of white, fissured rock. After half a mile we found a level glade where scarlet poppies and blue forget-me-nots thrust up through long, lush grass. I parked among them and carried the paper bag with our lunch into the shade of an almond tree.

While Kristy laid the food out and broke the bread into chunks I threw myself flat in the grass and listened to the silence: the pulse of crickets, birds chattering in some fruit trees up the hill, the distant hum of traffic in the valley, the ticking of the engine as it cooled.

'We don't have a knife,' Kristy said, 'have you got any bright ideas?'

I found a wide-ended screwdriver in the toolbox and gave it a sanitizing wipe with a bunch of grass. Kristy used it to paste a strip of bread crust with a rich, creamy cheese that was filled with what looked like tea leaves and which smelled like something rather nasty in the bilges. I made a face.

'What's this?'

'Try it and see.' It had a strong, tangy taste that was oddly refreshing and tickled the back of my nose.

'It's herbal goat cheese,' Kristy explained, handing up the bottle of wine. 'Can you open this?'

We drank straight from the bottle, the strong red wine somehow making the cheese taste clean and sweet.

'You're a typical Englishman abroad,' Kristy accused. 'Any excuse to eat out of a packet or a tin, preferably one stamped Made In Britain.'

'Not typical,' I said defensively, 'just a dull bachelor in need of care and attention.'

'And education,' Kristy went on. 'I'm always stunned by the English campers we see down here in the south of France, eating Golden Cling peaches out of a tin when you can buy individual fresh peaches twice the size and half the price in the street markets.' I said nothing, but thought of the small fortunes I had spent on tins of peaches in French supermarkets.

The chunky liver paté had a strong garlic flavour and was so delicious that I ate it straight off the end of the screwdriver, washing it down with gulps of wine. A gentle breeze rustled the long grass. There was hardly a cloud in the sky. The greenhouses of Villa Maddalena might have been on a different planet.

Kristy picked a dandelion, twirled it thoughtfully between her fingers, then got up and stood it in one of the vase-like carburettor-intake trumpets that jutted through the bonnet of the car. She sauntered back to me with a grin and sat down again, breathing in deeply through her nose.

'Mmmm, I love the smell of France,' she sighed. 'Can you smell it?'

I sniffed deeply and wrinkled my nose.

'Ash-trays, that's what I can smell.'

'Nonsense! It's wild lavender and sage and thyme growing on the hillside. There is nothing like the scent of wild herbs in hot sunshine.'

'What about an acre of blue chrysanthemums?'

'That's different. You know, if I had all the money in the world I would have a big garden near the sea where I could grow anything I chose without having to worry about selling it to make money. And I would fill it with wild herbs so the air smelled heavenly, like this.'

My dream marina on an island off the Costa Smeralda would look well with a garden around it, I thought, closing my eyes dreamily. But it was hardly a subject I should discuss with Kristy, for it was her island. I pictured the two of us together in my boat, heading out of the port of Yarmouth and turning through the Needles for destinations unknown. If the blue chrysanthemum withered and died tomorrow I would still want Kristy to be with me, but how could I say so when she had the key to a large fortune in her kitbag?

For a soldiering man, bed-mates had been relatively easy to find, particularly when I had fast sports cars and a boat to smooth the way. But finding a partner had been a different story. Mine had been a bachelor's world of boats, cars, engines and one-man sleeping-bags, and I had increasingly become the envy of my disenchanted friends. Mortgages, commuting, and nine-to-six jobs seemed a high price to pay for the privilege of getting your end away whenever you pleased, and my attitudes had hardened still further when every passing month brought news of yet another friend's marriage going on the rocks.

Since meeting Kristy life had been exciting but also it had been richer. In the space of half an hour I had learned to appreciate the perfumes of Provençe countryside, bought garlic paté at a roadside shop, and discovered herbal goat's cheese. Small things, but big enough to cherish for ever.

The irony was that if the bright sunshine and half a bottle of wine was all we had in the world I could give Kristy a smacking kiss on the mouth and tell her I loved her. But as long as Kristy had the Blue Hurricane in her kitbag I thought I should keep my feelings to myself. It was Kristy I wanted and needed, not her money or even her island, and it was becoming increasingly important to me not to risk making fundamental mistakes that could screw up another chapter of desires and aspirations.

When Kristy did speak it was far from what I expected to hear.

'I'll knock your head off,' she said impishly.

I opened my eyes to see her with a tough plantain stem in one hand. She had picked another and was holding it out to me. I took it and said, 'Bags first shot.'

She held her seed-head out horizontally and I flicked it with a hard, whistling crack. Hers remained intact; mine was decapitated. 'One to me,' she said. I picked another and she knocked its head off. 'Two up! What are we playing for?'

'Strip forfeits?'

'All right,' she said with a wicked grin. My next shot was a winner. 'Okay, what shall I take off?'

What a question! 'Better start with your left sandal,' I suggested.

I lost my shirt, shoes and socks, then Kristy lost her other sandal and her shirt. My next one her slacks and as she slid them off her long brown legs I saw that she had her yellow bikini underneath. Obviously, however, she thought the game had gone far enough. She did not pick another plantain stalk but lay back in the grass with a contented sigh.

'I could sleep all afternoon,' she murmured.

'Why don't you do that?' I suggested, patting her shoulder and missing, as I got up, the look of puzzled disappointment that crossed her face.

Dusting myself down, I unbuckled the Healey's bonnet straps and while Kristy snoozed in the sun I made a thorough inspection of the engine, looking for anything that might spell trouble at some awkward moment on the long drive to the Channel coast. While Kristy had the blue chrysanthemum my feelings for her had to be muzzled, but if anybody else took it from her it would be over my dead body.

Half an hour later I slammed the bonnet down harder than I intended and Kristy sat up. The sleep did not seem to have done her much good. Her eyes looked puffy and she rubbed her face with an open hand as if trying to wipe away a headache.

Carefully she collected the remains of our lunch and the bottle, and I realised guiltily that I would have left the litter concealed in the long grass. Then she dressed, and took the precious plastic bag out of her kitbag and opened it. The inside of the bag was speckled with moisture. I asked what she was doing.

'Letting it breathe,' she replied tersely. 'The leaves and stem will rot in the condensation if I don't take care of it.'

'How long will it last like that?'

'Easily a week, as long as I'm careful.'

I strapped the bonnet down and wiped my hands on a clump of grass. 'We had better make a move soon,' I said.

Kristy glanced at her gold wristwatch. 'What time do you think the banks shut?'

'Tons of time,' I said, 'but I've got more than enough cash for now.'

'I need some,' she said, wrapping up the chrysanthemum root again. 'How far is Marseille?'

'Forty-five minutes, I should think, if we get a good run.'

'Good, let's go.' Her manner was brisk and jumpy. She clambered into the car, pushing my hands away when I tried to help with the difficult seat-belt, cursed when she discovered that she did need some help after all. On the main road I found a gap in the traffic and blasted away, skidding the wheels in the gravel and throwing Kristy sideways in her belt.

'You're like a small boy with this thing,' she complained testily.

Ignoring the remark I drove more slowly and carefully. Noise and vibration and the thrust of acceleration can be fun for the driver of a powerful sports car but hell for a passenger.

When, with the best will in the world, I could not avoid braking sharply for a van that came from nowhere on my right, Kristy made an impatient noise in the back of her throat. She looked pale and strained and I concluded she was suffering from a relapse of the blues. When I asked if she would like to stop at a café for a cool drink she waved me on irritably, her mouth a thin line again and her pretty eyes bleak and narrow.

Traffic was busy and we had to stop at an endless number of red lights. Kristy stirred uncomfortably as the driver of a lorry alongside us at one intersection leered down at her. I gave him a murderous look and he made a circle of his thumb and forefinger. The lights changed and I hammered the Healey away, trying to get ahead, but at the next red light the lorry came up again and the driver tooted his horn while Kristy stared frostily straight ahead.

In a nervous gesture she glanced at her watch.

'There will be several trains to Paris tonight. I've decided to take one and go on from there to Calais and Dover. You have been very kind, and I'm most grateful, but now I can carry on alone quite easily ....'

'That's ridiculous!' I protested. 'If your cousin knows by now that he has got the wrong plant he is bound to come after you, and staking out the railway station or watching your mother's house would be an obvious thing to do.'

'You're being melodramatic,' she snapped. 'How could Ronald or Bruno possibly know I am in Marseille? In any case, he would never rob me in broad daylight, he just doesn't have the nerve.'

Refraining from pointing out that it would be dark in a few hours, and that Ronny had displayed plenty of nerve in the past two days, I asked how she would get

152

the blue chrysanthemum through Customs without the certificate showing it was virus-free.

'Not even you could help me with that. There is as much chance of being stopped in Dover as anywhere else. I will just walk through and hope for the best.'

Her sudden change in attitude left me at a loss. The memory of what I had been hoping for during the picnic stuck in my mind like a bad novel. Somehow I had to snap her out of this mood of depression.

We were close to the *centre ville*, driving slowly in the outside lane of a wide, tree-lined boulevard. A group of teenagers started to cross the road ahead, one spinning a set of car keys in his fingers, another holding two un-licked ice creams. They stood in a line between the lanes of traffic, edging in their toes as the Healey approached. I slowed, reached out with both hands, snatched the two ice creams, then accelerated away and turned through a gap in the traffic into a side-street. Chuckling, I handed one of the ice creams to Kristy.

She was sitting upright in her seat, cheeks flushed, eyes blazing like her grandfather's.

'You bastard, that was a filthy trick worthy of somebody like Ronny – you have been seeing too much of him!' Before I could do anything Kristy had twisted the ignition key out and thrown it out into the gutter.

Quickly I declutched and coasted into the side as the engine died. Kristy wrestled with the stiff catch of the seat-belt then climbed out and picked up her kitbag.

'You would be a better person to know,' she spelled out with soul-destroying candour, 'if for once in your life you stopped putting on an act.'

Struggling out of the car was not easy with melting ice creams in my hands. 'Kristy, hang on ... !'

'Go and play with your rotten engine,' she hissed, and ran off into the crowd.

I dropped the ice creams into the gutter, found the keys near the front wheel of a Citroen Ami forty yards back along the street, and strode back to the Healey with perplexity and disappointment hardening into a bitter rage. Kristy had every right to do what she wished, but her manner of doing it had driven a spike into every single one of my soft spots.

Five minutes of enraged driving brought me out at the *vieux port*, the great oblong harbour, guarded by twin forts, in the centre of the city. The sight of literally hundreds of yachts and small fishing-boats moored to rows of floating pontoons revived my spirits a little. This was one of my favourite Mediterranean harbours; I had been here one Bastille Day, moored in the centre of the old port, while the city exploded in fireworks. It was a dreadful city to visit by car, but by boat Marseille was pure magic.

Cruising along the quayside streets I wrestled with the options I faced. I could return to Julian's flat for the night and see if he had a job that would keep me occupied until Jon Van Blommenstein could be reached at the villa and I could find out whether he wanted me to continue the voyage to England. There were enough kids with backpacks knocking around the south of France to make the crewing problem easily solved. It did seem the best thing to do. The decision cleared my head and I began to feel better.

Kristy was probably right. She stood a good chance of reaching England safely and I saw little point in chasing after her. Damn her and the bloody flower, anyway. I had enough problems of my own to think about, and if Kristy thought I wasn't good enough for her, let her stew in her own juice.

The next lights were at red and it was a long wait. Huffily I stared along the bonnet, chewing my thumb, seeing not the traffic milling past my nose but Kristy coolly and methodically destroying the four remaining blue chrysanthemums as Bruno Feraldi and his heavy mob ran towards us. She had nerve all right. But she must be as mulish as her old grandfather.

A horn blared behind me. The lights were green and

I had been day-dreaming. Again the horn, not so much impatient as challenging. In the mirror I saw a bright green Porsche 928. When it drew alongside, the delectable and suddenly memorable girl photographer peered out at me with a pert, come-and-get-me grin: Fritz.

The Porsche was fifty yards in front and moving like greased lightning while I still fumbled into gear. As I shot away, leaving twin puffs of tyre smoke on the road, a pair of slender fingers appeared through the open sun-roof of the car ahead and formed an elegant but unmistakable v-sign. So that was how she wanted it!

When I caught up she made a sharp right down a side road. A pedestrian who had just dodged the Porsche leapt for his life a second time as the Healey hurtled straight at him.

I straightened up and earned a second mocking signal through the sun-roof.

Gritting my teeth, I started to drive.

Given rough treatment and driven with hob-nailed boots, *Ma Biche* could knock spots off anything on the road, even a woman's lib-mobile like a Porsche 928. Or so I thought.

Fritz jigged through the back streets and fought a way out to some dual carriageway but we were a bit careful about driving too fast in the city limits and I glued the Healey's nose to the Porsche's tail as we raced for the open road like dog sniffing dog in the park. At a roundabout I all but lost it when Fritz did what I least expected and shot around it a second time. Then she led up a slip road to the autoroute. At last we could open up. The wind beat my ears and the engine sang a wild and happy song as we whipped along the fast lane doing an easy ton with scarcely a car's length between us. A couple of gendarmes on motorcycles, travelling in the other carriageway and unable to turn because of the crash barrier in the centre, stared at us and one of them

155

lifted a radio hand-set mounted on the tank between his knees. Fritz saw it too, for she peeled off to the right and took the next exit. At the toll booth she dangled a ten-franc note from her window and sped away with her change. The toll collector waved me on. Fritz had paid the bill.

Skirting a large dull town called Aubagne, sharp left off the main road on to the N96, pell mell through narrow streets of a place called Gémenos with a nasty four-wheel skid in the market place where the cobbles had been hosed down. Then hard acceleration up a lane between shuttered houses and into open country, the sun sinking behind us and the parched escarpments of the Massif de la Sainte Baume turning pink in its glow.

With part of my mind I was venting disappointment and rage at the way Kristy had ditched me. Angry and sore, I was intent on catching the girl in front to compensate for my hurt feelings and injured pride. But it was with only a small part of my mind that I figured the *Go-Fast* journalists would know where Ronald Blom could be located, and if he happened to be still in France then Fritz would lead me to him.

Twisting in and out of ravines, curling round hillside cuttings, always climbing steeply, the road was only a little wider than the cars that took its corners with one wheel in the scenery. To keep up with the Porsche's low and well-sprung profile on the bumpy surface I had to work like a cowboy riding a bronco. Then the road came out in a sweeping right-hander and I saw a chance.

Digging in the spurs, I jabbed down a gear. The Healey rocketed inside the Porsche but there was a trench across the road where a pipe had been laid and covered in again. With a scream of metal and a spray of sparks the low-slung silencers scraped the tarmac. For an instant I eased up and the Porsche sprang ahead. Again the v-sign.

Jesus wept!

A racing driver treats a series of bends as one, lining

up from one apex to the next to find the line that enables him to come out of the last bend at the highest possible speed. An ordinary driver treats each bend individually. Fritz evidently had no racing experience. As I took my own line through the corners the Healey's front end she saw weaving close behind her in the mirror had an unsettling, hypnotic effect and I could sense that Fritz was unnerved. Then there was a series of gentle bends snaking around the side of a hill and though each one was blind I could see as we came down on them that the road was empty. Before she knew it I had the Healey along-side, then ahead.

But what I had not seen from further back was that workmen had been painting the white centre-line and marked it with rubber cones. I tweaked the wheel and let the Healey run over a long line of cones so they were crumpled beneath the spoiler and spat out the back in all directions, like depth charges. It was enough to distract Fritz from the problems of the next bend.

In a car like a Porsche 928, you can take a corner a bit too fast and think, this is fun. Do the same thing in my Healey and it's, Oh Christ!

But you have to keep your nerve.

Fritz took the bend too fast. Panicked. Braked shar-ply. Skidded. The green car whipped round like a dog bitten by a flea in its mechanicals. For a moment I thought it would spin off but the car recovered itself as Fritz touched the accelerator more by instinct than anything else and straightened the skid. The car snaked from verge to verge as Fritz recovered from her fright, then coasted to a stop.

'Boo!' I said with a chuckle. 'Are you okay?'

'You're supposed to be in Sardinia!'

'I was; where's your boy friend?'

'I told you he is not my boy friend.'

'Okay, so which cliff did you push him over?'

'I haven't seen him: he shot through in the Dino.'

Problem solved, I thought with relief. Fritz put a

cigarette in her mouth with slightly trembling fingers and in the flare of my Zippo looked up at me, green eyes mocking.

'I know a nice little *auberge* down the road where you can buy me a drink. Among other things.'

'For a sexy bird who pays my motorway tolls,' I said gravely, 'I would buy a drink. And other things.'

She chuckled and reached for the ignition key.

'Watch out, you might have to.'

Okay by me, I thought.

It was an elderly Provençal farmhouse with large wooden shutters, several terraces, and an orange tiled roof. Its picturesqueness was not even marred by the red neon sign that spelled out its name, *L'Auberge Pilon*. The parking spaces were shaded from the sun by a long roof of rattan and grapevines. In the lobby, odours of fresh bread, early strawberries and piquant sauces floated out of an open door leading to the kitchen. Opposite was the dining-room, where a dozen tables under crisp linen and jugs of flowers awaited the evening's business.

I sniffed appreciatively as Fritz tinkled the bell on the small counter.

'I'm starving.'

'So am I,' said Fritz with a provocative look, 'but let's have something to eat first.'

The Madame bustled out, smiling a good-natured welcome and wiping her hands on a white apron. Fritz spoke good French and soon we were upstairs in a large and homely bedroom which had a view over the mountain around which we had raced. Fritz bounced on the bed, which sagged but did not creak, her eyes flashing messages like Aldis lights.

I approached her with a glint in my eye but she got up, linked her arm through mine, and said maybe we should eat first – 'Then there won't be any interruptions.'

'Anything but herbal goat's cheese,' I said, thinking with a pang of Kristy stretched out in the grass.

As if she had read my thoughts Fritz asked casually, 'We glimpsed you on the way into town; what happened to the peachy girl you were with?'

'Just a hitch-hiker,' I temporized, but I was distracted from thinking about the implications of the question by the crackle and howl of exhaust noise in the carpark. As we went down the stairs to the lobby I was disconcerted to meet the two motoring correspondents working for *Go-Fast.*

'Here's that hot-arse with the Healey 100-S,' said Graham Wilson as he came through the door, his hands tucked in the back pockets of his jeans so his elbows flapped like wings.

Still wearing the black Dunlop rally jacket, now with the addition of string-backed driving-gloves, Alec Dempster was right behind him. He nodded in a friendly way, his mouth tightening in a leer as he noticed the way Fritz held my arm.

'I'll have to get myself an Austin,' he said, 'obviously a Ferrari doesn't rate.'

'It's only the way you drive it, Twinkle-toes,' Fritz taunted.

'Christ, what's wrong with his driving?' Graham Wilson demanded. 'I had the XJ-S coming up here and Alec was so far ahead I didn't even get a tail light to follow.'

The bearded Philip Fanselow, a slender briefcase under his arm, pushed into the small lobby we were crowding.

'What's the trouble?' he asked. 'Bar closed, or something? It can't be. Hell, that Corvette is twitchy on bends, it was all over the road.' He nodded to me, shooting an appraising glance from under wiry, grey-flecked eyebrows, then said to Fritz, 'You didn't bend the Porsche, did you, love?'

'Quit fussing, Phil,' Graham Wilson told him. 'That thing is as easy to push around as a pram in a park.'

'I don't think pushing prams is your forte, is it love?'

Fritz giggled coyly in response to Fanselow's teasing. As the editor pushed his fingers wearily through his hair I glimpsed a Mercedes insignia embroidered on the silk lining of his expensive leather jacket. The calf-skin briefcase under his arm sported a VW badge. A small tape recorder swinging from a thong on his wrist had a Ford roundel on its speaker. I wondered what was on the man's toothbrush.

'Do you know everybody?' Fritz asked me.

'By reputation, yes,' I smiled.

'I saw your Healey outside,' Philip Fanselow said. 'It made me think of one of those First World War biplanes, all string and good luck.'

'She flies well,' I said.

'Tally ho, chaps, dirty Fokker at twelve o'clock!' Dempster made machinegun noises in his throat and sprayed me with bullets while the others looked on stonily. Apparently tolerances in the team were wearing a bit thin.

Fritz disengaged herself from my arm and pointed to a door off the dining-room.

'That looks like the bar: I'll have a Pernod.'

'Where are you going?'

'I need to cock a leg.'

'Not your department,' Fanselow said, winking at me. 'Come on then.' He led through to a small, cosy room with windows facing the view and blue and yellow Richard ashtrays set out on half a dozen tables with red gingham cloths. A timber-built bar with a few high stools faced the windows. Alec Dempster tossed his rally jacket in a corner and tapped out a Stuyvesant on his thumb; his suit was wrinkled from several days at the wheel and I wondered how he didn't melt and run away in a puddle. The editor asked him if he had got some good stuff during the day.

'I'll have to sort out the figures: the Dino is ahead, of course,' the writer said.

'The standing quarter-miles were fantastic,' Graham

Wilson added.

Listening to their shop talk while drinking *bière pression* I realised they had been collecting data for comparative performance charts showing the acceleration, top speeds, braking-power and fuel consumption of the different cars. Though I felt relaxed and was enjoying the nuts and bolts chat, something made me uneasily conscious of lurking trouble but I could not pin down just what it was. In any case, I told myself, Kristy would be aboard a train by now, rattling up the Rhône Valley in a *couchette* with the blue chrysanthemum under the pillow. But it was to quell this uneasiness that I slipped into the conversation a remark that brought the writers up with a squeal of tyres.

'What's happened to the governor?' I asked. 'Pissed off to London, I hear.'

The sudden silence should have triggered alarm bells but my batteries were flat. Wilson spoke up first, darting nervous glances at the others through his owlish specs.

'Bet your life he's shacked up with the most beautiful doll on the Riviera.'

'Why do you say that?' I asked.

His tone sticky with mock envy, Wilson replied, 'He always is.'

'Or says he is,' Dempster added sourly.

'What about Fritz?' I asked. She had come into the bar to collect her drink then gone off to take a phone call when the Madame slid open a window in the wall and called her name through it.

Alec Dempster chuckled mischievously. 'Oh Fritz! She travels standby.'

Graham Wilson laughed. Philip Fanselow looked frosty. I asked, 'Who does Ronald Blom think he is, Biggles?'

Fanselow set his glass down with a bang. 'He's no comedian, but I must admit he does pay the bills,' he said, adding as if it was a short prayer, 'so far.'

Fritz came in and beckoned Philip Fanselow who left, saying it was probably London on the line. I took the opportunity to ask the two writers more about Ronald Blom but they did not want to talk about him and turned the conversation round to my Healey. We talked saloon car racing for a few minutes then Fanselow returned, darting me a frankly curious and bewildered look as I drained my glass and went to join Fritz in the dining-room.

It was much later before the significance of it dawned.

The dinner was fabulous. Onion soup dripping with *gruyère*, steak *au poivre* singed over a bundle of herbs that filled the room with pungent smoke and made our eyes water, a red *vin de la maison* so smooth and rich and light that it lined your throat with silk. Over blackcurrant water-ices, then cognac and coffee, Fritz told me how she had been photographing each of the cars in scenes reminiscent of Impressionist paintings.

'It's fun because you have to be rather more than just a photographer,' she explained. 'You have to visualize, organize, extemporize. It's quite satisfying. Tomorrow is the last day of shooting, then we have to get all the stuff back to the colour lab.'

I learned how Fritz had photographed the Jaguar on the beach at Les Saintes-Marie-de-la-Mer next to some fishing boats pulled up on the beach and positioned exactly like the ones in Van Gogh's famous painting. Then the Porsche was pictured under the pine tree Gauguin had painted at Antibes, and the Corvette in a market place at Nice.

'We had the extras put up umbrellas and stand around under a hose so it looked like the umbrella picture by Renoir, but it was a job getting the right colours. I had to use special filters and even now I'm not sure it was right.'

I remembered the painstaking care with which Fritz had photographed the cars at Toulon, and asked if the pictures in the yacht marina would be used. Fritz shrugged non-comittally.

'Probably not: Ronny borrowed one of Julian's boats last year in return for some publicity and the whole day there was really just a pantomime to make Julian think Ronny was at least doing something. The model was awful, anyway. One of Ronny's cast-offs.'

'Poor Julian,' I muttered. 'Sounds like a con job.' Fritz smiled.

'It's a living, that's all.'

She took my hand across the table.

'Are you feeling strong?' she whispered huskily.

In the bedroom she flung herself back on the bed and for a bad moment I thought she had passed out.

'Hey, don't go sleep!'

'No chance!'

Her arms came up, I kissed her and she pulled me down, one leg wrapping round the backs of my thighs. I broke free and started to undress her. She cupped her hands over mine and pushed them away.

'Let me,' she whispered, 'Special Swedish'.

Her fingers slid the shirt off my shoulders and she pushed me down on the bed, running her hands over the muscles of my chest, massaging strongly.

She paused and I opened my eyes to see her peeping through the half-open window and undressing. Her breasts were small and perfect, branded with pale shadows where they had been covered by the eye-patch bikini. She began to unbuckle my belt.

'Did you know,' she asked, 'that in France eighty per cent of the women get on top?'

'How do you know a thing like that?'

'It's the sort of thrilling information you get out of reading a magazine like *Go-Fast*.'

'Really! Does it tell you what they do in Sweden?'

'In Sweden we sit on the gatepost.'

'What does that mean?'

'I'll show you ....'

There was a knock at the door. Fritz at once slipped into her clothes. When I sat up she put a finger to her lips.

'Don't worry, it's probably the old dame from the hotel, another phone call perhaps.' In a louder voice she called, '*Attendez*!'

Fully dressed, she slipped her feet into her shoes, picked up her Gucci shoulder bag, tugged the key from the inside of the door where I had left it, and went out, calling, 'Sweet dreams, passionflower!' through the narrowing gap.

The last I saw of Fritz was a contemptuous two fingers as the door clicked and was locked.

Two minutes later, still only half dressed, having wasted time rattling the door handle and shouting through the keyhole, I pushed the window open wide and leaned out just as four pairs of headlights turned out of the carpark. One car blared the first few bars of Colonel Bogey on its air horn.

Four cars! The penny dropped.

Fritz had said Ronald Blom had shot through in the Dino. But Wilson had said the standing quarter-mile measurements he had made at the circuit were fantastic, especially the Dino.

By good luck or good management, Kristy and I had been spotted while driving into Marseille. Perhaps Ronald Blom had been in the car with Fritz and followed Kristy on foot while Fritz had lured me up here into the hills. Then she had telephoned him at some rendezvous, or he had placed a call knowing where she would be. God, I had to be quick!

Throwing on a shirt I scrambled out through the window, slid down the tiles, fought my way through the vines covering the pergola and dropped to the terrace below. The Madame glared disapprovingly but her expression softened when she realized I had been jilted; a lover's tiff was something she could understand. But when I asked at what times the express trains left

Marseille for the north she wagged her finger back and forth across my nose.

'*Rien de trains, Monsieur, tous sont fermés jusqu'à minuit.*'

'But why ... I mean, *pourquoi Madame*?'

'*A cause de la grève.*' Then I remembered the dock and rail strike that had been in the wind when I had come over from Southampton. There were no trains running until midnight. I glanced quickly at my watch. Nine-forty.

The Healey was under the rattan-covered carpark where I had left it. I reached for the door to fling myself into the driving-seat and got the shock of my life.

No driving-seat.

No door.

No steering-wheel.

The Healey had been systematically dismembered into at least a hundred different components which were laid out as neatly around the wheel-less body shell as an exploded diagram. Nothing appeared to have been broken and all the parts were present.

Except, of course, my tools and the torch batteries.

Kristy sat stiffly on a wooden bench in the concourse of the *Gare St Charles*, a pulpy brown mark edged with scarlet spreading over her cheek and a thin line of blood glistening where a signet ring had broken the skin. Pushing through the onlookers I saw a bored gendarme entering details in a notebook. An English girl tourist was victim of a bag snatch. So what, didn't it happen every day? What was lost, Ma'moiselle – toothbrush, under-wear, travellers' cheques, passport, Instamatic, souvenirs?

'Who had a go at you?'

Kristy started at the sound of my voice then sprang up and flung her arms around me.

'Thank goodness, I've found you!'

'Are you okay, is anything broken?'

Gingerly Kristy fingered the flaming bruise. 'There's nothing rattling about and I seem to have all my teeth. The gendarmes are searching the back streets.'

'Tell me what happened.'

'I had to wait in the station for hours, because of the go-slow. Then I was walking along the platform for the train that is scheduled to come in around one o'clock when I was knocked over in the crowd and my bag was snatched. I shouted and grabbed hold of him but he smashed me down with his fist.'

'Ronny?'

Kristy closed her eyes as if the name itself caused a stab of pain.

'And Bruno. They came one each side of me.'

The gendarme closed his notebook as I took Kristy's arm and thereby accepted, he presumed, the responsibility. He saluted perfunctorily and joined his comrades who were coming down the platform. Empty handed, as I expected. Sprinting up the marble steps leading to the station, I had seen a red Ferrari Dino scorch away down the Boulevard d'Athènes.

It had taken nearly three hours to fit the Healey together. It was a monumental jigsaw job in which the pieces were wheels, tyre-valves, headlight-lenses, bulbs, spark-plugs, fuses. Even the speedo cable had been disconnected. I had worked like a one-man rally crew, holding a borrowed torch in my mouth and using simple handyman tools scrounged from the *auberge.*

Fortunately, a Healey is unsophisticated, assembled by hand rather than by machines. A skilled mechanic who knows his way round can change an engine in half a day and I had done it myself half a dozen times. I knew each part so familiarly that I had often boasted I could put the car together with my eyes shut. Now I was put to the test.

At any moment I had expected to discover the lack of some vital part that would keep me grounded until the garages opened in the morning, but when I found something missing, such as a headlight bulb or a wheel-nut, I had been able to improvise or do without. I could almost read what had been in the minds of those who had set to work on the car while I was eating with Fritz, then getting busy with her in the upstairs bedroom: 'Let's tear the thing apart but we don't want to wreck it for the poor sod.'

Special Swedish indeed, by God!

Anger and burning embarrassment lent wings to my fingers. Even so, everything capable of being stripped by three reasonably competent mechanics in the space of forty minutes had to be re-assembled alone, and it was half an hour after midnight when I was at last able to run the engine up for a test. It ticked over lumpily and there was a leak in the manifold gasket which allowed exhaust gases to escape unsilenced so the noise racketed around the mountains as if a dirt-track meeting was under starting orders. Lights snapped on in the *auberge* and people shouted furiously from the windows as I strapped down the bonnet and with a squirt of gravel from under the tyres zoomed out on the road for Marseille.

The gendarmes' bravado and sympathy for Kristy evaporated with my own arrival on the scene. They inquired solicitously if she needed a doctor and said they would do what they could, but there was much shrugging of shoulders and it was clear they did not hold out much hope. Nor did Kristy, when I told her how I had seen the Ferrari speeding away. When she asked if I had followed it I squeezed her hand, saying, 'It was more important to find you.'

In a station café we had a couple of cognacs served with lumps of sugar in the glasses. Kristy picked out a sugar lump and sucked the sweetened brandy. Gradually some colour came back into her grey and battered face. With embarrassment I told her how I had diced with Fritz and had dinner with her while the Healey was dismantled, carefully omitting references to Swedish ways of sitting on gate posts.

'I don't understand how Ronny would find us so easily,' Kristy said.

Signalling the waiter to bring more cognacs, I went to the telephone at the end of the bar and dialled Julian's number in Toulon. He was cross at being woken at one-thirty in the morning but I told him briskly to shut up; this was an emergency. Just one question. Did Floribunda get in touch with him after we left this morning? Oh sure, missed us by ten minutes and wanted to know where we were heading so Julian told him Marseille, was that right, did he meet up with us okay?

'You could say so,' I said drily. 'Did he say anything else?'

'Only that he had drawn the Jaguar for the pace-notes scramble, whatever that may mean, but he seemed generally browned off. Why, what's up? This is a hell of a time to ring!'

Good night and thanks. I went back to Kristy and gave her the answer to her question.

'Ronny must have brought Bruno Feraldi over from Sardinia yesterday while we were at sea, and they staked out the ports. When they saw *Bonnie Jean* in Toulon they got on to Julian who said we were heading this way. They picked us up on the road, then, when you abandoned ship, the two men followed you and Fritz was detailed to take care of me. Simple!'

The phone call to Fritz at the inn, I realised now, had been from Ronny who knew where the writers were meeting for dinner. He had told them to keep me on ice at any cost. The *Go-Fast* boys had gone to work on my car, and as soon as they arrived at the station Ronny and Bruno had gone to work on Kristy.

'But why would the magazine people do a crazy thing like that?' Kristy asked. 'Taking a car to pieces is not the sort of thing you do for just anybody.'

'Ronny isn't just anybody,' I said. 'He could quite easily be charming enough to tell them it was an elaborate practical joke. He's also their boss. And a snake. It is a formidable combination.'

Kristy leaned over the table and kissed me lightly on the forehead.

'You're a sweet man,' she said shyly, 'and certainly no snake. You didn't have to come and find me at all....'

'I was a bit late,' I said lamely.

'But you did find me and I don't deserve such treatment. None of this would have happened if I hadn't been such a prig this afternoon. I feel so ashamed.'

'Forget it,' I said, knowing the shame was not all one-sided.

'What shall we do now?' Kristy asked, smiling gratefully at what she considered to be my forgiveness.

I was about to suggest that we drive on, but to where?

We had no idea at which hotel the *Go-Fast* team was staying, and I doubted that it would be *L'Auberge Pilon*. However there was a bed there, which would have to be paid for whether it was slept in or not, and as long as Fritz had left nothing incriminating under the pillow it seemed a good proposition.

Again lights in the inn snapped on angrily as the Healey, noisy as a chain-saw, drove into the carpark. A bad-tempered porter who had been dozing in the kitchen let us in and I packed Kristy into bed with a couple of Codeines. She fell asleep in a minute and I stretched out on the floor with the counterpane over me and dozed for a few hours. At dawn I got up closed the shutters to keep the room dark and tip-toed out to check over the car in daylight and try to re-pack the noisy manifold gasket.

The Madame took a dim view of my greasy hands, crumpled clothes and unshaven face when, at eight-thirty, I persuaded her to give me a breakfast tray for two. Bitterly and loudly she complained about the engine noise I had made during the night, until I took a carnation from a vase on the window sill and put it in the button-hole of her blouse. She chuckled and chased me out of the kitchen, emerging before long with a tray loaded to the gunwales with coffee, *croissants, confiture*, freshly-squeezed orange juice, and pats of home-made butter. I put the tray on Kristy's bedside table and opened the shutters, letting sunshine flood in. Kristy woke with a start and sat up looking round anxiously as if she did not know where she was. Then she stretched and smiled. The bruise on her cheek was an angry greenish-blue and had spread to underline her eye with a muddy-looking mark.

'You look as if you walked into a bus,' I said.

She poured the coffee. 'Some bus! But I feel better for a good sleep. Thank you for looking after me so well.'

'You do look perkier,' I assured her. 'What do you know about Impressionists?'

'If you want to buy one it will cost you a quarter of a million.'

'No, I didn't mean that.'

I explained about Fritz's assignment and how she was spending the day photographing the Ferrari Dino in a scene reminiscent of an Impressionist painting. Not by Gauguin, Van Gogh or Renoir but a fourth famous painter who worked around here. I said I had a strong feeling that where we found the Ferrari we would also find Ronald Blom.

Unless, of course, he had got on a plane and was already in England. But that was a risk we had to take. My hunch was that with his super-inflated ego, Ronald Blom would stick with the cars and this was confirmed by what Julian had reported when I rang him.

Kristy sighed. 'Sometimes I wish Opa had never developed the bloomin' flower. It didn't do him any good, and so far it has meant nothing but trouble for you and me.'

'Save your breath!' I snapped. 'What would your grandfather think if he heard you talking now?'

'We must live for ourselves, don't you think?'

I sawed at an imaginary violin and Kristy laughed, then became serious again.

'That's why I went off alone yesterday. At least, partly....'

Her eyes dropped and she blushed. It would have been easy to scoff but I waited in silence for her to go on.

'It seemed so melodramatic, insane really, rushing round corners on two wheels. Twice now you have nearly been killed, once by Bruno and once by Ronny, and now the Italian police are probably looking for you. I reasoned it was better just to get on a train here and step off at Victoria. It seemed the sensible way of doing things.'

'And now it is you who has been nearly killed,' I said roughly. 'It's lucky they didn't throw you on the track when the express came in. They could have done anything!'

However, I felt sure there was more to Kristy's change of mind than her explanation had covered, and had more than a sneaking suspicion it related to my behaviour during the picnic when I had ignored her and instead had tinkered with the engine. She had been hot for me and I had let her down. I tried to make her feel better about it.

'Well, it might have made sense if I hadn't been such a bloody fool and got hooked up with Fritz,' I said. 'But listen, today or tomorrow those four cars will head back for England and in one of them will be the blue chrysanthemum. We must find them, even if it does mean going round corners on two wheels.'

Glancing significantly at my watch, I went on, 'But if you are planning to spend the day in bed you may as well head back to the villa and start sweeping up the dead leaves.'

Kristy leapt out of bed.

'Give me five minutes for a shower. Could you buy me a toothbrush downstairs?'

The Madame was somewhat shaken to see a different girl come down with me but said nothing and contented herself with a look that could have blackened garlic butter.

It was pleasant tooling through the hilly countryside in the bright morning sunshine, driving so slowly that the Michelin map spread on Kristy's knees barely fluttered. I had stopped briefly to drop the windscreen, for one of *Ma Biche's* few original features was the 100-S windscreen that could be moved forward to an alternative mounting on the bonnet then raked steeply backwards until it was almost flat, so the wind blew in your face instead of buffeting the back of your neck and blowing your hair forwards. While studying the map Kristy turned her head from side to side to dry her shower-wet

172

hair in the gentle slipstream.

'I'm sure we can eliminate a lot of possibilities,' she said.

'Go on.'

'Well, I don't think they will travel all that far. It's unlikely they would return to Nice or Antibes. The editor would want variety in the article and so far they have photographed a beach, the sea itself, and a market place. The chances are that this time they will go inland, to a mountain or a waterfall. Some kind of landscape, I'm certain. Impressionists were keen on water lilies and willow trees and little bridges, but few paintings of that kind were done around here.'

I changed down a gear to negotiate some roadworks. 'So where does that leave us?'

'Perhaps the Camargue. We could look for Van Gogh's drawbridge, or find a row of cypresses writhing in the *mistral*....'

Casting my sailorly eye at the clear blue sky and the treetops whipping in the rising wind, I said, 'It might be their lucky day if it's a *mistral* they need.' Then I made my own small contribution to our worldly discussion of the arts. 'What about sunflowers?'

'Out of season, I'm afraid.'

'Oh,' I said, deflated.

Kristy grinned encouragingly and put her hand on my knee.

'Good thinking though.'

'Thank you very much. In any case, if they want variety they are unlikely to do Van Gogh twice.'

We crossed a main road to a smaller and twistier lane that led through a valley of orchards and ancient seignorial farmhouses standing at the ends of long driveways. The freshness of the morning colours looked good enough to paint.

'It's a gamble,' Kristy said, 'but I would bet we're left with Paul Cézanne.'

'Is that good or bad?'

173

'Well, Van Gogh was in Provençe only three years and spent half the time in a lunatic asylum. Gauguin merely passed through on his way to Tahiti. Renoir settled late in life at Cagnes, near Nice. But Cézanne was a son of Provençe. He painted here most of his life and is famous for his landscapes.'

'Sounds promising,' I agreed.

'It's a good day for Cézanne, so your photographer friend will be pleased. These misty blues and purples that fold over the hills like a veil. If you half-close your eyes and look through your eyelashes you begin to see the land forms and its colours as Cézanne did.... Watch out!'

I swerved to avoid a sheep that had darted out from the verge, invisible through half-closed eyes. We came suddenly to an intersection.

'Which way?'

'Look at the map and I'll explain,' Kristy said, and I pulled into the side. 'Cézanne didn't paint just one well-known picture of this area, he painted scores.'

With her finger Kristy drew a circle on the map around the city of Aix-en-Provençe, then tapped a mountain called La Mont Sainte-Victoire, east of the city.

'Many of his pictures have this mountain in the background; he painted it sixty-five times. If anything can be said to be the trademark of Cézanne it's Sainte-Victoire.'

'Which part of the mountain?'

'That's the trouble, he painted it from so many angles. We should start from Aix because that was where he lived, and search the back roads. The country is so hilly that the roads stick to the valleys and there are not many of them, not like lanes in the English countryside. We can cover them fairly quickly if we get cracking.'

'Okay, you read the map and I'll drive,' I said, slipping into gear. 'It's a long shot, but four cars like those are distinctive enough and won't have passed unnoticed. We can ask around.'

It was the beginning of a strangely magical day spent doodling through the byways of Provençe, quartering the lush, fragrant valleys that surround the 3,000-foot limestone massif of *La Sainte-Victoire*. All the time the great cross on its highest pinnacle, the cross of Provençe, stood high above us as if conferring a ritual blessing.

Stopping at service stations we inquired if a Ferrari Dino, a Porsche 928, a Jaguar XJ-S and a Corvette Stingray had been seen on the road, but we were not blessed with good luck. When I halted a pair of motor-cycle gendarmes they responded to the question as if I had asked whether they had seen God on a bike. Kristy questioned the barrier operator at a railway crossing on a busy road but he said he was busy watching trains, not cars.

By noon we had circled most of the mountain and driven a hundred miles over twisty, bumpy roads. Kristy purchased another al fresco picnic. This time it was country cheese rolled in grape nuts and a strong pork paté with another bottle of cheap red wine and we ate in a quiet shady spot up a cart track off the road.

'Aren't you happy?' Kristy murmured, her tone suggesting that the answer could not be anything but an affirmative.

I shook my head firmly. 'When I get your cousin Ronny backed up against a tree with a knife at his throat and that flower in my hand I'll be happy. Not before.'

She pulled a face. 'Don't spoil it. Forget about Ronny for a while, will you? Tell me about yourself. When you're living on your boat at Yarmouth what do you do in the evenings?'

'As a rule,' I said guardedly, 'I go to the pub.'

'Really! I bet you have your own pewter tankard with your name engraved on it behind the bar!'

She was teasing, but her aimless shot in the dark had been pretty close to bull's-eye. I wondered if she would

175

be disappointed, as I pictured the group of regulars around the back bar of The George and heard their slow, careful talk, smelled the cosy aromas of beer and pipe tobacco, and pork pies and pickled onions.

'Tell me about your friends,' she urged.

As closely as I could I described to Kristy the test-pilots who flew Islander aircraft from Bembridge, the hovercraft-engineers from Cowes, the boat-builders and sail-makers, the small band of paid yacht hands, the volunteer life boatmen who did other jobs locally such as building houses or selling vegetables. I told her of the retired admiral who grew chrysanthemums in a green-house the size of a tent and was secretary of the local lifeboat organisation, and the Trinity House pilots who took big ships in and out of the Solent.

'You haven't mentioned any women,' Kristy said.

'I haven't met any women worth talking about,' I said slowly, adding, as I twisted round to look at her, 'until now.'

Before I knew it she had melted into my arms. I held her tightly, stroking her soft hair. We kissed. Her sweet breath tickled my cheek. Here was a girl to talk about. And sing about. And shout about.

I felt a bit like a hovercraft myself, floating a couple of feet above the ground, as she broke away, lay sideways in the soft grass, and lazily traced my profile from forehead to chin with the tip of her finger. Her honey-brown eyes speckled with amber regarded me gravely and when I met her gaze she smiled and hugged me with that lovely smile lighting up her sore face. Had it been Fritz in my arms in the grass I would have had her half-undressed by now, but with Kristy it was different. We did not make love but held each other and with the scent of brittle-leaved herbs wafting in the air drifted into a contented doze.

A tractor coming up the cart track stirred us and I had to move the Healey to give it room. The young man at the wheel saw the flattened grass and grinned widely. I felt proud, not embarrassed, and laughed with him. Kristy frowned at the back of the tractor as it drove on and I felt a stir of uneasiness.

'What's the trouble,' I asked, taking her hand, 'feeling low again?'

'I'm so afraid you will get hurt, and when I hear you talking of putting a knife at Ronny's throat it gives me the jitters.'

I held her face in both hands and turned it up to mine. The bruise on her cheek was inflamed, the blue tinge turning black, and I carressed it lightly.

'All we want from your cousin is the plant he took from you.'

'I realise that, but even so....'

'If we don't do our best to get it back, you'll spend the rest of your life thinking back to the moment when you gave up.'

'But it's probably so pointless. If Ronny doesn't look after the plant it will die and even if it lives it may not be strong enough to grow commercially.'

'That's not what your grandfather thought,' I said crisply. 'He backed his judgement with his life and you have already done the same. Don't stop now. Whether the thing ultimately makes money is not the point.'

'If you say so.' Kristy's fingers strayed to the springbok brooch on her collar. 'I was only thinking of the villa. There is a whole crop of flowers going to waste, the car to collect, new cuttings to plant, and the funeral....'

'Those were yesterday's problems. Today we find Ronny and the blue-bloody-chrysanthemum. Okay?'

It was after five when we returned to Aix for the third time and took the N7 route out of the town to complete the last segment of our trip round the mountain. We had even stopped at the *Palais de Malte*, the art gallery in Aix, to look at Cézanne pictures in case they gave us some clues, but the young girl in the ticket office told us with some bitterness that all the Cézannes were to be seen in Paris.

Traffic was heavy, one lorry after another, and the Healey whiffled unhappily. Perhaps a hard spurt would clean her out a bit. There was an opportunity on the next straight and I pulled out. A white signpost on a pedestal appeared, indicating a turn-off to a place called Gardanne.

'Of course, Gardanne! Take it, go left!' Kristy shrieked. I wrenched the wheel around, earning a vicious blast of horns from the lorries, and stopped a few yards up the side-road.

'For pity's sake, can't you read a map!' I complained.

'It's Gardanne,' Kristy went on, ignoring my irritation. 'Cézanne did a lot of pictures there. I've been staring at it on the map all day without realizing. This could be it.'

Even through half-closed eyes I couldn't see what had attracted the great painter to the motley collection of red-roofed houses that straggled up the conical hill capped by a slender church spire. Perhaps, at the turn of the century, the flat lands around it were not built up with apartment buildings, ugly cement bungalows, and the blockhouses of modern light industry. We drove in and out of the place on each of the main approach roads and when we had finished, another forty miles on the clock, the sun was lighting the distant rocks of La Sainte-Victoire with tinges of pink. It was getting late for photographs and we were low on petrol.

At the next service station I ordered ninety litres of *supercarburettant* and spent the time while the tank was filled returning the Healey's windscreen to its upright position. I was threading the dip-stick into its socket when the attendant came back with my change. He whistled at sight of the big Chev engine with its bypassed turbo-charger and asked something in French.

Kristy translated. 'He wants to know how fast it will go.'

'About a hundred and fifty,' I said, writing the figures

in the dust on the bonnet as I strapped it down. He turned his mouth down, unimpressed. 'That's miles an hour, not kilometres,' I added.

Then his eyebrows did shoot up. Through Kristy he asked if I had modified the car myself. And would it beat the new Jaguar? I made scoffing noises in the back of my throat. What about a Porsche? Or a Dino?

Kristy twigged first and quizzed him sharply. 'All four cars filled up here an hour ago and headed south,' she told me. 'He says they passed towards Gardanne early this morning, too.'

The attendant got a vivid demonstration of the Bitch's capabilities as she scorched off the forecourt, touching forty in first gear before bumping over the gutter. It was good for morale but ultimately an empty gesture. An hour's start is a lot. Too much.

'Square one again,' Kristy muttered, reading my mind.

'Not altogether,' I said, struck by a thought. 'Fritz said she had a colour deadline coming up at the magazine and had to get get her films back to the lab.'

'So?'

'If you were a photographer working abroad, how would you get your films back to London in a hurry?'

We came fast over the saddle in the hills above the airport with the runway lights spread out beyond the nose as if the Healey were an Airbus on final approach. But it took us a great deal longer to wend through the side-roads and join up with the autoroute. The *mistral* I had forecast earlier was stronger here and it tugged at the steering as the Healey floated down the fast lane until the turning to *L'Aeroport Marignane* was signposted. The last three or four miles were a fast, dangerous, three-lane road of swooping curves and badly-marked passing-lanes that ran through the *zone industrielle* around the airport. Through a high netting fence encircling the airport I glimpsed a British Airways Trident taxiing to the end of the runway for take-off. Slowing, I hunted for the airport entrance. We would have to find the freight department, and if none of the *Go-Fast* team had called already we would set our own little ambush.

Kristy suddenly clutched my arm.

'What colour was the American car, the Stingray?'

'White. Look for a contoured marshmallow with tinted windows.'

'Convertible?'

'No, hard-top. A coupé.'

'Well, it's just gone the other way.'

There was a turmoil of headlights around us and a cacophony of blaring horns as I hurled the Healey round in a screaming 180-degree turn.

Accelerating hard out of the chaos, my eyes pricking from strain, I tried to make sense of the line of tail lights in the gloom ahead.

'Which one is it?'

'I'm not sure, but it was going at a good lick.'

'Right, keep your eyes peeled.'

A lot depended on whether the driver of the Corvette had seen us. I passed a long line of traffic, flicking the lights on full beam to demand road room.

'There!' Kristy pointed.

It was a hundred and fifty yards ahead, a white sub-sonic iceberg on fat, white-walled belted radials that sizzled like frying pans. I made up enough distance to worry the driver next time he looked in his mirror. Then the road narrowed suddenly to pass beneath the stone arch of an overhead railway bridge. A Renault 5 boxed along at thirty just ahead. Expecting to see the Corvette sweep past it, I put my foot down to follow. But its brake lights lit up like a Christmas tree and I could do nothing but accelerate hard and get ahead of both cars before the bridge.

Kristy glimpsed the driver. 'It's Ronny all right, and he's got somebody with him.'

So Ronny had drawn the Corvette straw today, and had Fritz tagging along with him as usual. I wondered what I would say when I met her.

Ahead lay an elaborate junction with three slip roads in quick succession. We could easily have been eluded had the 'Vette dropped back and taken any of the side-roads once we had passed them. But Ronald Blom's instinctive reaction to the sight of the Healey zooming by was to put his foot down and overtake with a beefy roar.

With its long, bulge-breasted bonnet, flip-up head-lights and deeply-recessed shiny-chrome wheels, the Corvette looked more suitable for the centrefold of *Playboy* than for the open road. It was a car for the American prairies, a long-legged pacer for freeways and dead-straight highways through level fields of corn. On a bend it wouldn't have half the Healey's sticking power, and that was not saying much.

The next bend was a down-hill right-hander. The 'Vette went into it at a cool eighty and I hung back, feeling instinctively that here it would come unstuck. It did. Its brake lights flashed, then the entire streamlined profile of the car lay across our headlights like a gasping fish as it slid sideways, streaming smoke from locked wheels. A good driver would never have braked in that fashion but Ronald Blom was rattled. Somehow he managed to lurch back into a straight line. There was a stop sign ahead with half a dozen cars waiting to turn on to a busy highway, their winkers flashing. The Corvette dangerously overtook them all, then swung out into the highway without a pause.

Nothing for it but follow. And hope for the best.

Startled by the sight of the Healey still on his tail, Ronald Blom darted down a slip road to the right. It twisted through a short tunnel beneath the highway, then both cars burst out on the edge of a carpark as huge as an asphalt football field.

The carpark sloped gently downhill and was studded

with high, slender pylons supporting clusters of flood-lights illuminating row upon row of herring-bone parking slots marked in white paint on the tarmac. At the foot of the hill, like a low grandstand, was a wall of light: the brightly-lit windows of a *Carrefour* supermarket. The flat-roofed building was so enormous you would not ask how many times it would fit into Wembley Statium, but how many Wembleys would be fitted inside the super-market.

Although the place was open for business, seven in the evening seemed to be a quiet time and the carpark was practically deserted, with only a couple of hundred of customers' cars bunched near the building's twin sets of main doors. Supermarket trolleys were scattered about where shoppers had left them after loading up their cars and driving away. Some had blown on their sides and others sailed erratically down the hill, pushed hither and yon by the wind. Otherwise, we had the arena to ourselves. No pedestrians in sight. No gendarmes.

As the Corvette cruised across the carpark, looking for a way out, Ronald Blom made a fundamental error. There were only two exit roads and both were near the same end of the carpark. My end. The Corvette was trapped.

Gleaming beneath the sodium lights the big car swung in a circle and halted. I killed the headlights and also stopped, facing the other car at a distance of about one hundred yards across an empty space as wide and empty as a skating rink.

Before I could stop her, Kristy snapped open her safety-belt and climbed out.

'I'm going to have a word with him.'

'No, wait!'

'I know Ronny, he's not that ruthless!'

But she had no chance to get near him for the 'Vette started to move. With headlights on full beam it drove straight at me at about thirty miles an hour.

Evidently Blom's plan was to sniff right up to the

Healey then suddenly turn one way or the other and get past. But which way would he turn?

With a few seconds to think I reasoned he would turn the nose of the Corvette to the left, for like any other continental or American car it had left-hand drive. When risking a side impact a driver would instinctively turn so the collision point would be as far from his own body as possible.

The oncoming headlamps were little more than five yards away when there was a shriek of tyres as Blom stamped on the gas pedal and hurled his car round in a tight turn.

At the same instant I flashed my own headlights on full beam and jerked my foot off the clutch. The Healey skidded round, its spinning wheels juddering on the tarmac. The two cars smacked together and ran side by side. Raced on. Touched again. Beaten, the Corvette swung away down the hill once more.

Gaining speed, it streaked among the cars parked near the shop entrance, travelling at a good eighty. Turning to face down hill again, I caught intermittent glimpses of it flashing like a missile over the dark asphalt. Now Blom was going to storm through by brute force, knowing that to throw the lightweight Healey in front of the heavy Corvette would be suicidal.

At the far end of the carpark the car swung round and then doubled back towards me. It dashed through the cluster of parked cars once more. As its tapered snout came into view again I saw a weird conga-line of shopping trolleys catapult suddenly into its path.

There was a series of loud bangs, like an ack-ack gun firing. Half a dozen trolleys hurtled into the air, turning over and over, their silvery wire frames sparkling beneath the lights. One trolley became lodged beneath the car's front end and the crushed metal streamed volleys of sparks.

The big car went out of control.

It spun between a belt of small trees lining the edge of

the carpark, slid neatly between the steel pillars standing at intervals along the shop's wide front entrance, and with smoke streaming from its locked tyres crashed tail-first through the plate-glass doors.

There, it spun again through a hundred and eighty degrees and dived nose-first through the next set of automatic sliding doors. They had no time to open. Glass sprayed like a bomb-burst.

Inside the vast store, the car clipped number forty-four of a long row of orange cash desks, demolished a circular display stall dispensing olives, gherkins and pimentoes from half-barrels of pickle, and came to rest beneath a rack displaying eighteen hundred pairs of children's flame-proof pyjamas.

9 : FOUR QUI PASSE

The supermarket was as brilliantly-lit as a stage. From my seat in the dress circle I saw Ronald Blom helped from the cockpit of the Corvette with the kind of stunned and close-lipped courtesy that might be accorded an enemy pilot who has just crash-landed in the town he bombed. I coasted the Healey into a parking slot near the shattered main doors and wondered how long it would be before Ronny got a pitchfork, or more appropriately a can of beans, rammed up his fundamental.

Though dazed, he did not appear to be hurt; nor was anybody else. A couple of women wept copiously after narrow escapes. Shoppers and blue-coated assistants crowded round the wreckage. In one of the sliding doors a large slice of plate-glass hung suspended, like the blade of a guillotine ready to drop.

As Kristy joined me, I said, 'It looks as if your cousin might lose his head.'

'Oh no!'

But he was saved from a possible lynching by a bleeding nose which gushed so vigorously and dramatically that it drew a gasp of sympathy from the crowd.

Thinking aloud, I said, 'We must get to the car in case the flower is there. If not, there's bound to be some clue as to where we can catch up with the others.'

'I'll go and look.'

'No, not you.'

'Far better me. I am his cousin.'

The hoo-haa of klaxons speeding along the road from the airport began to be heard, then a pair of ambulances and a police car flashed into the floodlit carpark. As Ronald Blom was taken care of by a white-coated ambulance attendant and given cotton wool balls to stuff up his nose, Kristy worked through the crowd until she was near the Corvette.

I lit my pipe and perched on the bonnet of a Peugeot 504 to watch the pantomime as she exchanged words with an overalled maintenance man staring bemusedly at the mess he had to clear up. He shrugged disinterestedly and Kristy brazenly dragged open the heavy door of the wrecked car and got in.

Finding a briefcase on the front seat she emptied the contents of the glovebox into it, sifted rapidly through the map pockets, fumbled beneath the seats, and searched the parcel shelf. No blue chrysanthemum, but that was hardly surprising. It could be anywhere. In this car. In one of the others. In Blom's pocket. But there was no way we could frisk a man flat on his back on an ambulance stretcher with cotton wool up his nostril and three gendarmes craned over him like vultures. After only a few seconds Kristy was out of the car again and worming her way out through the crowd. Catching sight of her, Ronald Blom shouted and tried to rise from the stretcher but the ambulance man pushed him back with an angry word.

Kristy was just a few yards away, walking up the slope towards me, when the wry smile playing in the corners of her mouth turned suddenly to a look of horror. The back of my neck prickled. In the same instant I remembered that Ronald Blom had had a passenger in the car.

As I dropped one shoulder and threw myself forward in a somersault a spanner whistled past my head and clanged on the 504's bonnet. Under the impetus of the blow my attacker staggered forwards with a grunt of alarm. I was on my feet in an instant and butted him solidly in the soft folds of his overflowing belly. Breath whistled through his teeth and he doubled up. More by good luck than good management, my knee thudded into his jaw and Bruno Feraldi dropped heavily into the shadows between the cars.

I fell on him, bunched his shirt in my fingers, and found it took all my strength to wrench him half-upright so I could hit him again.

As he rolled over groggily I noticed with some satisfaction the sticking plaster and iodine covering the rip marks on his cheeks.

Kristy ran up. 'John, are you all right?'

'Get out of the light,' I told her, pushing her away. 'There's life in the bastard yet.'

'What are you going to do?'

I signalled her to wheel over a shopping caddy which I chocked against the Peugeot's bumper. Bruno weighed a ton, but after searching him and finding nothing useful I managed to hoist him on to the bonnet of the car then, using it as a loading ramp, slide him into the wire basket. His head lolled over the front end and his splayed legs over the back. The whole thing rocked as he struggled to sit up but I back-handed him sharply across both cheeks and steadied the trolley to stop it from overturning.

'This one is for Kristy,' I said, and with all my strength pushed the trolley downhill and let go.

On well-oiled rubber wheels it trundled fast, teetering briefly on two of its wheels as Bruno struggled to unwedge his hips, then coming down again four square.

Its little wheels singing and gathering speed fast, it sped over the pedestrain crossing then hit the gutter and capsized. The Italian was thrown out violently. He skidded painfully across the concrete on chin, elbows and knees and slithered to a halt at the feet of a startled gendarme.

'Oh drat!' Kristy muttered, 'I do like to have my shopping parcels wrapped.'

Beneath the forecourt lights of an Antar service station

up the road we turned out the contents of Ronald Blom's briefcase. Cigarettes, book matches, Sealink ferry timetable and open-dated hovercraft ticket for car and driver, hotel receipts and restaurant bills, notebook showing the Corvette's petrol input, half-used packet of Entero-vioform and another of Durex Featherlite, three tape cassettes, various maps, binoculars in a monogrammed case....

Kristy peered at the faded gold initials embossed on the leather. '*P v. B* – last time I saw these they were in the glovebox of our Mercedes.'

'That's all the proof you need,' I said.

The bitterness in her voice was sad to hear as she whispered with a catch in her throat, 'I don't need any proof.'

One of the maps had been refolded and held open with paper clips so the Provençe area was displayed for quick reference. Several place names had been underlined. Toulon, Nice, the Ricard circuit, Gardanne. The country roads from Marseille to *L'Auberge Pilon* had been traced in Biro and another ballpoint line heavily underscored the name Arles, a town forty miles west, in the Camargue. Scrawled alongside it was written, '*des Arènes* 20:30'. Kristy said there was a Roman arena or colosseum thing in the centre of the town, so the name written on the map might be a café or hotel and should be easy to find.

I glanced at my watch. It was nearly eight already.

'If that is tonight's rendezvous then Ronny is going to be rather late.'

'I don't suppose they will go without him,' Kristy observed.

I started the engine and pulled out.

'Let's hope not.'

The road across the marshy Rhône delta was flat and straight. Black-green cypresses in silhouette waved in the wind, flooded lagoons and rice paddies glinted pale reflections of the starry sky, a black bull of the Camargue bellowed in a field. The master wind of the *Midi* tugged at the steering and spilled round the corner of the windscreen into the cockpit with a shrill whistle. Helpless in its grip, flying bugs whirled through the headlight beams.

Slowing at an intersection, I remarked casually to Kristy that it must have been a strong gust of wind indeed that had shifted all those shopping trolleys and got them rolling at just the right moment.

Kristy studied the map with sudden zeal.

'In fact,' I went on, 'it must have taken a damn good shove to get them going.'

'Call it an act of God,' Kristy said. 'Ronny's had it coming to him for a very long time.'

Arles is an ancient city on a knoll beside the *Grand Rhône.* At that point it is broad, sluggish and the colour of strong tea. Following the small map in Ronald Bloom's *Guide Michelin* we entered by the Boulevard des Lices, a street with wide, tree-shaded pavements alive with tourists strolling among the souvenir shops and drinking at open-air tables served by waitresses in colourful *Camarguais* costumes.

Kristy directed me to turn right and took me through a maze of narrow old streets. In the Healey's brilliant headlamps I caught glimpses of old churches, sculpted stone lintels, mossy fountains and cobbled alleyways that had been built for horses, not motors.

Before long we came out in a square called Place du Forum. It was not large, with cafés, hotels and bars on four sides, and tables and chairs set out beneath umbrellas on the paved central area. Tall, thick-limbed plane trees were hung with coloured lights and there was a statue of an old man with a walking stick and an overcoat behind a spiky iron railing. No other cars were in the square, so parking was easy. I switched off and breathed deeply.

'Now I do smell ashtrays,' I said.

'Me too!' Kristy laughed. 'Come on – according to the

189

map, the arena is up this way.'

After spending all day at the wheel it was good to walk. We strolled past a wrought-iron fence surrounding a stone amphitheatre. Kristy paused to read the notice describing it, and explained that it had been constructed by the Romans before even Rome herself had an amphitheatre.

'So were the drains, by the smell of them,' I observed.

'Quite likely,' Kristy added seriously, and I was astonished.

Hurrying on to escape an unpleasant odour we came out suddenly at the arena, an immense oval structure of pale, weathered stone built like the Colosseum of Rome with an outer wall of great arches standing in tiers. Spanish-style posters advertising forthcoming bullfights adorned the entrance gates.

On the far side of the arena a sign written in mediaeval script across the front of a cosy-looking corner restaurant with a first-floor balcony told us we had found the *Hostellerie des Arènes*. Its ground-floor windows were leaded and even from a distance we could see diners sitting at tables covered with red and white checked cloths, the lights and candles sparkling on wine bottles, glasses and silverware.

The upstairs balcony had half a dozen tables set out beneath green and blue umbrellas; each table had a candle in a tall, narrow-waisted glass funnel. And sitting at one table next to the balustrade, talking animatedly and watching the traffic moving beneath them, was the *Go-Fast* team: Philip Fanselow, Alec Dempster, Graham Wilson, and my late friend and co-star, Fritz.

From the shadows of an arch we watched a waiter bring two tall green bottles to the table, each one speckled with chill dew. After showing the labels to Philip Fanselow, who nodded approvingly, he pulled the corks. A second waiter brought an ice bucket on a stand. My mouth watered and my stomach began to grumble.

'It looks like they're settling in and Ronny won't be here for a long while yet,' I observed, thinking it was probably his car that they kept looking out for. 'What is a *hostellerié*, restaurant or hotel?'

'I imagine it's a restaurant with rooms,' Kristy replied.

'So they might have booked in for the night.'

'Possibly. I'll go and find out.'

Mingling with a crowd of Dutch teenagers, Kristy crossed the road and went into the restaurant. I caught my breath as the waiter tapped Philip Fanselow on the shoulder and said something in his ear. The editor looked surprised and stood up, wiping his mouth and dabbing his beard with a napkin, then followed the waiter inside.

With relief I saw Kristy coming back. 'No, it's just a restaurant, there are no rooms.'

Philip Fanselow returned to his table looking worried. Fritz cracked a joke but he silenced her with a terse remark that made the two motoring writers sit up and crane forward to hear more.

My guess was that Ronald Blom had just got hold of them by telephone and dropped his bombshell. The Corvette was a wreck and Ronny would be along as soon as he could fight his way clear of the *flics*. I saw Fanselow sink dejectedly into his chair then shrug impatiently and make a curt remark that caused Alec Dempster to shut his mouth with a snap. Then Fanselow flicked his wrist to illuminate his digital watch, a gift from Toyota, I suspected, and he beckoned to the waiter who came out with a bundle of menus which he passed around the table.

'Good, they're digging in,' I said, taking Kristy's arm. 'Are you hungry? Let's see if we can get a table.'

The *maitre d'hotel* was anxious to seat us at the one vacant table on the balcony. Fluttering his eyes at Kristy he said it would be more romantic, but we could not have that at any price and I persuaded him to give us the table that was just inside the windows which overlooked the balcony. The *Go-Fast* table was just the other side of the glass, but we were concealed from it by the café-style gingham curtains hanging from rings on a thick wooden pole halfway up the window.

As Kristy studied the menu I spun my knife idly and wondered what our next move should be. Before long Ronald Blom and perhaps Bruno Feraldi would come into the restaurant, but they might not spot us because our table was dimly lit and in a corner behind others. The group would undoubtedly leave together. There had been nothing in Ronny's briefcase, apart from the open-dated hovercraft ticket, to suggest their next destination. Julian had mentioned something about a pace-notes scramble, but seemed as mystified about it as I was. It was likely they would drive north in the morning, or during the night, but which route would they take? If they happened to split up it would be impossible for us to keep tabs on all four cars and we would have to find out, somehow, which one Ronald Blom was driving.

'It's a fantastic menu!' Kristy smacked her lips. 'What are you going to have?'

'You're the expert, I leave it to you.'

'Really?'

Flattered, Kristy spoke swiftly and decisively to the *maitre d'hotel*, quizzing him about the preparation of different dishes. As he turned to go after jotting the order on his pad I stayed him with my hand and told Kristy, whose French was miles better than mine, to ask if there was a small boy in the kitchen who might do an errand for a couple of francs.

The youngster who approached a few minutes later was about ten years old, skinny as a stick, with very short cotton pants and a yellow t-shirt bearing the emblem of the University of Alabama. Kristy explained what we wanted. He nodded seriously and skipped off.

With a flourish the waiter set down large brown

earthenware dishes so hot that the parsley butter spluttered as it ran against their low rims. Laid out in little hollows in each plate were a dozen snails in their shells. A long thin loaf of crusty bread cut into diagonal slices and soaked in garlic was put between us on a wooden board.

'Have you eaten snails before?' Kristy asked, seeing my doubtful look. I shook my head and she showed me how to pick up the brown and yellow shell in a pair of curiously-shaped tongs and extract the fleshy meat with a small, long-pronged fork. Steeling myself, I dipped the repulsive thing in the butter and tasted it. Not bad. Mopping up the butter with a wad of garlic bread, Kristy said, 'I could eat *escargots* every day of the week.'

'You'd get fat,' I teased.

'Probably, but who cares?'

'I do.'

'Oh,' she said with a delighted grin. 'In that case only Mondays to Fridays.'

Reaching over the table, I squeezed Kristy's hand. 'You're pretty good as you are.'

'Even with a black eye?'

'We're a matching pair.' Kristy chuckled and withdrew her hand as the waiter poured the wine for me to taste. *Listel Rosé*: light and sharp, but fresh and cleansing after the oily snails.

The waiter was clearing the plates away when I was struck by an idea. I asked him if it was possible to open the window to let in some air.

'*Mais oui, mais oui,*' he said eagerly, '*mais seulement un peu, à cause du Mistral.*'

Then he fumbled beneath the hem of the curtain and edged the window open a few inches while saying something so rapidly that I could not catch it. Kristy translated.

'He says that on the sixth day of the *Mistral* a man is allowed to murder his wife.'

'How long has it been blowing now?' I asked.

'Five!'

The curtain billowed gently in the draught which came through the open window, carrying with it the voices of the *Go-Fast* crew.

At first it was difficult to catch much of what was said because our waiter returned with the *entrée* fat quail smothered in wine sauce containing large sweet grapes. Then new potatoes and thin green beans. In a low tone I complimented Kristy on her choice, going through a mime of licking my chops, then I put a finger to my lips and bent an ear to the open window.

There was trouble in the *Go-Fast* camp. Strident and indignant, Alec Dempster was saying: 'Fiddles be damned! Everyone in Fleet Street does it, it's a recognized perk in the industry. You've approved my expenses often enough, Phil, so what are you talking about?'

'That's right,' Philip Fanselow cut in smoothly. 'It's a recognized perk until somebody wants to get rid of you, then it comes down to straight fraud. If you wanted to argue the point you wouldn't have a leg to stand on, and you know it.'

'But everyone fiddles expenses,' Graham Wilson protested.

'Even you,' Fritz accused.

Her remark was aimed at Fanselow, who said, 'Of course I do, and I'm in the same boat as you with a great deal more to lose. We have to go along with the bastard. I don't know what he is up to, or where that slob Italian he picked up fits into the picture, but if you overturn his little apple-cart now the sky will fall on your heads. So just... well, cool it. None of us is doing anything illegal.'

The quail was as good as it looked and I carved off another mouthful as the conversation outside the window lapsed. Then Alec Dempster said in a worried tone, 'It's not drugs then.'

'That's a scary notion,' Graham Wilson said, a tremor in his voice.

Fritz spoke up: 'Expenses fiddles are not the least of your worries, you know.'

Wilson: 'And what's that supposed to mean?'

Fritz: 'Do you think Ronny didn't see you and Alec sneaking your birds out of the disco last night?'

Dempster: 'Meaning what?'

The speculative lift of Fritz's eyebrows was silent but I could imagine it only too well. 'How is the little wife back home, Alec?'

'Christ, have you got photographs, or something?'

Fanselow rapped the table sharply with his knuckles. 'Cool it is what I said! Just bend at the knees and the shocks won't be too bad. Don't make waves for yourselves, it's early yet.'

Wilson: 'What's he got on you, Phil? Been finding teenage boys in your bed?'

There was a pregnant pause then Fanselow chuckled without much humour.

'Have another drink and shut up! Ronald Blom just happens to own my magazine, isn't that enough?'

We were picking the bones of the birds when the little boy returned and spoke earnestly with Kristy.

'He's found the cars in a courtyard off the Rue du Four Qui Passe, which runs down the back of here,' she told me. Then she added with a worried look, 'He says another car, a big white one with a dented front and side, just parked down the street.'

As I handed the boy a five-franc coin Ronald Blom came up the stairs and looked around. I turned away, concealing my face behind a glass of wine which I held in both hands with my elbows supported on the table, and made urgent signs at Kristy that she should not turn around. Walking with a limp, Blom went out on the open balcony. He had found a clean shirt to replace the bloody one and for once was without the silk cravat around his neck. He had hollow rings under his eyes and his pale, gingery face looked tense and drawn. Through the window I heard chairs being rearranged around the table.

'Give me a glass,' Blom said. 'By God I need a drink!'

'What happened?' Fanselow asked in a worried voice.

'Lost control and went into a shop window. That thing handles like a prairie wagon, no road-holding at all. But it's still mobile.'

'How are you going to tell that to General Motors in London?'

'I'm not,' Blom retorted. 'You are. Writers are supposed to be good at fiction, and you're in charge, that's what you are paid for.'

'What about your Italian friend?'

'In hospital with concussion.'

Kristy and I exchanged looks. My mind raced. I wanted to listen to the conversation but now there was a golden opportunity to search the cars for the flower. Coming to a decision I poured the last of the wine.

'Get the bill as quickly as you can, we've got things to do,' I said.

'What about sweet and coffee?'

'Some other time.'

As we left the restaurant, careful not to be seen from the balcony, the loud toll of a church bell reminded me how I had been startled by the bell at Villa Maddalena, and I remembered Van Blommenstein's friendly greeting and shrewd eyes. Now I had an opportunity to fulful my obligations to him, as long as Ronald Blom's appetite occupied him long enough.

Rue du Four Qui Passe was a narrow, one-way street slanting down the hill beyond the restaurant. After fifty yards we saw on our right the courtyard which the boy had described. A tiny lane opened into a cobbled square just big enough to park and turn half a dozen cars. It was shut in by tall, pleasant houses with flowery window-boxes and louvred shutters. Lined up with their noses facing the stone wall were the red Ferrari, green Porsche and blue Jaguar.

Pulling Kristy into a shadowed doorway, I said, 'Look, we may not have much time. Which car do you think I should search first.'

'How should I know?'

'I thought you might have inherited some of your grandfather's second sight. It's your flower and I don't want you to blame me afterwards for making wrong guesses.'

'Get on with it!' she whispered, giving me a gentle shove. As an afterthought she added, 'Try the Ferrari, it's Ronny's style.'

'Okay, but you get up the street and keep watch. Let me know the minute they leave the table so I have time to take cover, I don't want another spanner round my ear.'

Each one of the cars was locked, which was only to be expected. I found a cobblestone and, feeling like a vandal, smashed the Ferrari's side window. The noise echoed frighteningly but no alarm was raised. When I got the door open my heart sank. If it took a New York narcotics squad four hours to go through a Jaguar XJ6 and nearly overlook forty-five pounds of hash concealed in the door sills, what chance did I have of finding a slim polythene bag which could be in any one of three different cars?

In the glovebox was a torch which made the job easier. Sitting on the ground and leaning backwards into the foot-well beneath the steering-wheel, I hunted round behind the dashboard, then searched under the seats, took up the floor mats, and tried all the obvious places such as the map pockets. I pulled the lever to open the engine compartment and spared valuable seconds for a professional and admiring glance at the great aluminium engine, its eight vee'd cylinders a model of mechanical excellence and supreme engineering craftsmanship.

Dragging my eyes from the beautiful object I slammed the lid down and searched the wheel arches and sub-frame. No luck.

I picked up the stone again and was on the point of giving the Jaguar the same treatment when I heard English voices talking in the street, getting louder by the second. There was no time to bolt.

'Where's Ronny got to?' Dempster asked peevishly, the sound of his footsteps slowing up.

'Talking to that English bird in the street,' Wilson answered.

'Trust him!'

Snapping off the torch I threw myself full-length in front of the Jag, lying flat on my back beneath its overhanging snout, one of its fat Dunlops not an inch from my ear. When the headlights went on I would be hidden from view. Until the car backed away from the wall.

My mind was racing. What the hell had Kristy been doing?

One man stood by the Jaguar's door rattling his keys. Fritz and another walked round the Porsche, kicking its tyres and looking it over. It was Philip Fanselow who discovered the Ferrari's broken window.

'Oh no!' he cried, slamming his fist on the roof. 'Look what some thieving bastard has done here!'

'Jesus, they made a mess of that,' Alec Dempster said.

'Is anything missing?' Graham Wilson asked.

'They must have pissed off when they heard us coming down the street. Look, here's the rock they used.'

'Careful, they might be still here!'

My heart froze as three pairs of headlights came on. Then I heard the footsteps of another man walking into the courtyard.

'Ronny,' Fanselow called, 'the Dino has been smashed up, the side window is broken.'

Ronald Blom swore obscenely. 'I'll fix that bitch if it's the last thing I do.'

'The Porsche is all right,' Fritz called out. 'What about

198

the Jag, Alec?'

'Bugger the Porsche,' Fanselow said with feeling. 'How will you explain this in London, and the Corvette all smashed up as well?'

Ronald Blom opened the door of the Jaguar and I heard his fingers scrabbling under the facia. There was a ripping sound as the plastic bag containing the blue chrysanthemum was detached from the bulkhead where it had been held with sticky tape.

'What *is* that thing you keep fussing about?' Alec Dempster asked him, screwing up all his courage.

'It's my private goldmine,' Ronald Blom answered coolly. 'Phil, I'm taking the Dino,' he added in a louder voice.

'Oh no, the 'Vette is yours today. We need to stick to the rota or everything gets screwed up.'

'You take it,' Blom said authoritatively. 'The cassettes have been lost from the Corvette so you had better take the spare set out of the Porsche. See you on the bridge.' He folded himself into the Ferrari and started the engine. The walls of the courtyard rocked with noise as he gunned the accelerator. The others followed suit, the hard-edged, air-cooled whine of the Porsche revving with the tone and tempo of an enraged Volkswagen. Then the smooth, whoofling purr of the Jaguar's twelve cylinders just above my head.

The Ferrari reversed out, then the Jag. As soon as it moved I sprang up and sprinted through the glare of headlights. There was a shout, indistinct in the storm of engine noise, then a blare of horns. Running for dear life up the narrow street I heard behind me the howl of an accelerating engine. My shadow grew long in front of me. I sprang sideways, tripped in front of the oncoming car, rolled over and over as the Ferrari's fat tyres missed me by a whisker.

The blackness of the street became bright with the red glare of the car's brake lights. A moment later it reversed fast back towards me. I leaped into a doorway. Realizing he had failed to hit me, Ronald Blom braked again then shot away down the hill followed by each of the other two cars.

The rasping of my breath was loud in the sudden quietness. A dim light flooded into the street from a high window as somebody looked out to see what all the noise was about. I heard footsteps and saw Philip Fanselow, relegated to the damaged Corvette, walking dejectedly up the hill behind me. My impulse was to talk to him, but first I had to find Kristy.

My blood turned to ice at the thought of what I might find. In a sudden panic, I ran painfully up the steep hill towards the restaurant and was passing a dark alleyway when I heard my name called in a whisper. Kristy was doubled up on the ground, her face white and beaded with perspiration, her arms folded tightly across her stomach as she rocked back and forth drawing breath in deep, shuddering gasps.

'It's all right... only winded... it's getting better.'

She stood up with difficulty and leaned against me, her breathing becoming steadier.

'He came out of the restaurant ahead of the others, alone, so I confronted him and tried to make him see sense. He was friendly enough. Until the others had walked on, then he pulled me into this alleyway and knocked me down and kicked me in the stomach. Said it was for what we had done to him at the *Carrefour*.'

Muttering curses I hugged her tightly then saw the dark form of Philip Fanselow passing the end of the alley. He jumped visibly when I called his name, and his jaw dropped as we walked out into the gloom of the street.

'Good heavens, it's you!'

'That's right, and I want to talk to you.'

'I'm afraid I'm in a hurry.'

'No doubt,' I said thinly, 'but I think you should listen. You should know what Ronald Blom is doing, before you make a fool of yourself. We need your help.'

The editor licked his lips and stared with dismay at Kristy's grey face.

'Did he do that?'

'Yes, and a lot more. You see....'

'Well, it's not my business. I'm sorry about your car: we thought it was a joke and went along with him for the fun of it. But now....'

'Now he's got you by the balls and you haven't the guts to stand up to him. He's a bully and he's wiping the floor with you, don't you see?'

Fanselow started walking away. 'No, I don't want to talk about it, I'm sorry.'

'Because he found a boy in your bed?' The editor froze in his tracks but as I stepped towards him he walked frenziedly away, almost running. I started to go after him but Kristy groaned, clutching her stomach.

'It's all right,' I said. 'We'll let him go. The poor little sod has been fingered, like the rest of them. Just walk as quickly as you can, but take it easy. We've got to get back to the car.'

The streets were busier than before, thronged with people in costumes, all of them heading the same way as ourselves, so it was difficult to force a way through. Lights were on in the houses, doors were open, and old women sat out on the pavements watching with bright eyes as the people swarmed past them. Echoing down the streets came the tinny sound of a brass band. For three minutes we had to wait, hemmed in and fuming with impatience, as the musicians dressed in white ducks and yellow blouses shuffled past in a ragged procession. They were led by a portly figure wearing sunglasses and a peaked cap who marched with his hands in his pockets.

The Place du Forum was hardly recognizable as the quiet square in which we had parked the car a couple of hours early.

It was crammed with people dancing under the coloured lights which had been switched on, the men in long white stockings, red and yellow tunics, and a variety of caps, the women in blouses with puffed sleeves, embroidered waistcoats and long flared skirts.

A second band played on the steps of the hotel at the top of the square, beating out an indistinct but lively old-fashioned tune under the direction of a massive major-domo who might have escaped from a bull ring. Gipsies had set up stalls selling *nougat, crêpes* and *frites.*

In the middle of it all, hemmed in on every side by crowds of dancers and spectators and completely immobilized, was *Ma Biche.*

An urchin sat in the driving-seat taking a hairpin at ninety-five and making enough noise to drown the band. I eased his sticky fingers off the wheel and lifted him out. He screamed and people turned to stare but a portly old man spoke to him sharply, then gave me a friendly salute and sat down on the mudguard. I leapt round the car, took his arm, and by sign language tried to make him understand that the car's frail alloy bodywork would bend under his weight. The Healey was in danger of being broken up by good neighbourliness.

The Frenchman must have seen something in the look on my face for he called back the little boy, instructed him at length, and with a gesture to me to hold my peace sat him in the car and gave him his walking stick.

'Don't worry,' Kristy explained, 'the boy will stop people sitting on the car. You had better give him something.'

I produced a couple of francs, which widened the little chap's eyes, and he lashed with his stick at a man about to lower his broad posterior on the Healey's comfortably rounded nose.

The band struck up again and people shuffled round us, everyone dancing with everyone, many simply dancing with themselves.

We found seats at a table outside a café and ordered red wine. As I put my arm round Kristy's shoulders she fell against me with a giggle and a sigh.

'You know, all this would be awfully funny if it weren't such a tragedy,' she said. 'This thing could go on for hours. There is a saying in Provençe that Christmas comes but once a year while Easter time is always here. There is always some kind of local saint to be honoured with a festival.'

'Any excuse for a party, eh!' I said.

Kristy was in good form for somebody who has kissed goodbye to a fortune and been socked in the stomach. When I asked how she felt she stared reflectively over the heads of the dancers.

'You can't feel sorry about losing something you never really had. If we did have the blue chrysanthemum, it would be Jon's job to grow and sell it, not mine. Just now, I'm rather relieved that the trail has dried up. Aren't you?'

I said I had mixed feelings about it and she leaned over and kissed me.

'Will you dance with me?'

After we had shuffled through a couple of numbers Kristy stepped back and looked me up and down.

'You're still boiling mad!' she accused.

'I don't take kindly to men who beat up women, even if they did go to a good school.'

'Forget about it,' she urged, squeezing my waist hard as if by doing so the black thoughts would pop out of the top of my skull. When the music stopped the next time we found ourselves near the band and we watched, waiting for them to strike up again, as the trombonists and trumpeters flicked spittle out of their battered instruments and a twelve-year-old kettle-drummer picked his nose with a white-gloved finger.

At a table nearby was a young couple in blue jeans, t-shirts, and sneakers. They had the earnest look of American students on a culture trip; between them on the table was a small Philips portable tape recorder on which they were taping the music.

It made me think of the three tape cassettes we had taken from the Corvette, and of Ronald Blom's remark, when the Ferrari's broken window was discovered, about a spare set of tapes that could be used.

Abandoning Kristy, I returned to the Healey where

the boy was still doing his stuff and took the tapes out of the briefcase: three ninety-minute cassettes, their labels plain but for numbers scrawled in black felt-tip pen – one, two, and three.

The American students were surprised but charming, and happy to co-operate. I bought them Pernods and they agreed to let me listen to a portion of one of the tapes on their machine.

For a few seconds there was only a hum as the leader fed through the sound-head. Then there was a click and a precise, clipped, male voice began: 'All right, here we go. We're on the *nouveau pont* at Arles, pointing west. Start your stopwatches at this point. Zero your trip meter. Now get set. Ready, steady, go! It's seven hundred yards of dual carriageway to roundabout. ... Go out on the Montpellier Road at twelve-o'clock....'

I pressed the fast-forward button then let the tape play again. 'Two hundred to half-flat left with descent. ... One-fifty to fork, go right.... Six hundred flat, over bridge, then half-flat bends left, right, left....'

Sixty pounds sterling in cash on the table, nearly all Kristy and I had between us, sealed the bargain. It was expensive, but we had bought a tape recorder. The band was forming up in the square, ranks of children and dancers in national dress taking their places behind it. I chased the little boy out of the car; nothing had been broken or nicked but the steering-wheel was stickily with *nougat*. When the old man gave us a wave, I beckoned him over and told a mystified Kristy to ask him to find us some children who would like to ride in the parade.

In no time we had three little girls in white frilly dresses sitting on the petrol tank behind the seats. They squealed excitedly as the engine roared. The old man took a bouquet of white roses that one of them was holding and tucked it under the windscreen wiper. Then, to the accompaniment of trumpets and kettle-drums, and escorted by marching echelons of children, the Healey joined the procession.

It was the worst drive of my life.

Speed was only half ordinary walking pace, less than one mile an hour. In a car built for hard acceleration and flat-out cruising it was murder. The engine misfired and coughed. The clutch heated and began to smell. Worriedly I watched the temperature needle soaring and soon wisps of steam drifted from under the bonnet. The Bitch was in one of her bloodiest moods.

At last the procession route doubled back and I glimpsed a deserted side-road. The children were happy to get out and walk ahead with the band. We forced a way through spectators who were disgruntled at being disturbed, and thankfully made our escape.

As we found our way to the bridge over the River Rhône I told Kristy about the tapes. Before a car rally event drivers went over the route preparing special notes in shorthand form. These pace-notes, as they were called, were read back by the navigator during the event, enabling a competitor to drive flat-out every inch of the way because he always knew what lay ahead and how fast he could take each corner as he came to it.

'These tapes must be talking pace-notes,' I explained. 'Instead of having them read over an intercom by his navigator, the driver puts the tape into the car's stereo and switches the machine on and off as he needs it.

'The switch part is what we don't have. It would be simple enough to rig one up, with a press button on the steering-wheel, but there's no time. You will have to do the job instead.'

'I expect I'll get the hang of it.'

'Just pray the batteries hold out.'

10:58pm. 0 miles ALL RIGHT, HERE WE GO. WE'RE ON THE *NOUVEAU PONT* AT ARLES, POINTING WEST....

From a standing start on the bridge high above the wide river the Healey bored into the darkness, headlights forging a tunnel of brightness in which we saw the signposts of a roundabout coming up. The engine sounded glad to cough the phlegm out of its throat. The temp. needle dropped at once and settled reassuringly in its normal position.

11:01pm. 3 miles ONE THOUSAND TO ABSOLUTE LEFT ... SIXTY TO FLAT RIGHT ... ONE MILE DEAD STRAIGHT THEN HALF-FLAT LEFT OVER BRIDGE....

Here was a short straight leading to a left-hand bend that could be taken at absolutely top speed. Then I had to slow just a little for a right-hander: flat speed was flat out, but not as flat out as absolute. The bend came out on a mile-long straight which ended in a sharpish left bend over a bridge, requiring half-flat speed.

After the lights of the town the level countryside seemed remote and inky black. It was like putting to sea from a brightly lit port. We were sailing out into a complete unknown. Moths and gnats rocketed like flak up the twin halogen beams. Squadrons of midges committed mass suicide on the windscreen.

Traffic was light. Farmers returning home in bouncing old Citroens. Some heavy lorries lumbering ponderously through the night. An occasional limousine. With the speedo hovering on the three-figure mark, other vehicles seemed as static as the red-topped kilometre posts that showed up in the headlights every twenty-five seconds.

11:27pm. 35 miles FILTER THROUGH CLOVERLEAF ON TO AUTOROUTE AND CONTINUE WEST FOR TWELVE MILES ABSOLUTE, TAKING SÊTE ROAD....

Kristy shouted the instruction into my ear, then switched off the recorder as I opened out on the autoroute, a clear twelve miles ahead. Slipstream made a solid canopy over the cockpit. The lights of Montpellier loomed over to the right, then dropped behind.

I was exhilarated now, the blood tingling through my fingers and toes, my hands living like separate beings on the polished wooden rim of the wheel. My head felt disconnected, a guiding satellite orbiting out and beyond. Hypnotized by speed and noise I was immune to the blast of the wind, the cold and damp air, the shuddering suspension and the fierce heat around the foot pedals.

What a drive this would be in the comfort of one of those super-cars, I thought enviously. Insulated from the hard wind in a comfortably upholstered cockpit with precise and forgiving steering, power-brakes, fantastic double headlights, and the driving instructions coming from the cassette at the touch of a button. And probably in stereo.

00:06am. 89 miles SIXTY YARDS TO INTERSECTION, TURN NINETY DEGREES LEFT ... ONE HUNDRED TO LIGHTS, GO STRAIGHT ON....

Skirting Béziers, Kristy relaying instructions like an automaton, her expression glazed, her body stiff and sore. Then out into the rolling countryside with isolated trees, vineyards, and no roadside walls or hedges to limit the view for miles ahead. A glorious high-speed route with the automatic voice never failing in its relentless attention to detail. I was able to drive that unknown country road as if it were a race-track. Soon I knew the raconteur's driving style well enough to adjust my own idea of top speed to his. I guessed he had reconnoitred the route not in a super-car but in a standard sports or GT car, perhaps a BMW, for I was discovering I could take certain corners faster than he advised.

Suddenly Kristy shook my shoulder. 'Tape's stopped!' she yelled. I slowed, the exhaust burbling beautiful music on the over-run.

'Batteries okay?'

Kristy peered at the indicator needle, holding it in the dim glow of the instrument panel lights.

'Yes.'

'Turn the cassette over.'

One side completed, five more to go. At this rate we

would be on the road all night. The realization made my limbs suddenly feel heavy. My eyes began to sting from the effort of staring ahead.

00:33am. 121 miles VERY SLOW LEFT ... OVER HUMP-BACK BRIDGE CROSSING CANAL THEN ABRUPT RIGHT....

Exhaustion had drained Kristy's voice of the bite it required to be heard over the roar of the engine. 'Say again!' I shouted, as the left bend came up and the headlights picked out the arched stone parapet of the bridge. Poplar trees lined the towpaths on each side of the canal.

The car made the turn with a lurching squeal but there was little time to brake before the bridge lay ahead like a launching ramp. On the other side of it the road turned sharply right to follow the canal.

The Healey sprouted wings and flew. All four wheels left the ground. Twenty feet beyond the bridge the car fell on the road with a crash that shook every bone and rivet. The tape recorder fell into the foot well. The fire extinguisher fell out of its clip. Dead ahead, the headlights picked out a wooden gate leading between the trees into a field. I aimed the nose straight for it. Timber planks snapped around our ears in a volley of reports as loud as gun-shots as we burst through them.

As the car slewed to a halt in the grass Kristy put her face in her hands and said, 'Gosh!' Which was the understatement of the year.

The car had not suffered a lot. The windscreen was still intact. There were no oil leaks. The front had some new dents and a headlight was cracked but still operating. The silencers had scraped the road with a terrifying scream but, remarkably, had not dropped off.

'That was awful,' Kristy said in a low voice. It was utterly quiet by the canal side, the black water mirror-calm. Ripples made a perfect concentric pattern as I soaked my handkerchief in the water to rub the bugs off the windscreen and headlights. While Kristy stretched I used the foot pump to increase the tyre pressures: at the very high speeds we were doing it would help to give the car better adhesion on the road.

It was essential to get moving but I was concerned about Kristy. Taking a towel from my kitbag I tucked it round her legs as if it were a rug.

'What I really need are ear muffs,' she said. 'The wind is so cold around my head.'

With my old woolly sailing pullover tied scarf-fashion over her head, the sleeves knotted beneath her chin, Kristy looked like the old woman who lived in a shoe. I tugged the seatbelt tightly around her until she squealed.

'Can you breathe?' I asked.

'No.'

'Can you move?'

'Not an inch.'

'Good, that's how it should be. You'll grow into the seat-belt after a couple of miles and it will be much more comfortable.'

'Have you thought,' she asked, 'that the tapes might guide us in a big circle and Ronny could be sitting in some bar at Arles laughing his rotten head off?'

'I thought about it,' I admitted, 'and decided not to think about it any more.' As I set about shortening the straps of the tape recorder's plastic case so it could be suspended beneath my chin I thought it was unlikely that the road would lead any way but north; Ronald Blom would want to get home, and he would not be wasting time going round in circles. Even so, it was a disturbing thought. With the tape recorder now hanging around my neck I turned the volume up to full pitch and slotted the microphone with its on/off switch into one of the round holes in the steering-wheel. Now I could operate the recorder myself, and Kristy could rest. 'All set?' I asked.

Kristy looked apprehensive and strained but nodded bravely. 'I suppose there are worse ways of travelling?'

'Maybe, but none faster.' Gingerly I drove back through the shattered gate and turned left on the tarmac.

The middle hours of that long night on the road became a series of disjointed impressions, like memories of a film: the petrol attendant at Carcassonne looking quizzically at the tape recorder as I pulled in to fill the tank; the sudden turning off the main road an hour past Toulouse; the endless stretches of straight, fast road, with no traffic, linking fast-asleep agricultural towns.

Kristy stirred from her doze as I pulled up to look at the map and figure out our position.

'Where are we?' she mumbled.

'God knows.'

'Can't we stop, John?'

'No.'

02:45am. 292 miles HALF-FLAT LEFT ... TWO HUNDRED FLAT TO VILLAGE SIGN CASTEL-JALOUX....

Running into light drizzle now: Atlantic weather. Our hair became lank, flicking heavily into our faces. The air smelled thinner, damper. The road became a skid-pan. I regretted the extra pressure in the tyres and cursed the rain-speckle on the windscreen because the wipers were u/s and worked only when we went over a bump and the connection was made in some loose wire.

Forests, lines of trees, farmhouses surrounded by wooden-rail fences, timber mills.

02:56am. 321 miles FOUR MILES STRAIGHT AND LEVEL ... ABSOLUTE LEFT THEN THREE MILES STRAIGHT AND LEVEL ... VERY SLOW DIP THEN LEFT OVER RIVER BRIDGE ... TWO POINT FOUR MILES STRAIGHT....

Driving was swift and easy but had long since ceased to be fun. I fluffed a gear change, stabbing the brakes so the car slithered. Kristy came awake and her voice had a sharp, steely edge.

'You're getting slow!'

That was good, coming from her, I thought grudgingly. Moments later I had to brake savagely on a sharp corner that the tape had not said would be covered with new cow-pats. A herd had taken a night-stroll through a hole in the fence and were scattered all over the verge, munching unalarmed as the headlights zig-zagged among them.

'Don't you want me to take a spell at the wheel?' Kristy shouted.

'No, I'm all right.' She couldn't drive this thing, I knew.

'You have to do better than that.'

'Can't you see I'm tired?'

'Let me drive, then.'

'Shut up and let me concentrate!'

The palest glimmer of the instrument lights played over Kristy's face as she sat up and began to drive every inch of the road in her mind.

'You could have taken that bend faster,' she accused, when I slowed because a corner looked tricky.

'I know it.'

'Don't give up now, we've come too far for that.'

Taking the next bend with fierce abandon, I yelled, 'I'm not bloody giving up!'

'I thought this car could go!'

'Be quiet!'

'It's the mother-in-law in me....'

Catching my furious look Kristy bunched her fists and thumped them up and down on her thighs.

'Drive, man, drive, drive, drive!' she chanted. 'I wanna go fast, fast, fast!'

The car waltzed through the next series of bends like a ball-bearing in a groove. Average speed crept up again as Kristy taunted me on, insisting that she have a turn at driving, criticizing my every move.

The irritation of it woke me up. The shouting and the tensions of anger restored my circulation and relaxed my mind. Soon we were both singing. I bellowed the words of the dirty songs I had learned in the army, falling silent at intervals to listen to the steady, measured voice of the tape recorder. Kristy joined in the choruses.

It might have been an absurd way for two adults to behave but at least I was alert now and driving like a fiend.

'Drive, you bastard, drive!' Kristy urged when I showed signs of flagging. 'Wake up, it's a straight mile, flog it!'

Crossing the busy N10, the main north-south highway between Bordeaux and San Sebastian, I realised we were headed for the coast of the Bay of Biscay. For miles at a time the road ran arrow-straight between level pine forests. Soon we could smell the salty tang of the ocean mingling with the fragrance of pine resin.

03:25am. 366 miles HALF-FLAT LEFT OVER LONG BRIDGE ... SIGNPOST CAP FERRAT AT JUNCTION, BEAR LEFT....

The voice on the tape recorder was slowing down, sounding metallic as the batteries ran out of juice. But we were well into the second side of the third and last cassette.

The road became narrow and twisty, following the shoreline of a wide bay of calm water. Kristy found our position on the map and said the lights of the town on the far side of the bay were those of Arcachon. We passed through shopping centres with hair-dressing salons, boutiques, boat shops. It was holiday resort suburbia.

03:56am. 398 miles ONE HUNDRED YARDS PAST THE CONCORDE OYSTER FARM ON THE LEFT LOOK OPPOSITE FOR LOW STREET SIGNPOST RUE JACQUES COUSTEAU AND TURN RIGHT....

I swung the wheel over and motored quietly into a sleepy residential street with bijou Spanish-style bungalows nestled beneath tall pine trees. I looked at my watch and then at the odometer. Four hundred miles in five hours, and only a fraction of it motorway or dual carriageway. It was an incredible *average* speed of around eighty miles an hour: quite impossible to achieve without the benefit of the tapes.

Sensing that we were approaching our destination I killed the headlights and drove on slowly.

04:03am. 400.5 miles FIFTY YARDS VERY SLOW TO DRIVEWAY ON THE LEFT WITH WHITE GATEPOSTS SIGNPOSTED VILLA MARROC....

The tape went dead. This was the end of the road.

I declutched and coasted past the entrance, then switched off. The pines swished eerily in the crisp breeze blowing off the ocean. I was about to ask Kristy what she thought we ought to do next when the peaceful silence was shattered by the loud blast of a horn from beneath the trees just inside the villa's gates. Then we heard the roar of a powerful engine firing and revving, the squirt of tyres biting on gravel, and a pair of dazzling headlights blinded our sore eyes as the red Ferrari skidded to a halt six inches from the Healey's nose.

Seconds later the Porsche sped out from the trees opposite and turned across our tail.

Ronald Blom got out of the Ferrari and in the abrupt silence after the engines had died said with a dry chuckle, 'You're a tardy little bugger, Montgomery, what kept you?'

The bungalow was furnished for hot summer days and reeked of varnish. Its polished floors, doors, bolted wooden shutters and Swedish-style furniture were all made of knotted pine. Even the fireplace was stacked decoratively with pine cones. Wrought-iron knick-knacks ornamented the white plaster walls.

While Fritz dealt with the cars, Ronald Blom took us into the sitting-room. I lolled back tiredly on the sofa and put an arm round Kristy's shoulders. This seemed to annoy her cousin, who complained, 'God, can't you

214

keep your hands off one another for five minutes?'

Kristy stirred angrily but I held her still, determined that we should remain cool. Nattily dressed as usual in white shirt and dark grey slacks with turn-ups, Ronald Blom lit a cigarette and snapped his lighter shut with a flourish.

'I must say, you're a relentless sod, Montgomery. As a matter of fact I'm not at all sure you haven't become something of a pain in the arse. I know Signor Feraldi would think so, the bloody fool. He's taking the cure in Marseille, did you know?'

'I'm sorry you're not there with him,' I said levelly.

He flopped in an armchair, smoking with short, nervous puffs. The cigarette was held deeply in the vee of his fingers so his hand covered the lower part of his face when he drew on the smoke. I noticed that his finger nails were bitten. He turned to look at Kristy.

'And I would have expected rather better form of you, my cousin. Not a credit to our grandfather's memory, I would say, dashing around Europe wrecking cars. It's all quite extraordinary.' He jabbed his cigarette in my direction and grinned superciliously. 'There's no need to lose your cool at your first sight of a pair of hairy bollocks....'

Kristy tore herself out of my grip and stood up.

'Don't you lecture me, you rat!'

Ronald Blom chuckled and also stood up, languidly blew smoke in her face, and touched the tip of each of her breasts.

'My word, we are grown up all of a sudden.'

Kristy slapped his face with a force that knocked him back into his chair. Rubbing his cheek thoughtfully he regarded Kristy with a semblance of respect.

'I suppose I did ask for that.'

'Yes,' Kristy said curtly.

'Well, look,' Blom went on, 'I think we should be sensible about this business. The bloody plant is no more your property than it is Montgomery's. We are both Van

Blommenstein's grandchildren and I am delivering the plant to my father, who is the heir.'

'Bosh!' Kristy snapped. 'Neither you nor your father inherits a bean. My brother Jon is the heir.'

Ronald Blom switched his orange eyes to me.

'Tell me, old man, what is your opinion of people who crawl up the shirts of their dying relatives in order to be left a quid or two in their wills? Pathetic, wouldn't you say?'

'This is ridiculous,' Kristy snorted. 'I have nothing to discuss with you.'

Ronald Blom shook out another cigarette.

'Then listen to me, and listen well. The blue chrysanthemum is in my possession and I consider it belongs by right to my father. Certainly a court would think so, if you had the nerve to take it that far. We plan to stay here today and tonight: you will stay with us....'

Fritz came in and tossed a small black object into Ronald Blom's lap. He held it up between thumb and forefinger.

'The rotor arm out of your Healey. When we arrive in Boulogne I will mail it to the post office here in the village. There is food in the fridge, and plenty of wine, all laid on for us by the chap who made the tapes, so you can remain here comfortably until it comes, then push off in your own time.'

'Sounds reasonable,' I said non-committally.

'Anything for a dirty weekend, eh?' he leered.

Fritz took one of his cigarettes.

'What do you think of the tapes?' she asked me. 'Ronny is going to market them through the magazine as a special offer for sports car buffs who want to have a big blow-out. What was your average?'

Her bantering grin became a grudging nod of approval when I said our average speed had been around eighty miles an hour.

'That's pretty good,' she said. 'Fancy pants here could only manage seventy-eight, and that was in the Dino.'

Ronald Blom looked disconcerted and made an excuse.

'That car doesn't like the awful French petrol, you know that.'

Fritz winked at me over Blom's head.

'How is your sense of humour, still surviving?'

'Barely,' I said.

Ronald Blom yawned.

'I'm worn ragged, time for bed. Come along, you two love-birds, I'll show you your room.'

It was a small bedroom with twin singles and its own bathroom.

'Pleasant dreams!' Blom said, and closed the door. There was a click as he surreptitiously turned the lock. The shutters had been bolted from the outside.

Kristy shivered. 'It's a sad and dreadful thing to say, but there are only two people in the world whom I really detest, and they have to be my cousin and his father.'

'Stop thinking about it and get some sleep.'

Kristy fell on one of the beds and pulled the counterpane over her legs.

'John,' she whispered.

'Mmm?' I was too tired to speak.

'I do love you!'

For a long moment I was too astonished to think of anything to say but my heart suddenly pumped several degrees hotter and a flood of tingling satisfaction and pleasure pulsed warmly through my whole body. I knelt on the polished floor beside Kristy's head and kissed her long and tenderly.

'You're terrific! I love you too,' I said. As she snuggled down I kissed her again then went back to my own bed but lay awake for a long time, bright headlights flaring in my vision and my mind restless with the realization that from this moment the course of my life was changed.

We were woken around noon by Ronald Blom, who burst in, whistling ostentatiously, as if he had been anxious to find us entwined. He carried a cup of coffee in each hand.

'Rise and shine, lunch in twenty minutes,' he said cheerily. When I rolled over and eyed him blearily he went on, 'Separate beds I see. I would have been in there, if I had been you, Montgomery.' Then he went out, singing to himself, leaving the door open.

Feeling immeasurably brighter for a sleep and a wash, Kristy and I joined the others in the kitchen. It was a big room with a pinewood trestle-table in an alcove. Windows looked out on a lawn and big pine trees shivering in the sea breeze. There were upholstered window-seats around three sides of the table, and stools on the fourth side.

Philip Fanselow smoked in the corner; with his Mexican medallion hanging outside his black roll-neck shirt he had the severe look of a mediaeval abbot and his hang-dog expression was suitably sour. He did not look at us as we entered but remained sitting sideways at the head of the table, staring moodily out of the window.

For once Alec Dempster had his jacket off, though he had apparently slept in his shirt, and he gave me a friendly grin while reaching out with one foot to kick the stools out from under the table for us. Graham Wilson's psychedelic t-shirt now had matching grubby patterns under the arms, and he sat beside Blom who banged his plate and spoon on the table and chanted, 'We want grub!'

Stirring a pot at the stove, Fritz snapped bad-temperedly, 'You will have to wait, I can't do everything at once.' She balanced on wooden clogs and wore a faded blue denim shirt and shorts so small and tight they might have been painted on.

As Kristy and I sat down on the stools Wilson asked what average we had made during the night drive and he screwed up his nose in amazement when I told him.

'Not bad for an old thing like that,' he admitted. 'I did eighty-three in the Porsche and Alec eighty-one in the

Jag.'

'What about the 'Vette?' I asked.

Fanselow scarcely looked round as he spoke. 'The wheels are out of alignment and I had to take it easy.'

Fritz poured soup into mugs and passed them round, then put a French loaf and some cheese on the table.

'I don't see why I should do all the bloody work,' she complained, 'I'm here to take pictures, not be your flaming cook!'

Ronald Blom squeezed her waist and brayed in a lofty tone, 'I must say you're a better waitress than you are photographer.'

Fritz glared, hands on hips. 'You're insufferable this morning!'

'It's the company I keep,' Blom said, sweeping his orange-fringed eyes round the table and sitting back with a swagger. 'Just look at my zulu cousin here: any moment now she will either burst into tears or spit in my face, I'm not sure which. And her lover, Captain Tenderhorn.... ' Blom made a mock naval salute in my direction, and went on, 'What she sees in him I can't imagine. You can tell from the look of him he will be a number two man all his life, the poor old fish.'

Dempster and Wilson darted sympathetic glances at me but looked away, troubled, as Blom simply glared at them contemptuously and stared them down.

Kristy broke into the crossfire, saying in a nanny-like tone: 'Shut up, Ronny, or I'll tell them how you used to wet your bed every night until you were seven.'

Fritz sniggered as Blom got to his feet.

'Not as wet as all that, my dear,' he said. And with a theatrical gesture he snatched open the fridge, took out a plastic bag containing the blue chrysanthemum, and held it up to the light. Then, satisfied with the gesture, he replaced it in the fridge. 'Looks healthy enough,' he said smugly.

'What *is* that thing you have been fussing about?' Fritz asked.

'My little souvenir of Sardinia,' Blom answered, leering at Kristy who met his eye frostily.

'Daresay it's marijuana,' Wilson hazarded, his tone betraying nervousness. 'You'll have fun getting that through Customs, Ron.'

'Oh no he won't,' Kristy cut in. 'Don't you know cannabis when you see it? That plant is just a plain old chrysanthemum, but it is an extremely valuable variety which my cousin stole from us in Sardinia. We want to get it back, and if you fellows had any sense of what was decent you would help us!'

Fanselow muttered thickly, as if to himself, that it was a private matter and nothing to do with him. At the same time, seemingly enjoying himself hugely, Blom sat forward in his chair and delightedly slapped the table with both hands.

'There it is, fellows, the damsel is in distress!' he taunted. 'Watch the gallant knights of the road leap to the pretty lady's rescue! Watch the pretty lady promise anything, anything, but oh, please, please, cut my bloody throat and save her honour. Eh? Good God, Kristy, I always knew that Dornford Yates crap you read under the bedclothes would turn you into a raving lunatic.'

Kristy ignored him but turned to the others.

'Do you always do exactly what he tells you?' she inquired cuttingly.

'Oh yes,' Blom interjected. 'They always do.'

The thick vegetable soup, made out of a packet, was piping hot so I left it and had a piece of bread and cheese with a glass of wine from a litre bottle that Fritz banged down on the table. A tense silence fell. Kristy ate with her eyes studiously lowered. Blom was amused about something, oozing charm and self confidence. The others remained edgy and out of sorts. I was testing the soup again cautiously when my lips touched something metallic. Wonderingly I explored it with the tip of my tongue as the level of the soup went down when I sipped,

220

but it was some time before I could be certain.

It was the Healey's rotor arm. In the soup.

Putting the mug down slowly I glanced idly round the table. Fritz had been watching me steadily and now she caught my eye and flashed a small, conspiratorial grin.

But why? I could not understand why Fritz would risk Ronald Blom's anger to hand us a means of escape – not on a plate, exactly, but in a cup. Had she broken with Ronny, or had he simply become such a pill that she could not swallow any more? Whatever the reason, it gave me a surge of hope. Under the table I put one hand on Kristy's thigh and squeezed meaningfully. She stiffened, taking the hint. Shaking his gold lighter out of its absurd velvet purse, Blom lit a cigarette and eyed us with amusement, his eyes glittering in the flame. He seemed to think we were a pair of performing chimps and I did not like his manner one bit. With an arrogant Ronald Blom we knew where we stood. Grinning genially like this the man seemed twice as poisonous.

When I had emptied the cup of soup I held it casually in my lap and found an opportunity to tip the rotor into my handkerchief. Fritz brought another litre of wine to the table. The writers were getting well oiled. I slipped one hand into my pocket and concentrated on moving the rotor round inside my handkerchief to dry it as best I could.

Then, as Ronald Blom cocked his head back to draw on his cigarette, I nudged Kristy's knee again and she tensed. Taking a strong grip on the edge of the table I stood up and with a huge effort and a Tarzan-style shout tipped the table into the laps of the three men opposite. With a sweep of my foot I knocked Ronald Blom's stool out from under him – and this time I did not catch his arm as he fell.

Fritz drew back out of the way, wide-eyed but not alarmed, for she had been expecting something like this.

221

Kristy snatched open the fridge, grabbed the plastic bag, and ran out. I followed, slamming the kitchen door on the chaotic scene and spending a few moments building a barricade of sofa and armchairs so it would be pushed open only after a struggle.

By good luck – or design, I did not stop to wonder – the Healey faced downhill and the bonnet-strap had not been buckled up. In the sunlight I inspected the rotor quickly, rubbed it on my shirt to ensure the contact point was completely dry, then fitted it in the distributor, clipped the top home, slammed the bonnet down without waiting to buckle it.

Footsteps were pounding in the house.

Kristy was already in her seat. I jumped in, turned the starter. For a breathless three seconds I thought the Bitch was going on strike. Then she roared into action. As Ronald Blom ran out of the house, the Healey tore away, machine-gunning his knees with gravel.

We drove all through the afternoon and into the evening. By a circuitous route we cut through Bordeaux, then settled on the main road north through Poitiers, Tours and Le Mans. Kristy was as happy as a skylark, singing, teasing me about my driving, telling me not once but over and over again that her pig of a cousin had finally been taken to market.

The sun was warm and bright, the green fields of France as pretty as a picture. We drove easily and rapidly with none of the tension that had marked the last twenty-four hours.

Well into Normandy, three hundred miles on the clock since making our escape, Kristy opened the *Guide Michelin* to find an *auberge* off the beaten track where we could put up for the night.

It was sunset when she directed me off the main road and through ten miles of rural by-ways to a quaint village on the outskirts of which was a converted farmhouse

with brown-painted half-timbering and a thatched roof –
Le Cochon Rouge.

A single magpie flew across our path as I swung in and
parked under a chestnut tree, but I thought nothing of it.
Right now the omens *must* be wrong. Kristy was excited
about our luck in finding the place.

'Doesn't it look attractive? And it has got two rosettes,
so we can celebrate in style.'

There was a room for us with a dormer window
overlooking an orchard. It had flowered wallpaper on the
ceiling as well as the walls, and the huge double bed had
immense pillows and a feather quilt. A bunch of flowers
stood in a jug on the wash stand and through the open
window we heard the billing of doves and the hiss of
farmyard geese.

As I stood looking out at the last of the twilight Kristy
contentedly put her arms round my waist and rested her
head affectionately against my shoulder. I turned inside
her embrace and we kissed.

'It's almost too good to be true,' she whispered. 'I
never thought it could happen.'

We kissed passionately and this time I knew the
moment was right. I loved this brave, determined,
resourceful and beautiful creature with all my heart. Her
body had been a temptation since I had seen her swimming strongly ahead of me to the island at Villa Maddalena. She reached up and unbuttoned my shirt.

'Don't you want to have dinner first?' I asked mock-
ingly.

She did not pause but smiled seductively. 'Do you, my
darling?'

We undressed each other in front of the window,
hugging and kissing in the soft, pastel light. Turning back
the cover she drew me to the bed. The blue chrysanthemum lay on the pillow, where I had tossed it. I caught
my breath at the sight of long legs, the arch of her slim
waist as she reached to pick it up.

'I'll just give it some air,' she said, untwisting the wire

from the neck of the bag.

'It's the Blue Hurricane or me,' I threatened, getting into the bed. My heart banged like a trip-hammer.

'Wait just two seconds.' She hurried over to the hand basin and put the bag under the tap. Naked and beautiful, she stood beneath the mirror lamp and tested the dampness of the roots with the tip of her finger.

In that instant, with a flash of foreboding, I knew what she would find. I knew why Fritz had secreted the rotor arm in my soup. Why Ronald Blom had been so cocky. Why the Healey's bonnet had been left unbuckled.

Kristy stiffened. She extracted the plant and held it out on the flat of her hand, its short stem upright, the tangle of roots hanging down through her half-spread fingers.

'You don't need to say it,' I said sickly, 'it's the wrong chrysanthemum, right?'

Kristy's eyes brimmed. She sagged on to the bed and fell against me, fists clenched in silent rage and frustration.

The humiliating episode had been engineered in its entirety by Ronald Blom. He had dug up a chrysanthemum from a neighbourhood garden, put it in a plastic bag identical to the other, then made certain we had seen it in the fridge as he taunted us. God, how he must have laughed, seeing me playing with the rotor arm in the soup!

I flung the useless plant out of the window. Kristy's arms came up around my neck and she pulled me down, kissing fiercely and breaking off only to whisper, 'Who cares, my darling, haven't we got each other?'

11 : LE TRUC

Morning sunshine streamed into the cosy room through the open window as I unfolded the road map on the wrinkled bed. Naked and relaxed, Kristy nestled against me. Running my hand up the length of her backbone I massaged the back of her neck affectionately, her soft gold curls brushing the back of my knuckles.

At seven-thirty the maid had come in bearing a tray laden with *croissants*, pots of home-made *confiture*, farm butter and strong coffee. When these had been dealt with and the tray lay on the floor beside the bed our bodies had drifted together and our loving was as freshly poignant as the first time.

Now, showered and wearing only my trousers, with Kristy's chin hooked over my shoulder, I had an urge to begin all over again. Kristy sensed it and kissed my neck, putting her arms round my bare chest.

I rustled the map meaningfully as she blew in my ear.

'Stop it, you're tickling.'

'Don't you like it?'

'Why did you stop?'

She fell sideways on the bed and laid her head on my lap.

'Let's just stay here. For ever and ever.'

Tenderly I stroked the hair back from her face, noticing that the dark circles had disappeared from beneath her eyes and the raw bruise was fading from her cheek. For the first time I felt I was seeing the real Kristy. But it was a spell that had to be broken. I patted her on the bottom.

'Go and have your shower, or we will be charged for

staying two days.'

While I drove slowly through the farm lanes, heading back towards the main road, Kristy sat up on the back of her seat to dry her wet hair. When we regained the N138 it tumbled around her shoulders in a mass of golden waves. She sat down in her seat and buckled herself in.

'Now I feel better – what next, Captain Blood?'

I tapped the open map. 'It just depends whether it was a deliberate red herring when Ronny said they were leaving the villa this morning. If they set off last night they will be in London by now.'

'I don't think so,' Kristy said. 'Ronny was all set for a love-in with Fritz. And the others weren't exactly preparing for a second night on the road, by the rate they were going through the plonk.'

'In that case,' I asked, 'which Channel port will they head for? The hovercraft ticket in Ronny's briefcase suggests it will be Boulogne, but if the ticket is interchangeable with the ferries they might sail from Dieppe or Calais.'

'Maybe,' Kristy said, 'but the hovercraft is more Ronny's style, don't you think?'

'If you're right then he must go through the city of Rouen; it is possible to circle round by the back roads but it will be difficult for him to cross the Seine.'

Kristy leaned over suddenly and kissed me.'

'What's that for?' I asked.

'Thank you,' she said. 'Thank you for what you're doing. Thank you because I love you.'

'You're a sausage,' I said, and pulled out into the traffic.

Three times Ronald Blom had physically beaten one or the other of us. Myself aboard the yacht, Kristy at the railway station and again outside the restaurant at Arles. Although it seemed a century ago now, the memory of the collision in the Channel, and how his father had screwed up my plans, still rankled. Half a dozen times, now, I had been made a fool of. It was a wonder Ronald Blom had not choked on his own laughter. I shifted uncomfortably in my seat as the memory of it twisted my gut. Kristy noticed and asked what the matter was.

'Nothing,' I said, 'just thinking.'

'Yes I know, I feel just the same. We won't let it happen again.'

Later, struck by a sudden thought, I said, 'You don't think they could have departed before dawn? They might have passed through Rouen already and be buying their duty-frees in mid-Channel.'

'You know what they say about the early bird getting the worm?'

'Well?'

'Ronny,' said Kristy, 'is too much of a worm to risk it.'

By noon we were in heavy traffic crossing one of the Seine bridges in Rouen. The wide, greeny-brown river was busy with barges, and a small yacht flying a red duster, its mast down on crutches, was forging upstream. In three weeks it would be on the Rhône at Arles, within a few miles of the Mediterranean, after cruising right through the heart of France on rivers and canals.

'I've always wanted to go to Paris by river,' Kristy said.

'We will,' I promised, 'my own boat is ideal for it.'

In my mind's eye I saw Kristy at the wheel as I trimmed the sails and we set a cross-Channel course for Le Havre and the mouth of the Seine. Blue Hurricane or not, I vowed it would happen.

In four hours my resolve had a crack in it as wide as the English Channel. Five or six miles north of Rouen, reversed into a gateway and partly concealed beneath a shady tree, we had found the ideal spot from which to watch a long stretch of the main road leading to Abbeville and the Channel ports. Traffic streamed into view on a sweeping bend, came up the hill towards us, then vanished over a brow where the road was marked with double white no-crossing lines.

I had spent some of the time checking over the engine and tyres, wriggling under the chassis to tighten the exhaust silencers that had been loosened by our wild leap over the hump-backed bridge and were bottoming more frequently and threatening to drop off.

Then Kristy had walked two hundred yards up the hill to a small shop, returning not with a classic Kristy picnic but some apples, biscuits and a couple of ice creams. She had also bought a bottle of champagne with which to celebrate when we got hold of the blue chrysanthemum.

'You're very certain,' I said challengingly.

'Yes,' she admitted quietly, 'Yes, I am.' On the grounds that we needed all the positive thinking we could get, I did not disagree.

Twice we snapped to attention, binoculars ready, when sports cars appeared in the distance at the bottom of the hill. One proved to be not a Ferrari Dino but an MGB-GT. The other was indeed an *olivgrun* Porsche, but an old model which had been resprayed a modern colour.

When I sighed dispiritedly, Kristy snapped, 'All we can do is be patient. If you have got a hunch you must back it all the way.'

I said it seemed pretty hopeless. 'It's a fair bet they have gone to Dieppe after all. There's a sailing at four every afternoon. Or maybe they're hitting the hot spots, in Paris.'

'Stop fretting,' Kristy said. 'Ronny's the laziest man in the world. Probably didn't even get up until noon.'

'Not if Fritz was in there with him,' I said, squirming again as my gut twisted, though it was for a different reason this time.

Kristy had the glasses to her eyes and I could hardly believe it when she said with elaborate casualness, 'Here comes one of them, at any rate.'

It was the white Corvette, driving steadily amid a group of saloon cars. Kristy handed me the glasses and as it loomed larger I saw Philip Fanselow alone in the cockpit. He failed to notice the Healey pulled up under the tree but sped on, pulling out for a view of the road ahead as he breasted the brow of the hill.

My fingers moved at once to the ignition key. 'Shall we follow?'

'The others will be along soon.'

'Perhaps, but if we follow the Corvette we can be certain of meeting up with them ultimately.'

It was a tough decision. Undecided, we stared down the hill. Kristy took the binoculars and focussed on the far bend.

'Here comes the green one!' she said with an edge of excitement.

The Porsche overtook a line of cars on the hill, swinging in just before its offside wheels touched the start of the double white lines. Graham Wilson was at the wheel, his pale face and straggly hair nodding to the beat of a tape on the stereo. Moments later the dark blue Jaguar was in sight, Alec Dempster driving with the inevitable rally jacket and string-back gloves.

Thoughtfully I pulled at my lip.

'You know, I'd have expected the Ferrari to be ahead of the others, not trailing the pack. It's the sort of thing that matters to a prig like Ronny.'

Kristy agreed but had nothing to add. In suspense we waited. Minutes ticked by as we glued our eyes to the road where it came into view a mile away. Five minutes. Ten....

'There's a faint chance,' I said, 'that if we go now we will catch up to the others. They're bound to stop for petrol at some point. It's worth a try.'

'Don't worry about Ronny, he just stayed behind for a quick one after breakfast, like we did. Or he's having a late lunch.'

'You're taking a risk,' I warned.

Kristy lay back in her seat and closed her eyes. 'When I count to three, the Ferrari will come round that corner. Are you ready?'

'Ready,' I said.

Kristy fell silent, her expression intent and her eyes screwed against the sunlight finding a gap between the leaves overhead. Then she counted, slowly and clearly. 'One... two....'

No Ferrari Dino.

'Two-and-a-half....' On that instant the low red wedge streaked round the curve. I switched on the ignition and started the engine in half a second. Kristy sat up with a jerk, wide-eyed and laughing. 'You see, I *am* psychic.'

'Is it Ronny? We'd better make sure.'

'Of course it is.'

She handed me the glasses. It was Ronald Blom all right, his face a pale oval behind swept-back tinted glass. Fritz was beside him, strapped in tightly and smoking.

It was a signature of Ronald Blom's driving that he crossed the double white lines on the crest of the hill, passing four cars, then darting in again as a lorry loomed up, angrily flashing its lights. Traffic thinned out further from the city and within a few miles I had worked the Healey to within a quarter-mile of the Ferrari's cropped tail. For twenty miles, travelling at a steady seventy-five or so that became ninety on the longer straights, we shadowed the red car. Then, at some roadworks which we came upon suddenly, it was no longer possible to hang back. The Ferrari had stopped at the end of a queue of traffic awaiting the green flag. There was no choice but to pull in behind.

At that moment I would have given a lot to have seen the expression on Ronald Blom's face. He must have glanced in his mirror just as it was filled by the Healey's bunion snout.

The Dino shook on its suspension as he twisted round his seat to look back at us through the car's narrow rear window. Grinning, I waggled my fingers at him. He gunned his throttle until the car howled, demonstrating anger, surprise and anxiety in one.

As the line of cars began to move he pulled out and roared along the newly rolled and level surface which had been closed to traffic prior to sealing. There was no choice but to follow. Roadworkers leapt to safety, waving their fists as our tyres gouged deep ruts.

After a few miles it became clear that the Ferrari Dino could not lose the Healey on a road with such a lot of traffic. Ronald Blom must have reached the same conclusion. Just north of a place called Neufchatel-en-Bray he indicated a left turn and darted to the right. The jink nearly made a fool of me but I crashed down a gear and managed to hurl the Healey after him.

It was a secondary road, well surfaced and nearly straight. It rose and fell as it arrowed across rolling farm country, ideal for what was going to be a straight test of speed. Blom put his foot all the way down and as the red car snapped ahead I reckoned the Healey might be able to keep up if it could stay in the tunnel of the Ferrari's slipstream, less than two lengths from its rear bumper.

Engine noise was left far behind but the wind pummelling our heads like a great surf wave breaking into the cockpit all but drowned us. At seven thousand revs the tachometer needle touched the red line. The old Bitch shook with effort as I cracked on every ounce of power, but to enable her to bottle round town flexibly I had de-tuned the compression ratio and in this form she had little chance of keeping up with the superior Dino as long as Ronald Blom was able to drive it half seriously.

Midway along the straight, my speedo indicating one hundred and fifteen miles an hour, the Ferrari pulled gradually ahead and the Healey was left to forge its own tunnel through the air. After that the Ferrari went ahead quickly, cutting through the air like a razor blade, and at the first rise was two hundred yards in front.

A church tower came in sight ahead. The Ferrari now half a mile away. It could lose us in this village.

'Find us on the map!' I yelled to Kristy.

The map wanted to fly away as she unfolded it but already we were in the village, howling through the little streets at seventy, then crossing the market place. There was an intersection ahead. Signposts pointed right to Gournay, straight on to Poix, left to Dieppe. Two small boys on the pavement peered up the Poix Road as if they had seen Father Christmas go by. Taking the hint, we tore off again and sure enough the Ferrari was there, in the distance, sniffing like a Dinky toy through the green counterpane of the undulating landscape.

Before long the road climbed through a series of bends then plunged down a steep hill. The road snaked in a series of shallow twists and turns and was marked with double white lines, but the bends were so gentle that the car could take a short cut across each corner.

The white lines weaved back and forth under the front wheels as the Healey leapt forwards and downwards. We roared through a copse of dark trees in the floor of the valley. Up the other side. Again the snaking bends and double white lines.

And on the ridge a dark blue Peugeot with a flashing blue light on its roof. The red Ferrari was drawn up alongside, a gendarme stooping to talk to the driver. A second *flic* waved me into the verge. He had binoculars round his neck and from this vantage point across the valley had been watching us crossing and re-crossing the double white lines.

'Crafty sods!' I muttered, pulling up as directed. Rapidly I fumbled in the glovebox for driving licence and passport. The gendarme inspected them cursorily, then wagged his finger at me, smiling fractionally beneath his thin black moustache and telling me that next time I would really get it in the neck.

The other gendarme straightened up. The Ferrari was being put into gear.

232

'*Prenez-garde, Monsieur,*' the *flic* said. I nodded, smiled, shrugged a Gallic apology. The Ferrari was moving away. The gendarme touched his cap, gave the Healey a curious and appraising look, then rapped the bonnet with his knuckles and said, '*Allez!*'

We left the Police trap in time to see the Ferrari speeding down yet another snaking hill also marked with double white lines. Safe in the knowledge that the *flics* were behind him, Ronald Blom again took the straight line through the bends. I was tempted to do the same but some sixth sense made me behave and I twisted carefully in and out of each bend, staying on the proper side of the road. The gap between the two cars widened formidably.

On my part it was lucky thinking.

At the top of the next hill was a police van and two more gendarmes with binoculars. This time Ronny stood outside the car and the *flics* were not being charming. One took details in a notebook and the other handed Ronny a plastic bag containing crystals.

Seeing the Healey pull in behind, Ronald Blom panicked. With a slap he sent the breathalyser spinning from the gendarme's hand and he shouted, '*Vous êtes tous des cons, du plus petit au plus grand!*'

Your average friendly cop doesn't like being knocked about. Nor does he take a benign view of four-letter obscenities directed at his force in general. Particularly by foreigners.

Before he could bat an eyelid Ronald Blom was pinioned from behind, handcuffed, and marched into the big police van, the familiar Citroen that looks as if it is made of corrugated iron and is known throughout France as the salad basket.

Fritz showed her licence to the gendarme and insisted on taking the car. They were disappointed at missing a chance to drive a Ferrari but had to agree. As the van drove away I backed the Healey across the Ferrari's nose.

Fritz glared at me frostily.

'They're taking him off for a blood test.'

'More than that, I should think. Give me your key, I want to search the car.'

'Search all you want,' she said, her smile snapping like pants elastic. 'Ronny's got that plant of his in his blazer pocket. You'll have a job getting it off him in gaol.'

Knowing Ronald Blom's destination for the first time with complete certainty meant there was no longer any need to hurry. We dawdled through the lush countryside, each of us lost in our own thoughts. I was remembering with anxiety how the Ferrari had walked away from the Healey, its low-drag body-beautiful just too sharp and too powerful. By comparison, the Healey was as aerodynamic as Mae West and with the engine detuned there was no hope of squeezing any more speed out of her.

Kristy was thinking of her cousin in a rather different way.

'Ronny was always so tactless,' she said. 'He is so heartless and brazen that sometimes I feel sorry for him. It's not really his fault that he is the way he is.'

'How can you say that after what he has done to you?'

'I don't know, but it's true, just the same.'

Seeing a faded Total sign hanging from a pole outside a farm building, and glancing at the fuel gauge which hovered at E, I pulled in beside a pair of ancient petrol pumps. There was a cobwebby office behind the pumps and beyond, in what was still used partly as a farmyard, a workshop littered with rusty agricultural implements and tractor accessories. The yard was enclosed on two sides by an open-fronted barn, and on the third side by a large old farmhouse. The buildings had low outside walls but high, steeply-pitched, tiled roofs.

Nobody came out so I tooted the horn and after a few moments there was a footstep on the cobbles inside the gate and a young man appeared, wiping his hands on the seat of greasy overalls.

I touched my chin with the flat of my hand to indicate that he should fill her up. He extracted the nozzle from the pump.

'Bet she goes like a bomb, this thing. Not a 100-S is it?' he asked.

'Oh, you're English!'

He grinned engagingly and we shook hands.

'Bob Henderson is my name. Did you see the Dino going like a bat out of hell just in front of you?'

'Yes, the gendarmes down the road thought it was their birthday.'

'Cripes, did they catch you? It's a diabolical trick, that. *Le truc avec deux pièges*, they call it, and they don't half come down on you like a ton of bricks.'

I explained how Ronald Blom had taken a swipe at the gendarme and been carted off in the salad basket. Henderson whistled.

'He's in for a tough time, you can bet on it.'

With his faintly Midland accent, open and friendly face, and horn-rimmed glasses, Bob Henderson was an unlikely figure to find serving petrol at a back-road service station in the middle of northern France. He was about twenty-five, and obviously pleased to be talking English. Waving his hand behind him, he said, 'Have a gander in the barn.'

The geriatric pump poured with the speed of an old maid's teapot so I strolled in through the open gate. Among piles of hay, wooden carts and sacks of chaff, covered with dust and pieces of straw, its metallic pale-blue paintwork spotted with chicken droppings, was the familiar fuselage of an Austin Healey 3000 – the real thing with wire wheels, wind-up windows, dark blue upholstery in real leather, and even a hood. A closer look revealed its tyres split and flat, a hen nesting in the passenger seat, and the carpets chewed by rats or cockroaches. When I lifted the bonnet, causing a landslide of powdery dust, I saw that the car had no engine. The exhaust manifold dangled beneath the bulkhead where it had been disconnected, rusty wires hung everywhere, and the radiator had dropped lop-sidedly on to the ground.

The petrol pump was still ticking slowly when I returned.

'What d'you reckon?' Bob Henderson asked.

'It'll be a big job,' I told him.

His shrug was truly French.

'Well, it is capitalizing just by sitting there. One day I'll put a motor in and get her on the road. You don't see many Healeys these days.' Petrol overflowed from the tank and splashed on the road. 'Oops, sorry!' He did a sum in his head as he screwed on the filler cap then told me the total and seemed disappointed when I showed no desire to linger.

The town was eight miles away and we located the two-storey, cream-painted *Gendarmerie* by looking for the inevitable umbrella-rib aerial mounted on a high metal pole on its roof. Fritz walked down the front steps of the building, making for the Ferrari, as we drove up. I saw a row of blue-shirted figures admiring her from an upstairs window, though whether it was the slim blonde with sprayed-on shorts and shirt, or the red car she was bending her bare brown legs to get into, was difficult to know.

'He has been charged with dangerous driving and resisting arrest,' she said curtly.

'Are they letting him out?'

'Not until he appears in court tomorrow morning.'

As she slammed the door I said, 'Fritz, how's your sense of humour?'

'Bugger off!' she muttered, and drove away to find a hotel.

'Which leaves us in the soup once more,' Kristy sighed.

Now that we were close to the Channel ports and off

the main road there were half a dozen different routes that Ronald Blom could take when he left court in the morning. If he left, that is. By the quickest route it was seventy-five miles to Boulogne, ninety-six to Calais. Or he could strike west to Dieppe, only forty-seven miles away.

The countryside, I knew, would be rolling and open, the roads straight, well surfaced, and very fast. Once Ronald Blom reached one of the Channel ports our chances of getting hold of the blue chrysanthemum were practically nil. English roads were crowded and the network of lanes so thick that he would easily lose himself.

If we were to be in with a chance of catching the Ferrari on the open roads of France, I realised, there was only one thing to do.

Bob Henderson was surprised but pleased to see us again as I drove straight through the gate into the cobbled yard behind the petrol pumps. When I asked if his Healey had straight-through exhausts he bent low to peer beneath its body shell and came up shaking his head.

'Do you think you could cod something up in a hurry?' I asked.

'I suppose so,' he replied doubtfully, 'but it might be a long job.'

'We've got all night,' I said.

His eyebrows shot up. 'Why, what's all the dash?' When I told him we had to catch the Ferrari he had seen earlier he muttered 'Christ!' But he was a true enthusiast. His eyes lit up and he wiped his hands excitedly on a piece of cotton-waste as if he could not wait to unstrap the bonnet and get started.

'Run her into the barn,' he said. 'I'll shift those bags of grain to give you some room.'

As he unstrapped the bonnet I asked, 'Do you think you might run to a bed for the night?'

'We'll pay for it, of course,' Kristy added hastily.

'That's no problem,' he said agreeably. 'The only

237

thing is my mother-in-law is a bit old fashioned, that's all. It will have to be two beds. But you would be very welcome. Come and meet my wife, she's making the cheese.'

It was an unusual match, the car enthusiast from Nottingham and the French country girl. They had met a couple of years before when Bob went to the Le Mans 24-hour race with a coach party from the factory where he worked as a fitter, and met Josephine at the hotel where they put up for the night. He had abandoned the coach on the spot (after watching the race) and had not been back to Nottingham since.

When I remarked that I didn't think things like that happened any more he looked embarrassed and Kristy jabbed me with an elbow, telling me not to be cynical.

Wearing a pink gingham apron which set off her apple-cheeked complexion and pretty black hair, and heavily pregnant, Josephine clattered out of the scullery on wooden clogs and shook hands shyly. An old tractor pulling some spiked harrows roared into the yard and we were introduced to Josephine's father, a short, square figure of a man so grizzled and weather-beaten he might have sprouted and grown in one of his own fields. His open-necked shirt beneath the braces holding up his baggy corduroy work-trousers revealed a barrel-chest matted with fluffy grey hairs. When he took off his flat hat, which looked as if it might have been a gift from Nottinghamshire, and followed us indoors, I saw that the top of his balding head was white and smooth, contrasting comically with the leathery tan of his wrinkled face.

His wife was big-boned, stout, and grave of face. The two old people said little but their bright eyes did not miss a trick and I could see they were fond of their hard-working, enthusiastic and considerate English son-in-law.

Bob Henderson explained in French what we were going to do and the old man nodded to himself, looking amused, while the old lady covered her mouth with one hand as she realized there were rooms to make ready and beds to air.

Josephine was delighted for her husband's sake and was already taking a handful of cutlery from a drawer in the big kitchen dresser to lay extra places at the long, scrubbed table. A bell rang at the back of the house and Bob Henderson excused himself to go out and serve petrol. I followed him out and rolled up my sleeves to get down to work but he chased me back into the kitchen.

'Get some grub and leave me to get things ready,' he said, 'then we can do the whole job without having to stop.'

It was a welcome idea and I took my place beside Kristy at the big table as Josephine carried a tureen of steaming potato soup over from the range. As she stirred it with an iron ladle its surface glittered with melted butter floating on a thick layer of finely chopped parsley, chives and onion. She served it in deep bowls of blue and white china. The old lady passed me a chunk of home-baked bread and her husband pushed over a tumbler of rough cider poured from a gallon jar which had no label and I assumed that it, too, was home-made.

It was the start of one of the best meals I have ever eaten. The potatoes had come off the farm and had a nutty flavour of the earth. The ham which followed the soup was home-cured and had been sliced from a whole side hanging from a ceiling-hook in the pantry. The cheese was home-made, as was the yoghurt which was poured over a bowl of magnificent preserved peaches. Romantic considerations aside, it wasn't hard to see why Bob Henderson had abandoned his coach trip.

Kristy rhapsodized over the tangy, fresh-tasting yoghurt, so different from the plastic muck sold in shops. The old woman's eyes lit with pleasure and before Kristy knew it she was being taken on a tour of the cellar to see the yoghurt plant that was kept going in big wooden churns.

In the workshop, Bob Henderson had set up overhead lights, laid out his tools and a welding torch, and removed the Healey's domed bonnet. He was exploring round the engine, hesitating to do anything, yet itching to get started.

'I'm afraid I don't know much about turbo-chargers,' he said apologetically.

The turbo-charger sat to one side of, and slightly above, the engine. It comprised two round iron casings joined closedly together so it looked like an immense yo-yo, and was connected to the engine by a nest of convoluted pipes.

Normally an engine gulps air into its cylinders by natural suction. A turbo-charger helps things along by pumping air into the engine under pressure. It is a turbine, or air pump, driven at high speed by a second turbine which in turn is propelled by the exhaust gases as they are expelled from the engine. The faster the exhaust blows out, the faster the turbines go, pumping more and more air into the engine to increase its power. The exhaust gases are exceedingly hot, so the turbine is constructed of alloys able to withstand intense heat.

The result of force-feeding the engine is that it must withstand stresses for which it was never designed. A turbo-charger is not practical for ordinary motoring and this was why I had always adjusted it to waste the exhaust gases, so that, in effect, the whole thing was bypassed.

What I proposed to do now in order to catch the Ferrari, I told Bob Henderson, was close up the waste-gate so the turbo-charger came fully into operation.

'Will it really make that much difference?' he asked.

'You could say so,' I explained. 'The engine is presently rated at four hundred and seventy-five brake horsepower. The turbo-charger will boost this by about fifty per cent. To well over six hundred horsepower.'

240

Bob whistled. 'Wow! Six hundred horses in a Healey. How will you hang on to them?'

'Tightly,' I said, fitting a spanner over the lock-nut of the waste-gate.

Adjusting the turbo-charger took only a short time but it made a lot of difference to the compression of the engine, so the four carburettors had to be carefully re-tuned and this was a long and painstaking process.

Meanwhile, Bob Henderson cut away the silencers from beneath the sub-frame and, using some of the exhaust pipe from his own engine-less car, rebuilt the system so the exhaust gases would blow straight down the pipe and would not be slowed by passage through the baffles of a silencer. However, the engine had to be quietened at least a bit, so he cleverly built two pop-riveted expansion chambers, one for each side. These were long metal boxes in the length of each exhaust pipe which gave the gases space in which to expand and lose some of their punch before they were blasted from the rear of the car.

Now, instead of making large American burbling noises, the Chevrolet engine had the throaty roar of a piston-engined fighter. Demented chickens scattered from the rafters and fled into the yard as I tweaked the throttle lever and the air boomed with a surge of power that lifted dust off the ground.

Sitting in the cockpit I watched the inlet-manifold pressure gauge, a round instrument that had been original equipment in a wartime Lancaster bomber. As the revs increased, the needle suddenly twitched to the 'boost' side of the zero mark, then began to climb round the dial as the turbo-charger responded to the increasing throttle and started pumping air into the cylinders. The car felt that it needed only the handbrake to be released and we would have lift-off.

Switching off the engine before it got too hot to work on, I heard a clicking sound in the yard and the murmur of conversation. By the light of a car headlamp rigged up high on the wall to shine on a sandy area of ground on the far side of the yard, the farmer and his daughter were teaching Kristy how to play *boules*. The old lady sat in an upright wooden chair by the wall, knitting as she watched.

Kristy stood inside a small circle scratched in the dust, held the heavy metal ball loosely in her right hand, then swung it back and forth with a straight arm and lobbed it in the direction of a small red wooden jack about thirty-five feet away. It landed in the dust with a thud, bounced, brushed the jack, then rolled another three feet and stopped. 'Bravo!' Josephine shouted, clapping delightedly.

With an air of thoughtful calm the old man stepped into the circle and played his shot. The dull silvered *boule*, not much larger than a cricket ball but one and a half pounds in weight, arched high in the air, landed three inches from Kristy's *boule*, and nudged it gently out of the way. '*La pousse-pousse*,' he explained, with a shy and proud grin – the knock-out.

While Kristy was coached in the game Drake had played with cannonballs on Plymouth Hoe, Bob and I twiddled the carburettors until the big engine's orchestration of power was as sweet as anything you would hear in the Albert Hall.

After we had been running the engine up and down for a time, Bob suddenly switched off the barn lights. 'Look,' he said, pointing at the turbo-charger. Its iron casing was white-hot, so hot that it was almost translucent, and the shadow of the turbine blades whirling inside it at something like one hundred thousand revs per minute was clearly visible.

'You're going to need an asbestos suit,' Bob warned as I switched off.

It was a worrying prospect, and the dull thud and clink of the *boules* intruded on my thoughts as I tried to work out a solution.

Then Bob Henderson tapped the aluminium bonnet

with a pair of tin-snips and raised his eyebrows questioningly. I nodded that he should go ahead. Carefully he cut a hole in the dome of the bonnet, leaving a flap which he lifted up and shaped in the form of a cowl so cool air would be scooped in and directed downwards on the engine.

'That's the best I can do,' he said. 'It should cool things down a bit. How's your *boule* arm?'

Together we walked across the yard.

'This is fun,' Kristy said, handing me a pair of *boules* to try. For identification they were engraved with concentric patterns of rings.

Awkwardly I stood inside the circle and aimed at the *bouchon*, a few yards away. My first shot covered twice the necessary distance. The second hit a bump and darted off to the left. Then Bob Henderson had a go and I realized there were two distinct styles of play. The old farmer was a *pointeur* or 'gun-layer,' who played with delicate finesse, placing his shot within inches of the *bouchon*. Bob was a *tireur*, a 'trigger-puller' or hit man, who could crack a walnut at ten yards. His speciality was knocking opponents clean out of the yard. It didn't sound much of a recipe for family harmony but, unlike croquet played on an English lawn, nobody seemed to get ruffled.

When the old lady came out with a jug of cider and some glasses we stopped playing and sat around in the crisp night air.

The farmer asked me whether we were all set for tomorrow.

'*Mais oui*,' I told him. 'Tomorrow – *la pousse-pousse!*'

12 : CUT....

Kristy shook my shoulder at a quarter to six and when
we went down the house was bustling as if everybody
else had been up and about for hours. In the workshop
Bob Henderson was already busy.

'I checked out the brakes for you and took up some
slack on the clutch,' he said, beaming through his round
spectacles and wiping his hands busily on a cloth. 'The
points needed a scrape and I put a rag over the plugs for
you.'

This was well beyond the call of duty and I didn't know
how to thank him enough until, suddenly inspired, I
suggested he take the Healey out for a spin.

'Really? I'd love to.' He grinned like a schoolboy.

'Of course. We ought to give her a test run.'

Gingerly he turned out into the misty lane and tenta-
tively accelerated. The engine, a bit cold, hiccuped at
low revs. When the road opened out more Bob glanced
at me, as if requesting permission.

'Go ahead,' I said encouragingly, 'but take it easy.'

Although there was a stranger at the wheel, I could feel
the tremendous surge of power as the turbo-charger
rammed air into the Healey's cylinders. Previously, the
car had been a wild, unruly, strong-mouthed creature
needing firm handling and the odd cuff over the ear to
make her behave. Now she had the heart and power of
a thing demented. It was not sport any more. Keeping
hold of her would be a matter of life or death. I would
be like Evel Knieval on his rocket, looking for a canyon
to jump.

Bob Henderson was having a thrill a second but I
doubted that he had depressed the accelerator pedal

more than an inch. It had five inches of travel.

However, his gentle driving betrayed a certain unevenness in the engine. Knowing that the quality of French petrol was poor compared with our own in Britain, I asked if we couldn't find some real five-star quality petrol somehow.

'Only at the airfield,' he said.

'Why the airfield?'

'The French av-gas is one hundred octane, about the same as five-star. It is the best petrol in the country but it's green, and that means you mustn't use it on the roads because the tax system is different.'

'Who says so? Could you fix it?'

He shrugged non-committally. 'It's worth a try. I know a chap who works there.'

The airfield was seven miles away, a quiet grass-strip with a single fluorescent-orange wind-sock hanging as limp as pasta from its pole, and a pair of Cessnas pulled up in front of a corrugated-iron hangar.

Top-quality fuel made all the difference but it had cost twenty top-quality pounds sterling passed under the counter, in addition to the price of twenty-five gallons of av-gas itself. On the way back to the farm we stopped twice to make final adjustments to the carburettors. Josephine met us at the gate to say that breakfast was ready.

Bob Henderson had instructed her well in the art of English breakfast making: masses of cold ham heaped up with scrambled eggs, toast and home-made marmalade, a big china pot of thick coffee. Kristy had a large plate of yoghurt, fresh out of the churn, with a spoonful of black treacle.

The last few minutes before departure I spent trying to reduce weight in the car. I removed the wheelbrace and jack, and the spare wheel, and left them in the workshop promising to return to collect them later.

'We don't really need this,' I said, brandishing Kristy's bottle of champagne and thinking we could leave it with Josephine as a thank-you present.

'Oh yes we do!' Kristy contradicted decisively. 'It's for tonight, when we celebrate.'

There was just one more thing to arrange before leaving. Seeing me hunting around in the barn, Bob Henderson asked what I was looking for. When I explained my problem he said he knew just the thing, and whispered to his father-in-law. The farmer came out of the house a few moments later with a pair of *boules* which he presented to Kristy with a shy bow and a twinkling smile.

Overcome by the old man's generosity, Kristy mumbled her thanks and then kissed the white patch on top of his head – it turned quite pink as the old chap flushed with pleasure and delight.

Then his wife brought out a tall white plastic pot containing at least a quart of home-made yoghurt which she handed to me, saying I was to make sure Kristy ate it because she needed fattening up.

Despite the overload problem there was nothing for it but to accept graciously, and I stowed the pot upright in the narrow gap between the back of Kristy's seat and the petrol tank.

Kristy looked fit and fresh. The bruises had almost disappeared. She wore faded blue-jeans that looked as good on her as anything Bond Street could offer. The springbok diamond brooch was pinned to the collar of a modish pink shirt of Thai silk, and a red Swiss-cotton scarf was tied in gipsy style at the back of her head. She looked ravishing, though in the circumstances I would have preferred to have seen her in bone-dome crash helmet, and Nomex flame-resistant overalls, gloves, socks and face-mask, like the racing drivers wear. The temperature of burning petrol, I knew, was 2,500 degrees Fahrenheit.

In town it was market day. The wide square was cluttered with stalls selling fruit, vegetables, cheeses and cheap clothing. We found a parking place with difficulty and just before ten o'clock waited across the square from the *hotel de ville* where Ronald Blom would be facing the beak.

It took only a few moments to locate the Ferrari Dino, parked between a dung-spattered Deux Cheveaux and a rusty old Panhard. But I was alarmed also to see the Porsche, Jaguar and Corvette parked nearby among the cars which had come in from the country for market day. Fritz had gathered the troops.

On edge from waiting, I rubbed my hands together and hoped the court session would not drag on all day.

'I feel like I'm going on a para jump,' I said.

'Me too,' Kristy said with a faint shiver.

'Well, keep calm. Let's not get our knickers in a twist.'

At twenty-five minutes to eleven, clean-shaved, with his ginger hair glossed back and blue blazer buttoned over stripped shirt and some sort of club tie, Ronald Blom stepped jauntily out of the town hall. I watched through binoculars as Fritz and the others met him on the pavement. Whatever penalty had been imposed, it seemed to worry him little. He dragged deeply on a cigarette, throwing his head back and exhaling a long plume of smoke straight up in the air.

A surly Philip Fanselow consulted what looked like a Sealink timetable taken from the breast pocket of his Mercedes leather jacket. As Blom glanced at his gold wristwatch I would have given a lot to have been a fly on the wall. What route were they taking? How would they cross the Channel, and from which port?

Watching her cousin's relaxed and confident manner, Kristy ticked like an old clock.

'He looks too damn pleased with himself by half,' she said worriedly.

'After a night in jug it wouldn't be surprising if he was let off with a warning,' I said. 'He is crafty enough to be perfectly charming when he wants to be, and if he said the right things....'

Ronald Blom went up the steps again and gazed around the square as if trying to spot the Healey. He returned to the pavement and for some minutes spoke earnestly with the others who looked fed up and argumentative. But as they split up and went to their cars, Fritz as usual going with Ronny, I knew that he had got his way. I grabbed Kristy's hand and tugged her towards the side-street where we had parked.

'Let's go, the wagon train is moving out.'

We caught up with the convoy just beyond the square: four super-cars driving modestly in line ahead, led by the Ferrari and trailed by two gendarmes on black motor-cycles who were seeing them off the premises. Hanging well back, we followed. A mile out of town the gendarmes swung into the verge, giving the battered Healey a surprised look as it went by, making a noise like a hot tractor.

Last car in the line ahead of us was the dark blue Jaguar XJ-S, driven by Alec Dempster. Spotting the Healey in his mirror he tooted his horn three times in what was evidently a pre-arranged signal. The formation zoomed ahead. I wriggled my big toe a fraction of an inch and the Healey sprang up to the Jag, intent on rape. While it was reassuring to be able to keep up I hardly needed to read the trademark on its number plate. The power in *Ma Biche* was quite terrifying: the turbo-charged powerboat engine in the old car was the equivalent of a jet engine in a Tiger Moth, and for the first time I became acutely aware of just how frail and old fashioned the old darling really was.

As I pulled out to overtake Dempster weaved the Jaguar across the road, blocking, while the other three cars pushed ahead. So that was the strategy. Before I even got a smell of the Dino's exhausts I somehow had to knock out the other three cars. And that would be difficult.

Relaxed and travelling first class, Dempster would know nothing of the Healey's metamorphosis into a

Q-car, but already he must be wondering. It was time he learned a little more.

Gritting my teeth I jabbed hard at the heavy clutch pedal, palmed the stubby gear lever down to third. The clutch lashed back. At 85mph the rear end squirrelled all over the road and my heart burped up for a frightened look through my bared teeth. In the time it takes to gulp, the speedo registered in three figures.

Surprised to see the Healey alongside, Dempster fed the Jaguar's twelve cylinders every millimetre of throttle and the huge car creamed alongside as if poured from a jug.

Neck and neck we came out of a gentle right-hander at 115 mph and raced into a dip. As there were no hedges dividing the arable farmland, visibility of the road ahead was extensive and we could use it like a race track. Uneven tarmac tossed the Healey as if it was riding a brick trampoline, while the Jaguar's suspension swallowed the bumps as if they were cream cheese.

The mile of straight road ahead rose to a brow. One of us would have to give way. The blue wall of the Jag's passenger door bulged so close that I could have signed my name in the dust. Out of the corner of my eye I saw its door handle edge backwards as the Healey gained. But not quickly enough.

The XJ-S was built to eat Japanese salesmen and now it was making a meal of us.

Leaning over, I shouted at Kristy, 'How's your throwing arm?'

'What?'

Taking one hand off the kicking wheel for a split second I demonstrated what I wanted her to do. She looked thunderstruck for a moment then got busy, released her seat-belt, picked up the *boules* the farmer had given her, and crouched with one knee on her seat and her body doubled against the onslaught of the slipstream.

No time to work out the ballistical problems of throwing a milled steel cannonball from one speeding car to another. On the clock: 118mph. The Jag's front tyre was so close that its block tread whistling on the road screamed in my ear like a dynamo. But the long and balefully sloping bonnet alongside offered Kristy a large target.

The first *boule* hit the bonnet with a thunderclap, bounced, and dropped over the far side. The second was the shot of a *tireur*. It rolled the length of the Jaguar's nose with a rumble like a grand piano skidding on castors, cannoned up the windscreen in front of Dempster's horrified face, then rolled off.

With only yards to run, we suddenly had the road to ourselves. In the cracked mirror I saw the mauled Jaguar limping into the verge, scarcely damaged but totally defeated.

Straight as string, the road cut through undulating fields of sugar beet and young wheat. The other three cars were bunched closely together not a quarter of mile ahead, slowing as if confident of seeing the Jaguar appearing once more in their mirrors.

Instead, they saw the Healey boring down on them like a jet-propelled soap-box. Its crude air-scoop was aimed along the bonnet like a rocket-launcher. I wished it were loaded, but now we did not have even cannonballs.

Sweeping up on the Corvette, we saw Philip Fanselow's grizzled and bearded head outlined in its rear window. Of all the cars this one worried me least because I knew it had front wheel trouble. And I thought the magazine editor was the driver least likely to take real risks on the road. The others might easily be persuaded by Ronny's charm and guile, and the excitement of the drive itself, to have a bit of serious fun. But the idea would not appeal so much to their boss.

My confidence soon evaporated. Philip Fanselow was too clever by half. He stuck to the legal speed limit and placed the 'Vette firmly in the centre of the road, straddling the white line exactly so he had to twitch his steering wheel only a fraction, one way or the other, to keep the Healey boxed in while the Ferrari and the Porsche raced ahead, diminishing specks of red and green in the far distance.

Belting herself in her seat again, the red scarf blown away by the slipstream, Kristy glanced at me worriedly. I could see what she was thinking but what could I do? The Corvette moved over to let an oncoming car go by then instantly took up station again on the centre line. The only good thing was that the temperature needle, which had shot up during the burst of speed to pass the Jaguar, was dropping again. At 80mph in top gear the turbo-charger barely ticked over.

Fuming with impatience I blasted the horn and flashed the headlights but Fanselow drove like an old woman going to church and nothing would shift him.

The long straight ahead ended in a series of shallow bends descending to a bridge over a small brook, then a roundabout. The main road left the roundabout in the twelve o'clock position, climbed in a right-hand curve, and disappeared behind oak trees growing on the other side of the valley. As we began our descent I saw the Porsche dart behind the trees like a supersonic aphid.

Fanselow accelerated over the bridge as if he expected me to overtake, then swung right, into the roundabout. But there is more than one way of going round a circle.

Seeing the chance, I shouted to Kristy to hold tight. Kick-kicked the clutch. Slashed down to second. Hurled the Healey into the roundabout clockwise, which is contrary to the anti-clockwise direction that in France is considered customary and proper.

Lorry drivers alighting from their cab at a *Routiers* café on one corner gazed open-mouthed. Attendants at a service station opposite, arrested by the highly-bred howl of the Healey's engine, stood and stared. So did a couple of *flics* lounging beside a dark blue 404 on the forecourt.

With elbows flailing I fought the wheel as the Bitch played her usual dirty trick of trying to whip around and bite the master. Muzzling her with full left-lock, I glimpsed the Corvette abreast of me on the other side of the roundabout. And a dark-green Mini with a loaded roofrack, which had emerged from the screen of oaks and was cruising down the hill towards the junction.

Somehow I managed to straighten up. Corvette and Healey came out of the roundabout side by side. I flicked on the headlights. Floored the accelerator. The Mini had British plates. It weaved indecisively, braked, then stopped dead. Having approached her first continental roundabout and figured out the correct way to go around it, the poor girl at the wheel was now flummoxed.

And also in my way.

In the split second that remained before I had to brake or take a detour up the embankment, the Corvette fell back. Discretion being the better part, Philip Fanselow opted out.

Thank God.

At the top of the hill the road straightened out for another long run through hedgeless vistas of barley and wheat. It was also empty, but for a van coming towards us. The road surface was so bad, however, that the Healey bucked like a cross-country jeep and about 105 mph was as fast I dared go. Which was not enough to catch two cars with superior suspension systems now so far ahead that they were out of sight.

Landmarks of a town began to show in the blue-white haze of the distance. Church towers and gasometers, factories, apartment buildings, chimneys. It was the town of Abbeville, from which half a dozen main and secondary roads radiated to all points of the compass.

If Ronald Blom had any sense he would have switched up a side-road by now and be lying like low. Even if it was not his style to go to ground, like a fox, he would try to lose us in the town.

Squeezing Kristy's hand encouragingly, I said, 'That's

two down.'

She nodded in a way that showed she would be glad when it was all over. 'How is the engine?'

'Hot.' The temperature was rising again rather fast. 'But don't worry,' I told her with a breezy confidence I was far from feeling, 'the old Bitch won't let us down now.'

The road dropped down the side of a gentle hill. The buildings of Abbeville took shape on the far bank of the Somme which we would cross in the valley below.

I reckoned we had sixty seconds in which to sight the Porsche or the Ferrari, then we would have to admit they had lost us.

But Van Blommenstein had put in a good word, if not with the angels, then with the local traffic controller on the railways. For at the bottom of the hill, running parallel with the river, was a railway line. And at the level-crossing the red and white pole barriers were just going up as we trickled down the slope to join the tail end of the traffic queue that had been waiting for a goods train to pass. In low gear we rattled over the lines, taking it easy for the sake of the rickety low-slung silencers. There was no particular hurry, for the Porsche and the Ferrari were now only a few feet ahead of us.

Certain of being able to lose us again in open country, Ronald Blom did not try to shake us off in the busy streets of Abbeville. Instead, he took a right turn on to a dual carriageway boulevard that bypassed the town centre and came out on the N1 highway heading north. A signpost indicated Boulogne 80 kilometres, only fifty miles.

The rolling chalk downs between Abbeville and Boulogne were our last chance, but we had to catch two cars. Nerves taut, eyes straining, fingers tingling, I hardly felt the warm wind spilling over the windscreen or noticed the beauty of the sweeping green landscapes beneath the bright sky.

Graham Wilson was a brisk driver. When I started to

pull up to the Porsche he rocketed away, closing up on the Ferrari and flashing his lights. Buzzing like a bee in a box, the Ferrari cracked on more speed. Both cars peeled off on a side-road that twisted through woods, a slow route through beautiful scenery, but all I noticed of it was the steady shower of dust and gravel thrown up by the Porsche's rear wheels as Wilson clipped every corner. Screwing the car into each bend with vigour and panache, Wilson drove like a downhill skier. The mawkish Healey could only follow and spit dust.

But the woods did not go on for ever, and when the road opened out again into the characteristic open and unfenced fields there was only one course left.

For the first time I depressed the accelerator its full five inches. And held it there.

With half an eye on the bomber's pressure-gauge, I saw the effects of the turbo-charger coming in, felt the punch of the cylinders being force-fed compressed air. Engine noise enveloped us in a screaming tidal wave. Heat coming through the floor from the exhausts caused beads of sweat to roll down my legs.

A line of poplar trees went by as a solid wall. The speedo touched 110 mph. Revs just under seven thousand. Whip-crack change into top. Roaring up the turbulence into the tunnel of the Porsche's slipstream. Its tail came up fast. Pulled out, now tunnelling our own hole through solid air. At 125 mph the Healey's impetus faltered, still making ground but less quickly.

Inch by terrifying inch up to the Porsche. Lit by the sun flaring through the open roof, Graham Wilson's face was set in a scowl of concentration. Cockpit instruments were reflected strangely on his owlish spectacles. He was a bloody fine driver. I sensed his determination and respected it. The next bend was coming up fast and I couldn't expect him to give an inch.

The Healey might well be able to overtake before the bend, but could I get the power-flooded old banger around it when I got there?

Something to celebrate, Kristy had said.

I burrowed my hand behind her seat and extracted the bottle of champers. The bottle was hot to touch. I thrust it into Kristy's lap and signalled her to take the wire off. She did it quickly and gave the cork a loosening twist.

I snatched the bottle and gave it a hard shake. Then lobbed it through the Porsche's open roof.

The cork popped with a loud report as the bottle hit the edge of the roof. Spouting hot champagne like a geyser it dropped into the car, soaked Wilson to the armpits, sprayed the inside of the windscreen.

There was a scream of tyres, heard momentarily above the howl of the engine as the Healey moved in front.

Three down, one to go.

Now there was nothing but three hundred yards of open road between us – and the Ferrari, Ronald Blom, and the Blue Hurricane.

Ferrari Dino 308 GT4 2 + 2.

Ferrari because it wears the black prancing horse emblem of a First World War fighter ace, which was adopted by Enzo Ferrari as the seal of magic worked on all his cars.

Dino after the *commendatore's* own son, the pride and joy of his life, who died of leukaemia in 1956 aged twenty-four.

Three-oh-eight: three hundred and eight millimetres of piston thrust, thousands of times per minute, developing two hundred and fifty-five brake horsepower at seven-and-a-half thousand revs.

GT4 for Gran Turisomo number four, a grand tourer in which designers, engineers and stylists have got virtually all their sums right.

Two plus two: two front seats, two back seats.

It is a tiny jewel of a car that is the nearest you get to motoring perfection this side of twenty thousand pounds. Or the other side, for that matter. In a Dino you do not listen to the quadrophonic sound but to the beautiful music of four scrambling camshafts and the faint excited gnashing of valve gear. You take off in an aura of whirring, clicking, lubricated metallic glory and move so low to the ground that if you bump over a penny you know by feel whether it is heads or tails.

Italian cars usually have the pedals too close and the wheel too far away, but the Dino is just right. A small leather-covered steering-wheel, the black horse prancing on a yellow disc in the centre; you steer with the wrists, precisely, like aiming a dart. The raked windscreen is such a sun-trap that without air conditioning the driver wilts like a cut flower.

The Dino's chisel-lip look is the artistry of Bertone. Simply, it is an intelligent modification of the fish shape. Artistically, it is an aesthetic concept: plain metal, smoothly-flowing line, unadorned.

This is a car that sticks to the road like rain. Handling and road-holding characteristics are impeccable. Its engine is so wonderfully flexible that in top gear you can bottle through town at twenty-five, or flash down the back straight at a hundred and sixty plus. The Dino goes as it looks.

Versus the Bitch. A once-upon-a-time Austin Healey thrust by an immense American engine out of a powerboat. A car with the sticking quality of a pair of skates, the body-and-soul comforts of a tractor, and such manoeuverability on very tight hilly bends that in Wales I had once been overtaken by a plumber's Mini-van.

But six hundred turbo-charged horses to the Ferrari's two hundred and fifty-five. And, well, a will to win.

It is not enouth to have just a fast car. The driver is not a piece of freight but one of the car's constituent components. As any racing driver knows, enthusiasm alone is not what wins races. What matters is the courage and skill to push the car all the way to what Stirling Moss called the ragged edge – disaster minus half a mile per hour.

Did I have that courage and concentration, and trust in the car? More to the point, did Ronald Blom?

As the Porsche vanished in a blur of bubbly I kept my foot hard down to draw up on the Ferrari. The next bend was so shallow that in a family car doing seventy, or in the beautifully balanced Ferrari at twice the speed, you would hardly know it was there. At 132 mph it came at the Healey like a hairpin and I knew how it felt to be Ben Hur in his chariot. All I could do was hang on to the horses.

Water temperature: climbing fast. Oil pressure: dropping. The heat round my feet was intense. Kristy propped her feet up on the transmission tunnel to stop them burning.

The Bitch moved like she had never moved before but it just was not fast enough. For five minutes we clung to the Dino as best we could. Down to 70mph for the sharper corners, building up speed again on the straights, driving like a demon. Soon the Healey's engine would boil and seize up. Or explode.

The fuel gauge plummeted as the precious green av-gas was soaked up at seven miles to the gallon. As the tank emptied the weight in the rear grew less and the car cornered better, which was something.

Glimpsing signposts to Boulogne, to St Omer, I lost all sense of direction. Just drove, thinking of nothing but keeping the car on the road and as close as possible to the thing that sneaked round corners ahead as lightly as an aerodynamic germ.

Then I was struck by an idea so simple, so basic, that I thumped the steering-wheel with rage at not having thought of it before.

Kristy glanced at me in alarm. I pointed to the knurled knob that held the windscreen in place on her side of the car and told her to undo it.

The windscreen jutted into the slipstream like an immense air brake. If it could be slid forwards to its

257

secondary mounting then reclined almost flat into its streamlined position we would get another eight or ten mph. It could make all the difference.

On a bendy stretch, clocking 75mph, I loosened the knob on my side. With only one hand, moving the windscreen forward proved nerve-wrackingly difficult.

Inevitably, I dropped the knob. I was left in the ridiculous position of steering with one hand and supporting a wind-buffeted windscreen with the other, unable to let go of either.

Then two things happened.

The Healey hit uneven tarmac and bounced into the centre of a sharpish bend that ought properly to have been taken at about 25mph rather than at more than double the speed.

And a ten-ton Saviem loaded with fertiliser and hanging well out over the centre line came round the bend towards us.

I let the windscreen go and ducked as it flicked over my head. Then I twitched the car into the grass verge. Hitting grassy tussocks it went up on two wheels. Came down with a thump that shook the windscreen off its single remaining mounting. Dropped one of its two loose exhaust pipes into the road.

As the lorry whipped past I cracked down two gears. The Healey dug her way out of the vegetation and lurched out of the bend.

Unsilenced, the engine noise was now hardly bearable. With no windscreen, slipstream blasted directly into our faces. Kristy put her hands over her ears and bent her head below the level of the dash, her mouth working as she protested her terror, but I could hear nothing of what she said.

A man would have to be mad to put up with this, for the sake of a flower.

The exhaust pipe had snapped just below the foot-well on my side. Super-hot gases and sparks blasted the under-side of the floor-pan. The rubber mat beneath the pedals began to melt. The carpet over the transmission tunnel smouldered, filling our eyes with stinging smoke.

In his mirror Ronald Blom must have seen something amiss. The Ferrari was perceptibly slowing. If we crashed or blew up he would want to come back to gloat.

It was his fatal error.

We were close enough to see the prancing horse on its yellow badge when Ronald Blom realized that despite the smoke and the unbelievably strident noise he was in danger of being overtaken.

135mph ... 137 ... 138....

Even above the noise I could hear Kristy screaming. 'Stop it, stop it!' Or perhaps I couldn't hear. Just knew.

The turbo-charger pressure gauge read twenty-four inches of mercury. Air was being pushed into the cylinders at a pressure of twelve pounds per square inch.

Almost lying in my seat to keep my head low in the slipstream, steering with straight arms and my legs arched high because the floor-pan was glowing red, my eyes began to smart from the smoke and the acrid fumes of burning rubber.

139 ... 140....

This was ten-tenths. Right on the ragged edge.

And at the end of this straight we would have to stop.

But the Ferrari was no longer holding. The Healey gained. I pulled out to pass.

One hundred and forty-two miles per hour on the clock.

Dear God.

I prayed Ronald Blom would not try to block.

Through the tinted side window I glimpsed Fritz burying her face in her hands.

The windscreen came level. Then the wide sloping

bonnet. But we were running out of tarmac. At 146mph we ate up road at 214 feet per second.

Halfway down the straight. Ten seconds to do something.

We had no gun. No lassoo. No more runway.

Then Kristy came up with the large pot of farm-grown yoghurt. Nicely cooked by now.

I spiked the lid of greaseproof paper against the handbrake button. Held the pot over the side of the Healey. Flung it downwards with all my strength on the Ferrari Dino's streamlined red nose.

Carried by the slipstream, the junkety tide of curdled milk spread along the bonnet and slid up the curved windscreen as smoothly as cream running over the back of a hot coffee spoon.

In a blink the Ferrari was no longer there. With windscreen smearing uselessly, Ronald Blom panic-braked.

With relief I lifted my foot off the accelerator and the supersonic boom in which we were riding began to die. It was difficult to brake because the pedal was sizzling hot. I hoped the fluid had not boiled away.

In the mirror I saw the Ferrari hit the grass verge, spin, hit the other verge, then vanish behind a williwaw of dust.

13 : AND DRIED

Blinded by something resembling an enormous seagull dropping, the Ferrari Dino had waltzed out of control across the wide grass verge, hit a bump, spun, and run backwards into the only barbed-wire fence for miles. The noise of the crash stampeded a herd of black cattle across the field. When I reversed up in the Healey and got out they were still running.

The silence after I switched off was acute. Just the pounding of hooves becoming fainter and the outraged squawking of a pair of magpies circling over a silage heap.

Two for joy....

The Dino's nearside front wheel was bent at an odd angle beneath the wing so the car was down in one corner. The rear end had crunched a heavy fence post.

Running, I wrenched open the passenger door and saw Fritz bowed in her seat, frightened, shocked, semi-hysterical but not injured. With seat-belts and high-backed, suede-covered seats the occupants had been well protected.

Ronald Blom got out of the car with the set, ruthless, fearful look of a man one step from throwing himself under a train. Like wasps, his opaquely orange eyes darted aimlessly. A violent red flush rose thermometer-like through his white face as his temper came up to the boil.

Staggering, wiping his down-twisted mouth with the back of one hand, he came round the front of the car. In his other hand was the gun I had seen once before, when Bruno Feraldi was waving it around in the greenhouse.

261

So he had got it back from the Carabinieri.

The wasp eyes alighted briefly. His voice shook with rage yet was menacingly controlled.

'Listen, old man, you've bitched me around quite enough. I need your car so give me the keys.'

Instinctively I had taken the keys from the ignition when I switched off and was holding them in my hand. Now I lobbed them into the grass at his feet. In a reflex gesture that was hardly public school he spat in my hand as he stepped back.

'Bastard! Pick them up!'

I reached forward and sensed the down-swing of his arm as he tried to swipe the top of my head with the heavy butt of the big revolver.

As I dodged, Kristy struck the plunger of the two-kilo-gramme dry-powder fire-extinguisher which she had removed from its clip in the Healey. Coarse white sand jetted twenty feet, spraying Ronald Blom in the face and chest. I went for his knees. Sharp grains of sand fell thickly in my hair, ears and down my neck as he toppled on the mown grass, shielding his eyes with his arms. I tore the revolver from his hand and threw it away then got astride him, picked him up by the shirt front, and with a haymaker of a blow hit him squarely on the chin. With a grunt his head snapped back, his feet danced as he tried to keep his balance, and he sat down in the yoghurt on the Ferrari's bonnet.

Once turned on, the fire extinguisher could not be stopped and I shouted to Kristy to spray it on the Healey's smouldering carpet.

Ronald Blom shook his head dazedly, staring in disgust at the yoghurt mess on his hands: a picture of sagging *sang-froid*.

'Come on, hand it over,' I said.

'Hand what over, sport?'

I clicked my fingers impatiently.

'Cut the crap, you know what I mean.'

'God, you never let up, do you? You're like a bloody

boy scout!'

He looked round at Kristy, as if seeking support. She was holding the expended fire-extinguisher cylinder as if it were a loaded shotgun and liable to go off at any moment.

'Give it to him, Ronny,' she said coldly.

He cocked an eyebrow and met my gaze.

'Simply haven't got it, old chap.'

It was the affected 'old chap' that did it, the drawling, contemptuous, posturing voice that released a flood of vivid memories, of chukka boots thudding into my stomach aboard *Bonnie Jean*, of sparks whirling over the Villa Maddalena, of the Healey dismantled in a hundred pieces, of Kristy's grey face as she doubled up in the doorway at Arles.

With a shout of rage, I flew at him.

He was expecting it, of course. He rolled back on the bonnet, brought both feet up, and slammed them into my stomach. With a searing flash of agony I knew what a tyre feels like when it suffers a blow-out on the motorway. But as I doubled up I managed to lock my arms round Blom's legs and haul him bodily off the slippery bonnet on to the grass. My lungs seemed filled with red triangles. I fought hard for breath and through a red fog heard Kristy screaming my name. It was only as my breath came back that I realized I had my hands round Blom's throat and his eyes were popping, his face turning an unhealthy shade of purple. I had come within an inch of murdering the bastard without realizing it, and the shock made me let go. Blom rolled over with a groan, whispering 'Sweet Jesus!' and coughing.

I turned him over with my foot and told him to get up.

'You know what we want,' I gasped.

He pulled himself up to his hands and knees, then tottered upright and made a signal to Fritz who popped the Ferrari's boot-catch. Grimacing with pain, Blom lifted the lid and took out a large case made of shiny aluminium. He flicked the catches and opened it to reveal two cameras with an assortment of lenses and accessories lying in foam-rubber padding: it was Fritz's camera box. Fritz herself, pale-faced and scared, started to get out of the car when she saw what Blom was doing.

Too late.

Far from being at death's door when I released my thumbs from around his neck, Blom had been putting on the performance of his life. Now, as I reached across the car for the open camera case, he sprang aside and slammed the car's boot lid downwards to trap my hands. I jumped away to avoid being hit but Blom had the heavy Hasselblad camera body hanging from a strap in his hand and as I momentarily lost balance it whirled at me like a brick on a rope. The camera caught me a painful whack on the point of the shoulder then rang with an expensive breaking noise on the car's thin shell. Fritz screamed hysterically, pounding Blom on the chest so violently that he staggered backwards several steps. Then Fritz scrabbled among the lenses in the aluminium case, pulled out the plastic bag containing the plant, and lobbed it in the air.

I caught it neatly as she cried, 'Take the damn thing and leave us alone, for pity's sake....'

'Stupid bitch!' Blom yelled, darting forward in an effort to catch the plant, but Fritz stepped in his way and frantically ripped the broken camera out of his grip.

Kristy took the plastic bag from me, opened it anxiously, and shook the plant out into her hand.

'I think it ought to survive,' she said, after inspecting it critically.

'I suppose it is the right one this time.'

'Seems to be.'

'What about him?' I asked. Ronald Blom was trying to brush and scrape the congealed yoghurt and grass off his cuffs. The back of his blazer and the seat of his trousers were a mess.

'Leave him, John!'

'I want to tear the bugger apart.'

'No!' Kristy made as if to head me off, her face nearer to panic than it had been at any time during the frightening chase along the roads.

Ronald Blom leaned his rump on the roof of the Ferrari and beckoned at Fritz.

'Quick, give me a gasper!'

A dusty old Citroen 2CV, leaning as it rounded the corner like a dog cocking its leg, braked sharply. The red-faced farmer at the wheel began to pull in at what he thought was a road accident. I waved him on with a fierce gesture.

'Tell me, Ronny,' I asked conversationally, 'the property company with which you hold a consultancy – it is the one which holds Van Blommenstein's mortgage, right?'

At first he was determined not to answer but he read something in my eyes and nodded.

'What were you getting out of it?' I pressed.

'Only ten thousand and expenses.' His voice was husky and disinterested.

'And a percentage on the deal once you had delivered the place to them on a plate, eh?'

Blom shrugged. 'Only five per cent. Neither here nor there.'

'And what did you pay Feraldi to dynamite the water?'

'Two hundred quid. It was quite a cheap job, that one. But so easy....'

Far from looking the least bit humble as he spilled out these revelations, he became jauntily belligerent. The man was completely without shame.

'But why?' Kristy asked.

Blom laughed at her and my knuckles clenched.

'I never did understand why you were hooked on that patronizing, selfish, stubborn old twit....'

He was interrupted by the hum of a powerful engine

and the blue Jaguar swept into view, braking hard. It pulled up ahead of the Healey. Moments later the Porsche and the Corvette pulled in.

Philip Fanselow rocked on his heels when he saw the damaged Ferrari. The other drivers whistled, circling the lamed car and darting puzzled, dismayed glances. Not at Ronald Blom, who took no notice of them at all, but at me. Fanselow confronted me angrily.

'I suppose you're responsible for this too, you maniac! Where is your sense of humour, man? I mean, it's one thing having a bit of a dice on the road, but this, look at the damage!'

Facing him squarely and fixing him with a steady stare, I said through gritted jaw, 'Dice nothing! You elected to take part and you knew the risks. As for my sense of humour, it deserted me the first time I ever clapped eyes on Ronald Blom. But I can tell you one thing, it's coming back to me fast looking at you lot!'

Fanselow continued plaintively as if I had not said a word.

'The Ferrari is a tow-truck job, the Corvette will be in the body shop for a week, the Porsche smells like a pub at closing time, the Jaguar needs a new bonnet and the windscreen is cracked.'

'Bloody madman,' Graham Wilson muttered darkly.

'Incredible!' Alec Dempster echoed, the image of the steel *boule* rolling towards him evidently large and vivid in his mind.

Hands in pockets, cigarette cocked upwards in his mouth and smoke streaming away in the breeze, Ronald Blom strolled languidly away from the wrecked car as if he disowned the whole affair.

As I took Kristy's arm and led her to the Healey the idea of somehow immobilizing the other three cars crossed my mind. It would be poetic justice to take the rotor arms from their distributors and mail them to a *poste restante* address in Boulogne. That would slow them up a bit. But I did not have the heart. Perhaps Blom

266

was right, I would always be a number two man. Nor did I have a mind for detail. Like the loaded revolver still lying in the grass where I had tossed it.

'Wait one!' Blom's tone had a Sandhurst snap to it as he stood erect and faced us, the gun in his hand. The three writers gasped, shaken to the core by the sight. They stared, open-mouthed, as Blom approached Kristy and me and held out his hand. It was not me at whom he aimed the gun but Kristy, and I could see from the bright stare in his eyes that now he clung to sanity by a thread. The man was as sinister as a rabid dog. I gave him what he wanted at once.

'And the car keys. Nicely this time.' I handed them over and he grinned widely.

'There's a good boy.'

An expression of alarm crossed Blom's face as we heard the distant sound of a Police klaxon getting louder by the second, and he jogged to the Healey then climbed in.

Fanselow started forward. 'What the hell?'

I shouted at Blom: 'You can't drive that thing!'

With a finger on the starter he turned back to look at me over his shoulder and sneered, 'Don't make me laugh!'

The steadily growing sound of the klaxon was engulfed by a succession of loud backfires then the Healey's engine settled into a splintered howl. As Blom experimentedly marked time on the accelerator while finding first gear, the noise sent shrapnel through the eardrums. Fanselow and Wilson turned away, their hands over their ears.

I ran towards the Healey and shouted. It had the desired effect.

Blom quickly pocketed the gun, gripped the steering-wheel with both hands, and lifted his foot off the clutch.

Accustomed to the tamed refinement of the Ferrari Dino, he did not know the vicious, spring-loaded clutch pedal had a recoil like the kick of a blunderbuss. Not for nothing did you need to drive her with hob-nailed boots.

Nor did he know the Bitch had a mind of her own.

The car sprang away from rest like a predatory beast. Smack into the rear end of the beautiful Jaguar parked twenty feet ahead. The impact pushed the nose of the Jag into the tail of the Porsche which ran gently forward and bumped the Corvette.

Grand slam!

Stunned by the steering-wheel, Blom flopped unconscious in the driving seat but I reached him just in time to pocket the blue chrysanthemum before the Peugeot 404 with the blue light drew alongside with a loud squeal of tyres.

Like a motorway service station that has suddenly found its feet, the great blue and white Seaspeed hovercraft got up on its cushion of air. Self-importantly puffing out its black rubber skirts, it lurched in a crabbing turn down the concrete ramp and skimmed over the wide sandy beach of the hoverport at Boulogne, heading for England.

Sharing a pair of reclining armchair seats near the forward end of the starboard cabin, Kristy and I held hands with the candour of honeymooners. Not because we were demonstrative or frightened, but to reassure each other that this really was the last lap. In less than an hour we would be ashore at Dover, looking for a train to Victoria.

The tide was a long way out and for a few moments, as the hovercraft skimmed over the sand like some ethereal garage, we had a clear view ahead of the Channel waters. For once they were burnished a bright silvery-blue with hardly a ripple disturbing the mirrored reflection of the cloudless sky. It was early evening and the sun was getting low, flaring in our eyes as it bounced off the water. Then it was blotted out by clouds of spray that boiled around the windows like steam and the hovercraft began to pick up speed as it rounded the end of the breakwater.

The day had continued as nightmarishly as it had begun, but in a different way. Seeing Ronald Blom slumped at the wheel of the Healey, the intelligent gendarmes assumed it was he who had taken the roundabout the wrong way and nearly written off the British Mini. They took details of his name and address from Kristy as Philip Fanselow and the others laid him out on the grass and tried to revive him. Then the long white Citroen ambulance summoned by radio swished on to the scene. Blom had begun to return to consciousness as he was manhandled on to the stretcher and trundled into the back of the ambulance on rubber wheels.

Puzzled by the yoghurt smeared on the Ferrari's windscreen, the gendarmes questioned us at length but we closed ranks and played dumb in a British sort of way. Shaken by the sight of their guv'nor threatening to use a gun, and less under his influence now that he had been removed, the *Go-Fast* team were evidently thinking they had misjudged me. Kristy gave the police the lame explanation that a carton of yoghurt had fallen off a lorry as we overtook, and the others had backed her up vigorously. When Philip Fanselow broke what might have developed into a deadlock by waving his cross-Channel ferry tickets, the *flics* caved in and waved him off, concluding that if we were leaving the country in any case it would be good riddance and much less work. Though slightly damaged, the Jaguar, Porsche and Corvette were mobile; Fanselow told the Police he would arrange a tow-truck for the Ferrari when he reached Boulogne.

When the writers had disappeared in their three cars, taking a bemused Fritz along with them, the gendarmes helped me push the Healey on to the verge, then gave Kristy and myself a lift to Abbeville where they took a short, formal statement in writing and allowed me to use a phone to get hold of Bob Henderson. Driving his father-in-law's Renault van with a big box of tools in the back, he met us outside the *gendarmerie* an hour and a half later. When we had seen off a reviving bottle of wine together he drove us out to the Healey. The tow-truck had already arrived and was hooking up the Ferrari. Bob joked with the mechanics until they drove gingerly away, then helped me poke around the Healey. Not only was the front end stove in and the exhausts shot, but much of the wiring around the motor had lost its insulation from the heat. It was a miracle that it had kept going for so long. On Bob's suggestion I bypassed the turbo-charger once again, then limped the car six miles up the road to St Omer where Bob had a friend with a work-shop. Then he had delivered us to Boulogne in the van and left us at the hoverport. We had just missed a sailing, so it was a wait of nearly two hours for the next. At any moment, during the long wait, I had expected something to go wrong and had prowled restlessly while Kristy tried fruitlessly to make me sit down and be patient. With nothing to do my nerves had tinkled like Christmas bells, and when we finally got on board the thing there was another exasperating delay until the ramps were raised and the engines fired with a high-pitched, jet-prop whistle.

Now the hovercraft was moving fast and Kristy sat back in her chair with a deep sigh.

'Penny for them,' I said.

'I was just thinking that poor old Ronny will take a long time to live this down.'

'Ronny doesn't know how lucky he is,' I corrected. 'I was ready to snuff the sod. Would have done, if you hadn't been so squeamish.'

Kristy glanced at me worriedly to check that I was teasing her, and was reassured by the sardonic grin I painted rapidly on my face. She patted my knee.

'I'm glad you didn't. He will leave me alone now.'

'Don't count on it,' I muttered.

Disappointed at losing the view ahead because of spray I turned in my seat to look back along the cabin, hoping at least one window offered visibility. There was only a score of passengers in the long compartment running the full length of the hovercraft's starboard side. The seats behind us, for three rows back, were empty. Other passengers were scattered nearer the stern. A stewardess in a blue uniform with a red cap moved among them pushing a wheeled trolley loaded with cartons of cigarettes and bottles of spirits in presentation boxes.

It was the tilt of the man's head as he snapped a lighter to the end of a cigarette that caught my eye. The strange mannerism of jerking his head back and blowing a plume of smoke vertically into the air. The way he held the cigarette deep in the vee of his fingers.

He was a dozen rows back, wearing sunglasses. A cheap straw beach hat covered his ginger hair.

My mind reeling, I faced the blurred windows in front. The hollow in my belly felt as big as the Atlantic. Struggling to keep my voice level and calm, I said to Kristy, 'I'm afraid we've got company.'

'What do you mean? Who?'

'Cousin Ronald is travelling with us.'

'Oh no!'

It was Ronald Blom himself who answered, 'Oh yes!' He stood in the aisle, blocking us in our seats.

He had removed his sunglasses. Dark smudges showed where the bruises were growing on his cheeks from the beating I had given him. A large square of white sticking-plaster over a gauze pad covered the bump from the steering-wheel that had knocked him out. His hair was damp and slicked back: he had obviously freshened up somewhere. The silly straw hat was pushed to the back of his head and he was in shirt sleeves, the cuffs of his striped shirt held with oval links of thin gold. The cigarette jutted from the corner of his mouth and he narrowed his eyes against the smoke. He looked like a gangster in a pantomime, but there was nothing of Mother Goose in his burning eyes.

An Air France bag was slung on a long strap over his shoulder so it hung almost down to his waist. The zip was open, his right hand thrust inside, and I suspected it was neither his passport nor his traveller's cheques that he gripped in his fist.

Looking more than usually smug, he rested his free arm on the back of the seats in front and leaned over so the end of the airline bag pointed directly at my chest.

After the first startled moment of recognition Kristy sagged ashen-faced into her seat next to the window, turning her head away and staring into the pearly spray.

I nodded coolly.

'Hello, Ronny.'

The lumpy plastic bag in the pocket of my anorak suddenly weighed a ton. Without shifting his elbow he turned his left hand palm upwards, the meaning perfectly clear. I wished I had the nerve to spit in it.

Catching a whiff of unpleasant odour from his sweat-stained armpit I waved a hand in front of my nose. 'You need a bath, old chap.'

His voice snapped like the stem of a wine glass breaking. 'Come along....'

'How on earth did you get to Boulogne?'

'There are such things as taxis in France, you know.'

'Congratulations,' I said limply. But from my first close look at him I knew that Ronald Blom was far from being his usual dapper self. He had lost his cool. His eyes darted furtively behind the orange eyelashes drawn now into thin slits. The muscles of his jaw worked as if he were chewing on a gob of Juicy Fruit and his palm-out hand trembled. Sweat prickled his pale brow and I suspected the bump on the head was pounding like a pneumatic drill. He looked mean and dangerous, but while I turned all this over in my mind it was Kristy who spoke up.

'We're not such perfect fools as you suppose,' she said archly. 'The plant was wrapped up in a parcel and posted from Boulogne to an address in England. It will be there in a couple of days, and arrive in good condition. It was the ideal way of getting it through Customs.'

Blom pulled a folded paper from his shirt pocket and dropped it into Kristy's lap. As she folded it out he said, 'You should have given it to me: that's the sanitation certificate Feraldi got out for it. But I know you've got it, so....' He paused, then moved his right hand significantly inside the airline bag and I saw the pistol which I had last seen aboard the yacht *Bonnie Jean* when she was boarded in the middle of the night.

'Golly gosh, the two-gun kid!' I mocked. 'You would never use that thing in here. It's Dover we're going to, not Havana. You would be arrested as soon as you stepped ashore.'

The airline bag swung sideways a fraction and there was a sharp coughing noise, like the muffled popping of a cork. A round hole appeared in the upholstery of the seat in front. A strong smell of cordite issued from a similar round hole in the end of the airline bag as it moved and pressed firmly into my chest.

Frightened, I stared up at Ronny. His face was set and stiff, as if made of wax. His senses had deserted him completely.

'End of funny games,' he whispered. 'I want that bloody plant. I need it. Hand it over. Right now.'

The trolley loaded with cigarettes and spirits bumped against Ronald Blom's heel. Startled, he moved closer to the seats to make room in the aisle. The stewardess apologized with a plastic smile.

'Duty frees for you?'

Dropping my left hand outside the armrest I gripped the horizontal chromium tube forming the axle of the trolley, then stood upright, hurling the trolley upwards and forwards with all my strength.

The stewardess shrieked.

Ronald Blom leapt backwards, cursing, as cartons and bottles crashed around his feet.

'Hi-jacker!' I yelled. 'Stop that man, he's got a gun!'

It had the desired effect.

In struggling to retain his balance, Ronald Blom's right hand came out of the airline bag still holding the silenced pistol. The girl screamed again, cowering against the wall. I still had hold of the aluminium trolley. Made for use in aircraft, it was very light in weight. I held it in front of me then tossed it forwards. There was a tinny clang as a bullet passed through the thin metal and plucked at the padding of my anorak. My foot hit a rolling whisky bottle and I stumbled, sprawling face-down among the wreckage.

Ronald Blom thought he had shot me. In two strides he grabbed Kristy, shoved the pistol barrel into the pit of her stomach, spun her round, and dragged her back-wards down the aisle.

I lay doggo, collecting my wits, as the other passenger cried out in alarm, peering forwards to see what was happening. My fall had been so sudden that for a moment I, too, thought I had been shot and it took a few seconds of gingerly testing my limbs to check things out.

Blom and Kristy disappeared through a door leading to the car deck. I jumped up and saw him pushing her ahead of him up a steep narrow ladder leading upwards through a trapdoor. A notice on the bulkhead said Flight Crew Only.

In the cabin the stewardess, pale and weeping, had recovered sufficiently to lift a telephone headset to warn the captain. It would be too late for him to do anything, for Blom would have Kristy on the flight deck by now.

I had registered the look of utter dismay on Ronald Blom's face as he jerked the gun out of the airline bag and he realized he had gone too far to back out. I had intended it to be a neat trap but it was proving to be a disaster.

How could Blom get himself out of this mess? If the captain was prevented from sending out a radio message Blom might direct him to return the hovercraft to Boulogne, only seven or eight minutes away. When the landing ramp was lowered, and with his gun at Kristy's head, Blom stood some chance of getting away before the police were alerted.

But it was Kristy I was worried about. Blom was mad enough to shoot her out of hand, or in sheer panic. After a frantic search I found no other access to the flight deck. If I put my head up through the trapdoor Blom would put a bullet through it.

There might be one other way, however.

Halfway along the cabin was an emergency exit. I pushed through the white-faced passengers. Instructions on the door were simple. I yanked the handle in the direction of the arrow and tugged. The door swung inwards and upwards. A curtain of fine salt spray streamed into the cabin with the intensely loud scream of the engine and this, more than anything that had happened before, unnerved the passengers. There were screams of terror from the cabin as I hoisted myself on to the step. Squinting into the flying spray and the hovercraft's 40-knot slipstream, I looked out.

Below the windows was a ledge a few inches wide. Wind and spray lashed my body as I walked forwards past rows of liferaft cannisters and found a ladder leading to the roof of the vessel.

It was an open deck not designed for access during flight. There were no hand rails. Only a vast expanse of smooth aluminium, ribbed in places for reinforcement. Mounted on pods in each of the four corners of the deck were the 20-foot, four-bladed propellors which whirled in a barely visible blur. Below each pod were two elliptical air-intakes. Each was a semi-circular well, with a diameter of about eight feet, smoothly contoured for the best aerodynamic flow as air was sucked through them into the lift-fans revolving at high speed at the bottom of the holes. The lift-fans blew the air beneath the hovercraft's fuselage to lift it above the land or water it was travelling over.

Forward, situated above the vehicle ramp in the nose of the craft, was a square cabin with windows all round: the flight deck.

To stand on the windswept deck was impossible and with the vessel's ungainly lurching from one gentle Channel swell to another there was a real danger of falling overboard or sliding into one of the gaping air-intakes. Warily eyeing the propellor blades whirling within a couple of feet of the deck, I slithered forwards on my belly. Then I found myself beyond the reach of the spray.

The smooth metal beneath my body was no longer wet and slippery but warm and encrusted with dry salt. Peering forwards, I saw the white shirts of the crew on the flight deck and the standing figures of Ronald Blom and Kristy. Behind Blom was a narrow door leading into the cabin. If I could reach it there was a chance of catching him by surprise from behind.

I was ten feet from the door when Blom happened to look round. He saw me spread-eagled on the deck, lying flat to obtain every bit of friction I could on the smooth metal. He spun Kristy roughly in front of him and with his gun hand wrestled with the door catch. It whipped back on its hinges as the slipstream caught it and I found myself staring dry-mouthed up the barrel of Ronald Blom's pistol.

In the split second when his trigger finger began to tighten, Kristy bit the arm that encircled her throat. Ronald Blom's mouth widened in pain. Then, as he pinned Kristy against the door-jamb to alter his grip, she snatched the diamond springbok brooch from her collar. A heartbeat later it flashed in the sun as she jerked it free and jabbed the long pin into Blom's stomach.

He gasped and sprang backwards as if he had suffered an electric shock, then cuffed Kristy savagely with the gun. As she sank to her knees he lurched out through the door.

The slipstream punched him in the back and he was carried aft, running as he tried to grip with his feet on the deck, as if he were in the grip of an avalanche. I closed my eyes at the horror of seeing him blurred to a red mist by the scything props but some instinct must have warned him of the danger. He flung himself sideways, full length on the deck.

Springing like a tiger, I hurled myself on top of him. But he brought the gun round and got in a vicious chop that knocked the breath from my body and sent me sliding along the deck beyond him.

Scrabbling at the smooth metal and grunting with effort, I scuttled towards the ladder but Blom was already on one knee, aiming with a steady hand. His ginger hair was blown back by the wind, his silk shirt filled with air and billowed around his shoulders, its collar fluttering like a flag in a gale.

In a panic, I cast around for a way to escape. The ladder was still twenty feet away. No time even to take a running jump into the sea. I darted a stricken look at the flight deck. An officer stood in the open doorway, looking out at me. The captain's right hand was moving up to the throttle control levers mounted on the bulkhead above the windscreen.

Blom had to be delayed for just two seconds.

There was no point in trying to speak above the scream of the engines. I held up one hand as if beseeching him not to shoot and with the other tore at the Velcro strip that sealed the pocket of my anorak. Blom held his fire.

I drew out the plastic bag containing the blue chrysanthemum and held it out to him.

A look of satisfaction crossed his face. I could see him

thinking that he could still reach safety, with the flower that was a passport to a fortune.

The captain's fingers gripped the throttles. I saw his arm jerk back and pushed myself tight against the deck.

The pitch of the engines changed. For a long second I watched in fear as Blom reached out for the plant with one hand and made ready to fire a bullet at my head with the other.

With no air-cushion to support it the hovercraft sank down towards the surface. Solid water snatched at the metal frames forming the base of its fuselage platform.

With a surging crash the great hovercraft ploughed in.

In moments its speed was reduced from sixty knots to zero.

Forewarned, there had been time for me to arch my fingers round a protruding rib of aluminium. But Ronald Blom found nothing to grip. He toppled sideways, sliding rapidly along the smooth deck. His fingers scrabbled at the domed rivets.

His shins swept over the gaping lip of the air-intake. With a look of absolute terror he realized his predicament.

But he could do nothing to stop his violent slide. His legs dropped down into the hole. The smooth aluminium moulding swallowed him to the waist.

For a brief moment he managed to slow himself but the impetus was too great. Feet first, face down, he slid over the rim of the air-scoop.

I caught a last glimpse of his fingernails cutting furrows into the paint. Then he was gone, leaving only a lingering scream, higher pitched even than the jet noise of the engines, instantly cut off as he hit the smooth bottom plate of the revolving fan.

Violently his body was flung outwards by centrifugal force until brought up short by the twelve angled paddle-blades.

At twelve hundred revs per minute, Ronald Blom spun-dried to death.

14 : IN THE PINK

It was the calm before the storm. Yarmouth Harbour made the best of a peaceful Friday afternoon before hordes of toy boats crammed into the place during the coming Bank Holiday weekend. Dick Johnstone, the hobbit of Yarmouth, stood on the quayside looking down at *Windycap* as I sloshed a bucket of sea water over the specks of diesel I had spilled on the deck while refuelling. Now, topped up with oil and water, her lockers and bilges filled with supplies, including cans of peaches, we were ready to go. Dropping the bucket into the locker abaft the wheelhouse, I let the lid down with a slam and dusted off my hands.

'Getting out before the mob arrives, eh?' Dick called.

'Damn right. If you haven't got a new set of batteries in that trumpet of yours you'll need them.'

Dick raised the loud hailer to his lips, pressed the trigger, and blew into the mike. The air filled with a loud whoshing noise. Then he grinned and asked jovially, 'Where are y'bound?'

'Anywhere warm. The Med for the winter, I guess.'

'Lucky man. Wish I was with you.'

'Thought I'd give you a bit more room to pack 'em in,' I said, walking up the pontoon and joining him on the quay. Nothing moved on the harbour and the Solent was deserted but for a ferry lining up for the entrance on its way in from Lymington. Although it was strictly against regulations I thought *Windycap* would not be in the way if I left her at the fuelling jetty for fifteen minutes but I checked it out with Dick.

'Okay if I leave her there while I see Jack?'

'Sure, but don't be too long.'

'Just give me a shout. Those new batteries will find me anywhere up the High Street.'

He chuckled and turned away to watch a sloop edge out into the stream. The crew coiled up the mooring-lines, her skipper industriously puffing a pipe and glancing anxiously aft to check there were no hang-ups in the shape of ropes trailing in the water which could foul his screw.

The paperwork took only a minute and Jack Collins, the Customs Officer, teased me genially.

'France again, eh? I'm surprised you're not going by hovercraft. You ought to get a free pass for life on that thing after what you did.'

'No chance, too blooming dangerous,' I said.

There was just time to pop in for a farewell pint, but it was not quite noon, the sun was nowhere near the yard arm even by Yarmouth standards, and the back bar was deserted. Suddenly, it was not just the taste of hops that made the beer taste unusually bitter.

It was just short of three months since Kristy and I had landed in England with that cursed flower. Eighty-one nights of waking suddenly in a cold sweat, the image of Ronald Blom's terror-stricken face vanishing into the hovercraft's giant air-scoop vivid in my mind and his scream ringing in my ears. Hailed as the man who attacked the hi-jacker single-handed, I had been chased ragged by reporters but, because of all the fuss of our arrival in Dover, the little polythene bag in my anorak pocket had got into the country without any questions being asked and there had been no need to show the phyto-sanitation certificate Ronald Blom had so considerately arranged before meeting his ghastly death.

Kristy had taken the plant to her mother's cottage in Sussex and nursed it to health among the tomatoes in her little back-garden greenhouse, then she had flown out to Sardinia for the funeral. Since then there had been two postcards, informative but cool. Kristy hoped I was well; Jon had taken over the nursery; they were both working night and day; their yacht was being sold where she lay, in Toulon, and did not need to be taken any further, but thank you for your help, etc. For myself, there had hardly been time to scratch together the bare bones of a living between avoiding the press, talking with police, and giving evidence at both the Coroner's Court and the special court of inquiry convened by the Board of Trade and Seaspeed to investigate the bizarre mid-Channel incident in which a man with a gun had been spun-dried to death.

In July I had bought a copy of *Go-Fast* and been amused by the glowing testimonials of the Porsche, Jaguar, Corvette and Ferrari which appeared in glossy colour on the magazine's front cover, and on half a dozen pages inside. The cars looked in rather better shape than when I had last seen them, on the roadside in northern France. Then the jet-set magazine was sold and merged with another title and I had heard on the grapevine that Philip Fanselow had joined a Japanese car-importing firm as a public relations officer. The talking pace-notes were never marketed, and in any case they were rendered obsolete when France introduced overall speed limits to reduce consumption in the fuel crisis.

Ronald Blom's father had continued with his plans to build a shop on a floating pontoon in the harbour and every time I saw it, which was a hundred times a day when I was at home, I was reminded of how I had been used. A fortnight ago the manager had absconded with the takings and a great deal of expensive electronic navigation equipment which was in stock, and now the business was up for sale. But I had lost heart. The idea of being a shop-keeper, even a maritime one with the tide under my boots, had palled.

It was on a delivery trip I had made from Dieppe, collecting a family cruising yacht that had been weather-bound after a holiday cruise, that I had telephoned Bob

Henderson. He had driven over in the Renault van with Josephine and their new baby boy. *Ma Biche* needed so much money spent on her, which I did not have and saw little prospect of getting, that Bob had towed her back to his barn where she was collecting dust and chicken manure. Once I reached the Med the Hendersons were planning to join me for a week's holiday, and we would decide what to do with the old banger.

In a sour and unhappy frame of mind I finished my beer quickly and mooched along the sunny quay eating a meat pie. Gleaming beneath a coat of new dark-blue paint, *Windycap* stirred restlessly at her single fore and aft mooring-lines as if sensing my mood. But now that the time had come to sail away I was strangely reluctant to do so. There was nobody on the quay to wave me off, nobody with whom to share the challenge and the fun of the voyage which lay ahead. It all seemed rather meaningless to cast off into a void, but I knew that Julian Simpson-Potter would steer enough work my way to keep me in pocket money, so my plan was to cruise south and see what developed.

It was only as I stepped aboard from the fuelling jetty that I realized *Windycap* had a visitor.

She sat in the wheelhouse looking out at me with a wide smile curling mischievously in the corners in the way I remembered so well. The springbok brooch sparkled prettily against the dark background of a navy-blue sweater. She wore bright yellow sailing boots on her feet, a faded red cotton scarf around her golden hair.

So complete was the surprise that I choked on a crumb and Kristy had to thump me on the back. Finally, with eyes watering, I managed to speak.

'Where did you come from? I'm all fuelled up ready to sail; you just caught me.'

'Thank goodness. I caught the ferry by the skin of my teeth as it was. Where are you bound?'

'How about Paris, to begin with?'

'Well....'

'You look marvellous,' I said, holding out a piece of pie. 'Want a bite?'

'No thanks. We....' She looked away, suddenly shy.

'Bad news?' I prompted gently.

'In a way, yes. We grew the flower all right.'

'And?'

'It wasn't blue.'

Stunned for the second time in as many minutes, I tossed the remains of the pie into the tide and stared at her. Kristy had lowered her head and now she peered up at me from beneath her eyebrows to observe how I was taking it. I sniggered, then guffawed. Seagulls screeching down for the pie crust joined in. So did Kristy. We fell helplessly into each other's arms.

'That's the craziest thing!' I said. 'So what are you going to do now?'

'Opa's will is caught up in a bureaucratic tangle, as you would expect in Italy, but he has left the islands to me and the villa with its land and business to Jon.'

'Is anything left of it?' I asked.

'Oh yes. Jon got his doctorate okay, and through his university contacts raised a lucrative research contract so he can develop the place as a botanical laboratory. Now we don't have to rely on masses of labour to keep it all going, just a couple of good hands whom we can pay well. And the sale of *Bonnie Jean* paid off the outstanding mortgage payments, so we're in the clear for the time being.'

'That's terrific news,' I said, 'but what about you?'

Kristy shrugged and said nothing but her blue eyes twinkled and the grin spread ever wider. My mind whirled.

'Look, you've got an island, is that right?'

'Officially there are two, joined up by that little strip of beach, don't you remember?'

'But you don't have a boat.'

'No.'

'And how do you propose reaching your islands without a boat?'

Kristy beamed another smile worth all the Blue Hurricanes in the world.

'I hadn't thought, I must admit. But it sounds a bit tricky, don't you reckon?'

'You've got an island and I've got a boat,' I said. 'And I still love you, more than ever.'

'And I love you, more than ever,' Kristy said.

'Let's get married.'

'Oh yes!'

'Got your toothbrush?'

'I'll use yours.'

'Cast off for'ard.'

'Aye aye, Skipper.'

In twenty minutes we were cruising southwestwards down a placid Solent. The red and white-banded lighthouse marking the Needles was clear on the port bow. The squat bulk of Hurst Castle lay off the starboard beam. A Thoreson ferry on its way in from Normandy steamed up the channel towards us at a good lick. This was precisely the spot where I had rescued Jon Van Blommenstein and his friend in their capsized Enterprise sailing dinghy and I wondered how differently things would have turned out had conditions been as smooth and summery on that day as they were now. Jon would not have landed in the drink. I would not have gone to Sardinia. Old man Van Blommenstein would not have foisted a disguised blue chrysanthemum on me. Helped by Bruno Feraldi, Ronald Blom would have stolen a worthless flower from his grandfather and smugly carried it back to England expecting to make his fortune.

With a practised flick of the wrist I moved the wheel a spoke or two to starboard to give the oncoming ship a wider berth. With one arm around my waist and her chin on my shoulder, Kristy stood beside me swaying to the gentle roll of the boat.

'That flower we brought home,' I asked idly, 'what

colour was it in the end?'

'Pink.'

'Oh.'

Kristy was amused about something and her arm tightened, giving me a little shake as if she was excited.

'What's up?' I asked, puzzled.

'You should know more about growing flowers.'

'Perhaps I will, before long. But you can't begin a honeymoon cruise with secrets. Come on, tell!'

'Okay, okay,' Kristy said, surrendering. 'You know what sort of person Opa was: old-fashioned, with a nineteenth century idea of a woman's place. He might think I was decorative and lovable, even a little bit useful, but....'

'But simple-minded,' I said, teasing.

'Not exactly, but you've got the right idea. He thought it was not proper to bother a girl's pretty little head with the problems of real life, and that was why I could only guess at the extent of his difficulties.'

'So?'

'Well, it explains why he never told me much about the flowers he was developing,' Kristy continued. 'I seldom went into his lab and he always had so many trial flowers on the go that I didn't give any particular one of them too much attention.'

'But you thought it was a blue flower all along. Did you never actually see it?'

Kristy shook her head. 'No. You see, the blue chrysanthemum is genetically impossible, it simply cannot be grown, and Opa probably thought I knew this. Jon certainly did. The idea of finding a blue chrysanthemum growing among our flowers as a sport was really just a kind of family joke. Some people dream of the day they win the pools, or make a killing with a premium bond. With us it was always the day we grew a blue chrysanthemum. It was a euphemism for any flower that made us rich.'

'But you took it seriously?'

'Yes.'

'And so did Ronny.'

'Apparently. But Opa did develop one variety which he knew would be enormously valuable and when it came to dying a flower that would make Ronny show his hand he chose blue because it was obvious and could not help be noticed. That was when you came along.'

The boat dipped into the high bow wave made by the passing ferry and a lick of water ran along the deck.

'But we're not as badly off as you might think,' Kristy went on. 'Everything we did was worthwhile.'

'How come?'

'The French have an expression for it: *nous nous portons à merveilles.*'

'You know what my French is like,' I protested.

'It means we're in the pink.'

'I still don't see the point.'

'Nobody has ever before grown a spray chrysanthemum that is the most perfect shade of coral pink. It's a Pink Hurricane. And worth at least as much as a hypothetical blue. Jon has raised a lot of capital on the strength of it and is putting in all kinds of equipment to propagate the cuttings. But the finder's royalties are separate.'

'What do you mean?'

My hand was on the wheel's brass-tipped centre spoke, and Kristy put her own hand on top of mine, squeezing my knuckles excitedly.

'We will need money to get your marina started on the island,' she said, 'and that is where it will come from. The royalties on the Pink Hurricane are all ours.'

All Futura Books are available at your bookshop or newsagent, or can be ordered from the following address:
Futura Books, Cash Sales Department,
P.O. Box 11, Falmouth, Cornwall.

Please send cheque or postal order (no currency), and allow 45p for postage and packing for the first book plus 20p for the second book and 14p for each additional book ordered up to a maximum charge of £1.63 in U.K.

Customers in Eire and B.F.P.O. please allow 45p for the first book, 20p for the second book plus 14p per copy for the next 7 books, thereafter 8p per book.

Overseas customers please allow 75p for postage and packing for the first book and 21p per copy for each additional book.